BLOOD LINE

BLOOD LINE

Lynda La Plante

**SIMON &
SCHUSTER**

London · New York · Sydney · Toronto

A CBS COMPANY

First published in Great Britain by Simon & Schuster UK Ltd, 2011
A CBS COMPANY

Copyright © Lynda La Plante, 2011

1 3 5 7 9 10 8 6 4 2

Simon & Schuster UK Ltd
1st Floor
222 Gray's Inn Road
London WC1X 8HB

www.simonandschuster.co.uk

Simon & Schuster Australia
Sydney

A CIP catalogue record for this book is available
from the British Library

Hardback ISBN: 978-0-85720-180-5
Trade Paperback ISBN: 978-0-85720-181-2

Typeset in Bembo by M Rules
Printed in the UK by CPI Mackays, Chatham ME5 8TD

I would like to dedicate this book
to Cass and Anne Sutherland

Acknowledgments

Special thanks and gratitude go to my hard working team at La Plante Productions for their committed and valuable support while I worked on *Blood Line*: Liz Thorburn, Richard Dobbs-Grove, Noel Farragher, Sara Johnson and especially Cass Sutherland.

Many thanks also to Nicole Muldowney, Stephen Ross and Andrew Bennet-Smith, along with the ever-supportive Duncan Heath and Sue Rodgers.

I would also like to say how much I appreciate the wonderful stars of the Above Suspicion series: Cirián Hinds and Kelly Reilly.

Special thanks to my literary agent, Gill Coleridge, and all at Rogers, Coleridge & White for their constant encouragement.

The publication of this book would not have been possible without the hard work and support of Susan Opie and the team at Simon & Schuster: Ian Chapman, Suzanne Baboneau, Nigel Stoneman, Jessica Leeke and Rob Cox; I am very happy to be working with such a terrific and creative group of people.

Prologue

The first blow to his head made his body lurch sideways, striking his face against the bedside cabinet. The pain was excruciating. As he tried to fend off his attacker, the punch to his ribs forced him back against the pillow. He couldn't even cry out – the gag made sure of that. Over and over again the punches slammed into his body, but now it wasn't a fist that hit him, it was a club hammer, and he could feel the bones in his face splinter. Blood seeped into his eyes and streamed from his nose as yet again the hammer struck, this time with such force that his head lolled over the side of the bed. Incapable of moving or seeing, he could feel the sheet being dragged over him and around his inert body, like a shroud. His attacker was using the blood-sodden sheet to slide him from the bed onto the floor. Moments later he realised he was being dragged out of the bedroom.

As he was dumped into the bath, the taps struck him and part of the sheet covering his face fell back, but still he was incapable of making a sound. Even when the water began to run over him he could do nothing to help himself. A terrible darkness swamped him as he sank into unconsciousness. Blood clotted his nostrils, and his mouth was swollen from the beating, which had broken his front teeth and forced them into his lip, and yet he was still alive as his body was rolled over and the sheet drawn away from him. The blood mixed with the running water, swirling down the plughole beneath his broken face.

Sometime later he felt something being poured over him, and hands patting and rubbing at his limbs. For a brief moment his mind woke as if there was a glimmer of a chance he would survive. This hope gave him the strength to try and move his limbs; he thrashed and kicked, but his attempts were thwarted as he felt hands squeezing at his throat. Then his head was wrapped so tightly that he could no longer breathe and there was no hope.

Chapter One

The small dapper man in the navy pin-striped suit had been waiting in the Hounslow police station reception for over an hour. He had not complained, but sat patiently reading his newspaper. When Anna Travis eventually walked into the room he folded the paper.

'DCI Travis?'

'Yes – and you are?'

'Edward Rawlins.'

Anna sat opposite him and apologised for keeping him waiting. The truth was she'd been so busy wrapping up an investigation for a forthcoming trial that she'd quite forgotten he was there.

'That's perfectly all right, and understandable as I did not have an appointment. Thank you for agreeing to see me.'

There was a pause. In many ways she was unused to such cordiality, but at the same time impatient to know why he had specifically asked for her.

'I work at the Old Bailey, I am an usher,' Mr Rawlins said quietly.

'Why do you want to see me?'

'I have watched you in court many times and you have always impressed me.'

'Well, thank you very much, Mr Rawlins, but could you tell me why you wanted to speak with me?'

'Yes. I think my son has been murdered.'

Anna opened her briefcase and took out a notebook. She demonstrated little reaction to his statement.

'Have you reported this elsewhere?'

'No.'

'Can you give me a few details? Firstly, what is your son's name?'

'Alan. He's twenty-six years old and lives with his girlfriend in a flat not too far from here.'

'The address?'

'Newton Court in Hedges Street. He occupied a ground-floor flat, it's number two.'

'When you say "occupied", do you mean he's no longer living there?'

'He's supposed to be. I believe all his belongings are still there, but I haven't been to the flat. I've just telephoned there many times.'

'His girlfriend's name?'

'Tina Brooks.'

'You said you believed your son has been murdered?'

'Yes. We speak at least twice a week and I haven't heard from him for nearly two weeks now.'

'This is unusual?'

'Very.'

'You haven't reported him missing?'

'No.'

'Well, Mr Rawlins, that is the first thing you should do. As he is over eighteen and until we have more details, specifically if you think a crime has been committed, then you should make a Missing Persons report.'

'Whatever you think is necessary, but Alan is a very

studious and caring young man. He has always kept in touch with me.'

'Have you spoken to his girlfriend?'

'Yes, numerous times. She in actual fact called *me*, asking if I had seen him as she was worried because he hadn't come home.'

'Did she give you any possible reason for Alan's disappearance?'

'No, just that it was unlike him.'

'Do you know if he has withdrawn any money from his bank account recently?'

'His bank said they're not allowed to tell me. I asked Miss Brooks if his passport was at the flat and she said that it was. Then later she told the police it wasn't there.'

'The last time you saw him or spoke to him, did he seem concerned about anything?'

'No. He said we should go and see a film one Sunday and that he'd check what was on and call the following week. He never did.'

'What work does he do?'

'He's a mechanic. He works for an auto-repair shop. I rang them, and they were surprised that they had not seen him. They too had called his flat to find out where he was, so it's been of some concern to them also.'

'Why do you think that something as bad as murder has happened?'

'Because this is totally out of character.'

Anna stood up. 'I can get a local officer from the Missing Persons Unit to take a report and investigate the disappearance, but they would have to make the decision as to whether it was suspicious or not.'

'But it's been almost two weeks already!'

'That may be so, but your son is over eighteen and in

many cases we discover that nothing untoward has happened. He may have decided to just take off for personal reasons.'

'It doesn't make sense, it's not like him to . . .'

'It has happened before. Did he have a good relationship with Miss Brooks?'

'Yes, they were going to be married. Well, that's what he told me, but that was six or seven months ago. He hasn't mentioned it to me or my wife since.' Mr Rawlins hesitated. 'That is the other reason I am deeply concerned. You see, my wife is suffering from Alzheimer's and Alan always found the time to talk to her. She is at home with a carer and he would make conversation with her several times a month, even though she has reached a stage where she doesn't really recall who he is or who I am, for that matter.'

Anna felt sorry for the dapper little man as he gave a sad small shrug of his shoulders.

'I'll push this through for you, Mr Rawlins, but as I said it will have to go through the correct channels as I am attached to the Murder Squad and not the Missing Persons Unit. It's they who will need to have all these details.'

'But I know something bad has happened. He wouldn't behave this way – he's a wonderful son.'

Smiling in reassurance, Anna extricated herself from the interview. She did as she promised, arranging for an officer from the local Missing Persons Unit to take a detailed report from Mr Rawlins, but then she became completely consumed by her preparation for the forthcoming trial. Mr Rawlins was not exactly forgotten, just filed away as he had no direct connection to her department.

Three weeks later, Anna saw Mr Rawlins again. It was at the Old Bailey, and he was ushering a prosecution witness into the court. She was about to skirt past him, not wishing to get into a conversation, when he hurried over to her.

'Alan is still missing – my son. You recall me talking to you about my son? I reported him missing as you instructed.'

'Yes, of course I remember, Mr Rawlins, but I have not been contacted by Mispers so I assume the case-file has not been raised to a high-risk category. I'm sorry, but unless I am officially tasked to investigate your son's disappearance as suspicious, there is nothing more I can do.'

Anna then headed into the court and Mr Rawlins turned away. She saw him a number of times during the remainder of the trial, but tried to avoid him as much as possible. Although she felt compassion for the little man, the reality was that she would be allocated her next murder enquiry and couldn't choose it herself.

As her trial veered towards a conclusion, Anna saw Detective Chief Superintendent James Langton coming up for a case in another court. He smiled warmly at her and she joined him.

'How are you doing?' he asked.

'Fine, thank you.'

Langton made no mention of the tragedy that had happened – the murder of her fiancé, Ken Hudson, a prison officer who had been planning to become a child psychologist. Ken had been killed by a prisoner, Cameron Welsh, who had become obsessed with Anna during a previous investigation.

'I've been meaning to call you, but I've had a shedload of cases to deal with,' Langton said apologetically.

'That's okay, I understand.'

He cocked his head to one side. 'Well, let's have dinner one night.'

'Yes, I'd like that, but I've been caught up on this case we're here for.'

'Time moves fast.'

'Yes, it does.'

She couldn't mention to him that time had, in fact, moved unbearably slowly for her, and that it had done nothing to heal her loss. Work had helped; she had thrown herself into her present case, outwardly succeeding in burying the gaping pain that sat inside her.

'Do you know Edward Rawlins?' Langton went on. 'He's a court usher here. Apparently his son Alan is missing. Shame – he was a lovely young guy. I met him a couple of times.'

'Yes, Mr Rawlins actually spoke to me about his concerns.'

'Bit more than concerns – it's been almost six weeks now. I said I'd find out what Mispers have come up with.'

'I'd better get back in – the prosecution are summing up.' She was eager to leave.

'I'll call about dinner. Bye now.'

Langton moved off. He was very aware of the case she had headed up, her first as Detective Chief Inspector. It was a cut-and-dried investigation, one he knew would not place too much pressure on her as the suspect had admitted his guilt. Langton had also monitored her handling of the investigation, even down to making sure she had a team around her who had worked with her previously. Not that she had any intimation of all this; he had deliberately chosen not to be too visible. Anna was heading up her first murder enquiry, and though he was fully behind her promotion to DCI, he felt she needed time to acclimatise herself.

Ten years ago, Langton had been emotionally bereft at the unexpected death of his first wife, so he was more than aware of what Anna was going through. He himself had returned to work almost immediately after the death, but it had remained a painful scar that even now affected him deeply. Although he and Anna had once been lovers, and although he was now married once more and with children, the psychological trauma still troubled him. In fact, he often thought it stunted and overshadowed his life. He had therefore attempted to encourage Anna to take time out, but she had refused, just as he had done all those years ago. He had deliberately made sure her enquiry was one he felt she could handle.

Anna returned to court and after two days the jury gave their verdict of guilty to murder and not manslaughter as the defence had argued. Case closed.

Anna was packing up the incident room with her colleagues when Langton appeared. He first congratulated her on the successful outcome of the trial and then asked if he could have a private word.

As DCI, Anna now had her own office. She suspected that maybe he was going to ask about the dinner date, but instead he brought up the Misper enquiry regarding Alan Rawlins. It was on the same turf as her last case and he suggested that she take a look at the possibility that Edward Rawlins was right, and that his son was not missing, but dead.

'I'm basically looking over it because I like the man – have known him for years – so can you talk to Mispers for me and see what they have to date? If it looks as if it could be high risk and a possible murder, I'd like you to oversee it.'

'What is the general consensus?'

'Well, according to his girlfriend there was a possibility he had someone else and was about to leave her. She thinks he was seeing another woman and just took off. There is no movement in his bank account, nor any contact with the place he worked at – and apparently it is totally out of character that he would go away without letting his dad know. To be honest, it does have a bad feeling about it – at least in my estimation – so check it out for me, please. And if you want to retain the same team you've been working alongside, go ahead.'

'Will do.'

Langton again mentioned that they should have dinner together one evening, but as before made no date. He had had a few words with her team and had received only positive feedback. It appeared, at least on the surface, that Anna was dealing with the crisis in her personal life, perhaps even better than he had done himself.

The following morning, Anna selected a clean white shirt and navy blue pin-stripe suit to wear. Looking in the mirror she noticed that the suit jacket had a stain on the lapel and the shirt could do with a quick once-over with an iron. She thought about how much she had neglected her appearance since Ken's death and decided it was time to try and smarten herself up again, so she changed into a brown jacket and black trousers. Impatient to get to work, to give the team briefing on the disappearance of Alan Rawlins, she didn't bother to iron her shirt and placed the navy suit in a plastic bag to drop off at the dry cleaner's.

Anna briefed the team explaining that the Missing Persons report virtually said what Langton had told her:

they had found nothing incriminating and had no evidence to indicate foul play. They suspected that Alan Rawlins had simply decided to take time out, and although they had interviewed his girlfriend and his workmates, no one could give any reason for his disappearance. His current passport was missing, but there had been no withdrawals from any of his accounts. Anna's team was a trifle confused as to why they had been brought in to investigate the case, and Anna suggested that it was down to Langton's intuition and friendship with the father of the missing young man.

'If we uncover any possibility of foul play we'll act on it,' she told them at the briefing, 'but I think uppermost is showing an interest and seeing if Mispers have missed any lines of enquiry. If not, we can then move on and out of this station as planned.'

Anna, accompanied by her DS, went to meet Tina Brooks that afternoon. Newton Court was only fifteen minutes' drive from the Hounslow police station, a 1980s modern-build with six flats, a garage each, parking spaces and a well-kept horseshoe drive and forecourt with tubs of plants. The reception area was neat and clean, but with no resident doorman, just a plaque that listed the occupants of the six flats.

Tina Brooks opened the door to flat two with hardly a beat after Anna had rung the bell. She was an exceptionally attractive young woman, with thick, dark-reddish hair scraped back from her face and caught in a scrunchie. She had big dark eyes, wide cheeks and full lips, and a small sculptured nose. Barefooted, she wore a pale blue tracksuit and had a white towel around her neck.

'I was out running, so please excuse me.' She gestured for them to follow her into the lounge. The flat was very tidy, with white walls and pine furniture. Nondescript paintings and prints hung on the wall. The large coffee table had a bowl of fruit on it, with a couple of fitness magazines beside it.

'Can I offer you tea or coffee?' she asked them.

'No, thank you. I am DCI Anna Travis and this is Detective Sergeant Paul Simms.'

They both sat on the sofa, while Tina chose a beige armchair opposite. Paul Simms was rather skinny, with curly blonde hair that gave him a baby-faced appearance, but he in fact was one of the best officers Anna had worked alongside. He took out his notebook as she kicked off the interview, asking Tina to give them details of when she had last seen Alan.

'It'd be almost eight weeks ago, the fifteenth of March. He called from the garage where he works and said he had a migraine. He knew I wasn't due at work until later that day.'

Tina explained that she ran a hair and beauty salon and on Mondays only ever did a half-day as she was open until late on Saturdays.

'I drove to his garage and collected him. He often had these headaches and didn't like to drive, so he left his car there and I brought him home. He said he just wanted to get into bed and draw the curtains, and I think he took some painkillers to help him sleep it off. When they came on, his headaches could last for hours, sometimes a couple of days. I wasn't that bothered because he had had them before; I just made him a flask of tea so that if he felt like it, he could have a cup later. I put it on the bedside table; he had an ice-pack on his head and I said that I'd phone him in a while and see how he was. I got home just after six or maybe a bit later. I had tried his mobile a couple of times beforehand, but he didn't answer. I just presumed he was sleeping it off.'

Paul wrote copious notes as Anna listened, not interrupting as Tina went on to describe how, when she got home, the bedroom door was closed so she made herself a salad, not wanting to disturb him, and didn't check on Alan until around eight o'clock. She said he wasn't in the bed and she presumed that he had felt better and gone to collect his car from the garage. At around ten or ten-thirty she called his mobile again, but got no answer and left a message. She eventually went to bed and waited.

'I must have fallen asleep because it was about three o'clock when I realised he had still not come home. I came in here, thinking that maybe he had slept on the sofa so he wouldn't disturb me. I waited until around seven-thirty in the morning to call his work, but he was not there and the other mechanic who worked with Alan told me he hadn't returned there or collected his car.'

Paul lifted his pencil to indicate he had a couple of questions. He first asked if the bed had been remade when Tina had come home from work and she said that she thought the covers had just been put back, but it wasn't exactly made up. He then asked for the name, contact address and phone numbers of the mechanic and the garage Alan worked for.

'Stanley Fairfax owns the garage but he's never there, and the sort of head mechanic's name is Joe, although I'm not sure of his surname.'

Tina gave the phone numbers and Paul wrote them down as Anna looked around the rather bare room. Tina told them how she had contacted Alan's father to ask if Alan had gone round to see him, but Edward said he hadn't heard from him. She then explained to Anna and

Paul that she had continued to phone around all his friends, the garage again, and that his father had rung her a few times.

'Nobody had seen him or heard a word from him,' she concluded.

Anna leaned forward. 'Mr Rawlins said that you had found his passport, but according to Missing Persons you said that it was not here at the flat.'

'Right. I looked in the drawers in our bedroom and I saw Alan's passport and I told his father it was still in the flat. It wasn't until I spoke with the Missing Persons officer that I looked closer and realised it was an out of date one and his current one was actually missing.'

'Did Alan go abroad a lot?'

'Maybe once a year. We went to Spain for a holiday and Turkey once, but he didn't go frequently. He did spend a lot of his free time in Cornwall surfing. Most of the time we didn't have the money because we were saving up to get married and buy a place. We only rent this flat.'

She wrinkled her pert little nose. 'I suppose it's obvious, but we didn't want to waste money doing this place up.'

'Has Alan ever left before without leaving you a contact address?'

'No, never. I agreed with his father that this was totally out of character for Alan, since he was always very caring and thoughtful. But . . .' She licked her lips.

Anna waited and eventually Tina gave a sigh.

'I had been a bit worried about him. I mean, not too much, but he'd stayed late at work a lot recently and one time I phoned when he said he'd been at work, but the garage was closed so it wasn't the truth.'

'So what did you think?'

'Well, I started to wonder if there was someone else,

another woman, but he only did it once or twice, and when I asked him about it he said that he was working on his own car. It's a 280SL Mercedes – an old one – and he was always doing this and that to it. He planned to do it up and then sell it to make a big profit as he'd got it cheap.'

'This was the car he used to go to work in?' Paul asked.

'Yes, but the bodywork needed respraying and the engine was a bit dodgy – well, that's what he told me. It's a convertible and I know he was getting a new soft top as the old one was damaged.'

Tina went on to say how she had gone to Alan's garage and was told that if he didn't show up for work, Mr Fairfax would have to replace him. Alan's car was still parked there and they had not heard from him. His mobile phone had been left inside the glove compartment.

'Which is why he didn't answer when I called,' she said, and got up to open a drawer in a side table. She took out the mobile and handed it to Anna, adding, 'It'll need recharging.'

'Tell me about his friends.'

'Alan's?'

'Yes.' Anna found it strange that Tina was so unemo-tional – helpful, yes, but she showed no sign of distress. Everything was very matter-of-fact. She had left the room to return with Alan's address book and passed it to Anna.

'He didn't have that many close friends, and we didn't really socialise that much as we were saving up. We spent most of our time together watching DVDs and didn't go out a lot.'

'Did he drink?'

'Not really, just the odd glass of wine.'

'Drugs?'

'Good heavens, no. Alan was very straitlaced; he didn't even like taking the medication for his headaches as he said it made him feel woozy.'

'What about enemies?'

'What do you mean by that?'

'Did anyone have a grudge against him?' Anna then glanced at Paul, indicating she was leaving any further questions to him.

'No. You only had to meet him to know that he was a really nice guy. He hated confrontation of any kind – took after his father. They were very close.'

Tina then went at some length into how good a relationship Alan had with his parents, and how caring he was towards his mother, often phoning her two or three times a week and visiting her.

'She's in another world, doesn't really know who anyone is. It's very sad, but he adored her and he was an only child. He reckoned he owed his parents a lot. They'd paid for his education and I think his dad had given him the money for the Mercedes.'

'What about his bank balance?'

Tina got up again and crossed to the same drawer, taking out copies of their bank statements. They had a joint savings account – of just over seventy thousand pounds.

There was a current account that was used to pay the rent, and into which Alan's wages were paid directly, so it was clear how much he withdrew to live on. Not a lot. Tina also had a separate account for her beauty salon; this was overdrawn by thirty-five thousand.

'We saved the seventy thousand between us. Alan did well out of doing up and selling on old classic cars and the salon had a good turnover being in Hounslow High Street.'

'Your salon looks in trouble,' Anna said quietly.

'Yeah, well, it's the recession. We do hair, nails and beauty treatments, but when money is short, women don't make appointments. I think the business is picking up though – thank God, as I'm on my overdraft limit and the bank doesn't like it.'

'Do you own the salon?'

'No, I only rent it – but on a five-year lease. I work hard, but like I said, it's been a bit worrying, which is why I've been spending so much time there and taking a cut in wages. I really want to make it successful.'

'How long have you had the salon?' Anna asked, still glancing over the bank statements.

'Almost two years. Before that I was a beautician at Selfridges in Oxford Street. I employ two good hair-dressers, one a stylist, and the other can do beauty treatments as well as hair. I've also got two trainees plus a girl on reception, and business is picking up. Well, you can see that from the accounts.'

Anna suspected that Tina's business probably had a far bigger turnover than she wanted to reveal and she was using the overdraft as an excuse to hide the fact.

Tina told them all about her salon, about buying the equipment and redecorating, and how Alan had helped, spending many nights working there before she was ready to open. When she ran out of things to say, Anna spoke again.

'Let's go back to your feelings that Alan may have been seeing someone else.'

'Well, like I said, it was just because I caught him out lying about working in the garage. I never found out if he *was* seeing someone else – it was just a suspicion, and now obviously I think it could have been more.'

'Why is that?'

'Because he's disappeared,' Tina said, tight-lipped with impatience.

'When you discussed these late nights with Alan, how did he react?'

She shrugged and said that he just told her she was being stupid, as he was working on his Merc and if the phone wasn't answered at the garage it was because he was outside.

'So he didn't get angry – you didn't argue?'

'Alan wasn't that type. I don't think we ever really had a cross word, to be honest, which is why I don't understand how he could just leave me without saying something.'

'But he hasn't taken any money?'

'Not that I know of, but when he sold the cars he did up it was often for cash deals.'

'What about his clothes? Has he taken anything – a suitcase even?'

'I can't be certain. I mean, I don't know every item of clothing he's got – but I suppose he could have taken a few things.'

'Have you checked?'

'Yes, of course. I told the Missing Persons officer his washing bag and toiletries have gone, but I wouldn't really know exactly what clothes were missing.'

'Why didn't you report him missing?'

'I thought he might have gone off with another woman and I was waiting for him to contact me. When his dad said he'd reported him missing, I thought he'd done the right thing.'

Anna stood up and asked to be shown around the flat. Tina looked at her watch, saying she wouldn't have much more time as she had to shower and get to work. She led them down a narrow corridor and gestured at a small box room.

'We use this to store a few things as it's so small.'

Anna looked into the room. A single bed and a desk stood beside a row of fitted wardrobes. There was the same beige carpet in there too, and matching curtains.

'Did Alan have a computer?'

'No. He was always going to get a laptop, but never got around to it.'

Tina then led them to the master bedroom. This was as nondescript as the rest of the flat. It contained a king-sized bed with a duvet and a Moroccan throw across it. The double wardrobes were crammed with Tina's clothes and shoes. Alan's side had only a few things in it; a couple of suits, shirts, and in a row of drawers were socks, under-pants, two pairs of jeans and three T-shirts.

Anna thought that a man of Alan's age would have had more clothing, particularly informal wear.

'What sort of casual clothes did Alan dress in?'

'Mostly jeans, black or blue denim with a white or blue T-shirt. I don't know how many pairs of jeans or T-shirts he had so that's why I don't know exactly what clothing he could have taken.'

'What about work–clothes – mechanic's overalls?'

Tina nodded and said they were kept in the small utility room as he would take off his dirty clothes and put them straight into the washing machine when he returned from work. They trooped in there to look, and sure enough, there were some work-boots, a couple of denim jackets and jeans and two oil-stained overalls.

The kitchen was immaculate, with a juicer on the Formica top and a bowl of more fresh fruit. Nothing looked as if it was used very often, and the cream and black floor was highly polished, as was everything else. Anna sniffed; there was a distinct smell of bleach mixed with a heavy lavender room spray. They next went outside to look into Alan's garage. This was almost as neat, with all his equipment hanging on hooks and Tina's VW parked inside.

Anna said little as they drove back to the station. When Paul brought a coffee into her office he said, 'You're very quiet,' putting the drink down on her desk.

'Yeah. Tell me what you got from the interview.'

'Not very much. I think she's a bit of a clean freak. Their flat might be rented, but it was as if they had just moved in – everything spotless and nothing out of place.'

'Bit like her,' Anna said, sipping her coffee.

Paul sat opposite and flipped open his notebook.

'Nice cash deposit. Joint account, so I suppose she can fix her overdraft in her beauty salon.'

'That would only leave thirty-five thousand which isn't a big deposit for first-time buyers.'

'Depends what size place you're after, I guess – I've only got about two grand saved. She makes Alan out to be a really boring guy – never argued, never a cross word, hardly ever went out, didn't drink or take drugs. He sounds too good to be true. Unless he did have another woman stashed somewhere.'

'Well, if he did,' Anna said, 'he wasn't taking out extra money to pay for her, and the fact that there's been no money withdrawn from any of the accounts is worrying. I don't think we can walk away just yet. We'll do a few discreet interviews at his place of work and . . .'

'Maybe the hair salon. If he was helping Tina do it up

he'd have come into contact with the other females working there, so you never know – he might have run off with one of them.'

Anna nodded, but she doubted it.

'Okay, we'll start with his place of work,' she said. 'Check out a few of the friends too and see if they can come up with anything.'

'What about talking to his parents?'

'Doubt if they can shed any more light on his disappearance. In fact, his father asked me to look into it weeks ago.' She sighed.

'So we have no motive . . .'

'Unless there is something we overlooked. Let's get a list of the calls and texts on his mobile.'

Paul left Anna to finish her coffee. She hadn't mentioned her gut feeling to him – that she didn't like Tina. Even though the girl had been helpful, she showed no emotion. Tina and Alan were arranging to buy a place and get married in a few months' time, and yet she hadn't shed a single tear or even appeared anxious. It was almost as if she just accepted that she'd never see her fiancé again.

Helping their enquiry was one thing, and it would mean a couple more days of legwork checking out Alan's friends and so on, but with no hint of anything untoward having happened, Alan Rawlins could remain on the Missing Persons files along with the thousands of other people.

Anna put in a call to Langton and gave him the details of their meeting with Tina. He listened without interruption until she said they would give it a couple more days before moving on.

'Okay, give me your gut feeling,' he said.

She hesitated. The fact that she had not liked Tina was not enough for them to instigate a murder enquiry. She repeated that they did not have anything incriminating or anything that hinted at foul play. It was a possibility Alan Rawlins had just taken off; it had been done before.

'Yeah, many times, but carry on. As you said, give it another couple of days.'

Langton was about to end the call when Anna asked him, 'What's *your* gut feeling?'

'You need a body,' he said and laughed. As always he hedged the issue. 'We should have that dinner soon.' Then he hung up.

Anna replaced the phone and sat back in her chair.

'It's all too neat,' she mumbled to herself. She closed her eyes, picturing the flat. It was as if there was deliberately nothing out of place. If there had been some kind of alter-cation or an argument, something that had forced Alan Rawlins to take off, maybe all evidence of it had been tidied away. According to Tina though, nothing unusual had happened, apart from Alan returning home from work that Monday morning with a migraine. If he had, as Tina suspected, simply walked out on her, there had to be a reason.

Anna left the station. Even though she had suggested to Paul that they leave Alan Rawlins's parents out of their round of interviews, instinctively she knew they needed to talk again to Edward Rawlins.

Chapter Two

Edward Rawlins was not at home when Anna called, but his wife's carer answered the door. She was a heavily built Jamaican woman wearing a blue overall, and when Anna asked if it was possible to speak with Mrs Rawlins, she gave a shrug of her big shoulders.

'She's just got her tray, but you can come in and see her. Mr Rawlins is usually home around this time. I'm Rose.'

The house was dark and with a lot of reproduction antique furniture. It was like a 1970s time-capsule. The walls were a yellowish-brown, with faded flowery wallpaper and sagging chipboard shelves. The avocado shagpile carpet looked equally worn and faded. Anna followed Rose up the narrow stairs to the landing. Rose opened the door of a front bedroom, which was oppressively hot; the heat seemed to waft from the room as the door opened.

'Kathleen, you've got a visitor, dear.'

Anna entered the large room, which contained a lot of dark pine furniture, along with a big television set and stacks of magazines and books. The double bed had a cosy chenille bedspread and frilled pillows, with matching curtains at the windows. Kathleen Rawlins was sitting in a wing-back chair with a tray on a small table in front of her. It held a bowl of soup with a bread roll, sausages with mashed potatoes and gravy, plus a childish jelly with Smarties on top.

Kathleen was surprisingly young-looking; her face was unlined and her natural wavy brown hair was pinned back with two coloured slides. She had large washed-out blue eyes that made her vacant expression childlike.

'I don't think I can manage all this, Rose dear. Can you take the sausages away. I'll just have the jelly.'

Rose removed the plate and bent over the frail woman.

'You didn't eat your lunch either, Kathleen. Just manage some soup, will you?'

Kathleen glanced coyly at Anna and gave a sweet smile.

'She's so bossy, but I'm not that hungry.'

Rose thudded out and Anna drew up a chair. She wasn't sure how she should start, watching Kathleen's small thin hands try to wield the heavy soup spoon.

'Here, let me help you.' Anna took the spoon and gently held it to Kathleen's lips. The older woman sipped and then gave that glorious childlike smile.

'She should have taken the soup away; it's pea and I hate pea soup.'

Anna moved it aside and placed the bowl of jelly closer. Kathleen picked up a small plastic spoon and managed a mouthful.

'I don't know you, do I?'

'No. My name is Anna, I'm a policewoman.'

'Oh, you don't look like one – no uniform.'

'I'm a detective.'

'Oooh, that's nice. I've never met a detective before.'

Anna smiled, watching as the plastic spoon scooped up the jelly with some Smarties. Kathleen crunched them and went back for another mouthful.

'You like jelly?' Anna asked.

'Not really. I like the sweeties on top.'

'I'm here to ask about your son.'

The wide blue eyes stared at Anna and then the woman's face crumpled.

'I have a son, but . . .'

'You haven't seen him for a while, have you?'

'What is his name?'

'Alan.'

'Yes, Alan – my son is called Alan.'

Kathleen turned to a dressing-table and pointed with the spoon to where there were many silver-framed photographs. Anna got up to look at them. They were family pictures, the young Kathleen smiling to camera and very obviously heavily pregnant, another with her husband and holding a small toddler. They went from a schoolboy smiling with a bicycle to a young handsome teenager, with the same blue eyes as his mother, but even from the photographs there was a shyness about him.

Anna picked up one and returned to sit beside Kathleen. It was, she surmised, probably quite a recent one. Alan was carrying a surfboard, so perhaps it had been taken abroad or in Cornwall, as Tina had mentioned he went there. He was tanned and smiling and looking more confident than in any of the other photographs.

'He used to phone you, didn't he?'

Kathleen nodded, scraping the bowl for the remainder of her jelly.

'He is a very good boy. I never had any trouble with him and he comes to see me, but not for a while I don't think. Do you know where he is?'

'I am trying to find him.'

Rose barged in with milky tea in a plastic cup with two handles.

'Do you want one?' she asked Anna.

'No, thank you.'

Rose cleared the tray and placed the tea on the little table.

'Did you see Alan recently?' Anna asked her.

'No, not for weeks. He would drop by here sometimes after work to see his mum – always brought flowers and she likes jelly babies so he'd bring them for her too. She gets confused now and I don't think she's realised how long it's been, but it's almost seven or eight weeks.'

'How did you get along with him?'

'Me?'

'Yes. The last time you saw him, did he seem out of sorts or worried?'

'No, he was always cheerful. Well, it was a bit put on for her because he was actually very worried about how his father would cope. She's got worse, but whenever he came she would brighten up.'

Kathleen held the plastic tea cup with both shaking hands.

'I just said how much you liked the visits from Alan.'

'I'm not deaf, Rose – no need to shout at me.'

Rose lifted her eyes to the ceiling.

'This lady is a detective, Rose.'

She threw a look to Anna and walked out.

'She treats me as if I'm deaf, but it's not my hearing that's the problem. And she always puts too much sugar in my tea.'

'Did you meet Alan's fiancée?'

'Who, dear?'

'Your son's fiancée, Tina?'

'Is he coming?'

'I don't know, but did you meet his girlfriend?'

Kathleen nodded and plucked a tissue to dab at her mouth.

'She's rather common, but I never said anything to him. She wanted to cut my hair, but I didn't want it short, I've always had long hair. She asked if I had it dyed. "My hair is natural," I said, "and my husband has always liked it, and he sometimes brushes it for me when I go to bed."'

'So you didn't really approve of Tina?'

Kathleen's pale eyes looked confused. 'Who, dear?'

At this moment there was the sound of the front door and Edward Rawlins called out, 'I'm home!' Anna heard him running up the stairs and the bedroom door opened. 'Rose said you had a visitor and—'

There was such a bereft look on his face when he saw Anna that she realised he had thought it was his son.

Anna stood up to shake his hand.

'I am so sorry,' he said. 'Rose was eager to leave and she just said we had a visitor. For a moment . . .'

He attempted to hide his emotion by crossing to his wife and kissing her.

'How are you, dearest?' he asked.

Kathleen looked confused again and he sat back on his heels beside her. 'It's Edward, dearest,' he said gently. 'It's me. Have you had your tea?'

'Not yet. Rose is bringing it up.'

Edward turned to Anna and suggested they go downstairs and leave Kathleen in peace. She said in an aside to him that Rose had already brought up his wife's tray.

'I know she forgets when she has eaten, or forgets to eat. Do go down and I'll join you in a moment.'

He turned back to his wife, 'Do you need the toilet?'

Kathleen nodded. It was as endearing as it was wretched

27

to see him help his wife from the chair, but it was too late. Anna could hear him saying he would get her a nice clean nightdress.

Downstairs, Anna was unsure which room to use. She pushed open the door to what looked like a comfortable lounge with a television and gas fire. The furnishings were not as worn, but looked well-used, and there was a tray with a napkin over a plate.

Edward eventually joined Anna and asked if he could offer her a glass of sherry, and although she didn't want one, she agreed. He was such a sprightly little man, fetching crystal glasses, opening the bottle and placing a small table at Anna's side. He glanced at the covered tray.

'Rose will have opened another tin of tuna. She means well, but I sometimes wish I could tell her that I'd prefer to make my own supper. She even manages to mangle the tomatoes.' He moved the tray away and sat, then lifted his glass and sipped the sweet sherry.

'Your wife must have been very beautiful,' Anna began.

'She was. To me she still is, but I don't know how long the Social Services will help me, keeping on a carer like Rose. Still, I'm sure you are not here to be privy to our problems.'

His puppy-dog eyes were like a spaniel's as he asked, 'Do you have any news of Alan?'

'No, I'm afraid not, but I interviewed Tina today.'

Mr Rawlins nodded and sipped his sherry again.

'Your wife wasn't too keen on her.'

'Did she tell you that? Well, that surprises me. Kathleen never says a bad word about anyone. She only came here a couple of times. Kathleen's problems started a while ago, and in the early stages, before she was diagnosed, we didn't understand her mood changes. She could sometimes say things totally out of character, and she and Tina didn't hit it off.'

'She remembered that Tina was a hairdresser.'

'Ah yes. That's sometimes so hard to understand – how she can suddenly recall mundane things and then forget the important ones.'

'She didn't like her – did you?'

'To be honest, I had hoped Alan could do better, but he seemed to dote on her, so who was I to say anything? Often, the less said the better, and I sort of hoped that in time he would see for himself.'

'See what?'

'She's a bit of a pushy girl and I know he helped finance her salon, but then when he said they planned to marry I suppose I just accepted it. He is such a shy boy and I thought that having her with him might give him a bit of a confidence boost.'

'Did it?'

'I don't know. He was always very busy and saved every penny as they were buying a house together. I helped him buy this old Mercedes and he was doing it up to sell. We'd done a couple of other cars and he'd always made a profit and split the proceeds with me. He's as honest as . . .' His voice started to crack. 'I'm sorry, I just can't seem to accept the fact that he's disappeared. It just doesn't make any sense.'

'Tell me, did he have another, secret girlfriend?'

'No, not that I know of, but then he wouldn't have told me. Well, I don't think he would have because deep down he knew that we were not too keen on Tina.'

'Take me through the last time you saw him.'

Mr Rawlins took a deep breath. He explained how they

had sat with Kathleen and then come into the lounge to discuss what they should do about future care.

'He said he was worried about finances and I said I wouldn't allow her to be taken into a home, that I'd cope somehow. With Rose here it's not that bad. The only thing is, she leaves at six when I get home, so it means I am sort of trapped here every evening – not that I mind, but it's hard not to be able to even go out for the odd pint, and then weekends I have her.'

He sipped his sherry.

'I said to Alan that if the worst came to the worst, I would sell this house. I own it outright, no mortgage or anything, and it's worth quite a lot of money. I'd be prepared to sell and scale down, maybe rent a place where I could look after Kathleen. This has five bedrooms and . . .' His voice trailed off.

'Did he ask you for money?'

'Alan? Good God no, he earns a good wage, and I know if I ever needed help he wouldn't hesitate.'

'Are you aware if he had any enemies?'

'Not that I know of. He's not the type to make anyone go against him; he is, whether it's a good sign or a bad one, very much like me. I have always hated confrontations and he is the same. He'd walk away from a fight.'

'Did he and Tina fight?'

'That I couldn't tell you. We only ever went to the flat the once when they were moving in. Well, I did, Kathleen never saw it. It seemed very modern, but the rent wasn't too high.'

'Did you ever hear him say he had argued with anyone?'

'No. I've never known him to get on the wrong side of anyone, not that he can't take care of himself.'

'How do you mean?'

'Well, that was where he met Tina — at the local gym. He works out a lot, he's very fit, and he goes for a run every morning. He is a fine strapping lad, but even though I would say he could take care of himself, if he needed to, I have never known him get into any fisticuffs.'

Mr Rawlins topped up his sherry, offering to pour Anna another, but she put her hand over her half-filled glass.

'When you first came to see me, you said that you felt your son had been murdered,' she said quietly.

'Yes.'

'But from what we have just discussed, there doesn't seem to be anything to indicate to me that that could have happened.'

He took a deep breath. 'All I know is this. I had a good caring son, a boy who never missed seeing his mother or phoning me to check how I was dealing with it all. Alan had arranged for us to go and see a film, which meant he would have fixed up a sitter for Kathleen. We'd done it a couple of times and it was the only chance I had to get out — not that I am complaining, please don't think that. He said he would call me back when he'd checked what was on, and that was the last time I spoke to him. That was almost eight weeks ago.'

'Yes, I am aware of that.'

'Eight weeks, when there was never a week that passed when he didn't contact us. All the way through when he was at college, even when he was a teenager, Alan was caring and thoughtful. I love my son, Detective Travis — he is my best friend and he is also someone I admire, and this silence, if you can call it that, is totally out of character.'

He stood up and he had two pink spots on his cheeks.

31

'I will sell this house; I will do anything I have to, even if it means hiring private investigators, to find out what has happened. I know he has taken no money and no clothes, not even his mobile phone, but when I first spoke to her, she said his passport was still in the flat. Now she has changed her story again and said to the Missing Persons investigators that it's not there.'

'It would appear, Mr Rawlins, that your son may have left of his own choice as his toiletries, some clothing and passport are no longer at his flat. Miss Brooks phoned you when Alan first went missing and it could be that you have misunderstood some of what she was saying at the time.'

'I haven't always been a court usher, DCI Travis. I was a qualified engineer and section manager for a very reputable company. I am not a silly old man who misunderstands what he is told, I have a strong bond with my son and I know when something is wrong.'

Anna got up. It was time to leave. She didn't want to become embroiled in his suppositions since, unless they found any incriminating evidence, she would have nothing else to do with the case. She was really embarrassed when Mr Rawlins moved close to her, too close, and she had to step back.

'Please help me find out the truth. If he is dead, I will have to cope with it; if he has been murdered I want to know why, and more than that, I want to know who killed him – because, so help me God, that is what I believe has happened. Alan has been murdered.'

Anna could feel the room closing in on her and she was desperate to get out.

'Will you help me?'

'Mr Rawlins, I *am* helping you and I will continue to

investigate your son's disappearance, but without any evidence to support your belief that he has been murdered—'

Edward Rawlins interrupted her, shouting, 'Are you telling me that without a body you can't treat this as a murder enquiry?'

'I am, Mr Rawlins, asking you to be patient. I will do everything in my power to hopefully reach a conclusion.'

Mr Rawlins was at the door and she was unable to walk out of the room.

'A conclusion? What do you mean by that?'

'Exactly what I said. So far we haven't found any evidence that suggests your son was murdered.'

'He has been missing for almost two months, isn't that conclusive proof that he is dead?'

'No, it is not. Now please move away from the door, Mr Rawlins. I do understand why you are distressed, but it can't help the situation. Please let me leave.'

He crumpled and covered his face with his hands.

'I am so sorry, so very sorry. Please forgive me, I apologise. I'll show you out.'

Anna hurried down the dank hallway as Kathleen called out from upstairs, not her husband's name, but Alan's.

Anna sat in her car, shaking. Her head was throbbing and she couldn't wait to get home, away from the smells, the obsessive, dapper, desperate father, the vacant blue-eyed mother. She began to think that if she had been in their son's shoes, she might have upped and gone. Their desperation clung to her and she even contemplated the idea that perhaps Alan had discovered Tina was not the woman he wanted to marry, his parents suffocated him with their neediness and he had just, as in numerous other cases, decided to disappear.

On returning home Anna ran a bath and contemplated washing her hair with a colour enhancing shampoo that she had bought months ago but never used. She read the details on the bottle about how it would boost her natural hue but decided not to bother. Lying soaking in the hot water she wondered if her lack of interest in her appearance was down to her own apathy or the fact that she felt she no longer had anyone to glam herself up for.

In her own fresh bed with a scented candle burning, Anna lay wide awake. Had Alan Rawlins planned his disappearance? If so, they would need to unearth some clue. He appeared to be above reproach – honest, hard-working and caring – but had this shy, yet fit young man had a hidden agenda? Would he, being such a good person, be prepared to walk away from his hard-earned savings?

Again Anna put herself in his place, in that dark house with two needy parents who seemed to have no one else in their lives but their beloved son. She then thought about the featureless rented flat he shared with Tina Brooks, a dominant woman. He'd paid for her salon and yet knew his parents didn't like her – only two visits in all the time they had lived together.

Anna recalled the many photographs in Kathleen Rawlins's over-heated bedroom of their perfect son, and she had to agree he was handsome, with his mother's blue eyes and thick wondrous hair. One photograph stuck in her mind, of Alan carrying a surfboard, looking tanned and muscular, smiling. Anna blew out the perfumed candle, certain that she was correct: Alan Rawlins had arranged his own disappearance, in order to be free of them all.

'You must have been working late or came in very early,' Anna said as Paul handed her a list before she could even take her coat off.

'Early, but I couldn't sleep. There's something about this Alan Rawlins that doesn't sit right. Maybe it's his girlfriend Tina – she doesn't ring true. Look, these are all the people I've arranged to interview. We now know that his mobile was pay-as-you-go, but the calls and texts don't show anything suspicious and pretty much fit with what Tina told us.'

Anna looked down the list, adding up how long it would take to interview everyone.

'Listen, Paul, I've given it a lot of thought and I've come to the conclusion that this is all a waste of time.'

'But didn't *you* think that something didn't add up?'

'If I queried everything that "didn't add up", we'd never get anything done, and quite honestly, I don't think I'm prepared to spend much more time on this. We've not actually been allocated Rawlins's disappearance as a murder investigation; Mispers are still handling it.'

'Yeah, along with how many hundreds of other missing persons? He's just going to be a number, Anna. That washed-out beige on beige in that flat gave me the creeps.'

'Look, I'll tell you what. We'll sift through these people on the list, but as far as I am concerned, that is going to be that.'

'I think you've changed your feelings since yesterday.'

Anna sighed and gave him a brief rundown of her meeting with Alan's parents. Paul wagged his finger, smiling.

'So last night you did have the same feelings as I have?'

'No, last night I was hesitant, but after talking to Mr Rawlins I came to the conclusion that, given the circumstances, Alan Rawlins has simply taken the easiest route out of all the pressures.'

'What pressures?'

'That he had maybe made the wrong choice of girlfriend and that his parents were too needy and he'd just had enough.'

'You think.'

'Yes, that is exactly what I think, and to be honest, if I'd been in his situation I might have been tempted to do the same thing.'

'But you don't know for sure if that is what he would have done. You are just surmising or putting yourself in his situation.'

'Don't make me repeat myself, Paul, but yes, that is exactly what I'd have done. There is not a scrap of evidence that gives us probable cause for a murder, and I don't know if you checked about any life-insurance policies . . .'

'I have.'

'And?'

'Alan Rawlins had a life-insurance policy for fifty thousand pounds,' Paul stated.

'Well, you know it takes years before someone can be declared dead after disappearing, and I can't see Tina as the type to hang around waiting.'

'Why should she when she's got their joint bank account?'

Anna headed towards her office. Over her shoulder she told Paul to book out a CID car so they could get started.

'Already done – your carriage awaits you downstairs, ma'am.'

Irritated, she turned back to him. 'Just give me a minute, all right?'

The first place they went to was Metcalf Auto in Staines Road. It was a small business, but it looked as if they were busy. There were four cars for sale on their forecourt, two workshops with cars waiting for repairs, and inside the main garage, a Volvo was up on a ramp being checked out by two mechanics. Inside the small office cubicle, which contained just a desk and swivel chair, was the head mechanic, Joe Smedley. He was well-built and dark-haired with a thick beard that made him look like a gerbil. He had an equally thick growth of chest hair that spouted from the open neck of his overalls.

Anna introduced herself and Paul, and having nowhere to sit they both stood in the doorway. Joe got up to shake their hands and showed himself to be surprisingly short.

'Is this about Alan?'

'Yes. We'd like to ask you a few questions; hopefully we won't take up too much of your time.'

'You take as long as you need to. We've all been worried sick about him; he was one of my best mechanics. I've already had to replace him – couldn't keep his job open any longer as we're so busy. Since the recession began we've had a lot of work, as customers who used to change their cars regularly now just keep the old ones and get them repaired. It's been good for us.'

'Tell me about the last time you saw Alan, Mr Smedley,' Anna said as she glanced around the rows of documents pinned up on a cork board.

'It'd be the Monday, a good few weeks ago now. I'll have it in my diary, the exact date. He came to work as usual – always on time he was, sometimes he'd be here a lot earlier to work on his own car – but if I remember correctly, he was over at the fridge in the garage taking out a bottle of water. He looked a bit wan. I asked him if he was feeling okay and he just said he had a bad headache.'

Smedley scratched his thick beard and opened a drawer in his desk, taking out a diary.

'About a couple of hours later he came in here and said he was feeling really bad and could he use my phone. He said he felt he should go home, but didn't want to drive himself. He called Tina, asking her to pick him up. Then he went out and sat on the forecourt with the bottle of water.'

Joe passed over his work diary to show Anna the exact date, and where he had written that Alan had left work.

'Tina arrived, he went over to her car and got in, and that was the last time I saw him. When he didn't turn up for work the next day I just thought he was still feeling bad so I didn't call Tina until the day after. No, wait a minute . . .'

He scratched at his beard again.

'She called here first, asking if Alan had come in to work. I said he hadn't and that I wondered if he was still sick, but she hung up. I rang a couple more times because as I said before, we're busy and we needed him here, but he never rang back and she said she hadn't seen him.'

'On that Monday, was he acting strangely?'

'What do you mean? All he said to me was he had a headache and he looked a bit off-colour.'

'How about other times previous to that Monday?'

'I don't understand.'

'Well, had he acted out of character?'

'No. He was a quiet one, though. He wasn't a drinker

and he never socialised with either me or the other mechanics, but he was a hard worker and a nice bloke.'

'Did you meet Tina on any other occasions?'

'Not really. I'd seen her, obviously; she'd collected Alan a couple of times when his car wasn't roadworthy. She'd just pull up, toot her horn and he'd drive off with her.' He shrugged. 'To be honest, I think she thought of herself as being above the rest of us. They never even came to the bit of a do we had over last Christmas, but that wasn't my business.'

'Did he have a locker?'

'Yeah, it's at the back of the garage. Used to keep some of his clothes here and change when he turned up for work.'

'Can we see it?'

'Course. I've not emptied it, just in case.'

'Just in case of what?'

They followed Joe out from his office across the garage.

'Him coming back to work. I miss him and I tell you something – he's been working on that Merc of his for months. He is planning to sell it and should get a good price, maybe not a lot right now, but if he holds onto it it'll get a nice wedge as it's in great nick and he was just waiting for a soft top to be delivered.'

Joe took out a large ring of keys as they approached a row of thin lockers. The two mechanics working on the Volvo looked over then returned to work. Inside the locker was a pair of greasy stained overalls, a pair of oil-streaked trainers and a couple of jumpers. On the top shelf were manuals and auto-repair magazines. Paul checked the pockets of the overalls and flicked through the magazines. They found nothing personal; in one pocket was a packet of aspirin and a folded handkerchief.

'Do you know if everything was all right between Alan and Tina?'

Joe hunched his shoulders and gave a wide gesture.

'I wouldn't know. He was a very private guy. Like I said, I only met her a couple of times. I think they were going to get married, but he never really even discussed that with me.'

Joe led them out of the garage and towards the workshop storing the cars waiting for repair. Covered in a green tarpaulin was Alan Rawlins's Mercedes and it was, as he had said, in very good condition. Joe went into a long explanation of what Alan had done, from respraying to fitting new engine parts. Even the leather seats had been re-upholstered.

'It's odd that he wouldn't want to take this, wherever he is. He must have spent weeks on it — in his own time, mind — but I know he was waiting for that soft top to be delivered. Maybe . . .'

'Maybe?' Anna prompted.

'I don't know. It's just not like him to take off without letting me know. He's worked here for five years and he's been a bloody good employee, always on time. In fact, he's hardly ever taken a day off unless for his holidays.'

'Do you know where he went on these holidays?'

Joe nodded. 'Well, I know he went on a sailing trip in Turkey once and a number of times he went surfing in Cornwall.' Joe gestured at the workshop. 'His board is back there. He said he didn't have much space in his flat and could he store it there. It was an expensive one, because I think he was pretty good at it. Do you want to see it?'

'I don't think so, thank you. What about his mobile phone?'

'That was in his glove compartment. I think Tina came round for it when I wasn't here.'

As they returned to Joe's office Paul said he would need to have a word with the other mechanics before leaving. Anna thought there was really nothing else she could ask him, but Joe wanted to know if she felt that something bad had happened to Alan.

'By bad, what do you mean?'

'Well, it's odd, isn't it? He's a good bloke, a hard worker, and for him to take off without a word to anyone isn't like him, so maybe something has happened to him.'

'Like what?'

'I dunno – he's got mugged or something. He was very particular about himself, always very spruced up. He wore a spotless white T-shirt under his overalls, even his jeans were pressed, and I know he worked out a lot in the local gym because he'd sometimes have his tracksuit with him. Even that was always pristine, and I don't know how many times he'd wash his hands. Sometimes he'd even wear surgical rubber gloves if he was doing up an oily engine, and—'

Paul interrupted him. 'You mind if I ask you something personal about Alan?'

Joe shook his head.

'Was Alan Rawlins gay?'

'*Gay?*'

'Yes.'

Joe stared at him, then laughed. 'Because of what I just told you about him? Well, if he was, he kept that well-hidden, and if you want my opinion, he was straight. He was getting married and there was no way he ever gave me any indication he was a poof. Is that what *she* says about him?'

'She?'

'Tina. I mean, she'd be the one to ask – right? Not that I have anything against them, but I've never employed one.'

'A homosexual?'

'Yeah. Sometimes this is heavy work, not to mention getting dirty and oil-streaked, so I've never had anyone light on their feet so to speak.'

Paul, irritated by Joe's comments, left the office to go and speak with the other mechanics.

'You said he worked out – do you know which gym?'

'Yeah, he used a local gym called Body Form in Inwood Street, next to the park, did a bit of weight-lifting and ran the odd marathon for charity so he was fit. He was also a good-looking fella, not that he ever made it obvious. In fact, I don't think he ever realised that he was a bit of a head-turner.'

'How do you mean?'

'Well, we had a girl in the office handling the calls a couple of years back. She had to go because we couldn't afford her, but she was all of a-flutter if he came anywhere near her.'

Anna smiled and said that he had been very helpful and she appreciated the time he had given.

'You never answered my question,' Joe said, following her out.

'I'm sorry, what question?'

'You're a detective and we've had people from some other Department for Missing Persons talking to us. What do you think has happened to him?'

'That is what we are trying to find out, Mr Smedley.'

As Anna returned to the car she looked at her watch and realised that talking to Joe Smedley had taken longer than she had anticipated. It was a further ten minutes before Paul finished speaking to the mechanics in the workshop and she could then see him in the garage yard talking on his mobile. When Paul finally returned Anna found herself even more irritated as he stated the obvious.

'Mechanics couldn't add anything interesting. We're running late,' he said to Anna as he got into the car. 'I called Dan Matthews, and he said he could wait – he's a graphic designer and we're seeing him in his studio. The other bloke, Julian Vickers, has had to put us off until later this morning. Just as well, as he's all the way over in Kilburn.'

'Why did you bring up that Alan might be gay?'

'Way the hairy man was describing him – the clean white T-shirt, pressed jeans, rubber surgical gloves, all that – he was a mechanic, for chrissakes. Plus him being a fitness freak – I just thought he might be a closet.'

'Really! Well, I don't buy that. Let's drop in at the Body Form gym Alan used. How long have we got?'

'Two hours.'

'Fine. Maybe we can also see if Tina is at work. I'd like to take a look at her salon.'

'Whatever you say. But it was just a thought about Alan.'

'Maybe best to keep your thoughts to yourself, Paul.'

They drove in silence for a while and then Paul asked Anna what she was thinking. She smiled.

'Just making a food shopping list in my head for later.' She didn't tell him what was really on her mind. Sometimes it felt as if she was acting on autopilot, that everything she said and did was just going through the motions, but she was really elsewhere, in some kind of lethargic haze. It was becoming one of those days where she was finding it hard to motivate herself to do anything, let alone her job.

The Body Form gym was small and almost empty. There were two fitness instructors sitting at a coffee bar in a glass-fronted area where some elderly women were having an aerobics class. Music was thudding out, but the rows of equipment were stationary. The weight room had one man lifting and he looked as if he was ready for a seizure. The manager, Benjamin Issacs, was a muscular giant of a man who was clearly into body-building as a daily ritual. He introduced himself as 'Big Ben' and then took Anna and Paul to his office and invited them to take a seat. He recalled Alan Rawlins at one time being very regular, but over the past six months he had only been in to work out a couple of times. He said he was always polite, not a mixer – and then 'Big Ben' laughed, observing that Alan was very different from his girlfriend.

Tina was still a regular customer, coming in two or three times a week. She would take the advanced aerobic sessions and spend a lot of time at the coffee bar being very friendly and chatting to everyone. In fact, she had been there the previous night. He did know that Alan and Tina had met at the gym and added that he was surprised when they became engaged.

'Why surprised?'

'Well, she was really outgoing and he was the opposite – very quiet and studious, came in to work out and then left. He didn't mix with anyone here, but she did. Yeah, Tina is definitely a mixer.' Again he chuckled.

'Give me a bit more detail on the mixer description?' Anna said, smiling encouragement.

'Well, not to slight her, but she did put it about a bit. She was sexy and she liked the body-builders; in fact, she went through the members like a dose of salts.'

'What about after she became engaged?'

'She behaved herself if he was around, but if he wasn't, she'd be flirting as usual.'

'With you, for instance?'

Ben nodded. 'Yeah, we had a fling a few years back, but I'm married with kids and it just . . . couldn't happen.'

'Anyone you know of recently who she was having a fling with?'

'No. To be honest, it's very quiet and we've had to let a couple of guys go. Business isn't as good as it was. We pick up more of an evening, but the daytime is virtually empty.'

'When she was last here, did she seem upset?'

'No, she was the same as usual.'

'Flirty?' Anna smiled.

'Look, don't get me wrong, it's just the way she is.'

'When was the last time you saw Alan Rawlins?'

'Like I said, a few months ago. He was no different, worked out, said a few hellos and left. When he stopped coming regular he cancelled his direct debit and just paid at the door.'

'Do you think he was aware that Tina flirted when she was here?'

'I don't know. They didn't always come in together and she was usually in the aerobic gym, not in the cardio or weight room.'

Anna thanked 'Big Ben' for his time and she and Paul left the gym. En route to the car Paul reminded Anna that the next interview was in Chiswick with Dan Matthews and then on to Kilburn to see Julian Vickers the deli manager.

'Will we have time to go to Tina's salon as well today?' Anna asked as Paul drove off.

'Might be pushing it but they don't close until six.'

Anna closed her eyes, sighing.

'Still working on that grocery list?' Paul enquired.

She gave a small smile, not opening her eyes. 'Laundry now.'

Paul drove for a while before he brought up what they had gathered from the gym.

'She put it about and he didn't seem to be aware of it. These strong silent types often have a long fuse that when it blows, it sky rockets.'

'What am I supposed to gather from that statement?'

'That maybe he found out and went ballistic and—'

'Paul, it's Alan that's missing – not Tina.'

'I meant that he blew up and decided that he'd had enough and walked out.'

'What – without his car and no money? And we've no credit-card transactions. I don't think he just walked out.'

'You're changing your tune?'

'No. I am more than ever beginning to think he planned to go. Like I said, he had his parents on his back, he fell out with Tina – which is even more likely, now we know she was a sexpot and had had it away with all the members of the gym. We know he was a shy introverted man, someone who hated confrontations so he took the easy way . . .'

They drew up at a small mews courtyard just off Chiswick High Road and parked outside *Matthews Graphic Studio*.

They climbed up an exterior circular iron staircase that led onto a small balcony with sliding glass doors which in turn opened into the large studio space. Dan Matthews was working on a Mac as they approached. He was slender, wearing a T-shirt and skinny-legged jeans that made him look like a drainpipe. He had large horn-rimmed glasses on and his mousy brown hair was cut short at the sides and long on top.

Anna knocked then entered and introduced herself and Paul, and thanked Dan for agreeing to see them. She went straight to the point of their visit, asking if he was aware that Alan Rawlins had disappeared.

'Yes, I know. Tina has rung me a few times asking if I've seen him, but I haven't for at least four months. It's really awful.' He looked at Paul. 'Ever since you got in touch I've been trying to think of everything we talked about, the last time we met up. He used to come here quite often; I've helped him a couple of times with some drawings for personalising his cars. You know, he was very good at respraying motor bikes as well as cars.'

'How did he seem to you when you last saw him?'

'Same as always. We've been friends since schooldays. He went on to engineering college and I went to art school, but we always kept in touch. Maybe not so much recently.'

'Why was that?'

'He got engaged and was caught up with Tina.'

'Are you married?'

'No.'

'Did you meet Tina?'

'Just the once. We went out for dinner in order for me to meet her.'

'And?'

'Well, she was not my type. She wasn't interested in anything we talked about and she didn't like the restaurant as she complained that she wasn't keen on Chinese food. She had a few too many glasses of wine as well.'

'So it wasn't a good evening?'

'No. It's always difficult when you don't get on with your best friend's partner. It wasn't that I disliked her, I just didn't think she was the right choice for Alan. He was a bit agitated around her, wanting me to like her, I suppose, and although I never said anything to him we just didn't see each other as regularly.'

Dan's eyes seemed large behind the horn-rimmed spectacles.

'What has happened to him? His father has phoned me asking if I've heard anything from him. Mr Rawlins was very distressed; in fact, he broke down in tears.'

'Yes, it's very difficult, but we are attempting to trace him,' said Anna.

Paul looked around at the artwork on the walls. He nudged Anna. There was a large acrylic painting of Alan Rawlins on a surfboard and he went across to look at it more closely.

'This is Alan, isn't it?'

'Yes. I did that after he brought me a photograph of when he was surfing in Cornwall. I thought I'd give it to him as a wedding present . . .'

'Did he know you were working on it?'

'Yes, and he was pleased. It's also a very good likeness.'

As Dan and Paul went and stood in front of the painting, Anna glanced around the studio. It was obvious why these two men would be friends: everything was neat and orderly, and Dan was clearly good at his job. She checked her watch.

'I think we need to go, Paul.'

Dan returned to stand beside her with his big, owl eyes blinking.

'What do you think has happened to him?'

48

'We're trying to find out.'

'But it's been eight weeks! Surely he would have at least called his parents?'

Anna turned to go down the stairs while Paul was shaking Dan's hand, thanking him for his time.

'Did you know his parents?' Paul was asking.

Anna sighed with irritation since Dan had already said Mr Rawlins had phoned him, so it was obvious that he did.

'Yes. I was often round there when we were at school. My mother worked so I'd spend a lot of time with them. Alan's mother always made us tea so my mum wouldn't have to cook anything when I got home. It's very sad what has happened to her as she was such a vibrant and fun-loving lady. Alan adored her. He was very concerned that taking care of her was too much for his father, and sometimes when he took his dad out he'd ask me to sit with her. They have a carer, but she leaves as soon as Mr Rawlins returns home and he's become housebound as a result.'

'Paul,' Anna called, heading down the stairs. He eventually joined her outside the studio as she waited in the car.

'Nice bloke,' he said, getting in.

'Yes, and easy to see why they would be friends.' Anna stared out from the window of the passenger seat, feeling hungry. They just had the next interview to complete, and then she could have some lunch.

'He's gay.'

'Pardon?'

Paul turned out of the mews. 'I said Dan Matthews is gay – he told me just as you left. He also said that Alan—'

'Don't tell me you were right?'

'No, what he said to me was that when they were in the sixth form he told Alan that he knew he was homosexual and was terrified of it. Apparently, Alan told him that whatever he was he should keep private as it was his life and no one else's.'

Anna looked at Paul. 'And . . .?'

'Well, it was just such a grown-up thing for Alan to say and the fact is that they remained friends. Dan's confession made no difference. The poor guy is really distressed; he was almost in tears when I left.'

'You got all that very fast?'

'Takes one to know one.'

'I'm sorry?'

Paul sighed and hit the steering wheel with the flat of his hand.

'Don't tell me you don't know.'

'Know what?'

'You must be the only person at the station who doesn't know, not that I am in any way embarrassed – to the contrary.'

'You're gay?'

'Ah, the penny finally dropped, has it, ma'am? Yes, I am.'

She giggled. 'I didn't know.'

'Well, now you do. Did you think that Alan was playing for the opposite team?'

Again she giggled. 'No, I didn't actually, but what do you think?'

'I reckon he was straight. Well, Dan said he was and I don't get the feedback that he was a closet. It was the painting that sort of gave me the hint about Matthews. Alan was bloody good-looking, wasn't he?'

'Yes, I suppose he was.'

Paul glanced at her. 'You have a very infectious giggle, ma'am.'

'Really?'

'In fact, it's the first time I've heard it. Wondered what it takes to make you laugh.'

Anna felt herself plunge into the void. It happened so quickly, she couldn't speak; her heart hammered and it took a huge amount of control to straighten out and push the overriding panic down inside her.

'After the next interview we should grab a bite to eat,' she said.

'Okay by me.'

Paul didn't even notice as he was concentrating on driving, but Anna's face was drained of colour and her hands were so tightly clenched her knuckles were white.

The next interview was with Julian Vickers, the manager of a small deli in Kilburn. The shop was stacked with all makes of cheeses and hams and imported Italian pasta, with a counter for takeaway sandwiches. Julian was a rather overweight young man with thinning hair and lovely blue eyes, wearing a white apron, and he was at least six foot three. He was openly friendly, and Anna and Paul watched as he sliced some ham for an elderly lady. When she left Anna flipped the door sign to closed and apologised to Julian, saying she needed to talk to him in private but would not take up too much of his valuable time.

'I have had calls from Al's father, but I haven't been in contact with Alan himself for five or six months. This is all terrible, and my wife and I were trying to remember everything that we discussed the last time he came over.

I've known Al since we were at school, and in fact I make up a hamper every Christmas for his dad because he likes his cheese and a good port.'

As he talked, Julian moved boxes of groceries off two chairs so they could sit down. He said that his friendship with Alan had been very important. His own family had suggested he was out of his mind to start a deli when he didn't know the first thing about it, but Alan had lent him money to open up, and Julian had proved to be successful even if he did have to work around the clock.

'So at this last meeting with Alan ...?'

'Right. Yes. He would sometimes come over on a Saturday night because I have Sundays off, and we'd try out all the new goods. The last time, we had some herrings marinated in ginger. God, they were bloody awful, made the eyes water.' He laughed and then his face fell.

'I know he was engaged, but he never brought his fiancée round, and often my wife would leave us alone to chat. We both worked out together – I may not look as if I do now, but we used to. We even ran marathons, which I couldn't do now. I run to post a letter and I'm knackered.'

'Did he give any indication the last time you met that anything was wrong?'

'No. We mostly talked about the Mercedes he was doing up as I thought I had someone who would be interested. In fact, he didn't stay all that long. He doesn't drink like me, just the odd glass. He's always been a fitness freak, but he said ...' Julian closed his eyes, genuinely upset.

'I tell you something a bit odd. He had asked before then if I'd be his best man, but the last time I saw him, he never brought it up so I didn't either. You never know, nowadays women come and they go, unlike my wife. I've been hoping she'd go for years.'

He laughed and then said that it was a joke.

'We've been married since I left college. We're expecting twins, which was something else me and Alan spoke about. Well, it's going to be a big financial situation for me and as always he said that if I needed anything, like a few thousand, he was good for it.'

Julian took out a handkerchief; his stunning blue eyes were full of tears, all jokes forgotten.

'I hope to God nothing bad has happened to him. He was one of the best people I know. Nothing was too much trouble for him, and as I said, he helped me start up . . .'

'Do you think he could or would just take off and disappear?' Anna asked. 'That maybe being a Good Samaritan became too much for him?'

Paul glanced at Anna. It was on the nail and Julian was already showing signs of distress.

'No. I personally could not think of any reason why he would do that. I know he worried about his parents, but he was earning good money. Although . . .'

Anna and Paul waited. Julian blew his nose and then tucked his handkerchief into his pocket.

'In all the years I have known Alan he *was* like a Samaritan – I'll give you that – but he was a genuine caring person. You could look at this big blonde handsome guy and think he'd be a real arsehole, but he wasn't. In fact, he was shy, never self-opinionated. I often wondered if there was another side to him, but I never saw it.'

'Or was it just he never showed it to you?'

'You find anyone with a bad word against him and it'd surprise me. I think he was the product of a very loving home. Any time you wanted, his mother would welcome you in, cook up a storm, and their house was always full of kids whose parents were not at home or working. His dad was terrific, arranging outings, packing us into his old Volvo, sometimes taking us off to Brighton funfair. He seemed to have an inside knowledge of the best fairs – Clapham Common, Wimbledon, Putney . . .'

Anna stood up and thanked Julian, but he wasn't prepared to let them leave his deli without making up a packed lunch of thick-wedged sandwiches and potato salad with sauerkraut, refusing to allow them to pay.

Anna and Paul parked at the back of Julian's deli in a small side street so they could tuck in and enjoy their lunch without being seen by the public. Paul ate hungrily, but Anna just picked at hers, her appetite gone. They had been given two bottles of a chilled ginger and elderflower drink as well, which was delicious. For a while they ate in silence.

'What are you thinking?' Paul eventually asked.

'I wish you wouldn't keep asking me that.'

'Okay – do you want to know what *I* am thinking?'

'If I said no, would it stop you?'

Paul took a big bite of the sandwich. He had mayonnaise dripping down his chin and he used one of the paper napkins to wipe it off.

'Well, go on.' She folded her own half-eaten sandwich back into its wrapping.

'I'll finish that off if you're through with it?'

She passed it to him.

'He's dead, isn't he?' Paul said, staring straight ahead as Anna drank from her bottle before screwing the cap back on.

'We don't know that. What we need to do is find someone who saw the other side of Alan Rawlins, because so far I think it's all too good to be true. No one is that perfect. He *will* have secrets – maybe dark ones. So in answer to your question, we need to find out what made this Samaritan disappear because, as I said last time, I don't believe he is dead.'

Chapter Three

The last interview of the day was at Tina's salon in Hounslow High Street. She had agreed to see them again on the condition they came late in the afternoon just before closing as she had appointments booked.

'Her fiancé goes missing and she's too busy to see us. The more I hear about her, the less I like her.'

'Maybe she's seen the dark side?' Paul said smiling, but Anna was not amused. Instead she told him they should head straight there. She felt tired and decided she would take off home later, after making up the reports with Paul in their incident room.

'Make up a report? But we don't have a case,' Paul said as he drove.

'Nevertheless we'll need to show what the hell we've been doing all day. Besides, Langton will want to know.'

'Whatever you say, ma'am. He's knee-deep in a big case – double murder in North London.'

She made no reply, instead brushed away the crumbs from their picnic lunch and wrapped their napkins into the small deli bag Julian had provided. She tossed it into a rubbish bin as they pulled up in a small car park attached to Tina's Beauty Salon. She remarked that it wasn't a very artistic title and the large neon eye coated in eye-shadow and false lashes was tacky.

The salon was surprisingly well-equipped. A section was given over to hairdressing, then there was a row of booths for manicures and pedicures. Another section, separated by white screens, was the massage and therapy area and there was a small staircase to the floor above with a sauna, sunbeds and spray-tanning room. A notice informed them that the sunbeds were out of order. The place was jumping. Four women sat under dryers, a girl was blowdrying a customer's hair and another was having her hair washed at the row of sinks.

'Well, she said she was busy,' Paul murmured as they stood by a small reception desk. The receptionist was a girl with a fake tan, a mound of hair extensions and thick false eye-lashes. It also looked as if she'd had breast implants. Her pink Tina's Salon overall hardly met across her bust, colliding with her name embroidered over the pocket – Felicity.

'Could you ask Tina if we could see her, please?' Anna showed her warrant card, not that it made much of a difference.

'Do you have an appointment?'

'We do.'

Felicity dragged a fake nail down the customer lists.

'Just go and tell her we would like to talk to her,' Anna ordered.

'I can't leave the desk and she's doing a wrap so I can't interrupt her for another ten minutes.'

Anna was not sure what a wrap meant, but Felicity continued, explaining it was a seaweed wrap and would be finished shortly. She then indicated a row of pink plastic-covered gilt chairs.

'You can wait there.'

They were only two feet away from the reception; it looked as if every inch of the place was taken up with all the various beauty treatments. As Anna and Paul sat down the girl offered the salon's brochure and said there were several offers at half-price.

'Do you know her boyfriend, Alan?' Anna asked as she pretended to scrutinise the treatments on offer.

'Yes, we all do and it's just terrible. Poor Tina has been in such a state about it.' Her pink desk phone rang and Felicity picked up, speaking in an over-modulated posh accent.

'Tina's Beauty Salon, can I help you?'

Anna and Paul listened as she made an appointment for hair extensions and learned that it would take at least four hours if it was to remove the present extensions; it would take longer if the caller required new ones.

Anna glanced at Paul, but he seemed enthralled by Felicity's ongoing conversation.

'If we didn't actually put your extensions in for you, you should come in and have the hair matched. We only use real hair. No, there would be no charge for that, but is what you've got in real hair?'

The row of customers waiting for their cuts and blow-dries began to thin out; the two girls were working as if they were on a factory floor. The thudding music, now on an Abba compilation, continued.

'I'll book you in for an afternoon then. What's your name?' Then Felicity looked at the pink phone in fury. 'I don't believe she hung up! Honestly!'

'Could you please ask Tina to join us?' Anna said testily.

'I can't. It's a seaweed wrap and you can't leave it half-done.'

Anna stood up and pointed to the partition. 'Is she behind there?'

'No, upstairs, but you can't go through, it's a private consultation.' Felicity moved from her stool and put her hand up. 'I'll go and ask her to come out, all right?' She left.

Paul glanced over to the hairdressing section, remarking, 'She must be coining it in.'

Anna nodded to a card on Felicity's desk. 'It's half-price day and a few of the customers look like pensioners; they get a discount as well.'

Tina came down the stairs at the rear of the salon, wearing latex gloves that looked as if they were covered in mud, and a rubber apron. She didn't look very pleased to see them.

'I'll be with you in ten minutes – I'm with a client.' She didn't wait for an answer, but returned upstairs. Felicity asked if they would like a tea or coffee.

'We've got a little rest room right at the back by the stairs,' she said, 'and there's a coffee machine. Just help yourselves.'

Little was the operative word. It was more or less a corner with more screens, a couple of chairs and a table with coffee cups and mugs and packets of biscuits. A girl in one of Tina's pink overalls was standing eating a sandwich and brewing up coffee. She turned as Anna and Paul sat down on the chairs.

'Excuse me, I've not had a break today. I was starving and my lady's under the dryer.' She had a mouth full of her sandwich and wiped it with the back of her hand. 'Do you want a coffee?'

'No, thank you. We're waiting for Tina.'

'Okay. Busy today since nine this morning. I had two perms—'

'What's your name?' Anna interrupted.

'Donna.' The girl bit into her sandwich again.

Anna showed her warrant card and introduced herself and Paul. It had little effect as Donna was now making herself a mug of coffee, stuffing the remains of her lunch into her mouth.

'Is this about Alan?'

'Yes. Do you know him?'

Donna turned and nodded. 'We all do – well, we know who he is, but ...' She lowered her voice and moved closer. 'What's going on? Tina told us he left her. She was in a terrible state.'

'Did he come to the salon?'

'No, but he used to pick her up sometimes and wait outside in the car park. I think we all scared the pants off him. We used to have a couple of guys working here, but they didn't fit in.'

Tina walked in now minus the gloves and rubber apron, but with her pink salon smock.

'Donna, your customer is taking her own rollers out!'

'Sorry, sorry, but I never got lunch.' She scurried out and Tina crossed to the coffee percolator.

'I did say I was very busy and for you to come later. I couldn't leave my client; these wraps have to be done correctly. I'm training one of the girls, but I'm the only one really qualified. You have to layer the thick seaweed emulsion, then do a complete body wrap, but not too tight because the heat makes the seaweed dry. You lose a few pounds all over; it's a very good treatment.'

Tina poured herself a mug of coffee and then leaned on the table. 'Have you any news?'

'No, I am afraid not. Have you had any contact from Alan?'

'No. To be honest, I've been working really hard and it's the best thing for me – helps me not think about it – but I've had to get sleeping tablets. Every time the phone rings my heart jumps. I had to tell his father to stop calling me – he was driving me crazy.'

'We've talked to a few of Alan's friends, but nobody has seen him for quite a while. I really wanted to ask you about something you said – that there could have been another woman.'

'Well, it's all I can think about, the possibility. He could be very secretive sometimes.'

'Can you give me an example?'

'Well, yes. That Mercedes, he never told me he'd bought it. We were supposed to be saving up to get married. I only found out when I saw some receipts for spare parts – they cost a fortune.'

'Did you argue about it?'

She sighed. 'Alan didn't argue. I mean, I could shout and carry on at him, but it never seemed to bother him. He'd ignore it, or what really used to get me furious was he would just walk out of the room.'

'That must have been very frustrating,' Anna said.

Tina shrugged her shoulders. 'Yeah, sometimes it was.'

Paul was flicking through one of the glossy magazines; he appeared to be paying no attention to what they were discussing.

'Did he ever get physical with you?' Anna asked.

Paul closed the magazine, looking directly at Tina.

'Alan? Never. And besides, if he had have done, I'd have given him as good. I told you, he was never confrontational and he hated getting into any kind of row.'

'Did he get annoyed about your flirty behaviour at the gym?'

She sighed with even more impatience.

'No, of course he didn't. I'm flirty here with the customers, as we do have both male and female. It's part of the job!'

Anna pressed on. 'If he was seeing someone, do you have any idea who it would be?'

'Not really. I never found the lipstick on the collar thing or blonde hairs on his jacket. It was working on that bloody car that he said was the reason he was out so late.'

She closed her eyes.

'I find this all upsetting, you know, because I have told you all this before, and if I did find out there was another woman he'd run off with, you'd be the first people I'd contact. I told that to the Missing Persons people. They've asked me the same questions over and over.'

'He used to collect you from here sometimes?' Anna noted.

Tina looked at Paul, who still hadn't spoken.

'Yes. When he took my car to work he'd drop me off here and pick me up. Not frequently because I never liked to get here as early as he needed to be at the garage.'

'Did any of the girls working here seem friendly with him?'

'No, no way. They're not his type; the Donnas of this world wouldn't be interested in him either.'

'Really.' Anna said it so quietly that Tina flushed.

'They're too young and Alan's so straitlaced and he didn't have much time for chit-chat.'

Felicity walked in. 'I'm sorry to interrupt you, Tina, but your client wants to see you.'

'Tell her I'll be two minutes.' Tina sipped her coffee and put the mug down. 'I'm gonna have to go and unwrap her. Is there anything else you wanted to ask me?'

'No. Thank you for your time.'

Tina hesitated, as if about to say something, then seemed to change her mind and started to walk out. However, she then stopped and turned back. Anna felt as if the woman was in some way rearranging her features or her emotions, since she was suddenly nervous.

'I am beginning to think he took off – you know, left me – because he was too afraid to tell me he didn't want to go through with the wedding. He would have been in turmoil about it; it's the only reason I can think of for him walking out the way he has done. It doesn't make it any easier, obviously not, and . . .' She broke off and took out a tissue from her pocket. 'I've been wondering how long it will be – you know, your investigation. I mean, when do you call it quits?'

'That would depend,' Anna told her.

'Depend on what?'

'Well, whether or not we trace him.'

'But what if you don't?'

Anna glanced at Paul, not wanting to get into the discussion herself. He took over. At last he showed some interest.

'It will depend on whether we uncover any evidence that gives us confirmation that Alan has met with foul play. Then it will become an ongoing murder enquiry.'

'*Murder?*'

Paul nodded and flicked his eyes to Anna, who was giving him a frosty gaze.

'Is that what you think, that Alan's been murdered?' Tina said shakily.

'We will look into every possibility.'

'But can you have a murder enquiry without a body?'

'If we suspect foul play, then yes.'

She sniffed and dabbed the tissue to her nose. 'And do you?'

Anna had heard enough. She stood up and turned to Paul, saying briskly, 'We should go; Tina has to unwrap a body.'

Paul could hardly keep his face straight, but he stood up and joined her.

'Thank you, Miss Brooks, for your time,' he said politely. 'We will no doubt be in touch if we have any news for you.'

Anna had already walked past and was heading into the main area of the salon.

'She doesn't like me, does she?' Tina sniffed.

'No, it's not that, it's just been a long day.'

'Tell me about it. And you tell *her* she could do with some treatments. A wash-in colour enhancing shampoo followed by a cut and blowdry would do her good, and I'll give her a discount.'

'I will pass that on to DCI Travis.'

Anna was waiting for him in the patrol car. He got in beside her, repeating what Tina had said.

'Cheeky cow, but she's right about me not liking her. I don't.'

Paul started up the engine and added that Tina had also said she would give her a good price reduction.

'Wild horses wouldn't get me into that salon.'

They drove off, heading back to the station. Anna was really irritable, twice snapping at him to take another route as they were heading into rush-hour traffic.

'Why don't you like her?' Paul persevered.

'Maybe because I can't believe a word she says, and after everything I've heard about Alan, it's no wonder he took off. Another thing, I wouldn't like to get into a confrontation with her. In fact, I find it really difficult to imagine the pair of them as a couple.'

'Love is blind.'

She made a derisive sound.

'You know, Anna, sometimes people under pressure and stress act in different ways, and by now she must be sort of getting used to the situation.'

'What do you mean by that?'

'Just that if he did take off, which now I'm beginning to think he did, then she's taken it on the chin and she's getting on with her life.'

'Doesn't work that way,' she said quietly.

'Okay, now it's your turn: what do you mean by that?'

'I don't want to go there, Paul. Just drop it.'

Since Ken's death, so long as no one brought up his name or his murder she was able to control the tide of emotions that welled up inside her, but whenever the subject was broached, grief would sweep over and drown her.

The incident room at the station was almost empty apart from a couple of clerical staff still clearing up from the previous murder enquiry. Anna went into her office where virtually everything was now packed up and sat at her desk. She typed out a quick report of the day's interviews, and having split the work with Paul, it took only half an hour. When he tapped and entered with his sheets it was just after six.

'You mind if I take off?' he asked as she stacked her sheets together with his.

'No, go ahead.'

'We on for tomorrow?'

She said that she wasn't sure as she would need to talk to Langton.

'You want me to take them over?' Paul offered. 'His station's not far from where I live, and I don't mind.'

'No, I'll drop them off to him. You got a hot date?'

Paul, who very rarely showed any campness, flicked his wrist, saying, 'Could be. So you'll call me?'

She nodded, placing the pages into an envelope.

Left alone, she picked up her briefcase, but in reality she didn't feel like going home. The conversation in the car with Paul had niggled at her, but the reason wouldn't rise to the surface. Maybe it was just frustration, but the fact remained that they still had no clues as to Alan Rawlins's whereabouts. Nor had they discovered any evidence to suggest that a crime had been committed.

Part of her felt that they had reached a dead end and she wanted to get onto another case, but there was that niggle. Perhaps it was her intuition, or as Langton would always ask, 'What's the gut feeling?' Truthfully, bar her dislike of Tina Brooks, she didn't have anything else that she felt would justify the continuation of her enquiries.

Anna left the station and drove to Highgate, where Langton was heading up a murder team. It was almost seven when she reached the local police station and parked in the private section reserved for patrol cars and police vehicles. She saw that Langton's rusted old brown Rover was as usual erratically parked, taking up two spaces. It looked as if it had even more dents than usual, and passing it she saw, left in the back, a child's booster seat. As always, whenever she caught a tiny piece of his private life it surprised her. She never found it easy to connect Langton with a whole world that didn't include her or their past relationship, and yet it was years now since they had been lovers.

The Duty Sergeant suggested she go straight up to the incident room. It was one of the new stations with all mod cons, unlike the one she was attached to. It was very different also in that even at this time of the day it looked busy; a couple of female DCs passed her in the well-lit corridor as she made her way along to double doors, following signs to the incident room. She listened outside at first, then, as she could hear Langton's voice, she inched the door open and looked in.

Langton was giving a big team of officers a briefing. All had their back to the door as she slipped in to stand at the rear of the large, very well-equipped room. There were rows of desks and monitors, a long incident board with photographs and details, and numerous clerical staff working on the periphery. Anna held onto her briefcase and looked around. She saw DCI Mike Lewis, DS Paul Barolli and, sitting side by side, Joan Falkland and DC Barbara Maddox. They had all worked with her on four previous cases. She felt a pang of envy that they were together and she was an outsider. Langton was pacing up and down, pulling at his tie.

'I think our victims have been chosen through a systematic and lengthy period of stalking and surveillance. I am certain he has been watching this family for some time. He had to know the husband's habits, that every other night he played snooker at his local club. He would have noted how long the husband spent there in order to have enough time to complete what he wanted to do. The crime was carefully staged to impact in the most traumatic way on the husband when he returned from the pub. I think the staging and placing of the bodies indicated that our killer is methodical and he wanted to shock. He could know this family – more importantly, know the husband –

and although it's just speculation at this stage, we concentrate on anyone who held a grievance against him.'

Anna had inched her way over to sit unobtrusively on a hard-backed chair left against the wall by the double doors. She listened intently, watching Langton pace the floor back and forth in front of the incident board, tapping the photographs of the victims and turning on his heels to face his team.

'This is a murder of sexual sadism. Our killer was organised. He planned these murders. He targeted his victims, he brought restraints and knives, and we have no weapons found at the victim's home. By the use of these restraints the element of control was uppermost in his mind, but something didn't go according to plan; that something was the husband returning home earlier than usual from his snooker game, which had been cancelled due to his friends having to work a late shift. So although victim one, the wife, is deliberately displayed and ready for viewing, his second victim, the twelve-year-old boy, is not. From the blood distribution along the walls in the kitchen and hallway, we can ascertain that the child tried to make a run for it.'

Langton stood in front of a large sketch of the outlay of the victims' kitchen, breakfast room and hall. He jabbed it with his finger.

'The boy was caught and dragged to the kitchen dining area – we have blood smearing and spattering against the walls. Forensics has given us a scenario that the killer rammed the boy's head against the side of a cabinet before tying him to the chair beside his mother. Pathology report indicates the poor kid thankfully would have been unconscious by this time.'

Langton loosened his tie. He was sweating and Anna

could see that his old injury to his knee was paining him as he paused to rub it.

'With three possible suspects the search warrants will be executed first thing tomorrow morning. Look for any items relating to sexual or violent behaviour – pornographic magazines, videos, books relating to true-life crimes, vibrators, clamps, women's clothing, underwear and so on. Look out for diaries, anything connected to this sort of violence. They could have police equipment, handcuffs, ropes, knives, so search their vehicles . . .'

He took a deep breath and glanced at his watch.

'Right, that's it for tonight. Weekend leave is cancelled. We work round the clock on this one.'

His team began to disperse, taking chairs back to their desks and talking quietly to each other. No one as yet had seen Anna, and she now stood up, waiting for the moment to speak to Langton. However, he was in a huddle with Mike Lewis and Paul Barolli. She decided that rather than wait in the incident room, she'd leave her notes with the Duty Sergeant downstairs. She also didn't feel like talking to anyone from the old team.

'DCI Travis!' It was Barbara. 'How are you?' Barbara was carrying her coat, eager to leave. She was always the first out if it was possible.

'I'm fine, thanks. This sounds like a nasty case.'

'Christ, it's awful. The victim's husband was an ex-detective working for a private investigation company.'

'Anna.' Joan now joined them and she had that sorrowful look in her eyes. 'How's things?'

'Good, thank you. I just wanted to pass this over to Langton.'

Joan turned and pulled a face. 'He's been sleeping nights here, as usual keeping us all on our toes, but I hear you got a good result – guilty verdict. Consensus was it was pretty well on the cards though, wasn't it?'

'Yes.' Anna felt hemmed in by the two women. If she left with them they'd want to continue the conversation so she stepped aside.

'Just want to give this to him.' She held up the file of her notes on the Alan Rawlins enquiry.

The two women left and Anna still hovered. She found it annoying that they seemed to think her last case was an easy ride – although it had been. Had Langton chosen her to head it up for that reason? She now suspected that was exactly what he had done. Her anger made her confident enough to walk towards him.

'Excuse me, sorry to interrupt. I just wanted to run these reports by you.'

Langton turned, surprised. 'Travis.'

Mike Lewis and Barolli both smiled, but Anna cut through any start of a conversation by handing Langton the file.

'Maybe talk about it tomorrow?' she said briskly.

'Hell, no. Come into the office. As I'm here we might as well deal with it all now.'

Mike and Barolli moved away, giving her those sad smiles that she loathed, and she forced herself to look back at them with a grin.

'Nice to see you again. Goodnight.'

Langton put his hand in the small of her back, guiding her towards the office section.

'You want a coffee?'

'No, this won't take long.'

The office was sparse, but very modern. Langton sat behind the desk on a leather chair and Anna drew up another equally new chair in front of him. He opened a pack of nicotine gum and then gave a sheepish grin, saying, 'I've given up, but I think I'm getting tooth decay from chewing so much of this stuff.'

'You should get the patches,' she said.

'Got them all the way up my arm.'

Anna watched as he flicked through the pages so fast that she doubted he was really able to read them properly. It took him about ten minutes. He looked well, she thought. Also, he'd put on weight, perhaps thanks to giving up smoking.

'How's that knee of yours?' she asked.

'Fine – just the occasional twinge. How are you doing?'

She managed a smile. He stacked the pages and replaced them in the envelope.

'What's your gut feeling?' he wanted to know.

'I knew you'd ask me that.'

He leaned back in his posh leather chair. 'So what's your answer?'

'I don't have one.'

'Mmm.'

'Can I ask you something about my last case?' Anna said abruptly. 'Did you handpick it for me because it was a no-brainer?'

'No such thing, Travis,' he replied immediately, 'but as a first-time DCI you had to be able to control it and not feel pressured; you needed to build up your confidence.'

'Is this why you've got me virtually working a Missing Persons case?'

'Is that what you think it is?'

She hated the way he turned a question around to another without giving her an answer.

'Looks like you have a big investigation going,' she said.

'Yeah – a very sick one. Mother and son found slaughtered, but the husband is an ex-detective and now runs a private investigation company. He's got a lot of enemies – unpleasant bloke, but nobody deserves to come back to his home to be confronted by such horror. He's under sedation.'

'You have suspects though?'

'Yes. He's been doing some work for a couple of nasty bastards, collecting their debts. Unbelievable! Works as a copper all his adult life then gets out and works for the other side.'

Langton patted Anna's file with the flat of his hand. 'You want to call it quits on this and hand it back to Mispers?'

'Yes, I think so. It's just been me and Paul Simms working it.'

'Ah, the gay cavalero. Good detective though.'

'Yes.'

'You get along with him?'

'Yes.'

'Very monosyllabic tonight, aren't you?'

She shrugged.

'You want a bite to eat?'

'No, thanks. I'm actually on my way home. Just dropped that in so you can see that I have been doing as requested.'

'I talked to his father yesterday,' Langton said quietly.

'I've been to his home, met his wife, his son's friends. He appears as you could see from the report, an all-out nice man.'

'Any buts?'

'Only that I have a bad reaction to his girlfriend, Tina Brooks, but I think that's just personal.'

'What about neighbours? You talk to any of them?'

'No, but we talked to his place of work, his gym – it's all in the report.'

Langton chewed hard on his nicotine gum, staring at her. 'You want to start on another enquiry?'

'Yes.'

He stood up and took the gum out of his mouth, tossing it into the rubbish bin.

'Okay. Tell you what I want you to do. Tomorrow, go and visit the neighbours and see if they have anything to add to the mix. Something in me doesn't quite accept your view that Alan Rawlins has just taken off.'

'Like what?'

Langton opened another piece of gum, walking round the desk to sit on the edge close to her.

'First his Merc. He spends months doing it up, ordering spare parts, bought it with his father to make money reselling it. Why not take the car if he was doing a runner. You now know his passport is missing; there's no movement in any of his bank accounts or credit cards, and from your interviews he appears to be a nice upright guy, loving family, good mates, he's not into drugs, he doesn't drink bar the odd glass of wine and nobody has a hint of any extra lady friend on the side. Correct?'

Anna nodded. He never ceased to amaze her. Although he had appeared merely to skim her report, he had somehow acquired the gist of it, and this became even clearer when he picked up the file and passed it back to her.

'The fiancée also asked how long you'd be digging around if there was no body – right?'

She nodded.

'Does that sound like a distressed lady? Her fiancé disappears and all she seems interested in is how long it will be before she gets her hands on the savings.'

'It's a joint bank account and doesn't need his signature.'

'Oh.'

'His life insurance is only fifty thousand so I don't think that would be a motive.'

'People have been killed for less.'

'Listen, he was a nice man, one who hated any kind of confrontation. I think, judging from what everyone has said about him, he seems to fit the profile of someone who would just walk away rather than get into any kind of emotional row.'

'Has he ever done anything like it before?'

'Well, no, not that I've been told.'

Langton chewed hard on his gum. Then he got up from the desk and yawned.

'Give it one more day then I'll get onto allocating you the next murder enquiry.'

Anna stood up and stiffened as he reached for her hand and drew close.

'You sleeping?'

'Yes.'

'I miss not having you around on a case.'

'Well, you could have me if you wanted.'

He laughed. 'In the literal term, I gather.'

She released her hand from his, saying, 'I'll be in touch. I'll still use Paul.'

'You make it very difficult, Anna.'

She looked up into his face.

'I keep wanting to put my arms around you, comfort you; you think I can't feel your troubled soul.'

'It's not troubled. I am just tired tonight. It's been a long day.'

'Have it your way, but like I keep on saying to you, if you need me I'm here for you.'

'Thank you. Goodnight then.'

He gave her a smile, nodding his goodnight as she

walked out. She held it together until she was sitting in her car and then she started to cry. It was like a fast release, and no sooner had she broken down than she was able to pull herself together and drive home.

Chapter Four

Anna took a double dose of her sleeping tablets and slept until early morning. The alarm woke her and she again had that feeling of lethargy, not wanting to get out of bed, get dressed or do anything. She felt that this time her mood swing was down to the dead-end case she had been told to investigate by Langton, and remembered her conversation with him the evening before and how he had said to give it one more day. As she turned to look at the time on the alarm clock she saw the picture of her father on the bedside cabinet and her mind rushed back to her childhood. She could see him standing at the foot of her bed and jokingly threatening that she was running late for school and had better be out of bed by the count of three or it was cold bath time. One, she threw the duvet back, two, she jumped out of bed, and by three, she was in the bathroom turning on the shower. As Anna looked at her glass-enclosed power-jet shower she recalled the dreadful avocado green fibreglass bath and matching tiles in the family bathroom. She jumped into the shower and straight back out again. She laughed out loud realising that in her rush she had turned it onto cold and could hear her father's voice saying, 'Got you this time, Anna.'

Refreshed she rang Paul to say she would pick him up

at the station at eight. Paul was waiting outside the station and when he was in the car Anna told him what Langton had asked her to do.

'Is that why the early-bird call?' he yawned. 'I was out until four a.m.' Paul was unshaven with dark circles beneath his eyes.

'Good date, was it?'

'No, but I went to Fire and danced my socks off and had a few too many vodka shots and slingers – that's when you knock it back neat.'

'Hung over?'

'Yeah, a bit. What was Langton's reaction?'

Anna told him and he listened without his usual interruption. Anna didn't add that she felt Langton was simply side-stepping the issue of her heading up a murder enquiry. It felt to her as if he was stringing her along, thinking he was giving her time to get over the death of her fiancé, Ken.

'Langton's up to his neck,' Paul said. 'You heard about the case he's on – ex-detective finds his wife and son shredded.'

'Yes, I know about it. I heard him giving a briefing.'

They arrived at Newton Court in Hounslow where Tina Brooks lived and parked up close to her garage so as not to create any problems for the other tenants. As before, the reception area was open and there was a caretaker polishing the floor. He continued working the machine as they headed for flat two.

'Nobody at home,' he said, looking towards them.

Anna showed him her ID and asked if he knew the couple living there.

'By sight, yeah. I wouldn't say I *know* them.'

'What's your name?'

'Jonas Jones, ma'am.'

'You work here regularly, Jonas?'

'Two days a week. I clean the reception, stairs, and if the tenant is away I collect their mail for them.'

'How long have you been working here?'

'Three years. I do all the owner's places. He's got three blocks of flats and I check them all out. The bins sometimes are overflowing and the council don't collect as regular as they used to.'

'Have you ever found anything suspicious?'

He wrinkled his nose and said he didn't know what she meant.

'Well, anything unusual?'

'Oh no. Just some tenants tie up their rubbish in black bin liners and if they don't put them in the bins, dogs or cats or whatever can scavenge and rip them open. You'd be surprised, we got foxes around here. Dunno where they come from, but I've seen big bushy-tailed ones.'

'Are you aware that Mr Alan Rawlins has disappeared?'

'Who?'

'The tenant of flat two. He lives with his girlfriend, Tina Brooks.'

'Oh yeah, I know who you mean. I didn't know he was missing. Where's he gone?'

Anna smiled and said they were trying to find out. She then asked for details of the other tenants. The caretaker walked over to a small desk and took out a list of names, saying that as he didn't do cleaning in individual flats he only saw them on odd occasions. There was an elderly Jewish couple in flat three, flats four and five were Iranians and flat six was a single woman.

'Could you tell me who owns the building?'

'You mean the landlord?'

'Yes, the person that owns this building.'

'Doesn't live here.'

'His name and contact number will do.'

'He's Iranian. Owns two or three blocks like this one and only ever comes over a couple of times a year. Prefers to live in his beach-front condo in Morocco.'

'And his name is . . .?'

'Mr Desai.'

'What about flat one?'

'Mr Phillips, youngish bloke, drives a nice Lotus and works in the City.'

'Is he at home?'

'I don't know. I've been polishing the floor. I'll be here for a while as I'm waitin' on a delivery for Miss Brooks.'

'What is it?'

'She ordered new carpet.'

'But isn't the flat rented?'

'Yes, but they are semi-furnished flats, rented with just the necessary. Tenants can bring in whatever else they need.'

They thanked Jonas and went towards flat one as he turned on his polishing machine again.

'That's odd, isn't it?' Paul said as he rang the doorbell.

When there was no answer, Anna suggested that Phillips was probably at work, and said they should go from flat to flat to see if there was anyone at home. She too thought it was suspicious about the new carpet, but said nothing.

They got no answer from flats four and five either. When they rang the doorbell of flat six there was the sound of a dog yapping. It continued its noise as they pressed the doorbell twice more before it was inched open.

'Yes?' The woman's face was partly hidden.

'Miss Jewell?'

'Yes? What do you want?'

Anna showed her ID and introduced herself and Paul. The door closed, the safety chain was unlinked and the door opened wider.

Miss Jewell was no more than forty, but she was frail and very thin. She held a small terrier under her arm with one hand over its mouth as it gave a throttled growl.

'Has there been a burglary?'

'No. Could we just talk to you for a moment?'

Miss Jewell reluctantly led them into a beige-coloured sitting room, which had a lot of shabby furniture unlike Tina Brooks's sparse flat. It was a smaller place in comparison, more like a studio, and, as it was at the top of the block, it had sloping ceilings.

Anna and Paul sat down as the small bedraggled dog was shut in the kitchen; it yapped for a while and then went quiet.

'Don't worry about Trigger, he doesn't bite, but he's a wonderful guard dog,' Miss Jewell said as she perched on the edge of a bright green bucket chair. If she sat back any further her legs would have lifted off the ground. Anna and Paul were seated on a sofa covered with blankets and shawls. They explained briefly why they were there and asked if she knew Alan Rawlins.

'No. I don't know anyone living here apart from Mr and Mrs Maisell, they're in flat three. There's also two families of Iranians, but I don't talk to them. They've only been here about six months.'

'What about the tenant in flat one?'

'I have never spoken to him, but he drives a big yellow car which makes a dreadful noise. I have also complained about the cooking smells from the Iranians. I don't like to cause trouble, but my little flat stinks of their fried fish or whatever they cook down there.'

'Do you know Tina Brooks who lives in flat two?'

'Oh, her? Yes, I've met her. She pushed some leaflets through my door about special offers at her hairdressing salon. I never used them; put them straight in the bin.'

'Tell me what you know about her.'

'Nothing, really. She's always quite friendly, but I wouldn't say I've ever had a long conversation with her.'

'And you never met Alan Rawlins?'

'Not really. I know she had a chap living with her – I obviously have seen him come and go – but I keep myself to myself, apart from Mr and Mrs Maisell. In fact, I just talked to them earlier as they were going to go shopping and they often get my little things that I need. I am registered partially blind as I have tunnel vision. Basically, what that means is I have no peripheral vision and I can only see straight ahead.'

Anna had heard enough. She glanced at Paul and they both stood up.

'Just one more thing, Miss Jewell: were the carpets provided when you rented?'

'Yes, throughout, and all the same colour. I think the owner must have got a deal on them as they are apparently the same in all the flats.'

'Thank you.'

'Look, we're not supposed to have pets, but he's such a good companion and he never does a naughty inside. I take him out first thing to do his business and there have been no complaints about me having him.'

She gave an odd look and eased herself off the bucket seat. 'It's not about me having a pet, is it?'

'No, not at all. We are looking into the fact that Alan Rawlins has disappeared.'

'Oh really? I didn't quite follow what you said earlier. Where's he gone to?'

Anna smiled, repeating what she had told the caretaker – that they were concerned. Miss Jewell said that she wished she could help.

'Do you think he's had an accident, or something like that?'

'Possibly.'

'Have you tried the hospitals? He could have been knocked down and got concussion and not remembered anything.'

'Thank you for your time,' Anna said, heading out, and Paul followed. As they went into the hall the yapping started up again and Miss Jewell banged on the door and told the dog to shut up.

Anna looked at Paul and said that was a waste of time. He suggested they try Mr and Mrs Maisell as they might have returned from their food shop.

'Why not,' Anna agreed.

'It's odd, isn't it, living cheek by jowl and nobody knows anybody else,' Paul commented.

'Yeah, but to be honest I don't know any of my neighbours. Do you know yours?'

'Not really. In fact, come to think of it, I wouldn't know them if I fell over them.'

'There you go.'

They rang Mr and Mrs Maisell's bell and waited, and were about to turn away when the door was flung open. Mrs Maisell was about four foot five and as wide as she was tall.

'I was just going to bring them up. Oh sorry, I thought you were Hester from upstairs.'

Anna did the introductions and Mrs Maisell ushered them inside. There were the same beige carpets, but theirs were covered by bright rugs of every shape and size, and the flat was crammed with furniture, paintings and bric-à-brac.

'Morris? Morris! Can you come out, love?'

Mrs Maisell ushered them into the lounge and it was like an antique shop it was so crammed with furniture.

'Sit down, dears. MORRIS?'

They heard him before he walked in.

'Don't tell me it was that ruddy woman upstairs, we've only just got back inside.'

'It's the police,' Mrs Maisell said, wafting her hand as an equally short squat man appeared with a grocery bag. He put it down and looked from Anna to Paul.

'Has there been an accident?'

'No, they're asking about that nice young man from flat two. He's gone missing.'

'I wouldn't mind going missing. We can't put a foot out of the door without that Miss Jewell coming down to ask us to pick up this or pick up that. She hardly goes out.'

'Don't be nasty, dear.'

'It's the truth though. And she shouldn't have that rat of a dog. No pets is part of the lease agreement. In fact, I don't think the landlord even knows she's got it.' Morris squatted down in a large comfortable-looking armchair as his wife scurried to stand beside him.

'Do you know Mr Rawlins?' Anna began.

'Yes, lovely chap. He helped start my car once and gave me a good deal when I took it into his garage. Something was draining the battery.'

84

'When did you last see him?'

The Maisells looked at each other and then both gave almost identical frowns.

'A while back, it must be.'

It was extraordinary as they talked to each other; it was as if Anna and Paul weren't present. They discussed somebody or other's wedding and decided that wasn't the right date. Mrs Maisell eventually said that it had to be a couple of months ago.

'I was putting rubbish out by the bins and he was coming out to go to work – well, I *think* he was going to work.'

'So you never really knew either Tina Brooks or Mr Rawlins?'

'No, not really.'

'Can you just try and recall if that last time you saw him he gave any indication that anything was wrong?'

Again the couple conferred with each other and then Mrs Maisell got up and went in a zigzag route across the cluttered room to open a drawer in a small carved mahogany desk. She rifled through it and brought out some flyers from Tina's salon.

'She put these through our letterbox, pensioners' special prices, but I've used Audrey for fifteen years.'

'That's no use to them, Bea, they don't want to know about hairdressing. It's where Alan's gone – that's right, isn't it?'

'Yes, Mr Maisell.'

'Well, we can't help you. I've never even set foot in their place, but like I said, he seemed a friendly sort of chap. Wait a moment, I've remembered now . . .'

They all looked at Morris expectantly.

'He used to jog in the morning – you know, run round

the block – and I was going to . . .' He sucked in his breath.

'I can't remember where I was going, but I know it was early.'

'The only time you've been out really early was when you went to collect Eileen from the station.'

'Oh yes, that's right . . . so when was that, Bea?'

Mrs Maisell got up and did another zigzag around the furniture to the desk and opened another drawer, taking out a diary. She flicked through it and then nodded her head.

'It was exactly ten weeks ago. She's his cousin and comes from Israel. She got the train from Heathrow to Paddington, that's right, isn't it, Morris?'

'Correct.'

Anna's patience was wearing thin.

'So on this morning you saw Alan, Mr Maisell?'

'He was doing those stretch exercises – you know, standing facing the wall and bending over to ease up the tendons. It was really early because it was quite dark still and I said to him . . .'

Again everyone hung on his words.

'I said, "You're an early bird."'

'And?' Anna wanted to grip him by his throat.

'He said it takes one to catch one.'

'Is that it?' Paul asked, becoming as exasperated as Anna.

'No. There's something else. I went to the garage, got my car and, as I was driving out, I saw him and he was kicking the wall, like a karate kick, and next minute he was punching it as if he was really angry about something.'

Mrs Maisell had been thumbing through the diary and she now had something to add.

'I met Miss Brooks a few weeks back – that's the last

time I've actually spoken to her. She was in Asda. The reason I remember is I go there once a month to buy those big bags of all-in-one dog meals. They're cheaper there than anywhere else – not for us, for her upstairs.'

'I wait in the car park,' Morris said, looking disgruntled.

'I was in the checkout queue and Tina, Miss Brooks, was in the next one, and you know it's always the same, you get in one line and see the other one moving up faster. I saw her and said to her I should have joined her because she started off behind me and then she was ahead of me and then at the till while I was still waiting. Something was wrong with the woman in front of me; her credit card wasn't going through.'

Anna felt like screaming. Paul stood up and asked Mrs Maisell why she recalled the incident.

'She had some big containers of bleach – four of them that were this big.' She indicated with her hands. 'I said to her, "I hope you're not doing tint jobs with those", like a joke you know, because she's a hairdresser, and she gave me such a look and then said she needed them for the salon as sometimes hair-dye won't come out of their over-alls.'

'Did you see any other cleaning liquids in her trolley?'

'I think she had some carpet cleaner.'

'Can you give us the exact date this incident occurred?'

'Yes, it was the sixteenth . . . or was it the seventeenth. Well, it was March and it was one of those days. I do the dog-food run every month. You'd be surprised how much that little dog can eat.'

Anna sat with Paul in her car. Neither had said much, but ideas were forming as they swapped information back and forth.

'Day or so after Alan goes missing, there's bleach, carpet cleaner?'

'Could be for her salon?' Anna suggested.

'No, she'd have one of those special cards for business bulk buys.'

'Then there's Alan's early morning run, punching out at the brick wall,' Anna mused. 'Doesn't sound like the same person we've been told about.'

'The new carpet order – why?' Paul looked at Anna. 'Kind of spoils the possibility that she bought the bleach to clean up evidence.'

'Unless she couldn't get rid of it? Blood and bleach stains are hard to get out of a carpet so she's now ordered a new one.'

'Shit, you going down that route, Anna?'

'Yes, and don't tell me you're not thinking the same thing.'

'Yeah, I am, I am – but we were there at her flat. Did you see any signs of there being a fight or cleaning up? There wasn't anything that looked out of place.'

'I could definitely smell bleach.'

Anna started the engine and said they should find out – visit the salon again and check for the bleach. If there was no sign of it they'd return to Tina's flat. She also wanted to interview Tina's next-door neighbour, the city slicker with the Lotus.

Feeling a hit of adrenalin kick them into action, they arrived at Tina's Beauty Salon just after twelve. From the outside it didn't look too busy and Anna suggested that Paul keep Tina occupied whilst she had a nose around.

Felicity recognised them and told them that Tina was not there, but was expected back early that afternoon.

'Thank you, Felicity. We just wanted to have a look around, if that's all right with you?' In case she didn't give permission, Anna flashed her ID badge. They both headed past the hairdressing section that had only one client under a dryer and another having a cut and blowdry. Donna was at the sink washing around the bowl with a water jet. She smiled at Anna.

'Donna, can you show me the kitchen area? I'd like to ask a few questions, and maybe you'd make us a coffee?'

Donna turned off the spray and checked her client under the dryer. Then she led them to the same area behind the screens, and went to the coffee percolator. 'There's still some fresh as I just brewed some for myself. As you can see, we're not busy today.'

'Tell me, how do you clean up the floor here?' Anna asked, looking at the black and white lino tiles.

'We wash it all down, either after work or first thing in the morning.'

'What do you use? It looks good.'

Donna pointed to a corner cupboard and said that all the equipment was stored in there. She added that she didn't actually do the sweeping up or mopping – that was down to the juniors. Anna opened the cupboard. There were two large plastic containers of domestic bleach and some polish called Kool Floors, a couple of ragged mops, two brooms, a bucket, and that was about all that fitted into the small corner space. She examined one of the containers of bleach and shook it. It was almost empty and the other one was full.

'When do you use the bleach?' she asked, closing the cupboard.

'Quite often. Sometimes there're drops of dye, and with wet hair these tiles are difficult to keep spotless. With all the cut hair and the traffic going back and forth it's often a mess with footprints, and she's very particular.'

'Tina?'

'Yeah. She doesn't use much bleach because of the smell so that's done at night after we close.'

'Where do you get the cleaning equipment from?'

'Dunno, Tina buys it. Do you want milk and sugar?'

'Thanks, just black for me with sugar.'

Felicity popped her head around the screens. 'Can you fit in a blowdry, Donna, no appointment?'

Donna nodded and Felicity disappeared.

'Where is Tina this morning?'

'No idea, but I don't think she has any appointments until this afternoon. We're always quiet midweek unless it's specials, half-price, like yesterday. That was pandemonium and we were short-staffed. A junior was off with flu and Kiara wasn't in.' Donna fidgeted and then said she should go and check on her client.

Left alone, Paul helped himself to coffee as Anna sipped the rather tepid cup she'd been given.

'This isn't fresh,' she complained.

'So what?' Paul snapped, as he had the start of a headache.

'This bleach is not from Asda,' Anna said.

He was about to check in the corner cupboard when a striking-looking black girl with a head full of cornrows walked in.

'Is that coffee fresh?' she asked.

'No – Kiara.' Anna looked at the name on her salon smock.

Kiara gave her a rather haughty look.

'Who are you? This area is for staff only, you know.'

Anna did the introductions and Kiara started to make up a fresh pot of coffee.

'Is this to do with Alan?'

'Yes.'

'All this is a bit strange, isn't it? Him taking off like that.'

'You knew him?'

'We all knew him, not that we had much to do with him. He'd wait for Tina in the car park sometimes, but he hardly ever came into the salon. He probably felt a bit self-conscious – I think he was shy.' She laughed.

'When was the last time you saw him?'

She sat down on one of the pink chairs and crossed her legs.

'It has to be at least three months ago. He and Tina were having a row, I remember that.'

'Where?'

'Out in the car park. I park my car out there and it was after closing so I was on my way home.'

'Did you hear what they were arguing about?'

'No.'

'You didn't hear anything that was being said between them?'

'Not really, no. They were sitting in his car, or it's her car – the VW – and she was shouting, but I was not going to get involved. I just got into my car and drove out.'

'What was Alan doing?'

'Sitting there. To be honest I always found them an odd couple – she's very volatile and she can really have a go at you, know what I mean? But he seemed a bit downcast. It was obvious who the boss was.'

'They were engaged to be married, weren't they?'

'Yeah. Well, she flashed a diamond ring around, and I know she was looking at property to buy.'

Anna placed her half-empty coffee mug down on the table.

'Do you think that Alan was the type to just walk out on Tina?'

Kiara pulled a face. 'I dunno.'

'Did you ever hear anything about there having been someone else he was seeing?'

'I wouldn't have liked to be in his shoes if she found out.'

'Why do you say that?' Anna asked.

'Well, like I said before, the lady has a short fuse and I wouldn't like to be caught on the end of it.'

'Give me a scenario when you have seen Tina angry.'

Kiara suddenly didn't want to answer any more questions, shaking her head and backing out.

'Look, I don't want to get in the middle of anything here. I know she's got a temper and we've all had to bear the brunt of it sometimes, but she's good to work for if you treat her right. Ask someone else, okay?'

Kiara left them and Anna helped herself to some of the fresh coffee Kiara had brewed, but not drunk. The next moment they got their own experience of Tina Brooks's temper. She almost kicked the screen down as she faced them.

'What the hell is going on here?' she demanded, hands on hips. 'Why are you asking my staff about my relationship with Alan? It's none of their fucking business.'

'We are just interviewing everyone who might give us some indication as to where he could be.'

'Anybody working for me would know we kept our life private. I told you this – in fact, I've been fucking accommodating to you two whenever you turn up, and from now on if you want to see me again, you ask to do so through my lawyer. Now get out of my salon.'

Anna put her coffee down and Paul drained his mug.

'Now – I want you out of here *now*.'

'You know, Tina, this isn't the best way—'

The young woman pushed Anna in the chest, interrupting her.

'It's *my* way. I've got enough pressure trying to deal with the fact he's walked out on me. I don't need this aggravation, I DON'T NEED IT.'

Anna walked out first and Paul followed quickly as they heard a crash of breaking china in the staff room. They both hurried through the salon, passing Donna blowdrying a customer's hair. She gave them a smile, but wiped it off her face fast as Tina strode after them.

'You want to talk to any of my staff, you ask me first.'

Anna opened the salon's door. Felicity at reception looked terrified as Tina told her, 'You hear me, Felicity? You don't let anybody in here without my permission – and that includes the police.'

She slammed the door after them so hard, Paul was worried it would shatter the glass.

Anna whistled and then smiled. 'Mmm, that was nice.'

'You look as if you are starting to enjoy yourself,' Paul said.

She laughed. 'I wouldn't exactly describe it as enjoyment, more like interesting.' Paul didn't say anything, but it was the first time he had heard her laugh properly. It perplexed him, because he had not found the interaction with Tina in any way amusing. On the contrary, it disturbed him.

'Next port of call?' Anna said as she started the engine. They were using her Mini rather than a patrol car.

'City banking company over by Liverpool Street,' Paul replied promptly.

'What's his name?' Anna asked.

Paul pulled out his notebook and flipped over a page to a name he'd taken down; the occupant of flat one.

'Michael Phillips.'

The journey took some time from Hounslow and Anna put the radio on. They sat listening to classical music on Radio 3. Paul's hangover was still resting like a low dull thud so he closed his eyes, hoping it wouldn't get any worse.

They parked and headed towards an impressive building close to the station. It had taken a while for Anna to get the doorman to allow them to park in the small private parking area. She showed her ID and said she was there on business and he gave her a sticker to place on the windscreen.

By this time Paul had asked a receptionist seated behind a large curved desk to contact Mr Phillips. She placed a call to the company of Aston & Clark Merchant Bankers and at the same time wrote down on two visitor's cards his name and Anna's. She slipped them into plastic covers with the phone hooked under her chin, repeating that she had DCI Travis and DS Paul Simms waiting.

'Mr Phillips is in conference room three. If you go to the fourth floor, his secretary will meet you outside the lift.'

Together Anna and Paul pinned their visitor cards to their lapels and waited by a small gate for it to open and allow them to pass through to the lifts. The security of the company was very obviously a priority and it wasn't until the receptionist had clicked open the automatic lock that they could pass through.

The glass lift had mirrored panels and thick carpet.

'This all smells of money to me,' Paul said, brushing a hand through his hair, looking at himself in the mirror.

'Well, he must have some if he drives a Lotus, but compared to all this Newton Court is a bit downmarket – and he's only renting.'

They reached the fourth floor and as the glass door opened to allow them to step out, a pretty blonde girl was waiting.

'Good morning. I am Sarah, Mr Phillips's secretary. He's just finishing a meeting – it shouldn't be more than a few minutes. Please follow me.'

They were led through a thickly carpeted corridor with numerous closed doors on either side. She reached the end and opened a door to conference room three. This was a corner room with long windows reaching from the floor to the ceiling. The table filled almost the entire space, with tubular steel and leather chairs surrounding it.

'May I offer coffee or tea?'

'Yes, thank you,' Anna said, crossing to look out of the window.

'Help yourself. There's also herbal and decaf coffee.'

Sarah walked out, closing the door silently behind her. Paul was making himself a coffee and stuffing his mouth with a fresh croissant.

'This is all very swish, isn't it? Do you want herbal or what?'

Anna joined him, looking over the neatly arrayed rows of all the various teas and coffees.

'I'll have a Columbia, black.' She picked up a chocolate digestive biscuit and took another look around the room. There was a stack of notebooks with sharpened pencils beside them with the logo of the company, A & C, entwined in navy blue. She carried her coffee to the table pondering which chair she should take, and decided to sit in the end one facing the door.

'That's probably the chairman's seat,' Paul said, wading through his second croissant.

Anna sipped the piping hot thick black coffee; it tasted good. Paul drew out a chair midway along the table with his back to the tall windows. After ten minutes and no show of Michael Phillips, Anna was getting impatient. They'd helped themselves to more coffee and biscuits and Paul had also helped himself to a couple of notepads and pencils. Then the door swung open and in strode the over-confident and very handsome Michael Phillips. He first crossed to Anna to shake her hand and then went to Paul.

'I'm not sure what this is about, but I apologise for keeping you waiting. Have you had coffee or—?'

Anna interrupted his flow, holding up her cup. 'Yes, thank you.'

He spread his arms, smiling. 'I sit down, do I?'

Anna was immediately on her guard, not liking his manner. 'As you wish, Mr Phillips.'

She then introduced herself and Paul, even though it was obvious he knew who they were. He chose a seat almost opposite Paul, but he drew the chair out far enough to cross one leg over his knee.

'How long have you lived at Newton Court?' Anna asked.

'Not that long, actually.'

'How long?'

'Eighteen months. It's a rental property.'

'Long way for you to come to work here, isn't it?'

'Not really. I have only been with this company four months and previously to that I worked in a Barclays Bank not far from Hounslow. I have no intention of staying there much longer, but I had renewed my one-year lease.'

He was very slender, wearing a good grey suit with a

pristine white shirt and black tie. He was also, Anna reckoned, about six foot two. He had very piercing dark eyes in a chiselled face, with strong cheekbones. His mouth was thin-lipped, which slightly diminished his handsome appearance, but he had thick glossy black hair parted on one side and had a habit of running his slender fingers through it. As she hadn't spoken for a while she watched him pat his hair, tossing his head back slightly.

'What is this about?'

'You are a tenant and live next door to a Tina Brooks and her partner Alan Rawlins?'

'Yes.'

'Are you aware that Mr Rawlins is missing?'

'Sort of, yes.'

'What do you mean?'

'Miss Brooks actually knocked on my door a while back asking if Mr Rawlins was with me, though why she would ask me didn't really make any sense as I hardly knew him.'

'But you did know him?'

'I'd pass him going to work and sometimes when I returned. He once asked me about my car and we chatted a bit, but I wouldn't say I knew him.'

'What did you make of him?'

'Make of him? I don't understand. I've just said I hardly even spoke to him.'

'When was the last time you did that?'

He lolled back in his chair. 'Erm . . . a few months ago.'

'What happened on that occasion?'

'As far as I can recall, I was coming into the block and he was leaving. He said hi or something like that and that's it.'

'What about Tina Brooks?'

'I know they lived together, but that's all I knew about them.'

'So you didn't socialise with them?'

'No. To be honest, I can't wait to leave, but it was very useful for me when I was at my previous job in Hounslow. I was working not too far away, but with all the present banking fiasco I was one of the first they let go, so I applied for numerous positions and got lucky here.'

'What exactly do you do?'

'Investments.'

Anna tapped her notebook and then gave a smile. 'You look fit, Mr Phillips. Do you work out?'

'Yes.'

'Do you use the same gym as Tina and Alan?'

He nodded and then ran his hand through his hair.

'I was a member at the local gym, but we have our own here in the basement so I didn't renew my membership.'

'So you must have met Tina there?'

'Yes, she was there on a number of occasions, I think, but like I said I didn't really know either of them and I used a personal trainer there so I didn't really mix with anyone else.'

'Did you ever hear any arguments between them?'

He sighed and shook his head. 'No. I'm not wall to wall to them but opposite, so even if they had argued I doubt if I'd have heard them. They live in flat two and I am in flat one.'

'Have you ever seen anything suspicious with regard to them?'

'No. I leave early and I get back around seven. To be honest, the block is a bit of a dead zone apart from some tenants above; apparently their cooking smells drift upwards. I don't think I've ever even met them. I know there's a woman with a small yapping dog and a Mr and Mrs Maisell who I've bumped into a few times.'

'But you didn't know either Tina or Alan well?'

'No. I've already said that I didn't.'

'Your flat is the same size as theirs?'

'Yes.'

'Quite large for a bachelor, isn't it?'

'Not at all. In fact, when I first looked over the place I was with a friend and it was sort of a maybe situation of us moving there together, but it didn't work out.'

'Girlfriend?'

'Yes.'

'So you're not engaged?'

'Been almost caught,' he grinned, 'but no, I'm single.'

'Do you have an ongoing relationship now?'

'No, actually I don't. I'm playing the field, as they say.'

'Did you ever play with Tina Brooks?'

His face tightened. 'No – and if there is nothing more you need to ask me, I should get back to work.'

Anna stood up and gathered her notebook and pen, which she had not used, and slipped them into her brief-case.

'What do you think happened to him?' Phillips asked.

'Well, we are trying to find out. Thank you for your time. Do you have a card in case we need to contact you again?'

When he stood up he towered above Anna and she reckoned she'd been out by a couple of inches; he was at least six foot four. He handed Anna his business card as he led them back to the lifts and waited until they stepped inside before moving off.

'What do you think?' Anna asked Paul, who had not said one word.

'I dunno. He seemed like an okay bloke, bit of the flash type, but he didn't come over to me like he was lying.'

'Did to me,' she said as they walked out to her car.

'How do you mean?'

'Come on – think about it. He's young and around the same age as Alan and Tina, lives on their doorstep, but never gets friendly, drives a Lotus, and we know Alan's a mechanic, et cetera, et cetera.'

'Are you sure you're not wanting him to be involved, because it didn't come across to me that he was lying. He was good-looking though, wasn't he?'

'Oh please.'

'In a hetero-very-sexual way.'

'We'll go back to the gym and ask them about him.'

'Then what?'

'I want our heterosexual neighbour checked out. See if he has ever come to police notice.'

'He's obviously earning a packet.'

'Did you look at his shoes?' Anna asked.

'His shoes?'

'Yes. Case I was on with Langton, we all missed our suspect and let him walk out on us, but Langton suddenly went crazy. It was the guy's shoes. He came in as a Drug Squad officer and we were all fooled.'

'What about his shoes?'

'Handmade by Lobb and probably cost more than my week's wages. Langton was correct; the guy hoodwinked every one of us.'

'So Mr Phillips has expensive shoes.'

'No, that's just it – they were rundown at the heels. And I didn't buy his story about why he's living out in Hounslow in a rented flat if he's working for that posh firm.'

'Maybe they're just comfortable.'

'I also want to check out his phones, landline and mobiles, see if he lied about not socialising with our Tina Brooks, check if there are any phone calls between them.'

'Yes, ma'am.'

'We also get a search warrant for Tina Brooks's flat.'

'You won't get it through without more evidence.'

'Want to bet? The bleach, carpet cleaner then the new carpet she's ordered – we'll get it through. As Langton's been so keen on us following this up, I'll get him to back me.'

They drove out of the parking area onto Bishopsgate. Paul was surprised by her newfound energy, unless it was down to the several cups of strong coffee, but Anna was buzzing.

'This is all getting very interesting, Paul. I know at first I was pissed off, but I'm changing my mind as it's possible Alan Rawlins isn't missing: I think he could have been murdered. Pity we don't have a body, but charges have been brought without one before.'

She gave him a smile and then returned to weaving in and out of the traffic, constantly using the car horn and swearing as they hit a snarl up by Ladbroke Grove. Paul felt very uneasy, and not just because of her erratic driving, although it did make him cringe back in his seat a few times, but rather because of her attitude. Anna seemed pleased about Alan Rawlins possibly being a victim. He himself was not so certain. They still had no real evidence to warrant a full-scale investigation, but he didn't feel like getting into any kind of disagreement, especially not with a hangover.

Chapter Five

It took considerable time to gain access to the phone records for both Tina and Michael Phillips, and it was not until 5 p.m. that the team acquired access to Phillips's bank accounts. Anna had left messages for Langton to call and she was becoming very impatient waiting for him to respond. She constantly badgered Paul for a result, but when he eventually did come up with the information it was disappointing. There were no calls to Michael Phillips from Tina's landline or mobile phone. Her listed calls were already noted as she had given details to Anna about where and who she had rung in an attempt to find out what had happened to Alan Rawlins. In response, Anna snapped, enquiring where the records of Phillips's calls were. Paul informed Anna that Michael Phillips didn't appear to have a landline but only a company mobile phone, so the records would take longer to compile and check. Added to that disappointment came the financial position of their 'suspect', as they were now referring to Phillips.

Paul was feeling really frazzled. Nothing had shifted his hangover headache, and spending so much time on the phone and then on the computer had made it feel worse.

'Okay – quick rundown,' he said to Anna. 'This is as

much as I've got. He did work for Barclays, but was one of the many made redundant. Previously he'd been with two other banks that went under. He's not had what I'd call a successful career. He lost half a million with the Icelandic Bank, but he got a leg-up with his present employers as his sister is married to one of the chief executives. The Lotus is leased, by the way, he doesn't even own that. So renting a place in Hounslow is about all he could afford.'

'So I was right about his shoes,' Anna said, folding her arms. 'Does he have more than one mobile?'

'I've not checked that yet. I'm still working on his business card number.'

She glanced at her watch. Paul could feel her irritation.

'What has Langton got to say?' he asked.

'He's not returned my calls, but you go off and come in first thing in the morning.'

'Thanks.'

Anna glanced through Paul's notes and was about to put in yet another call to Langton when the man himself walked into her office.

'I've not got long,' he said, sitting down. 'I'm really busy.'

'Well, excuse me, but I've been running around on this Alan Rawlins business and now I need your approval.'

'For what?'

'I want to get a search warrant issued to look over Tina Brooks's flat.'

'But you've been there, haven't you?'

Anna filled him in on the carpet order and the bleach purchase, and said that although she had interviewed Tina, they had not had a thorough or even part-detailed search of the flat.

'You didn't really need my authority, but if you now think that we have a murder then it will have to go through all the usual channels. What's more, you'll have to set up a new team as I've put the rest onto other cases.'

'I am aware of that, obviously. But as you oversee all the murder enquiries, do I get the go-ahead?'

He frowned and then stood up, stretching his legs and rubbing his bad knee.

'You able to cope with this?' he grunted.

'What?'

'You want me to repeat it?'

'No, I don't, but what makes you ask if I can cope?'

'Because as DCI you'll head the team. I can look over your shoulder, obviously.'

'When have you not? But I have handled my last case and—'

He turned on her angrily, leaning against the edge of her desk.

'Don't you get flippant with me! Just remember, whatever personal relationship we might have had, I am your—'

Equally angry, she stood up to face him, interrupting him.

'*Superior!* Well, you tell me if you wouldn't want a full investigation after what I've told you.'

'You have only circumstantial possibilities.'

She flopped back down into her chair.

'Oh, wait a minute,' she fumed. 'You have been the one wanting more details. Basically it was a Mispers case, but because you insisted I look into it, that is what I have done. And now that it looks like a murder enquiry, you start telling me to back off.'

'I did not suggest that.'

'What do you want – to get someone else to do it?' Anna demanded.

'I am just concerned about putting too much pressure on you. Right now I need all the people I have, but I can allocate another DCI to make further enquiries.'

'I see. So what has this all been about – give her something to occupy her mind, nothing too strenuous – because you think I'm not capable?'

'You are more than capable, Anna.'

'So what is your problem?'

'You, Anna. You have been through a terrible ordeal, your fiancé has been murdered, and as far as I can ascertain you have refused to take any time out.'

'What about the previous case I worked on and got a result?'

'Come on, it was a cut-and-dried case – of course you got a guilty verdict!'

She was so angry she could hardly look at him.

'I thought it was best as you had insisted on returning to work,' Langton went on, 'but now I am not so sure. I am worried about you.'

'Well, you don't have to be. I am fine! And what's more, I don't want anyone else taking over the Alan Rawlins investigation. If he is dead, I am damn sure Tina Brooks had something to do with it.'

'You have to be aware how difficult it is to bring charges without a body.'

'Give me time and maybe I'll find one for you!'

He glanced at his watch. 'I can't argue about this now. Get the search warrants and see what the outcome is.'

'Thank you.'

Langton found it difficult to deal with her. She was so rigid and so defensive, and he really didn't want to force her into taking a holiday. Yet she was suffering extreme emotional anguish of the kind he himself had experienced when his first wife had died, and he wanted to help.

She wished he would go. Now she'd got the permission for moving on with the case, she didn't want to discuss anything else. She looked at him, and then turned away because she didn't like the expression in his eyes.

'Listen to me, sweetheart. You lose someone you love, and no amount of work can help you deal with the loss. It takes a long time,' Langton advised.

'You've already told me this. Maybe you are projecting your own inability to come to terms with grief. I lived with you, James, and let me tell you, I have no intention of ever allowing myself to form another relationship until I am well and truly recovered from losing Ken. However, what happened with him is over, finished – and I just want to get on with my life, my career.'

He wanted to slap her, the way she stuck out her chin and clenched her fists at her side. He was only too aware of the fact that he had been unable to sustain a relationship with Anna. He had known he couldn't give her more than what he had to offer, and it had not been enough. Even now, married to his second wife, taking on her daughter, Kitty, and with a son, Tommy, he was still having extra-marital affairs. He also still held a passion for Anna. It was not reciprocated and he knew that, but he also knew that, given the opportunity, he would start up seeing her again – and what made it worse, he actually felt no shame even contemplating it.

She stared at him, waiting for him to say something, but he remained silent. She couldn't tell what he was thinking.

'I'm sorry. I shouldn't have brought up your personal

life. Sometimes I forget you are who you are,' she said quietly, avoiding eye-contact with him.

'That's okay, Anna, and I can see you've calmed down.'

'I have, and I want this case.'

He walked to the door and gave her a smile.

'You have it. Get a team organised. I'll forward the list of available officers and you can stay on here as it's the same location.'

'Don't I know it. I have to schlepp all the way from my flat at Tower Bridge. I sometimes wish I'd never bought the place – not that I've seen that much of it, but it's home sweet home. As you haven't arranged the promised dinner, maybe one night I'll have enough time to cook for you!'

She smiled, making a joke, but he walked out closing the door quietly behind him. The fact that she had the case made her buoyant for a moment, but then she felt the shuddering panic rise and couldn't get her breath. She broke out in a sweat, gasping before the tears welled up inside her. She rested her head in her hands. She wasn't over losing Ken, far from it. She'd had the lengthy trial of the killer of John Smiley, and then with only a couple of weeks' break, had taken on her last case. Almost a year had passed, but the thought of taking time out to dwell on the terrible way she had lost the future she and Ken had planned together made her fearful that she would never be able to recover.

Langton sat in his car. It had been a while since he had felt the twist in his gut like a scorching pain. He had sometimes wondered if he had embroidered on the love he had lost, that perhaps it had not been as perfect as he made it out to be. Inside his wallet he retained the small photographs of his adopted daughter, Kitty, and his son, but he still had the worn photograph of his first wife tucked behind their innocent little faces. Even now, years later, when these moments of grief descended, he felt almost incapable of moving. He looked at his first wife's photograph. If he closed his eyes he could hear her voice calling out to him that she would see him for dinner. He had been told she had collapsed and died four hours later, the undetected brain tumour that killed her leaving her with not a mark on her beautiful face. When he had seen her in the mortuary she looked as if she was peacefully sleeping.

He had never known with another woman the same deep understanding they had had with each other, and that sleeping face reared up as if to eclipse anyone he felt emotionally drawn to. This combined with a sense of guilt that he could never feel the same attachment to another woman. Even though he had remarried and now had a son, sometimes when he watched his boy sleeping, he felt an overwhelming sense of loss, thinking of what it would have been like to have a child with his first wife. Thinking what it would have been like if she had lived.

Anna had wanted from him commitment, children, and although it had been she who had instigated the end of their relationship, he had in many ways known it was never going to work. She wanted too much of him and he was incapable of giving it. His present wife was intelligent, very attractive, and had wanted stability for her daughter Kitty who adored Langton and now called him Daddy. It was almost a marriage of convenience. She had accepted what Langton could give her, and had not really contemplated having a child with him. Tommy was almost as much a surprise to her as he was to Langton. She had been sure it was the onset of the menopause, but when she discovered she was pregnant, Langton had proved to be very caring. He was a good provider, and although very much an absentee father, being so dedicated to his career, she accepted their marriage for what it was – a stable if unemotional relationship.

Unlike Anna, Langton no longer had the release of weeping; instead he waited for the pain to subside. It was still strong, but thankfully not as frequent or as debilitating as it had been in the past. He drove off and headed to Highgate, thankful that preoccupation with work cushioned the ghost that still haunted him.

Anna opened a bottle of wine when she got home and had two glasses before she made herself something to eat. She finished the bottle before she went to bed, and with the alcohol and the sleeping tablets she was able to get a full night's deep sleep. She often felt slightly heavy-headed in the mornings, but black coffee heaped with sugar made her feel wired enough to face the day. She was still losing weight and she had made a rather empty promise to herself that she would start to work out, but that had not happened. The thought that she might be running on empty and that it might have repercussions hadn't even crossed her mind. Instead, she was certain that she was dealing with losing Ken, dealing with it on her own terms.

By the time Anna arrived at the station, Paul was already there. They had a search warrant for Tina Brooks's flat, but before making use of it they first marked up on the incident board the case-file to date. Alan Rawlins had not been reported missing for almost two weeks after his disappearance. He was now missing for eight weeks. They had no sightings, no movement in any of his bank accounts, and no use of his credit cards. They were unsure exactly what items of clothing were missing and at first Tina had said to his father that she thought she had found his passport, but then changed it to discovering an old out-of-date one. Alan Rawlins's current passport and toiletries were definitely missing. Anna had also requested an all ports warning to see if Alan had taken a flight, rail or ferry out of the UK, but there was no trace of this being the case. It was not to say that he hadn't used a false identity to travel but she felt that this was unlikely.

Anna sat on the edge of a desk looking over the details she and Paul had so far accumulated. No witness had seen Alan Rawlins for the entire period he was missing. The occupants of the block of flats had little or nothing to do with either Tina or Alan.

The police had no note, no correspondence of any kind that gave them an indication that he had planned to disappear. The last sighting of him was therefore the day Tina collected him from his workplace at 10:30 a.m. on 15 March. He was unwell and had phoned her to ask her to pick him up and take him home. Tina stated that she had made him a cup of tea and left him to sleep off his migraine.

Underlined on the incident board was the need to check out what medication, if any, he had at the flat, also whether or not he suffered from migraines on a frequent basis, because found in his locker at the garage was a packet of aspirins. Tina Brooks said she returned from work around 6:30 p.m. on 15 March and Alan was not at home. She could not recall if the bed had been remade, but she felt that perhaps it had been. Visits to Tina's workplace had given no clue as to where Alan might have taken off to.

111

Interviews with his parents and close friends had revealed no hint that he had any intention of leaving Tina. Interviews at the local gym used by both Tina and Alan, and the tenant from flat one, Michael Phillips, revealed nothing untoward, bar the fact that Tina was very flirtatious and over-friendly with a few of the members.

They had no connecting phone calls from Tina to Michael Phillips on her landline, but the pair could have used mobile phones, and the team were still in the process of checking out the possibility that both Tina and Michael Phillips had lied.

Paul stood beside Anna, looking over the mark-up on the board.

'Not a lot really,' he said.

'No.'

'Just the purchase of the bleach and the carpet stand out as being odd.'

'Let's go over there and see what we can pick up from the flat.'

'I hope the new carpet's not been laid,' Paul said.

'As it was only delivered yesterday, I doubt it.' Anna picked up her bag and headed out. Paul was still very dubious and nowhere near as certain as Anna that they were now looking for a victim.

Anna was driving as Paul was on the mobile to Tina Brooks. He was very polite, asking if it was possible for her to be at the flat to allow them to enter; if not, they could under the warrant force entry to instigate the search. She was very rude and said that she would have to return from her salon as she was at work.

'We really appreciate it, Miss Brooks.'

Anna glanced at him and he shrugged.

'She's got a mouth on her, but she didn't seem all that worried about the search warrant.'

'Didn't she even ask why?'

'Nope, just said that it was bloody inconvenient.'

Tina remained belligerent as she let them into the flat.

'Why do you have to search the place? You've already been over it once!'

'I'm afraid we are considering that Alan Rawlins may be dead so we would like to do a thorough search.'

'Well, get on with it, but I can't stay long.'

'Thank you for your cooperation. When we were last here, the caretaker said you were expecting some new carpet to be delivered.'

'Yes, it's in the living room.'

Anna glanced at Paul. This was good. She asked why the carpet was being replaced and Tina rolled her eyes.

'I am sick to death of this beige colour. It also marks easily so I decided weeks ago to get some new carpet with a bit more colour, but it had to be beige again because it's in the bloody lease. Anyway, I am not going to stay on here longer than I have to, as it has sad memories.'

'We will try not to inconvenience you more than is necessary,' Paul said as Anna headed into the lounge. The new carpet was rolled up and left against the wall. There were a few stains around the coffee table, but they were not very noticeable. Together she and Paul moved around the room, opening drawers and cupboards. Tina was in the kitchen and occasionally walked in to stand in the doorway watching them.

'Did Alan have any medication for migraines?'

'No. He would just use paracetamol or codeine tablets.'

'Did he often have these headaches?'

'They went if he had a good sleep. I'd draw the curtains, make the room dark and that was about it really.' She returned to the kitchen.

There appeared to be nothing out of the ordinary in the lounge, not until Paul moved the sofa aside to look beneath it.

'Anna, come here.'

She joined him and he shoved the sofa even further away. There was a large piece of carpet missing which had clearly been neatly cut out, measuring about two feet by two. The dark black underlay was still in situ.

'Miss Brooks – Tina – could you come in here for a moment, please?' Anna called.

Tina came to the doorway.

'Can you explain why there is a large piece of carpet cut out from here?'

'Yes, I can. The sofa used to be against that wall.' She gestured across the room. 'Alan spilled a bottle of red wine and he couldn't get the stain out. He must have cut it out, I think.'

She pointed to the roll of new carpet. 'That's another reason why we have to leave a month's deposit with the landlord. If there's any damage when we leave, he uses it.'

'So you intended leaving before Alan disappeared?'

'Yes, I told you. We were looking for a place to buy – we were getting married.'

'I see. Thank you.'

Tina went back to the kitchen as they finished up the search of the lounge.

'Do you want a coffee?' she offered, from where she was sitting on a stool at the breakfast bar.

'No, thank you, but do you mind if we look in there? Shouldn't take long,' Anna said.

Tina picked up her coffee and walked past them to sit in the lounge. They opened the cupboards beneath the sink first, and Anna held up a container of bleach. It was half-empty and no other container was visible. There were scrubbing brushes and a bucket which all smelled strongly of bleach. Anna went into the lounge.

'You have a container of bleach in the kitchen?'

'Yes – what about it?'

'We have a witness who saw you buying a considerable amount of bleach and some carpet cleaner from Asda.'

'Yes. I use bleach to clean the floor in the salon. I use that one here to clean around the sinks and tiles in the kitchen and the bathroom.'

'And the carpet cleaner?'

'I used it to try and clean up coffee and food stains on the carpet so we wouldn't lose the deposit but gave up and ordered a new carpet.'

Paul finished checking out the kitchen and walked past Anna into the master bedroom. It really was a very nondescript tasteless flat, and the bedroom had the same beige carpet. He searched through the wardrobes and dressing-table drawers; they were as they had been from their first search of the place. There were also two black plastic bin liners filled with Alan's clothes, all folded neatly, with a tag attached to the bag which said *Salvation Army*. Paul had to remove each item and check it out.

Anna had by now completed a search of the small second bedroom which was used as an office. She found nothing, apart from the accounts for both Tina and Alan's mobile phones. As she went into the master bedroom, Tina approached her.

'Listen, I am going to have to leave. I've got appointments for this afternoon.'

'We won't be too long. I am taking these statements for the mobile phones. Is that all right?'

'Take whatever you want.' Tina went back into the kitchen to wash up her own coffee mug.

Paul indicated the black bin liners, saying, 'His clothes ready for the Salvation Army.'

'What?'

'His side of their wardrobe's empty.'

'Miss Brooks?' Anna said loudly. She pointed at the plastic bin liners. 'You are sending these to the Salvation Army?'

'Yes. They're Alan's clothes, no use to me, and if he comes back, serves him right.'

Tina walked off again, and Anna shook her head. Talk about lack of emotion! She sighed. They had found nothing. She looked around the room and then back to the bed. There was a bedside table on either side of the bed, each with a matching lamp. Anna noticed old indentations in the carpet on the right side of the bed.

'The bed and tables have been moved to the left. Push the bed back out to the right.'

Paul heaved at it. It was very heavy and he hadn't been able to see beneath as it had two storage units under the frame and mattress. It took him all his strength to move the bed, and Anna had to shift the other bedside table so it wouldn't get in the way.

'What have we got here?' Paul wondered, bending down.

'What is it?'

He pointed to an inserted square of carpet almost the same size as the section they had found missing beneath the sofa.

'Is it tacked down or glued?' Anna asked, close to him.

'Double-sided carpet tape holding it down.'

'Ease it up.'

Paul carefully drew the carpet up by one corner, pulling it away from the underlay. He sniffed. 'I can smell bleach.'

As he slowly peeled it back to reveal the dark waffle of the underlay they could see a large bleach-stained area. It was almost circular and had been scrubbed so hard there were bits of damaged rubber and weave exposed.

Anna stood up. She instructed Paul to get the local Scene of Crime officers to the flat to test the stain.

'There's no red wine on that bit of carpet you just lifted.'

Next, Anna drew the sheet from the bed, but there was no sign of staining on the mattress, duvet or pillows. Tina came and stood in the doorway.

'I am going to have to go. Have you finished in here?'

Anna turned to face her. 'No, Miss Brooks, we have not. We have found something very disturbing and we will need to get people here to ascertain exactly what—'

'What's that?' Tina demanded, coming further into the room.

'It is obvious that the carpet cut from your lounge has been used to cover damage in here.'

'Oh my God, I've never even seen that before!'

'I will need to interview you, Miss Brooks, at the station.'

'Why?'

'I think the staining on the underlay by the bed is due to someone cleaning it with bleach, maybe because it had Alan Rawlins's blood on it, so if you would agree to accompany me . . .'

'I've got nothing to do with that! I didn't even know it was there.'

'I nevertheless need to ask you to accompany me.'

'But I've got appointments!'

'You had better cancel them.'

The forensic team moved into the flat an hour later, and quickly ascertained that the underlay stain was bleach mixed with traces of human blood. They proceeded to roll back a wider area of carpet and then underlay, revealing heavily bloodstained floorboards. Due to the extent and density of the stain, even though attempts had been made to clean it with bleach, the Forensic Crime Scene Examiner believed that whoever had sustained the injury could have had a very severe wound. They also began examining the carpet in the lounge looking for any further signs of blood and the so-called wine spillage.

A very distraught Tina Brooks was taken in a patrol car to the station. Anna followed in her Mini whilst Paul remained at the flat to liaise with the forensic team as the premises were now being treated as a possible murder scene. Various items of clothing, the mattress and bedding, along with the neatly tied black bin liners of Alan Rawlins's clothes were removed to be tested at the lab.

Tina had been asked if she would like representation and she insisted that she wanted a solicitor present. This took a further hour as they waited for a Jonathan Hyde to arrive. Meanwhile Anna was checking if there were any blood samples known to have been taken from Alan Rawlins, in case the stain in the flat belonged to him, then they could match it. She spoke to his father, who seemed in a terrible way to be relieved that at long last there was some kind of result. Even the fact that it was possible his son had met with foul play meant he could stop hoping, he said. He wanted to know for certain, and he agreed that both he and his wife would give blood samples, to be able to prove whether or not the blood discovered beneath the bed was their son's.

Paul returned to the station to report that the forensic team were still at the flat, and that SOC officers were now doing an inch-by-inch search. This would include the garage and Tina's car, which they impounded. If Alan Rawlins had been murdered in her flat, then his body would have to have been removed. As Anna banked up the incriminating evidence, her adrenalin kept her going without having lunch or even a cup of coffee. She had not pressed charges against Tina, as at present there was no direct evidence that she had murdered Alan Rawlins.

Anna and Paul went into an interview room first to talk to Jonathan Hyde. They explained that his client was not under arrest as they were awaiting verification that the blood was that of Alan Rawlins and she would, at the present time, be simply assisting their enquiry. They gave details of the length of time Alan had been missing and the discovery of the blood staining. They also provided him with the information of his client's purchase of bleach, carpet cleaner and the ordering of new carpet.

Hyde then sat privately with Tina, explaining everything to her.

It was not until six-thirty the same evening that Anna got to conduct the first interview.

Paul sat beside Anna as she informed Hyde that she had not as yet received verification that the blood from Tina's flat was Alan's, and it would take more time to compare the blood with his parents' for a positive result. Anna was calm and relaxed, but Tina sat like a coiled spring ready to unwind. Although she was there to assist their enquiries,

Tina was cautioned to ensure that anything she did say could be used as evidence at a later date.

'We really want you to explain the discovery of the blood on the carpet underlay in your bedroom. Do you have anything to tell us?' Anna asked.

Tina shook her head.

'But you must have known it was there. The bed had been moved, a section of carpet had been cut out from under it and then replaced by a piece cut from beneath your living-room sofa.'

'I told you – Alan spilled a bottle of wine so he must have cut out the section of the carpet. He was always concerned what money the landlord would try and get out of us if we damaged anything. We were saving to buy a place of our own.'

'So did Alan subsequently insert the section cut from the lounge under your bed to cover the bloodstain?'

'I don't know. I've never seen it before.'

'How do you explain it then?'

'He must have done it when I was at work.'

'Miss Brooks, if we discover that the stain is in actual fact Alan's blood, how do you explain that?'

'I don't know. Maybe he had a nose bleed, something like that.'

'But surely the section of the carpet being cut out from beneath the sofa would have occurred sometime before you say he might have had a nose bleed. You claim that he spilled a bottle of wine – when did that occur?' Anna asked.

'A while ago, maybe a few months.'

'So when did he cut out the section of the carpet?'

'I don't know. As I just said, it could have happened after he had a nose bleed.'

'Did you cut the section of carpet beneath the sofa?'

'No.'

'When did you notice it had been done?'

'More or less when you showed it to me.'

'Why did you order new carpet?'

'Because I want to move and the landlord would make us pay for any damage. I tried a bottle of carpet cleaner but it wasn't much good.'

'When did you order the new carpet?'

'A week ago. It was on special offer.'

At this point Jonathan Hyde intervened. 'We appear to be going around in circles, Detective Travis. Surely until this stain discovered beneath the bed is actually verified as being Mr Rawlins's blood, I can see no reason to continue this line of questioning. My client has told you she was unaware of its existence and she did not cut any of the carpet herself.'

'Could you explain why you purchased a considerable amount of bleach shortly after Mr Rawlins went missing?'

Tina sighed. 'I told you why. I use a lot of bleach in the salon because it cleans up the spilled hair-dye and we've got black and white lino tiles.'

'The bleach container in your salon is a different make to the ones you purchased from Asda.'

'They were on special offer so as I was there I took the opportunity and bought them. I kept one at the flat – the rest I used cleaning up the salon.'

Hyde shook his head, saying to Anna, 'This is really all conjecture. Miss Brooks has explained why she purchased the bleach, for her salon, and some to use at her flat.'

'Was it not an attempt to clear away the bloodstain?'

'No, it wasn't, because I didn't even know it was there!'

121

'But you must have been aware that the bed had been moved – moved to cover the offending bloodstain.'

'I never noticed. Sometimes when I hoover I move it or Alan does. We try and keep the place immaculate because it's rented.'

'So you admit that you move the bed to hoover?'

'Yes, I just said so.'

'It's exceptionally heavy, with two drawers beneath the frame for storage. Did you get any help when you say you moved the bed?'

'Well, if I did, Alan would help me.'

'So you have not moved the bed for some time?'

'No, not that I can remember.'

Paul knew they were getting nowhere. He had remained silent watching Anna work over Tina, but it wasn't bringing a result. Mr Hyde obviously felt the same way as he tapped the table with his pen.

'I feel that my client has answered your questions and to be honest, unless you have proof that Mr Rawlins is deceased and not as Miss Brooks claims missing, I think she has assisted your enquiries to the best of her ability. If you have nothing further to add, I suggest that we terminate this interview.'

Anna really had no alternative. She closed her file and thanked Tina for her cooperation, but warned her that she might well want to interview her again when she got the blood results from the lab. She also made it clear that her flat was now a possible murder scene and she should make arrangements to stay elsewhere until the tests had been completed. Paul took Tina and Jonathan Hyde to the reception while Anna remained in the interview room, irritated because she knew she had perhaps jumped the gun. However, she hoped that putting Tina under pressure might produce a result as by now the woman must be aware of the seriousness of the findings in her flat.

Anna found Paul sitting on a chair facing the incident board.

'That was a bit of a waste of time,' he said.

'Maybe, but it might put the skids beneath her. Tomorrow we'll go over to the lab and see what they have for us.'

'I tell you what we need – a body.'

'You think I don't know that?' she snapped.

'Question is, where the hell is it?' Paul went on. 'If he was killed in the bed she couldn't have carried him by herself. He was a big guy, muscular, and must have weighed at least seventeen stone.'

'I know.'

'Which means she would have had to have help. The other scenario is, whilst she was at work someone else entered the flat, killed him and moved the body before she got home.'

'I don't buy that. Are you saying that this other person cut out the carpet, laid it under the bed, moved the body and she didn't know about it?'

Paul shrugged. 'I dunno, but if the blood *is* Alan Rawlins's . . .?'

'Not *if*. I am damned sure it is, and we'll be able to prove it when they get the results from the comparison with his parents' blood.'

'Well, until we are positive there's not a lot we can move on with.'

'I'll see you at the lab first thing in the morning.'

With that, Anna went into her office. She wrote up the report of the interview, but felt disinclined to contact

Langton. Tina was obviously her prime suspect. Although she had thought about Michael Phillips being a part of it, they had not a shred of proof that he was involved.

Anna used the wine and sleeping tablets combination to get another good night's sleep. She did make herself an omelette the next morning, but hardly touched it. By nine she was waiting at the forensic lab in Lambeth for Paul to arrive. Meanwhile work was still continuing at Tina's flat as the team searched every inch for further bloodstains and any evidence that Alan Rawlins was murdered inside the bedroom. Tina had given the address of Donna Hastings, the girl she was staying with until she could move back into the flat.

Whilst waiting, Anna went over and over in her head the possible scenario. There was no sign of forced entry, so did Alan know his killer? Whatever had occurred in the flat must have been very traumatic. It was possible that Alan had been bludgeoned whilst leaning over the bed. Had it been an argument that got out of control? Or was it a planned murder?

To dispose of a body was no easy feat. She surmised that Tina would have had to have help, but if it had been some argument that resulted in murder, why not call the police and explain that it was an accident? The financial gain for Tina was the seventy-odd thousand in the joint savings account, plus Alan's life-insurance policy. Surely that was not enough to commit murder? Tina's salon was on the surface successful, but Anna knew it was also in debt; nevertheless she had to be making a good living.

Anna rubbed her head and tried to think of the alternative scenario. Tina, with an accomplice, planned to kill Alan. The motive could be that she wanted out of the relationship and wanted the joint bank account for herself. That would mean it could possibly be a passionate relationship, but with whom? So far they had found no evidence to prove she was having any kind of affair. Okay, there had been some flirty behaviour at the gym, but nothing had surfaced from their interviews, to the contrary. Tina had claimed she was suspicious that Alan was leaving her for another woman, but so far there was no evidence of any other woman in Alan's life.

She was going around in circles again and she physically jumped when Paul tapped her shoulder.

'Sorry I'm late. The bloody tubes were up the spout.'

They headed into the forensic lab, where Liz Hawley was just arriving, also complaining of a tube strike. She was a middle-aged, rather rotund woman with straggly grey hair caught in a knot on the top of her head. She was also a very experienced scientist. As she put on her white coat she led them to her section of the lab.

'Right. First I'll deal with the cut-out area beneath the sofa in the lounge. We've examined the underlay that was left in place there, and there does not appear to be any wine staining. The section of carpet inserted by the bedside is not wine-stained and most probably came from beneath the living-room sofa. It looks like both areas were originally cut out with a Stanley knife, but the uneven ragged edges on the bedroom insert suggests scissors were used to re-shape it so it would fit.

'Now, onto the blood distribution under the inserted piece of carpet by the bed. I would propose that the victim may have suffered a severe head injury or possibly stab wounds causing heavy blood loss, as some areas of staining were so dense. Although attempts had been made to clean it up, the blood had soaked through the underlay onto and between the floorboards where it pooled and congealed underneath. The victim could have been on the left side of the bed when initially attacked, as ultra-violet light testing revealed some minute traces of blood spatter on the bedside wall. It would appear that a bleaching agent was used to wipe the wall and we also found some minute bloodstaining on the edge of the mattress. The sheet we removed from the bed has no blood on it so it's likely the original blood-stained one was destroyed or laundered. The pillows also have minute traces, but not the pillowcases.'

'What kind of weapon do you think would have caused the injury?' Anna asked her.

'Well, my dear, that is really for you to find out. It could have been a blunt instrument, knife or even a gun, but without a body for a pathologist to examine it's impossible to tell you. We have removed a few items from the flat for testing – a golf club, a baseball bat and hammer, but we haven't recovered any trace evidence from them.'

'So you wouldn't say all that blood could have come from a severe nose bleed?'

'No, definitely not with the heavily stained and pooled areas, but the staining on the pillows and mattress could have done. It would appear that whoever sustained the injuries lost a large volume of blood, which without immediate medical attention would probably result in death. Also, for this amount of blood to be found in one area, your victim must have been in a dormant position for quite some time, possibly lying over the edge of the bed or on the floor beside it.'

Liz moved along the workbench. 'We have recovered two hairs from one pillowcase and a semen stain on the bedsheet.'

This pleased Anna. 'That's good. We'll need to test if the hairs are Tina's.'

Liz picked up her notebook. 'We have received the blood samples from the parents, Mr and Mrs Edward Rawlins, for genetic DNA comparison to the scene stains.'

Anna waited, eager to know if their suspicions were correct and that Alan Rawlins was probably dead.

'There are a couple of problems though. Firstly, the doctor who took Mrs Rawlins's blood failed to secure the container properly, causing it to leak – which raises not only health and safety issues for my staff but also possible contamination. I will need another sample from her. In respect of Edward Rawlins's profile, I'm not entirely happy with the result. Sometimes things can go wrong and the results can be misleading, but I can't say at this stage that the blood from the flat did belong to their son.'

'What do you mean by misleading?'

'Well, in the past this type of DNA testing has some-times revealed that the offspring is not the biological child ...'

'What, you mean like adoption?'

'Possibly, but in this case the result of the genetic profile from the scene stains, when compared to Mr Rawlins's DNA, is questionable. He may not be the father.'

'I don't believe it! It's going to be difficult to find out.'

'Why is that? I have enough of Mr Rawlins's blood to run further tests, and once you get another sample from Mrs Rawlins ...'

'I meant find out who is the biological father. The mother has Alzheimer's and didn't recognise her son most of the time, or her husband.'

'Well, to be certain either way, I will need to run some further tests for genetic markers on Mr Rawlins's blood sample. As I said, sometimes mistakes can be made and you need to be one hundred per cent sure on victim identification for your investigation.'

Anna was about to leave, disappointed, when Liz tapped her arm. 'I'm not finished yet. There's something else.'

She led them to another section. Laid out were Alan Rawlins's clothes from the black bin liners.

'We didn't find any blood on any of the clothes, but we have retrieved a single head hair and the colour does not match the two hairs recovered from the bedlinen.'

Anna knew this was a very positive step.

'Can you get DNA from these hairs?'

'None of the hairs recovered have a root attached, but our best bet is to attempt to raise a mitochondrial profile for comparison. You inherit this type of DNA from your mother. However, the process is very time-consuming and can take a few weeks. Basically we have a very small cut strand of blonde hair from Mr Rawlins's clothes, but the two hairs from the bedlinen are reddish and possibly dyed.'

Liz checked her clipboard. 'We have also compared the DNA from the semen stain against the blood pooling and they do not match.' She gave a bark of a laugh. 'Looks like somebody else has been sleeping in his bed.'

Anna patted Liz's arm. 'This is fantastic, Liz. Thank you.'

'Sadly, there's no trace on the national DNA database for the blood or semen stains. There's some further scene examination I'd like to do and I don't want to proceed without your permission as there's a risk of losing evidence by this chemical testing.'

Liz produced photographs of Tina's bathroom: white bath, white tiles on the wall, white wash-basin, and the floor covered in more white tiles.

'It was just a tiny speck in the grouting between the tiles on the far side of the bath – and when I say tiny, I mean less than the size of a pinhead.'

'What?'

'Blood. Although the use of bleaching agents is common in a bathroom and the speck of blood could have got there for a number of reasons, the smell of the bleach was very strong, considering Alan Rawlins has been missing for two months now.' Liz showed them the photograph of the pristine bathroom, indicating with a pen where she had found the minuscule bloodstain.

'There is the possibility that bleach has been used to clean up blood in the bathroom, and I want to use Luminol to detect any remaining specks that are not visible to the human eye. It's a chemical spray that has to be used in darkness and which reacts with the haemoglobin in diluted bloodstains, causing them to glow a bright blue. It's more commonly used in the US. However, the problem is it can damage genetic markers and also give false reactions to a number of things, but further tests to determine blood on anything recovered can be done in the lab. I personally only like to use it as a last resort, but have had positive results in the past – and as they say, nothing ventured, nothing gained.'

'Do it,' Anna said confidently.

'Jolly good, I will get onto that.' Liz closed her notebook. 'Now then, last but not least. This is just my intuition from experience on a previous case. I think the victim was killed in the bedroom, possibly subsequently wrapped in the sheet and carried into the bathroom, then placed in the bath to be dismembered, as it's easier to dispose of body parts rather than the whole corpse. We found no saws or knives that may have been used for this, but it is a possibility. Using Luminol might help us to determine if this scenario is correct, but for now it's over to you to see if you can find anything that might have been used to kill or dismember the victim.'

'Christ, that was some session,' Paul said as they headed back to the station with Anna at the wheel.

'She's one of the best and it sort of makes you . . .'

'Sick?'

'No – more and more aware of what went on inside the flat. What I can't get my head around is the motive. It can't be money, it's just not enough.'

'I dunno – about a hundred grand would see me right.'

'But would you kill for it?'

Paul frowned, clearly finding it hard to come to terms with what they had just been told.

'Why kill him? Why not just leave?' he said. 'They weren't married – it doesn't make sense to me.'

'It's got to be passion.'

'Passion? Jesus Christ, that doesn't work for me. Passionate enough to beat the guy over the head, maybe dismember him in the bath and then go out and dump whatever remains they have? That's not passion: to me, that's cold-blooded murder. And like we keep saying, the motive isn't there.'

'I think it's passion,' she insisted.

'Well, all I can say is what kind of passion have you been involved with because I can't see it.'

'All right, think: they have DNA from the semen, plus hair from the bed which was not the victim's. So whoever it belongs to has to have had sex *after* Alan was murdered. That's passion, sick as it sounds.'

They drove in silence for a while and then Paul sighed.

'You know we still don't have a positive that the blood was Alan Rawlins's? Well, I've got another scenario. What if . . . no, no, it wouldn't work.'

'Go on,' Anna prompted.

'Okay. What if we discover that it wasn't Alan Rawlins's blood by the bed? What if *he* was involved in the murder instead, and *he* cleaned it all up and then went missing afterwards?'

'That's impossible.'

'Yeah, that's what I thought, but Liz said the blood was not a match for the semen found on the bedsheet − so what if the hair and semen in the bed were Alan Rawlins's, but the blood on the floor under the carpet was someone else's.'

Anna digested what he had said, mulling it over in her mind.

'He was fair-haired, right? Liz said the hair found in the bed was reddish-dyed. It could be Tina's, but either way we have to get him identified,' she said quietly.

'Well, if the genetic blood comparison doesn't give it up we don't have Alan Rawlins positively identified. There're no hairbrushes, combs or razor to help us either. That in itself is odd, but not if he packed them up and took them away with him.'

'Shit,' Anna muttered under her breath.

'Added to this,' Paul went on, 'it could mean that Tina genuinely wasn't aware of what went on in the flat, that she didn't know about the blood under the bed nor about the cutting up of the carpet.'

'What about the bleach?'

'She uses it at the salon, we know that.'

Anna bit her lip. 'So what you are saying is that Alan Rawlins committed the murder, cut up the body, moved it and then, knowing what he had done, went on the run?'

'Yeah. Is it possible?'

'You are the one suggesting it,' she snapped.

'Well, what do you think?' Paul asked.

'I think,' Anna hesitated, 'that before we get into this mad conjecture we need verification that the blood was Alan Rawlins's. If the further tests on Edward Rawlins's blood reveal he is not the biological father, we revisit Mrs Rawlins. Maybe she can remember if she had an extramarital fling that resulted in the birth of Alan.'

'We need to arrange for a police doctor to get another blood sample from her anyway,' Paul said, yawning. 'It doesn't make sense.'

'Well, as Liz said, there can sometimes be a blip in the blood testing, so again we have to wait for confirmation.'

'This is a big step up from looking for a missing person, isn't it, ma'am?'

'You said it. We've got us a full-scale murder enquiry.'

Chapter Six

Faced with the evidence from the Forensic Department, Anna and Paul needed to work out their next moves. Now that the case had opened up, Anna felt it was time to put together a full murder team, so she spent the rest of the morning finding a couple more detectives, along with some clerical staff to begin coordinating all the interviews she wanted to take place.

Liz Hawley had left a message that she would not be doing the Luminol test until the following morning, as the fingerprint team had not quite completed their examination. She also reminded them that she needed the further blood sample from Mrs Rawlins.

After a quick lunch, Anna gave a briefing to the new detectives, DC Brian Stanley and DC Helen Bridges. They listened attentively as she explained the investigation to date. Finishing on Liz Hawley's developments she opened the briefing for any questions. Brian Stanley, a thick-set dark-haired officer with unfortunate eyebrows that met together in the centre of his forehead, was an old-timer and had sat with his legs spread wide, resting his elbows on the front of the hard-backed chair he had turned around.

'You get any feedback that the victim could be homosexual?' he asked.

Anna said that she had at one time contemplated the possibility, but had no evidence that he was.

'If you take out money being the motive then it's got to be some kind of passionate incentive to kill,' Stanley persevered.

Paul was bristling due to the man's tone, but said nothing.

'Yes, we have also discussed the motive situation. There's not a lot of money, but murders have been committed for less,' Anna pointed out.

'But if we do get the information from Forensics that a body was severed in the flat, that doesn't have the feel of a monetary gain. To dispose of a body it takes planning as well as cleaning up afterwards.'

'Well, we do have to wait to get that verified from Liz Hawley as she will be testing tomorrow morning,' Anna informed him.

'If this murder was not one of passion but for money, then could it be premeditated? Guy gets off work early and makes sure his girlfriend leaves the flat. Have you come up with any kind of trouble in Alan Rawlins's background?' Brian asked.

'No – to the contrary,' Anna told him. 'From the people we have interviewed he appears to have been a very decent, hard-working, studious man. He was kind and thoughtful, but shy – someone who kept himself to himself, who didn't drink or use drugs.'

'Sounds too good to be true,' Brian smiled.

'Yes. We have also been informed that he was a man who hated confrontations,' Paul said, becoming more irritated with Brian Stanley who now hitched up his trousers.

'That wouldn't match with the Jewish couple. Didn't the old boy say he saw him kicking the hell out of a wall?'

'Correct. So maybe Alan Rawlins had more to him than we've been able to uncover,' Anna replied to diffuse the tension between Paul and Brian.

Brian Stanley had a habit of lifting his forefinger into the air to attract attention.

'These body-builders at the gym he frequented . . . were they gay?'

'Didn't seem so to me, far from it,' Anna replied, glancing at Paul.

'What about this guy who lives in flat one – did he come over as a shirt-lifter?'

Anna gave Brian a disapproving glare. Paul was tight-lipped with anger, but still he remained silent.

'No, he did not. You can see from our investigation that he's had quite a chequered career. Lost his life savings in that Icelandic bank crash and now works for the company listed. Apparently his sister is married to one of the chief executives so she might have had a hand in giving him work. He's a very good-looking young man, by the way.'

'At no time has anyone from the block of flats seen these two together – Tina Brooks and Mr Handsome?' Stanley asked.

'No, they have not.'

'We get anything from the phones? Have they been calling each other?'

'No. We've checked out both landlines, although Phillips hardly uses his. Tina's mobile has been checked but we are still waiting on Mr Phillips's, so we don't yet know if he contacted her – maybe at the salon's a possibility, but it will take a long time to scroll through the hundreds of calls there.'

'You got Alan Rawlins's mobile from the glove compartment in his Merc at the garage, correct?'

'Yes, it's on the board,' Paul said briskly.

'Just wondering why it's taken so long to check out his calls.'

'I have checked them and there was nothing untoward.' Paul looked over to Anna and again she interjected.

'We have only just found out we have a possible murder case. Now unless there is anything else, Brian, we need to move on.'

Brian took out a black-covered notebook and muttered that he would get onto the mobile companies ASAP. It was now the turn of DC Helen Bridges. In her mid-thirties, she was a quiet woman with a pleasant manner, wearing glasses.

'Was Tina Brooks ever unhelpful?' she wanted to know.

'No, but she was always very edgy, especially when we went to the salon,' Anna told her.

Brian Stanley put up his index finger again.

'Have we obtained any CCTV from Asda or verified that the bleach she bought was on special offer? And did she also buy the salon bleach from a different company?'

'She admitted to buying it as she said they use it to wash the floors in the hair salon.'

'But there was a semi-full one in the flat when you did the search?' Helen said, reading up the case-file notes.

'Yes.'

'That means if she bought four large containers, three and a half have been used up?'

'Correct, Helen.'

Brian now did his finger in the air again.

'That has to mean she was involved in the cleaning up of the bloodstains. If she wasn't, surely she would have noticed that there was a lot of the bleach missing, and said something about it?'

'Yes, that is correct,' Anna said, watching Brian make a laborious note in his book, again muttering that he would check that out and contact Asda. Helen half-rose from her chair then sat back down again.

'Do we have any photographs of Tina Brooks?' she asked, flicking through the file. Anna sighed.

'No, we don't, but we have that surfing picture of Alan Rawlins.'

There was a guffaw from Brian Stanley and he suggested that they get a decent head shot of him ASAP.

Anna brought the session to a close by outlining what the team would be working on the following morning. She suggested that the new detectives continue to familiarise themselves with the case-file to date before leaving for the night.

She had just returned to her office when Paul knocked and walked in.

'That bastard with the eyebrows gets on my nerves. At least he should have them plucked.'

'Just let them settle in before you allow him to get under your skin.'

'He's already under it, the homophobic prick.'

'Paul, that's enough. It's been a long day and I don't know about you, but I'd like to get home and recharge my batteries.'

'Yeah, okay. What about the interview with Rawlins's parents? You said you wanted to talk with the mother.'

'We wait for the second blood-test results.'

'Fine. See you tomorrow then.'

'Goodnight, Paul.'

Anna waited until he had gone before she sat back in

her chair. From her desk she could look into the incident room via the semi-closed blinds on her window. Helen and Brian were standing by the incident-room board, conferring. Mr 'Eyebrows' might be a pain in the butt, but he was very experienced, and from the way the case was opening up she knew she would need all the help she could get.

The next morning, Anna learned that there was a further delay in using the Luminol. The forensic team were waiting until the extensive search of the flat was finished, to avoid damaging anything the fingerprint team might still uncover. Liz Hawley had also contacted Anna to say that she was still doing more work on Mr Rawlins's blood, and asked if a further sample had been taken from Mrs Rawlins. Anna rang the Rawlinses' home, but the carer answered to say that Mr Rawlins was at work. Anna tried the courts where Edward Rawlins worked as an usher, but had to leave a message as his mobile was turned off.

Impatient to get on with the day, she had another delay when Langton came into the station. She could see him conferring with Brian Stanley and waited for him to come into her office.

When he eventually left Stanley and walked over to her office, he cocked his head to one side.

'Well, well. This is getting more interesting, isn't it?' he said.

She nodded.

'You know until you get that blood matched with Alan Rawlins's, there's not a lot you can do.'

'I am aware of that, but do you know the problem?'

'Yes,' Langton said. 'I've looked over the board.'

Langton was wearing a very smart suit and his usual pristine shirt, but she noticed a stain on his blue tie. It amused her, because he was very obviously unaware of it. She knew how much he prided himself on always being well turned out. He sat down opposite her, popping some nicotine gum in his mouth.

'If you prove it is Alan Rawlins and get further proof that his body could have been dismembered, it's putting a heavy slant on the investigation. Alternatively, if it is *not* his then it's a further complication – like who the hell is it?'

'Going with the scenario that it's not Alan's blood, it would make sense why he did a disappearing act,' Anna said.

'Ditto if it was him cut up, but to date there has been no discovery of weapons. I think you should go ahead with the Luminol test as soon as possible, because if it is proven that there was a bloodbath in that bathroom, it really ups the ante on your enquiry.'

'You are not telling me anything I don't know.'

'Suspects? You still have Tina Brooks in the frame?' he enquired.

'Yes, but with reservations. It's possible that after she left Alan at home and went to work, someone else came to their flat and either killed Alan or some other person, and had the evidence cleared up by the time she returned from work.'

Langton chewed hard on his gum.

'I don't buy that,' he said. 'There's no sign of forced entry. Then there's the bleach, the new order of carpet and the squares cut out of the old. I think she *is* involved.'

'We have no proof that she was,' Anna said quietly.

'I know that.'

'I also think I jumped the gun by bringing her in for

questioning, as we didn't really gain anything from the interview bar the fact she denied any involvement.'

'She also had Jonathan Hyde representing her – a good operator. Did she bring him on board herself?' Langton asked.

'No. She lucked in as he was the duty solicitor.'

'Motive? What are your thoughts on that?'

'Well, we have discussed the joint bank account and the life-insurance policy; added together it's quite a substantial sum, around a hundred and twenty thousand, and although her business is doing well now, she's admitted to being up to the limit on her overdraft. Somehow I don't buy money as the motive.'

'You checked it out? If she's in debt, she might be getting in deeper.'

'No, but I have been there and it looks like she's got a good turnover and employs quite a lot of staff.'

'Check it out.'

'Will do. The other motive that I've been toying with is that perhaps Tina was having an affair with someone, and whoever that was could be implicated. But to date we've not found any evidence that she was seeing anyone else. We know she had quite a reputation at the local gym, but we've checked with all the instructors.'

'There was a semen stain found in the master bed – right? Tina said, didn't she, that Alan was possibly seeing someone else? So it could be his?'

'Yes. But we also know it doesn't match the DNA from the blood pooling. So the victim might not be Alan Rawlins. I am checking out if the semen could belong to the neighbour, Michael Phillips, who is single and very handsome.'

She hesitated because the single hair also discovered in

the bed was not the right colour match for the dark, glossy-haired Phillips. She scrawled a note to remind herself to get a hair sample for DNA from Tina, plus recent photographs.

'Any witness that saw them together?'

Anna looked up and Langton repeated the question.

'No,' she replied. 'But there's one odd thing that sort of takes away from Alan being the submissive non-confrontational type. A neighbour saw him kicking out at the wall close to their flat and punching it. This was a few days before he went missing.'

'Or was cut up.'

'Right.'

Langton stood up, taking out the chewed gum and dropping it into her waste-basket.

'You know, we have a result over in Highgate – brought charges last night. Bastard's a real psychopath, but whether or not he'll be fit to stand trial is another matter.'

'Congratulations.'

'Thank you. I think what you need to do is obviously get the ID of the victim ASAP and dig around into any sexual deviancy. Old Brian reckons Mr Rawlins was homosexual. One of his close friends you interviewed was gay, right?'

'Yes, but I disagree. I don't think Alan was gay.'

'Well, you never know, and if he was, he maybe didn't want it known. Anything come from Forensics from Tina Brooks's car?'

'No. We're waiting on Liz to get back to us.'

'You know what's interesting?'

She cocked her head to one side and smiled, saying, 'I am sure you are about to tell me.'

'The fact that after a murder was committed close to or

on the bed, someone had sex in it. Now that's deviant . . . Look along those lines, Anna, and uppermost try to find out what happened to the body.'

'I intend to.'

'Good.'

He stood staring at her for a moment and then went to open the door.

'Good work.'

'Thank you.'

He hesitated and turned back.

'Just one more thing. As we're on top of this case I've been overseeing I was wondering if you'd like Mike Lewis transferred over to your investigation.'

'No. I want to see how the team I've got pans out before bringing in anyone else.'

He gave her a small smile and opened the door.

'Well, you know where I am.'

Anna was left irritated by his offer. As a DCI she didn't need another one of her rank looking over her shoulder. Langton was enough.

'By the way,' she said, 'you have what looks like an egg stain on your tie.'

He lifted it up and swore, walking out scratching at the stain.

Her desk phone rang. It was Edward Rawlins returning her call, very concerned about his wife giving another blood sample.

'She was very distressed about having it done the last time. Is it necessary?'

'Yes, I'm afraid it is.'

'But surely you can determine whether or not it is Alan.'

'Unfortunately the first sample taken from your wife

leaked, and the genetic combination of the blood from both parents is required for examination by the scientist.'

'I see. In that case, I suppose you have to do what you have to do, but I don't understand why.' He couldn't continue. She heard him give a muffled sob.

'It's possible, Mr Rawlins, that it might not be your son's blood,' Anna said gently.

'Jesus God, this is all dreadful. I am leaving work at three today so I will be at home for when the doctor comes to take the sample, but as I said, my wife is very distressed. She doesn't understand what is happening. I told her it was for some new medication to try and calm her.'

'The police doctor will endeavour to make your wife feel as relaxed as possible,' Anna assured him.

She then rang Liz Hawley to say the further sample from Mrs Rawlins would be taken late afternoon and she would have it brought up to the lab as soon as possible.

'The fingerprint team have finally finished,' Liz told her, 'so I will be starting on the Luminol testing first thing in the morning.'

'Did you find anything from Tina Brooks's car?'

'That's not my department, but I'll check for you.'

'Thank you.'

Before she hung up, Liz asked if Anna would be bringing in any suspects' DNA samples for a comparison with the hair and semen.

'It's on the cards. I'll let you know.'

Anna replaced the phone. They would require a mouth swab and hair sample from Michael Phillips. She decided that she would handle that personally as it was imperative they either implicate or eliminate him. However, as they had no evidence against him, he would have to agree to the tests and he'd be entitled to refuse.

Anna sat with Brian Stanley at his desk and explained that he was to make further enquiries at the Body Form gym used by Tina, Alan and Michael Phillips. She was about to walk away when he held up the offending finger.

'You know, we really need to get that crime-scene blood identified, because if it wasn't Alan Rawlins it's gonna shed a whole different light on our enquiry.'

'I am aware of that and it's in the mix for today.'

'Another thing, we need more updated photographs of Alan Rawlins. If it isn't his blood, then he's missing. I've got onto Mispers about it and they have a couple of shots they are sending over. They were given to them by Tina Brooks, but I wondered if we had his driving licence.'

'We don't. We didn't find one.'

'Wouldn't the DVLC hold double photographs nowadays if he had a recent new licence?'

'I believe so.'

'Right, I'll check with them. And what about Tina? We should have a photo of her. It helps when looking over any CCTV we may seize.'

'I'll ask her to hand one over.'

'She's not staying at the flat until it's given the all-clear, so do you have a contact address for her?'

'It's on the board, Brian.'

'Right, thanks. Have we sniffed around for any new life-insurance policies, only the one we have been checking out was made a couple of years ago. Maybe there's a newer one?'

'Check it out then.'

'It's just that I find it odd. I mean, I'm in my forties and I haven't got one.'

'Nor have I, but Alan Rawlins appears to have been a particularly cautious man when it comes to money.'

'Particularly anal if you ask me.'

Anna's patience with Brian's offhand derogatory remarks was wearing thin. She raised her voice to show her disapproval of his comments.

'Just get on with it, Detective Stanley!'

'Okay, I'll get started.'

'Thank you.'

Anna returned to her office. Stanley might be very experienced, but he was starting to get under her skin; however, she had to admit he was working the case. She wondered how Paul and Helen were getting on interviewing the remaining names in Rawlins's address book. She called Paul's mobile, but it was turned off so she sent a text message. Once that was done, she left the station to go to talk to Michael Phillips.

Paul and Helen had been criss-crossing London. A number of the names were dead ends as the people had moved or gone abroad. By mid-afternoon they had successfully interviewed six. Four had not seen or spoken to Alan for a long time and could give no indication of what might have occurred. They did all repeat what an exceptionally nice person he was; most had been to school or college with him and none appeared to be very intimate friends, but almost all of them said that after his relationship with Tina had begun they had seen very little of him. None were very enthusiastic about her, but at the same time felt that if she made Alan happy it was none of their business.

The fifth person they interviewed was a librarian called Alison Bisk. She was an attractive blonde, but the type of woman who doesn't know how to make the best of herself. She was wearing a very plain jumper with a woollen skirt that reached her calves, and comfortable shoes. She was at first startled by their appearance at the library and then shocked when they said they were interviewing everyone who knew Alan, as he was missing.

'Missing?'

'Yes, Miss Bisk. If we could go somewhere more private we'd just like to ask you about your friendship with Mr Rawlins.'

They went into a small reading room, where Paul explained that they were looking into his disappearance as it was possible it could be due to foul play.

'What do you mean?'

'He has been missing for some considerable time and we have found things inside his flat that give cause for concern.'

'But I haven't seen him for maybe six or seven months.'

'You knew him well?'

She nodded.

'What can you tell us about him?'

She chewed her lip and then did a small nervous cough. 'We used to go out together so I did know him very well.'

'Tell us what you know about him.'

She sighed and then explained that she and Alan had lived together in her flat, and that at one time she had felt that their relationship would eventually lead to marriage.

'I don't want to say anything bad about him. You see, we were together for almost three years. He was always a very caring and loving person. He could be a bit obsessive about saving money, but he wanted to buy a place of his own – you know, he didn't really like living at my flat. He halved the rent with me though, as well as saving for the future. It was a future I believed I would be a part of, but ...'

She looked down at her hands, twisting her fingers together and releasing them.

'He went on a surfing holiday to Cornwall,' she continued. 'I couldn't go because my holiday dates didn't match his. I knew something was wrong when he phoned me from there.'

'Wrong? What do you mean?'

'Well, he sounded different — distant. He said he was having a wonderful time, but he just didn't sound like the Alan I knew. He phoned me maybe four times, but I could feel he was different. I can't really explain it, but I sensed it, as I was very much in love with him. Anyway, the Saturday he was due to come home I'd bought a special dinner and even though he didn't really drink I'd got a bottle of rosé wine.' Her eyes welled with tears.

'Go on, Miss Bisk, please. This is very helpful.' Helen felt for the girl; she was obviously still very hurt.

'I was in the bath and I had my hair in rollers because I wanted to make myself look good for him when he got back, but he came home earlier than I expected. He was so tanned and his hair was very blonde and he leaned on the bathroom door and . . .'

She searched for a tissue and dabbed her eyes.

'He was like a stranger. He said that he still loved me, but he was no longer *in* love with me and would be moving out.'

She began to rip at the tissue.

'I was in shock. I couldn't believe that in just two weeks he could have changed so drastically, and then there were these calls from *her* – she had the cheek to call my flat and ask to speak to him. I knew whoever it was had to be the reason he was leaving, but he wouldn't tell me anything. It took two weeks for him to clear all his belongings and he left.'

'When exactly was this?'

'Four years ago.'

'But you said you saw him a few months back.'

'Yes. He would often stop by and see how I was, or a couple of times he came here to see me at work. He never really explained anything to me, but I knew he had moved in with that woman in Hounslow. I never went there and I never called him. It was always him that contacted me, but not for us to get back together – just to see how I was. I think he felt guilty for the way he had treated me.'

'When you saw him, did he appear to be in good spirits?'

'How do you mean?'

'Well, was he depressed or moody, and did he say anything derogatory about his latest girlfriend?'

'No. I never felt I could broach the subject with him. To be honest, I hoped he would come back, but he never even suggested it. I used to see his parents on the odd occasions at Christmastime. I'd take them a little gift. They were the sweetest people and I think they were upset at the way he had treated me. I don't think they liked his new girlfriend.'

'Did he ever seem angry?'

'Oh no, Alan was such a calm person. He did dress differently, more fashionably, and he seemed more handsome, or maybe that was just me. I missed him so much and like I said, I think he did feel guilty because we had been very serious about each other. In fact, one time he asked if I wanted to start a family and I obviously said that I would, and after he had left I found . . .'

Again she started to weep. Paul and Helen waited.

'I didn't drive and he had started to arrange driving lessons for me. I found in a cupboard the L-plates he had bought for me. On one he had written a message about having a baby soon. I never took my test. I still don't drive – silly, really.'

Paul got into the driving seat and looked at Helen.

'"Silly, really". Bloody sad, more like it. She's a nice-looking girl if she did more for herself.'

Helen shrugged. She had found it rather pitiful that Alison had not got over a relationship that ended years ago.

'Didn't get much from her though, did we?' Paul said.

'Well, if I remember, in a statement I read, Tina said that Alan used to go surfing a lot, and according to Alison he seemed changed when he returned from one of his holidays there. Maybe we need to look into the surfing friends.'

'Not got any. We've only one more bloke to see and that's his address book finished.'

'Maybe the last is the best – or is it the other way round?'

'I dunno, but we've got to go all the way to Kingston. The guy runs a car wash on the A3. His name is Silas Douglas.'

'A car wash?'

'Yeah. Not really sounding like the Silver Surfer, is he?'

'Who?'

'It's often the way great-looking guys on surfboards are called. I read it somewhere – you know, all bronzed and blonde-haired.'

'Oh. I thought it was a sort of *Marvel* comic character. Maybe this Silas Douglas is one. I can always live in hope!'

Paul laughed.

*

The car wash turned out to be a small business employing six Polish men. The ramshackle four-car port had hosepipes and buckets and polishers, with a seedy office at the back.

'Bet you these guys are making illegal benefit claims as well,' Paul said.

Helen agreed and was astonished that customers were paying up to thirty pounds for a total valet service.

'All this cash must make a nice income, enough to employ six guys.'

They knocked on the glass door to the office, but were unable to see in as it was covered in posters for firework displays and local events. Then it banged open and they were confronted by a well-built man wearing a baseball cap with a greasy ponytail sticking out the back.

'Yeah?'

Paul introduced himself and Helen and said they had called earlier. 'Are you Silas Douglas?'

'Oh right, right, come in. I'm Sal Douglas and excuse the mess. Shift anything off the seats; it will all end up on the floor anyway.'

He had a very upper-class voice that belied his appearance in baggy torn jeans and a T-shirt. Lined up against one wall were four surfboards, expensive ones, and there was another one lying on a bench with pots of paint.

'I'm customising that for a client. Wants, believe it or not, Shaun the Sheep. Bloody stupid, but you do what you have to.'

'Shaun the Sheep?' Paul asked, shifting a stack of magazines onto the floor.

'It's a kid's cartoon, little runt of the sheep herd that gets up to all crazy things, so I guess he's now going to be surfing.' Sal sat behind the muddled heaped desk and grinned.

'What do you want? It's not about the bloody neighbours' complaints, is it? I've got a licence to run this place – in fact, I own that block of flats, but they don't seem to understand, and these used to be the old garages.'

'We're here because we know you were friends with Alan Rawlins.'

'Who?'

'Alan Rawlins.'

Sal leaned back in his chair, rubbing his head. 'I know him, do I?'

'He has your phone number.'

'Alan Rawlins? Has he bought a board from me?'

'I don't know. He did go surfing in Cornwall.'

'Ah well, maybe I met him there. Come June I pack off to my place near Newquay and don't come back until the end of summer.'

'He was a big fair-haired man, about six foot,' Paul said as he took out the only photo they had of Alan on the surfboard. 'Aged twenty-six.'

'Oh Christ yes, I know him. Terrific guy! I taught him. It's a few summers back, maybe three or four, and he went on to use some of the other bays with the real big waves, fearless. To begin with I thought he was a no-hoper, but ...'

Sal pulled at his ponytail. 'I didn't know he was called Rawlins, but there you go, I meet a shedload of guys every summer.' He then gestured to a wall calendar. 'I teach. First I make them use the gym, as you've got to have strong leg muscles – lot of squats – but above all balance. Yeah, I remember him now.'

'He's missing.'

'What?'

'I said he's missing'

'In Cornwall?'

'No, from his place in London. Do you know where he stayed when he was in Cornwall?'

'No, there's loads of hostels, B and Bs and other cheap places.'

'What can you tell me about him?'

'Nothing more than I just did.'

Paul looked to Helen and she was making notes. 'Did he have girlfriends when you met him?'

Sal shrugged his shoulders. 'I couldn't tell you. I have my own clan there, but there are lots of bars they all use and if it's bad weather, which it was this bloody summer – a downpour almost every day – they always hang out at a place called the Smugglers. It's a beach bar and café.'

'When was the last time you saw Alan Rawlins?'

The big man gave a wide-armed gesture. 'Look, I didn't even remember his name. I don't think he was around last summer. I can't honestly recall.' He held the photograph in his big hands. 'No, he wasn't. In fact, it had to have been a while ago, maybe a couple of years, because the board he's using here was one of mine. It's an old hire board, used to mark them at the front with a large black S and a number, so I knew who was out on the water with one. You can just about make out S three on this board. The one he's surfing on is old stock that I sanded down, re-sprayed and sold on about two years ago. He could have even bought one off me, but I can't be certain as I've sold so many over the years.'

Sal passed the photograph back.

'When you were teaching him you said he was a nice bloke, so you can recall that much about him. Is there anything else?'

'Listen, if they pay me they're good guys. You'd be

amazed how many kids bounce cheques, give nicked credit cards, but if I remember correctly, he was sort of straight – know what I mean?'

'So you wouldn't know if he mixed with any specific people?'

'No. Wait a minute, hang on.'

Sal got up and crossed to an old filing cabinet. It was in as much of a mess as his office as he hauled open one drawer after another. He then took out a dog-eared file and sat at his desk, again sweeping papers aside. He opened the file and began sifting through a stack of photographs. Paul and Helen waited patiently as Sal continued taking out a wedge of prints, flicking through them and picking up more.

'I tell you what I'm looking for. Often at the end of a season or the end of a group teaching course, 'cos they pay for ten or twenty lessons at a time, I get a class photo and sell them copies. I would say that the photo you've got of him was taken by a bloke I've met. He earns a buck or two …'

'What's his name?' Helen asked.

'It was Sammy – yeah, Sammy Marsh. I say *was* 'cos he did a moonlight last year owing rent and Christ knows what else. I think he disappeared to Florida, but he's not been seen since.'

He produced a slightly creased photograph and scrutinised it.

'Yep, I'm right – at least, I think I am. Isn't that the same bloke in the middle?'

Sal passed the photograph over. There were four men, all suntanned and athletic-looking, wearing wetsuits. The two at the end of the line held up surfboards with S One and S Eight written on them. They all had their arms around each other's shoulders, smiling to the camera.

Paul and Helen glanced at the photograph. Turning it over they saw it had a faded stamp, *Sammy Marsh*, with his phone number.

'Do you recall the names of the other surfers with Alan?' Paul asked.

'You must be joking! That was taken years ago, and like I said, the guys come and go every summer.'

'Do you mind if we keep this?'

'Not at all. It's no use to me.'

Paul stood up to shake Sal's hand. The latter's grip was so strong it made him wince.

'Thanks for your help.'

Driving back to the station, Helen jotted in her notebook.

'You know something strange?' Paul said thoughtfully. 'It was obvious that Alan liked surfing, but we've not found any wetsuits, flippers or whatever they use, and no surfboard at his flat.'

'Well, Sal said he hired one of his,' Helen noted.

'That was a few years ago, right – and he also said that Alan went off to take in other bays. He had to have become very proficient so he could have bought his own board.'

'I suppose so.'

'The other thing: we should look into any information we can find about where he stayed in Cornwall. There's nothing in his address book, is there, but if he went there regularly, wouldn't you think he'd have contacts? I have when I go to Wales. I rent a cottage and I've got loads of addresses and phone numbers.'

'Yeah, we can have a nose around. Also, from what Alison said, you know how careful he was about money, saving to buy a property – same scenario with Tina

Brooks, saving to buy a flat of their own. So we have this careful guy saving his pennies for what seems like years before he lived with Tina.'

'Yeah? So what. I've been saving all my adult life and I've not got a pot to piss in,' Paul said.

'He earns good money as a mechanic, fixes up vintage cars and sells them. The Merc is one, right?' Helen asked.

'True. Apparently he made a big profit when he sold the cars. Cash in hand as well.'

'I doubt Tina puts every client through the salon books, so with his money from doing up the cars ... I guess saving the seventy thousand between them wouldn't have taken long.'

'Yeah, maybe not.'

'In fact there could be more somewhere if it's cash. How much rent did he pay?'

'I dunno.'

Helen closed her notebook and stared at the back of the photograph.

'Maybe we should run a check on this Sammy Marsh.' She turned it back to look at the four surfers. 'Handsome-looking guys. I might think about a holiday in Cornwall.'

Paul laughed. 'You're not the only one. I was thinking of doing that myself.'

'Do you surf?'

'No. I'm not that interested in the surfing.'

'Honestly,' she giggled, punching his arm.

Anna had been waiting in reception at Michael Phillips's company, Aston & Clark, for fifteen minutes. The receptionist eventually said that he could see her. She passed Anna the security badge and repeated that she should go to the fourth floor.

'Yes, thank you, I remember,' Anna said curtly.

The same secretary was waiting as the lift opened and she led Anna down the corridor, this time to a different room, but with an identical table and the same offer of coffee and tea placed on a sideboard with two flasks of hot water.

'Please help yourself. Mr Phillips shouldn't be a moment.'

'I hope not.' Anna sat down, not bothering with refreshments.

It was another fifteen minutes before Michael Phillips finally swept into the room full of apologies. He was wearing the same suit as before, but with a pink shirt with a white collar and cuffs, and a blue silk tie.

'I am so very sorry, but I had an important meeting and I couldn't leave. You should really have made an appointment as I have meetings almost back to back today. I'm afraid I will have to make this short.'

'Really?' Anna was fuming. 'Well, Mr Phillips, that can easily be done. I am simply here to ask if you would be willing to give us a DNA sample.'

'*What?*'

'You can come to the police station at a time convenient to you, but the sooner the better as it is very important.'

'What do you want it for?'

'I am investigating a murder, sir, and I need to eliminate you from my enquiry.'

'Hang on, hang on – murder? I don't understand.'

'We now believe that Mr Alan Rawlins . . .'

'But I thought he was missing – right?'

'Yes, but we have found evidence that leads us to believe he may have been murdered.'

'But I don't even know him!'

'Nevertheless, Mr Phillips, as you are a very close neighbour we require your DNA to eliminate you from my enquiry.'

'That's all I bloody am, for Christ's sake – a neighbour. I didn't know him and I find this all very intrusive, never mind inconvenient.'

'I would be most grateful if you would agree.' Anna was trying to keep calm.

'But I don't have to?'

'No. That is your prerogative, but as I said it would assist my enquiry if you would agree.'

'I don't. If you want anything from me, you get it via my lawyer because I find this outrageous. I did not know Alan Rawlins.'

'What about Tina Brooks?'

'No. I have already told you. Of course I do know *of* her – it's obvious as we are neighbours – but that is as far as my relationship with either of them goes.'

'So you are refusing?'

'Yes.'

Anna pursed her lips, trying to be controlled. 'You must be aware that by refusing to assist my investigation it appears to be very suspicious.'

'It can appear, but I am still refusing.'

Anna picked up her briefcase. 'Good afternoon, Mr Phillips.'

She walked out, leaving him sitting in the centre of the board room, where he remained for some time before returning to his office.

Anna was still seething by the time she returned to her office. She knew that without any implicating evidence against him, Phillips could legally refuse to give a DNA sample.

By now, Paul and Helen had returned from their interviews and were marking up the incident board with their details. They pinned up the photograph of the group of surfers. Brian Stanley came back and he too wrote up a report. He tapped the photograph.

'I still say Alan Rawlins was a shirt-lifter. Very friendly with each other, aren't they?'

Paul bit his tongue, refusing to rise to the bait. Stanley continued, 'I've been at that pansy gym – load of wankers there. First they wouldn't even let me look in Rawlins's fucking locker.'

'We'd already checked it,' Paul said stiffly.

Stanley turned on him and produced a bag with the bottle of aspirin.

'I took this. I want Forensic to check out if they really are aspirin. I think the guy might be on steroids.'

'Why do you say that?' Paul demanded.

'Because the muscle rippers there are using – I'd put money on it. One of them is a weight-lifting idiot that got right up my nose.'

'He could see you as competition, could he?' Paul said sarcastically, looking pointedly at Stanley's beer gut.

At this moment Helen signalled to Paul. She had run a check on Sammy Marsh and it proved to be interesting. He had previous convictions for possession with intent to supply and supplying cannabis, for which he spent a short spell in jail. He was also currently wanted by the Devon and Cornwall Drug Squad for importing and supplying cocaine.

'He did a runner just before he was about to be arrested. They found a substantial amount of ecstasy tablets and skunk cannabis plants, and two guys already under arrest implicated him in a six-kilo cocaine deal. Street value, quarter of a million.'

Paul looked over the printed sheets. 'They got any idea where he ran to?'

'Nope. Possibly Florida, just as Sal told us, but that was last summer and there's been no sighting of him since then.'

Stanley did his irritating raised finger gesture.

'Here comes the boss.'

Anna perched on a desk listening to Paul and Helen's accounts of their afternoon and then to Brian Stanley's. When they had finished, she asked what they felt was a positive outcome. She looked to Paul first.

'Well, I don't know about outcome, but what we discussed between us was the possibility that Alan had more money saved somewhere, even though we've found no evidence of this at his flat. We also have found no surfing equipment, wetsuit or board, which if he was a keen surfer he should possibly have. The other thing is that we might try to trace these other guys in the photograph and also check out possible places where Alan might have stayed when he was in Cornwall. Again, from his address book we have no contact numbers for there. We now know that the man who took the photograph, a Sammy Marsh, is a convicted drug dealer who's on the run from the local police.'

Anna took a deep breath. All the new information could give them a clue to where Alan Rawlins could be, if he was alive. She picked up on the detail that his ex-girlfriend, Alison Bisk, had noticed a remarkable change in Alan on his return from his surfing holiday.

'It could be that the very clean-living Alan Rawlins had

an introduction to drugs there, but we have no evidence of that.'

Stanley did his usual finger.

'He might have come out of the closet there as well – good reason to leave his girlfriend.'

'I don't really buy that. He went to live with the very strident Tina, so whether or not you think he might be a latent homosexual, and—'

Stanley pointed to the surfers' photo. 'All very cheesy-looking blokes,' he said.

Paul was about to explode, but Anna nipped it in the bud.

'No evidence that they were, as you say, "cheesy" guys. They all look very heterosexual to me, but let's see if we can track them down. That will mean going to Cornwall, but it would be easier if we had some evidence that Alan did have a usual place he stayed at. So . . .' She sighed. 'We found no indication of anything connected to Cornwall at his flat, but I think we might have to check with his parents. He was a regular visitor, so maybe he kept details there. That needs to be sorted.'

'What about Michael Phillips?' Stanley asked.

'He has refused to give us a DNA sample. However, if we find any evidence that shows he is lying to us then we can arrest him and if necessary take his DNA by force. Have we any news, Brian, on the mobile phones? Any calls back and forth to Tina Brooks?'

'Nope, but I've not got all the billing details yet.'

'Make it a priority, please. What about the Asda CCTV?'

'I'm waiting for the manager to get back to me.'

'Well, chase it up. Tomorrow we should get Liz Hawley using the Luminol test at the flat and we are waiting on the new sample from Alan's mother to hopefully identify the blood from the flat as his.'

Anna called it quits for the day and returned to her office as her desk phone rang. It was Liz Hawley and it wasn't good news.

'I'm sorry to tell you this, but we are unable to give you a positive result. Mr and Mrs Rawlins are *not* the biological parents of the person whose blood was found at their son's flat.'

'Shit,' Anna muttered.

'Sorry.'

Anna replaced the phone. This was not good news. They still had not confirmed the victim's identity from the blood. She couldn't believe it. If their son was adopted, why didn't they say so? It didn't make any sense. But if it wasn't Alan Rawlins's blood, then whose was it? She was just about to leave the office when her phone rang again. This time it was Mr Rawlins asking if she now had proof that their son had been murdered. Anna chose her words very carefully, saying that there was a delay, but she would like to talk to him. He told her that he was not working the following morning and he could see her at his home.

'How is your wife?' she asked.

'She's calm now, but she got into a dreadful state. She doesn't understand, you see. In fact, it's very difficult. She told me that Alan had been to see her. She doesn't remember that she hasn't seen him for nearly two months now.'

'I am so sorry, but I also wanted to ask you, did Alan keep any papers or belongings at your house?'

'Yes, in his bedroom. I told the officers who took the original missing persons report about his room. They had a quick look in it before they left.'

161

'Sorry, they seem to have left that out of their report. Would I be able to take a look?'

'Yes, of course. He used it sometimes when he stayed over. It's always been his room.'

'Thank you very much, Mr Rawlins. I'll see you tomorrow.'

She dropped the receiver back, leaving her hand resting on it. Looking through the blinds she could see the remainder of the team packing up for the evening. In prime position was the photograph of Alan Rawlins with the surfers. Handsome, smiling, tanned and fit, he also looked relaxed and happy. Was it his blood? Did the gentle and calm Alan Rawlins really have another side to him, perhaps another life that had resulted in murder?

Anna shut off her office light and made her way out to the car park to head home. Preoccupied and troubled, she went over in her mind all the new information. Although she was unaware of it, this was the first time she wasn't thinking about her own situation, about Ken. Her commitment to work was slowly eroding the pain. She also felt hungry for the first time in quite a while and decided to stop off and buy a hamburger and chips.

With her takeaway still in the carton, Anna poured herself a glass of wine. When she shook up the tomato ketchup and squirted it over the French fries, it didn't make her think of whose blood oozed into the carpet. That came later as she tried to sleep. She had no body. She had a murder and no identification of the victim. Her original suspect, Tina Brooks, was no longer top of the list, but was now on the back-burner, along with Michael Phillips . . .

It was the first night she did not use sleeping tablets, just a couple of glasses of wine. She wanted her brain to work as it used to, on a sort of automatic pilot knitting the evidence together to produce an insight into the case. Drifting into her subconscious was a photograph she had seen in the Rawlinses' lounge. It was of Alan's mother standing in a garden, shading her eyes as she smiled to camera. She was obviously pregnant. Anna couldn't understand why the tests seemed to indicate otherwise, but she would find out – and it was not a meeting she was looking forward to.

Chapter Seven

Anna rang the bell to the Rawlinses' terraced house. She had begun the day at Tina's flat watching Liz Hawley setting up her equipment. She'd then had to rush off for this meeting just after nine. But now she had to wait a while before the door was answered. It turned out that Rose had an emergency at her home and so Anna was greeted by a close friend of Mrs Rawlins. Freda Jackson was a woman of about the same age as Kathleen, but rather more smartly dressed, and she introduced herself before asking Anna to go into the lounge. Along with Rose having an emergency, Freda also informed her that Edward had been called to replace someone at court.

'It's this wretched flu,' she said as she indicated for Anna to sit down and then closed the door. 'And I don't think Kathleen is really up to talking to you. She's been very confused.'

'It's extremely urgent that I see her, even if only for a moment ...'

'I really don't advise it. And Edward insisted that we should arrange the meeting for another time.'

Anna stood up as Freda herself now sat down.

'I know what this is about,' the woman said. 'Edward told me.'

'Then you must realise the importance of clearing the situation regarding their blood tests. It is imperative we find out if it is their son who is the victim.'

'This is a very delicate and personal matter and I want you to know that I only have both their interests at heart. I have been Kathleen's friend for many years. We grew up together and in many ways we have been like sisters, which makes her present predicament even more distressing. In some ways it is best for Edward not to be present.'

Anna slowly sat down again.

Freda wore a pleated skirt and nervously ran her fingers along the sharp creases.

'I obviously want you to regard what I am going to tell you with the utmost confidentiality. Would you agree to that?'

'Do you mind if I call you Freda?'

'No, not at all.'

'Well, Freda, this is a murder enquiry. I will do my best to, as you ask, treat whatever you tell me with confidentiality. However, if it also has connections to my investigation then I can only promise that I will try to respect your request.'

The doorbell rang and Freda stood up.

'I think that'll be Rose. She said she would try and get here as soon as possible. I've given Kathleen her breakfast, but she needs changing and . . . excuse me.'

Anna watched Freda scurry out as Rose called that it was her, obviously having her own key to enter the house. Anna waited as they had a conversation in the hall and then Freda returned. Hovering at the door, she asked if Anna wanted a cup of coffee.

'No, thank you. I would really like to hear what you have to say.'

Freda closed the door and sat opposite Anna again.

'Kathleen and I have been friends since schooldays, as I said. We were like sisters, which neither of us had. I have three children, all grown up now, and we both married around the same time. I'd been married about three years before I had my first, a girl, and then shortly after I had my next two. Kathleen would always visit and she was a wonderful knitter – she made such lovely things for my babies.'

Anna glanced at the clock on the mantel, wondering where this was all leading, but she didn't want to look impatient.

Freda continued, 'They'd been married about five or six years and Kathleen was desperate for a child, as was Edward. At that point he was working for a sales company – the job took him away for weeks at a time. Anyway, they had numerous tests and it was whilst he was away that Kathleen told me that she had visited a fertility clinic. In those days there weren't as many as there are now, and it was quite a new thing really.'

'Please go on.'

'Oh, this is awful! You know you keep secrets, never believing that one day you will have to tell them, and it *was* very secret. I also promised on my babies that I'd never tell a living soul, but . . .'

'Please, Freda, tell me what you know.'

'Well, at first Kathleen was told that Edward would not be able to conceive a child as he had a very low sperm-count. She had received the information whilst he was away and never told him. After a few months during which she had numerous tests, she went into the Chelsea fertility clinic for a laparoscopy, which is an operation to check if your ovaries are functioning properly. They discovered that she had a cyst and some other problems, and doubted that she would ever be able to conceive naturally. It was a dreadful time for her and it broke her heart.'

Freda continued to pinch the pleats in her skirt.

'About a year later she came to me, and this is when I promised to never repeat it to anyone else. She had been to a private fertility clinic and got IVF treatment using a donor's eggs and a donor's sperm.'

Anna said quietly, 'Did her husband not know?'

'No. She kept it secret from him. She sold some diamond and gold jewellery she had inherited to pay for it. I think she had a few appointments before she became pregnant, and she only told Edward after the worrying first three months were over.'

'And he still has no idea that Alan is not his biological son?'

'No, none at all.'

'I think he will have to be told, Freda. He's very impatient, obviously, to know if we can identify Alan as the victim.'

'Oh God, it will be so difficult! You know he never questioned that Alan wasn't his. He was such a handsome child and his eyes by chance were mirrors of Kathleen's — beautiful blue eyes.'

'Did Alan himself know?'

'No. Kathleen never told anyone, apart from me. I think it was because she carried Alan and gave birth to him, and it didn't ever become an issue. You know how terrified she was to give a blood test? It was as if somewhere in her sad befuddled mind, she has guessed that the truth might come out. She was even more upset when they sent the doctor here to take another sample. It would also now be impossible to trace the donors as the clinic closed down years ago. Whether or not they would keep any files on record after this length of time is doubtful.'

Freda sighed and Anna quickly glanced at her mobile as she had received a text message. It was from Liz Hawley requesting she contact her immediately.

'I'm afraid I have to go. But first—'

'Could *you* tell Edward?' Freda interrupted.

'No, I am afraid not. It will have to come from you.'

Freda stood up and walked with Anna to the door.

'She was a wonderful mother, and as I said, Alan looked like her and he dotes on her. He's such a good boy. This is all very sad, isn't it?'

'Yes, and I am sorry for you as I am for Edward, but he does need to be told,' Anna insisted quietly.

'Yes, I understand. Thank you for being so kind. I will tell him this afternoon when he gets home.'

As they entered the hall there was a shrill cry from the top of the stairs. Kathleen was standing holding onto the newel-post. She had on a fresh nightdress and looked frail and frightened.

'Freda? Freda, is that you?'

'Yes, dear. I'm coming right up to see you.'

'I thought it was Alan – I'm expecting him. He'll want something to eat. I know he's coming to see me.'

'I'll look after him, dear. You go back to bed.'

Anna saw Kathleen's helpless, pleading, beautiful blue eyes, so similar to those of her beloved son. Rose guided her away from the stairs back to her bedroom.

'There is something else, Freda. I believe Alan had a bedroom here? I really need to look over it, if that would be possible. Mr Rawlins said it would be acceptable.'

'I am sorry, but I couldn't allow you to, not without Edward being here. But Alan did often stay with them.'

'I understand. Please ask Mr Rawlins to contact me.'

Anna was more than ready to leave. It was all so wretchedly sad, not to mention a major hiccup for her case.

Liz was standing outside the block of flats having a smoke when she saw Anna drive up, and she gave her a thumbs-up. Stubbing out her cigarette as Anna got out of the car, she eagerly told her that they were ready to start the Luminol testing.

'I've waited because as I've told you, using Luminol can destroy or degrade the DNA markers in the blood. We have made some progress though in the hallway.'

'I have news for you too. The reason the genetic tests on Mr and Mrs Rawlins's blood samples didn't match is because Alan was an IVF baby – third-party donors, so no inherited DNA.'

'Ahhh. I wondered what the problem was. Throws up a larger one, when you think of how many children are now born via IVF. Any hope of getting the records of the donors?'

'No. It was nearly twenty-seven years ago and the clinic has closed down. The wretched part of it all is, neither Edward Rawlins nor Alan know the truth.'

'Oh dear. That's going to be a very sad revelation for the father.'

'Yes. Nobody else knew but the mother's best friend, and she kept the secret.'

'Until now . . .'

'Yes, until now, which is a real screw-up for us as we have no way of identifying whose blood it is. It might not even be Alan's.'

'That does pose a problem, for us as well. Anyway, shall we go inside?'

'Talking of blood, can I ask why, if there was so much under the floorboards, there was no smell?'

'Number of reasons really. The replaced bit of carpet, and the bleach, would suppress it; and then you have the air current under the floorboards which would have dried it out very quickly.'

Liz led the way into the flat across the stepping plates. She had two forensic assistants waiting, both suited up with goggles hanging round their necks and face masks on.

'Okay, due to the fact we have found so little visible blood, apart from in the bedroom, we're mixing a Luminol solution that will increase the intensity of the glow reaction with very minute traces of blood.'

Anna got dressed in the white forensic suit, complete with her own goggles and face mask. The assistants finished preparing the mixture in a plastic spray bottle and then proceeded to close all the curtains and turn off the lights while the photographer set up his digital camera on a tripod. Liz gave the go-ahead for them to spray the Luminol on a section of the narrow hallway leading to the bathroom.

'At first I didn't think we'd get anything from here because, as I said, I thought the body might have been wrapped in the bedsheet, but . . .'

As one of her assistants sprayed the Luminol, four clear marks began to emit a striking bright blue glow and the photographer started taking a long-exposure picture.

'The iron present in any blood catalyzes the chemical reaction that leads to the blue glow, revealing the location of the blood. We have a smear on the door and another on the edge of the frame. There's no sign of any finger- or palm-marks, and as you can see they are quite low down. Their direction is towards the bathroom and from the pattern I'd say the body was carried from the bedroom in a blood-stained sheet that brushed against the door and frame.'

'My God, it's like a child's glow stick.' Anna looked at the marks previously undetected by human eye.

'The walls and doors have been cleaned, which is why these marks were unseen until now. The bleach briefly glows very bright but fades fast, whereas the blood glow lasts for about forty seconds. Now the bathroom . . .'

One of the assistants went in followed by the photographer, with Liz and Anna standing behind them. Since the bathroom had no exterior window and the lights were off, it was very dark. The white tiles, white surrounds of the bath, white wash-basin and white toilet were unmarked.

'As the mixture is water-based we use an aerosol solution on tiles to avoid runs. We'll start on the far edge of the bath where I found a minute trace of blood.' Liz briefly indicated the area with a torch.

Nobody spoke as the Luminol reacted to some blood-spatter patterns that went about twelve inches up the tiled wall beside the bath. Next they sprayed the bath itself, resulting in a blue glow around the taps, plughole and down the side of the bath onto the tiled floor and edge of the toilet pedestal. Smears, spatter and wipe-marks were now visible on these areas and the wall behind them.

'Oh my God,' Anna said quietly.

'Bloodbath, isn't it? Experience has taught me it's not uncommon for a body to be cut up in a bath, and the Luminol results in here certainly go along with that theory. Now just back out slightly and remain on the stepping plates in the area just outside the bathroom door. I would say with this much distribution, and even though I have seen a lot worse, we might get some footprints.'

Anna, the photographer and the two assistants shuffled backwards and hovered in the hallway as Liz moved a stepping plate to one side and sprayed the Luminol on the area below it.

'Yes, we have one. Not a lot of detail, just the heel, but keep backing out and we may get more from the hall area.'

There were no further footprints or any drag marks, which Liz again suggested was because the body could have been wrapped when carried. Only when the dismembering began would there be extensive blood spillage in and around the bath.

'I'd say the victim was dead before the dismembering, otherwise the blood-spatter patterns would have been higher up. Nevertheless, you would still get a substantial leakage from the torso.'

Anna felt faint. 'I'm going to have to go outside for a minute,' she said.

'I'll come with you. I need another fag.'

Liz gave her assistants instructions to remove the plug-hole and u-bend and to check the exterior drains to see what they could find – perhaps some hairs or body tissue – then went out for some much-needed air.

Anna gasped. The thought of what had happened in the bathroom made her feel like throwing up. Liz took out her Marlboro Lights and lit one. She then passed over the pack to Anna.

'I make the excuse that smoking disguises the stench, but nowadays we're not allowed to light up anywhere. You want one, dear?'

'Thank you.' Anna didn't usually smoke that much, but needed something to calm herself down. The nicotine made her feel light-headed.

'Talking about stench, I know there is a strong smell of bleach and some awful flowery spray, but usually if a body's left decomposing there would be a much stronger odour,' Liz said thoughtfully. 'I've been wondering ... You are thinking that the victim was bumped off just after the last sighting of the chap, correct?'

'Yes.' Anna exhaled and coughed.

'Well, whoever did the tidying-up had to have taken some time. You don't get it all cleaned so easily. Plus areas of the carpet have been washed as well and they are bone dry, excuse the pun.'

'We are taking it from the day Alan Rawlins went missing as being the probable time of death. That was the day he was last seen, but he wasn't reported missing for two weeks.'

'Ah well, the body could have been in situ for that time and would smell a bit, but I haven't got any whiff of decomposing flesh. That's a very pungent smell.'

'Yes.' Anna nodded, still trying to stop herself feeling queasy.

Liz inhaled deeply. 'You know, maybe the killer is someone with some kind of medical or forensic knowledge. There were no hairbrushes, toothbrush, razor or anything where we would have been able to test for a DNA match. Unless they watched a lot of *CSI*.' She gave a short barking laugh.

Anna checked her watch, beginning to feel better.

'I'm going back in there now. Are you joining me?' Liz asked.

'No. I think after what we have discovered here I should get back to the station,' Anna said.

'Righty-ho. I'll send in my report sometime tomorrow.'

Anna returned to her car. She hated the lingering smell of the cigarette on her fingers, and even though feeling less sickly she sat for a while with the air conditioner on and the windows open, taking deep breaths.

On the drive to the station Anna now had to move Tina Brooks back into number one position as the prime suspect. There was no way the young woman could not have known what had taken place in her flat. Anna also had a timeline now that made no sense. Perhaps Alan Rawlins had been murdered on the day he left his garage due to a migraine, which Tina had said was the last time she had seen him. Yet from what Liz Hawley had said, the victim could have been murdered any time in the two weeks before he was declared missing. Anna then had to consider the semen stains and hair on the linen removed from the bed. If there was a considerable time between the murder and the sex antics that went on in the bedroom, possibly two weeks after, where was the body? And now without any weapons or witnesses it was becoming more and more of a nightmare jigsaw puzzle.

In the incident room there had been little development. Paul had been trying to trace anyone who knew the drug dealer Sammy Marsh, but had come up against a brick wall. They were asking the local Cornwall police to help trace his last residence or anyone who could help with their enquiry. They had looked for any rental flats or houses linked to Alan Rawlins, but so far they had had no luck. Brian Stanley was also coming up against one false lead after another, and was still waiting for Michael Phillips's mobile phone records. If he and Tina were in contact with each other, there was no proof of it.

Helen had been to Tina's salon and had brought back three photographs of her. They were posed pictures of her that Tina used in the salon, and these were now pinned up on the board. By the time Anna had given the team the update from the flat, they were stunned. She also gave them the news that it was still not possible to get identification from the blood found at the flat.

'He was not the biological son so we will not get any matching DNA from the Rawlinses' blood samples.'

'What about anything from his parents' home? Did you check that out?'

'Not yet.'

Stanley glanced at Helen and it irritated Anna.

'It wasn't convenient for me to do so this morning, Brian, so you can wipe that expression off your face. Anyone thought to get a DNA from Tina to see if it's her hair found in the bed?'

Brian looked at Helen again. She shook her head.

'Get it sorted, would you?' Anna snapped. She took a deep breath to calm herself down. 'We really need to get more information on Alan. We're back to square one, but what we do know now is that the place was a bloodbath.'

'Do we move Tina Brooks up to prime suspect?' Helen asked.

'Yes, but until we get more evidence we leave her hanging.'

'Well, if she cut him up she deserves to be.'

'Thank you, Brian, but I am now very sure it would have taken two people to move and dismember the body, dispose of it, clean the flat, and so we place Michael Phillips back up alongside Tina.'

'But we don't have a shred of evidence linking him to her or to Alan Rawlins!'

'Then let's try and find it,' she said crossly.

Helen signalled to her that she had a call. It was Edward Rawlins.

'I'll take it in my office, Helen. Thank you.' She dreaded talking to him. By now she was sure he would have been told the truth.

'Mr Rawlins, thank you for getting back to me.'

'I am sorry for the wasted time. You have my sincere apologies, Detective Travis – that is all I can say.'

'I understand, Mr Rawlins, and now I really need to come and talk to you again because I need to see the bedroom that Alan kept at your house.'

'Yes, of course. I am at home now so whenever is convenient to you.'

'Thank you. I will come over straight away if that is acceptable.'

'Yes, of course it is.'

She replaced the receiver. Her heart went out to the dapper little man whose voice was so strained, and for him to apologise to her for what must have been the most devastating news touched her. It must have felt as if he had lost his son twice over.

Paul knocked and said they had made some headway; they'd traced a possible contact who knew Sammy Marsh. After a series of calls to Cornwall they had been given the address of the flat owned by Marsh that was still unoccupied. They also had the details of a contact of Marsh who was closer to home, serving time at Wandsworth Prison.

'Good. Interview this guy. What's he in for?'

'Drug dealing. Got an eighteen-month sentence, small stuff, but he did at one time share the flat with Sammy. His name is Errol Dante. He's got a record for previous drug and assault charges, but nothing major. The most major thing about him is he has fifteen illegitimate kids with a variety of women. He's a Jamaican overstayer recommended for deportation on completion of his prison sentence. He travels around seaside towns with fairground workers.'

'See what you get from him and ask if he can identify any of the guys in the surfing picture.'

'Will do. I'll go with Helen, is that okay?'

'Yes, and tell Brian to continue trawling for any other contacts in Cornwall. If we have to go there we don't want a wasted journey.'

'*You* tell him. He's so far up my nose and he won't like me passing on details.'

'As the DS you're his line manager, so deal with it.'

Anna was just about to leave to see Mr Rawlins when Langton phoned in. She spent a considerable amount of time explaining all the new developments and he listened without interruption until she told him they could not make any positive identification.

'Why not? You've got his parents giving blood samples. You can't waste time – it is imperative you—' She interrupted him to give the reason why not. He was stunned.

'Jesus Christ, I didn't know that. Can you imagine how many people are giving birth with donors? It's going to create a big mess and we could have God knows how many victims unidentified in years to come.'

'I am just going to meet with Mr Rawlins. We might get something that'll help, as apparently Alan still used a bedroom at his parents' home.'

'What? Bit late in the day. Why hasn't that been checked out?'

'I've only recently found out and it wasn't in the original Misper report.'

'Let me know if you uncover anything.'

'Yes, sir!' she said sarcastically. She knew it was a slip-up, that with luck could be rectified, if she did find anything that could help identify Alan Rawlins as the victim.

Anna drove reluctantly to the Rawlinses' house as she knew how distressed Edward was, and now having to search the room that his son kept there was not going to help matters.

Mr Rawlins opened the front door before she had time to ring the bell.

'Come in. Could I have a private word with you?' he said immediately.

'Yes, of course.'

He looked very pale and nervous as he ushered Anna into the lounge.

'I want to ask you if the information regarding my son's birth could be kept confidential.'

'Yes, of course I will endeavour to respect your privacy. I am sorry that you had to find out in such circumstances. It must be very upsetting for you.'

'That is putting it mildly. I found it hard to believe, even harder to realise my wife has kept a secret from me all these years. It never entered my head that Kathleen could have been so devious. I have to come to terms with it – I have no choice – but nevertheless I am hardly able to accept it. Alan is *my* son; whether or not my biological offspring, I could not have wished for a better . . .'

He hesitated. 'He had his mother's eyes – clear blue eyes. I never questioned that he could not be her child, and he was very like me in so many ways. The hardest thing is for me to understand the fact that Kathleen was too afraid to tell me the truth. It wouldn't have mattered. I loved him, treasured him as she doted on him, and now with this awful situation, not knowing if he is alive or . . .' He broke down.

Although impatient to see Alan's bedroom, Anna was aware of the need to be considerate and said that if he found it disturbing to be present during the search then she could do it alone.

'He used it when he stayed over. In fact, we hardly ever went in there, only to clean or remake his bed. It's as he left it. During the time he's been missing I have sat in there praying.'

'Have you removed anything?'

'No. It's his bedroom and it's private. It's always been his bedroom. If Rose needs to rest she uses the spare room next to our master bedroom. Sometimes lately I've also slept in there because Kathleen is . . .' He paused. 'She's incontinent,' he said sadly.

Anna stood up saying she didn't want to take any more of his time. He nodded and led her into the hall. They moved up the stairs.

'I can do this on my own, Mr Rawlins,' Anna reiterated. 'I don't want to add to your distress.'

'Yes. I won't stay with you. I'll just show you the room. I have the keys.'

'Is it locked?'

'No, but his desk drawers are and he has a small safe.'

'I really appreciate this, Mr Rawlins.'

They passed the master bedroom and Rose turned to smile. She was spoon-feeding porridge to Kathleen, who was sitting up on a chair close to an electric fire.

'Rose, I am just showing Detective Travis Alan's room. Is she eating today?'

'A little. She's been changed and we had a shower, didn't we, Kathleen?'

Kathleen had her mouth open for the next spoonful like a fragile bird, her eyes vacant and staring ahead.

Mr Rawlins gestured to a closed door. 'That's the spare room. We are going up to the top floor now. It's two rooms. We always intended knocking them into one to make it a larger bedroom, but just never got around to it.'

He opened a door at the end of the corridor that led to a narrow staircase. Anna followed him up onto a narrow strip of landing with two doors side by side. He opened one, stepping back.

'This is the bedroom and the room next to it was where he used to do his homework when he came home from school. He turned it into a little office. These are the keys I mentioned you'll need. Could you leave them on the table in the hall when you leave?'

'If I need to take anything away, Mr Rawlins, I'll fill out a property report and ask if Rose could check and sign it. Would that be okay?'

'Yes, yes. Take whatever you think necessary.'

Anna stepped into the bedroom. It had a musty smell.

'Let me open a window,' Mr Rawlins fussed. 'It smells stuffy in here.'

'Please don't bother. Thank you for the keys.' Anna held out her hand and he passed a key ring with three small keys attached.

'Although we had these I would never invade his privacy. They were kept for emergencies only. He was very particular about this being his private domain and I respected that.'

'I am sure you did. Thank you, Mr Rawlins.'

He hovered at the door for a while before turning back and heading downstairs. She crossed to the slanted window and eased it open, and from there she saw Mr Rawlins walking down the path and out onto the road below. She drew a deep breath, relieved, and was now able to take in the room.

The single bed had an orange duvet, matching orange pillowslips and a white bottom sheet. Beside the bed was a small chest of drawers. On top of this were two photographs of his parents, an alarm clock and a small glass dish with some loose change. Hanging from the walls were framed certificates for swimming and gymnastics, and two insipid water-colour paintings depicting an empty beach with sand dunes. They both had a scrawled signature: *Alan Rawlins, Holiday, 1995*

The wardrobe just fitted beneath the slanted roof. It contained very few items; a tracksuit and a leather jacket, and folded neatly were two pairs of grey slacks and two pairs of black lace-up shoes. In a dressing-table the drawers contained three neatly folded laundered shirts, underwear and socks. Anna carefully removed each item, checking beneath and around them before replacing them. In front of the bed was a rag rug which covered a worn fitted carpet in pale green. She looked beneath the rug and under the bed, but apart from a layer of dust there was nothing else. She stripped the bed back, but the sheet and duvet cover still had creases as if the bed had been freshly made. It was a room devoid of any real personal items bar the paintings and certificates. She sat for a moment on the bed, looking around, trying to get some sense of the boy, the young man who had stayed and used this room from his childhood. It was such an empty room and probably used for exactly what Mr Rawlins had stated: somewhere to sleep when his son came to visit.

Finding nothing of interest – no hairbrush or combs that could give them a possible DNA sample – she walked out, closing the door, to enter the room beside it. She was surprised. It was very bright with quite a big window newly framed as if it had been made larger to give good light. The walls were painted white and there was the same green fitted carpet and two arc lamps either side of a good-sized desk. The computer, printer and telephone extension were all covered.

Leaning on one wall were two surfboards. They were expensive ones and both covered with a fitted black zip-up bag. Hanging up was a wetsuit, and placed neatly beneath it were goggles, flippers and a snorkel in a plastic square container. Two posters of surfing in Florida were hanging behind the desk. To one side of it was a filing cabinet with three drawers.

'So this is where you hung out,' she muttered, but before she opened up the drawers in the desk and the filing cabinet she made a thorough search of every corner of the room.

Her heart jumped when she found a man's leather vanity bag. Opening it, she was hoping to find a hairbrush, comb or razor, but all it contained was some aftershave lotion, shampoo and conditioner, expensive French mois-turiser and hand cream. The containers were all clean with no residue around the caps; another insight into a fastidi-ous man's personal belongings. There was a small leather case with scissors, a nail file and a bottle of self-tanning lotion inside. In another container she found the round surfboard-wax packets, again neatly wrapped and carefully stored. In a second part of the vanity case were numerous vitamin bottles and a packet of condoms.

Anna replaced everything in the exact position she had found it. Next she opened a cupboard beneath the large window. Inside were weights, a wall bar and a folded bicycle. There was also a Nike bag containing swimming trunks and gym gear.

Whenever she came across any clothing item she did a thorough search for evidence, but the neatness and orderliness of everything proved to be unhelpful. She didn't find one stray hair.

Sitting on the chair behind the desk, Anna ran her finger along the wood that was covered with a film of dust, which was good because it proved nothing had been touched or removed. The drawers either side of the desk were locked. She selected a key to open them and then tried the other two, but the drawers remained steadfastly locked. None of the keys fitted. Anna got up, took the manicure set and removed the nail file. She worked on the lock of the right-hand drawer for some time before she heard the click and was able to slide it open. It contained a neat stack of body-builder's magazines and surfing magazines. She checked the dates and they were all at least six months to a year old. She flicked through each, but found nothing. Disappointed, she closed the drawer and went to work on the second. Frustratingly, this took considerably longer to open. She refused to give up, even when the nail file became bent. She rattled the brass handle, sat back and slapped the top of the desk with the flat of her hand. She next tried to prise the lock with the small sharp nail scissors and got down on her knees to be on eye-level and only when she was that close did she see the scratches. Had someone else also tried to break into this drawer? She looked at the one already opened and could see the same telltale scratches.

'Someone else has had a go at this,' she muttered.

Sitting back on the desk chair again, she selected the nail file and this time rammed it into the lock as far as it would go. She then twisted it sharply – and bingo, it clicked open! She was certain she would find something, but pulling out the drawer, she found it contained only more magazines.

'Shit.' Then as she flicked over the first couple, tossing them to one side she saw the erotic pose of a muscular man. The cover was torn off, but she didn't have to look too far before it became obvious that it was a gay man's pornographic contact magazine. There were four more magazines of the same type and these she stacked to one side to remove from the room.

Pleased with her findings, she also found three DVDs pushed to the back of the drawer. They had sexual titles: *Well Hung, Gorgeous Orgies* and so on. She also placed these on top of the magazines to remove.

Anna rubbed her hands together and now turned her attention to the filing cabinet. The small keys fitted each drawer so she opened the bottom one first. There were files attached to a sliding rod and these all listed vintage vehicles, purchases of spare parts, price lists and contact numbers for sales. Each of the cars bought and repaired and customised by Alan were listed in a separate file. Photographs showed the vehicle before and after, and beside them the price it was bought for and the price for which it was sold. She was astonished at the amount of money an AC Cobra had made, and this was matched by the selling price of a Ferrari, a 280SL Mercedes and a Maserati. She worked out that Alan had made about four hundred thousand pounds from the sales. She could see by the dates that these sales covered a period of five years. Listed were the amounts he had paid to his father and the amount he had kept for himself. Considering how much they knew was in the joint bank account with Tina

Brooks, it was obvious that Alan either had a separate bank account or a very big cash haul.

Anna removed the files and stacked them for removal along with the magazines and DVDs.

Drawer two was full of receipts that had been pinned together. On each one was a neat Post-it note listing dates. It took a while for her to match some of the receipts to material from the bottom drawer. They were mostly for the purchase of spare parts, from spark plugs to hub-caps and steering wheels. There were also extensive costs from a leather upholstery company for repairs and rebuilding of car seats. This secondary business Alan had run in his spare time was extremely well organised and detailed.

She noticed that some of the writing on the Post-it notes was different, and drumming her fingers on the side of the desk she made a mental note to get a sample of Mr Rawlins's writing. She was certain that he was the other person. This would mean that he too was making a considerable amount of money on the side. Many of the purchases were cash and no tax or VAT documents surfaced. Had Mr Rawlins been up here in the room, concerned about it getting out just how much money he was being paid by partnering with his son in his little business?

Anna now opened the top drawer. This had more personal items, with piles of surfing locations and holiday brochures for Florida, the Bahamas, the Cayman Islands, Spain and Portugal, plus rentals in Newquay and numerous estate agency listings for properties in Cornwall. A few had red rings around them and all were in the vicinity of three to five hundred thousand pounds. She was unable to find anything that indicated that a purchase had been made. There was nothing that connected Alan to Tina's flat or any mention of her. There were no bank statements; no cheque books and no credit-card statements, unless they had been removed.

Anna swivelled from side to side in the desk chair. She took off the hood from the computer. She knew it would have to be examined and hoped it would give more insight into Alan Rawlins. So far, all she had basically gained were details of the income from the sale of the cars, the gay pornographic magazines and DVDs. She was certain that their possible victim led a separate life from Tina. Anna had no indication that Tina was aware of it, but neither had she as yet discovered a motive for Alan's murder, unless his girlfriend had found out that he led a double life. The question was obvious: was that sufficient motive to kill?

Chapter Eight

Errol Dante was enormous, at least six foot four, with dreadlocks down to his waist. He also had the most pungent body odour that permeated the prison's small interview room. Errol had three gold teeth, and a gap between two of them that made him have a lisp. With his strong Jamaican accent it was very difficult to understand what he was saying.

Although it was not easy, Paul and Helen had established that he had lived in Cornwall for a period. He first denied ever being there or knowing Sammy Marsh, but when told that they knew he had shared a flat with Marsh, he did a swinging head move.

'Oh yeah, fink it was 'im dat I know. I rented a caravan from 'im.'

'Did you also know Alan Rawlins?'

'No man, dunno 'im. I gotta work in da kitchen. I don't need dis hassle. I'm helpin' cook de grub here.'

The thought of this man cooking in the kitchen with the heat and his body odour was sickening to even contemplate.

Paul first showed him the photograph of Alan Rawlins. Errol kissed his teeth. 'Na, I dunno him.'

They next showed him the photograph of the surfers,

which led to a long ramble about when he worked at the Hotel Jolly in Antigua and he ran the water-skiing on the beach.

'This was taken in Cornwall, Mr Dante.'

'Look a lickle like Antigua to me, man.'

'So are you saying you never met any of these men?'

'I dunno. If dey was in Antigua maybe. I meet a lotta guys from da Carlisle Hotel; dey don't have water-skiing or ski-boats der.'

'You admit that you knew Sammy Marsh.'

'I dunno 'im, man.'

'You lived in his flat. We know you shared his flat in Cornwall – he was a photographer.'

'Ohhh I dunno. I crash out maybe on his floor. He's not a good guy, lemme tell you he's not a good guy. I rented this shithole of a caravan.'

'Why?'

' 'Cos I'm just tellin' how it is. Stitch you up, man – know what I mean?'

'We know he dealt drugs.'

Errol swung his dreadlocks again and shrugged his shoulders.

'We know you were arrested on a drug-related incident, Mr Dante.'

He blew out his cheeks. 'He informer, man. I was just smalltime, bit of hash here, lickle weed der. Him disre-speck me, man. Fockitup. Me no know 'im, right?'

Paul was immensely frustrated. He slapped the table with the flat of his hand. Then leaning forward, he shook his finger.

'We know that you *do* know him – and let me tell you, Errol, we're not here for a drug-related incident. We are here because we are investigating a murder.'

'If he dead, man, I wanna shake de killer's hand.'

'It's not Sammy Marsh who is the victim – it's someone else.'

'Me no know. Lot of people want dat man out of der hair. He was an informer, you hear me? I get picked up and I done nuthin. Fuckin' stitched me up, man.'

Helen tapped Paul's knee beneath the table. He was becoming so agitated and she wanted to have a try.

'Errol, we are here asking for your help. We are not connected to any Drug Squad. We are just trying to trace this man.' She pushed Alan's photograph forward again. 'We believe that he is a murder victim and we are simply asking if you knew him.'

She then moved the group shot of the surfers across the table. 'We also need to identify these men with our victim. We know that Sammy took this photograph because his studio stamp is on the back of it.'

Errol kissed his gold-capped teeth again.

'Him long gone, lady.'

'Yes, we know that, but could you give us any other contact from Cornwall who might know who these people are?'

'He was a piece of shit. He hadda finger me. They come to my woman's place in Brixton. Cornwall is a shit-'ole, stinking rain every day.'

'Well, maybe you should try and help us get Sammy back – pay day, and if you help us we can talk to the Governor here . . .'

'I dunno where he is, lady.'

'But you know people in Cornwall that knew him – right?'

He nodded and sucked his teeth again.

'Me no inform on 'im, even though 'im a pussy-'ole.'

Paul gave an exasperated sigh. He was so tense he wanted to reach across the table and punch Errol. Helen gave him a look, warning him to stay calm, but he took no notice.

'If you say he tipped off the cops about you, what's it to you?' he snapped.

'A lot, brother, a fuckin' lot. That's all I'm sayin'. He's a batty man like a mean prancin' lickle shite.'

'He's a what?' Helen asked, incredulous.

'Let's just say he'd not screw *you*, woman.'

'So you are not going to help us even though we're saying that if you do we can help you?' Helen battled on.

'G'way! Yuh no pull ma strings.'

Tight-lipped, Paul picked up the photographs. 'Well, then we'll just encourage the powers-that-be to send you back to Kingston, Errol. It's on the cards – you know that. You've got no right to even be in this country.'

'I'm gettin' married so you can't diss me, brother.'

'Who to – the mother of your fifteen kids?'

Errol gave a wide grin and laughed. 'Na, but she ain't no juvie either. I'm gonna have a legit reason to be in this country so I am not helpin' nobody to come out and slit me throat.' He jabbed the air with a thick filthy finger. 'You git outta ma face. I not talkin' no more.'

That was it. Paul stood up and replaced the photographs in the file. He looked to Helen and then crossed to knock on the interview door for the guard to open it. Errol turned and grinned.

Helen hurried to join Paul. The interview was over, but they still had to speak to the Governor, who informed them that Errol had requested permission to marry whilst he served his sentence, as his girlfriend was pregnant. The Governor at first refused to give any details, claiming it was against regulations, but he brought out Errol's prison files, then left the office, giving the excuse that he needed a moment to speak to someone. Paul grabbed the opportunity to have a look at the request for a marriage licence. Helen was stunned to see him act very fast, jotting down the name and address of Errol's intended. He was back in his seat by the time the Governor returned.

'Everything all right, Detective Simms?'

'Yes. Thank you for your time and for arranging our interview with Mr Dante.' They shook hands.

As they drove out of the prison gates Paul started to relax.

'Her name is Sandra-Dee Fallow; address in Brixton.'

'That was a bit naughty,' Helen observed.

'Yeah well, that bastard wouldn't give it up. The Governor, thank God, was more cooperative. Let's go and see her now.'

Anna waited as Brian Stanley removed the computer from the Rawlinses' house along with the magazines. Rose had glanced over the list of items Anna had written down for her to sign and show Mr Rawlins on his return home. Anna also asked if she knew if anyone had taken anything from Alan's bedroom and office, but the carer said that she had never even been up the stairs.

'Has something bad happened?'

Anna watched her sign the release form.

'Their son is still missing.'

'I know that, but I mean since?'

Anna looked surprised. 'How do you mean?'

'Well, it's not my business, but Mr Rawlins has asked me to talk to the social services to find a home for Kathleen. He wants her to go in as soon as possible. It'll affect her badly. At least here she sort of knows where she is, and to change her environment will make her very distressed.'

'I didn't know. It will obviously be a very private matter between them.'

'Yes, of course. It's sad though, isn't it? Yesterday she was certain that Alan had come home.'

'Why?'

'She could hear him, she said, moving across the ceiling. He used to stay in the rooms above hers. She said he was back home.'

'Did Mr Rawlins go up there?'

'I don't know. He was at home so maybe he did. I didn't hear anything, though.'

Anna was about to walk out when she paused. 'Have the rubbish bins been collected at all?'

'I don't know when the binmen come.'

'Are the bins out by the kitchen?'

'Yes, just beside the back door. There's three wheelies, but we really only ever use one.'

'Thank you.'

Anna hurried into the kitchen, opening the back door to find that the bins were lined up as Rose had said. She opened one, which smelled of urine and stale food. She shut the lid and tried the second. She looked inside to see a black bin liner tied very tightly. There was no rotting food stench so she lifted the bag out. Untying the knot she looked inside and saw it was filled with magazines and more DVDs similar to the ones found in Alan's room. She retied the knot and carried it back into the house.

'We're taking this as well, Brian. Are we all set to leave?'

'Yep. I'll get the computer over to Tech Support and see what they get from it. What's in the bag?'

'You'll enjoy sifting through it all back at the station.'

'What is it?'

'Wait and see.'

Heading towards her car, Anna was unsure how she felt about the nursing home for Kathleen and the fact that Mr Rawlins must have opened up the drawer to remove the pornographic magazines and DVDs. He obviously was unable to get access to the drawer that had taken her so much time to open. She sighed. Poor man. His beloved son goes missing, then he finds out he wasn't his biological child, and then he uncovers further details about his blue-eyed boy that he probably would have preferred not to have known. But did he also remove evidence? She knew she would have to question him again, but the next time she wouldn't be quite so accommodating.

Paul and Helen were at a highrise council estate in Brixton where flat number thirty-four looked in disrepair. The side window by the front door was boarded up, the letter box had a plank of wood nailed across it and the door itself looked as if it had been kicked in numerous times. They rang the bell, but it didn't work, and then Paul hammered with his fist. Eventually the door was inched open with the chain still attached. A bleached-blonde woman peered out asking what they wanted. Paul showed his ID and asked if he could talk to Sandra-Dee Fallow.

'Whatcha want to see her for?'

'Are you Sandra-Dee Fallow? We've been to see Errol and he gave us your address.'

The safety chain was removed and the door opened wider.

'First off, it's just Sandra, so lay off the Dee bit, I fucking hate it! Mother gave me the name after that stupid song in the film *Grease* . . . "Look at me, I'm Sandra bloody Dee", she said in a mocking childlike voice.

'We need to talk to you, Sandra, it won't take long,' Helen said, smiling.

Sandra opened the door further and glared at them. 'What you want to talk to me about?'

'Could we please come in, Sandra?' Helen said pleasantly.

The woman stepped back, allowing them to walk in. Helen went in first with Paul following.

'I was lying down. I've been ever so sick.'

Sandra was also very pregnant. She was wearing a short nightdress with a sweater pulled over it, and her belly stuck out.

'I think it was some curry I had last night – got terrible heartburn.'

She led them along a filthy hallway to an equally dirty room with no carpet and broken furniture. There were also a number of toys and a pushchair.

'You have children?' Helen asked.

'Yeah. 'Cos I was so sick they're wiv me neighbour. She's ever so good.' She had an inch of dark growth in her bleached hair and was around thirty, but she was still a very pretty woman with a round face and full lips. Her eyes were dark with thick lashes that looked as if she just continued to apply black mascara on a daily basis without ever removing any, making it seem as if she had panda eyes.

'How many children do you have?' Helen continued.

'Two, boy and a girl. If it wasn't for the social services helping me out they'd be in foster homes. Their dad's not around. Dunno where he is and I hope he rots in hell.'

'So you're married?' Paul asked.

'Nah. You want to sit down?'

They sat on a bow-legged sofa amongst Barbie dolls and tractors, and Sandra sat in a sagging armchair.

'You are engaged to marry Errol Dante, aren't you?' Paul took a plastic truck out of his back.

'Yeah. This one is his.' She rubbed her stomach.

'How long have you known him?'

'About a year or so. What's this about?'

'We are investigating a missing person and we have some photographs we wanted to show you from when Errol was in Cornwall.' Helen kept her voice very quiet and relaxed.

'Yeah, that's where I met him. I used to work as a wait-ress. In fact, I wish I'd never left to end up in this dump. I had a nice rented caravan there.'

'So when Errol left Cornwall you came with him?'

'Well, not exactly. He came to London before me and then I packed up everythin' to be with him.'

'How many months gone are you?' Helen asked.

'Seven. Feels like a year, I'm tellin' you. I wasn't like this with me others.' She puffed out her cheeks.

'Would you mind looking at some photographs to see if you recognise anyone on them?' Paul opened his briefcase.

'Yeah. Is this to do with that little bastard Sammy Marsh?'

Paul glanced at Helen.

'It is actually, because we know he took the photo-graph ... this one.' Paul passed over the photograph with the surfers.

Sandra peered at it and then pulled a face. 'Nah, dunno them.' She turned it over in her hand to look at the studio watermark print.

'We reckon that Sammy tipped off the cops about Errol and that's why they picked him up.'

'But Sammy has disappeared, hasn't he?'

'We believe so,' Helen said, passing the photograph back to Paul.

'Is it him what's missing? 'Cos I know a lotta people would like to strangle him. He was a really nasty little sod.'

'Errol shared a flat with him, didn't he?'

'I wouldn't call it sharin'. He dossed down on his floor then we met and he moved in wiv me and the kids.'

'Can you look at this photograph?'

Paul now passed her the single shot of Alan with his surfboard. Again Sandra gave it a good look-over, but shook her head.

'I didn't really mix wiv them.'

'There's a café called the Smugglers . . .'

She leaned forward. 'Which one? There's quite a few called the same name. The one in Newquay is very nice, and then some are a bit cheap, know what I mean – summer openers. They close 'em down for winter.' She jabbed her finger at the photograph. 'Yeah, that's where I worked.'

'Did a lot of the surfers use it?'

'Yeah. It's right on the beach and open all hours.'

'Do they do drugs there?'

'They do everythin' – it's a bit of a rough place. Sammy used to be kingpin. He could get you anythin' you wanted.'

'And you never saw any one of these guys in the café?'

The young woman shifted uncomfortably. 'Me back is killin' me,' she said. 'I think if you don't mind you should leave.'

'Just take another look, love. We really appreciate this,' Helen said encouragingly.

Sandra suddenly became cagey, shaking her head. 'I'm not getting into anything, not in the state I'm in. I've said enough. I don't want no trouble.'

'Do you think you would get into trouble?' Paul said.

'I could, and I'm not wanting to start yakking on about any connections to Sammy. He's someone you don't mess with and I got to look out for Errol and the kids.'

'Is he looking out for you?'

'Yes, he fuckin' is. At least he's gonna marry me, said he's gonna take good care of me when he gets out.'

'I hope he keeps his word. He has fifteen other children, did you know that?' Paul replaced the photograph into his briefcase.

'You are fucking joking, ain't ya!' she gasped. 'He's got no others.'

'You sure he's not just using you to be able to try and stay in the country?' Helen wished Paul hadn't been so abrasive.

Sandra heaved herself upright. 'I want you to go. Go on, both of you!'

'He's an illegal immigrant, love. The judge recommended him for deportation.'

The girl pursed her lips and then flopped back down again. Paul was unsure how to proceed, but Helen moved to stand by Sandra.

'Can I get you a glass of water, love?'

'Yeah. In the kitchen there's some bottles in the fridge. Thanks.'

She closed her eyes. 'To be honest, you know what? I don't care any more. If what you say is true, where does that leave me?'

Helen returned with an open bottle of water and handed it to Sandra, who sipped and then burped loudly.

'There's no way I should've had that curry,' she hiccuped.

Helen stood by her and patted her shoulder.

'Could you just have another look at the photographs, love? The person missing is this blonde guy, the one in the middle. It's nothing to do with Sammy Marsh, we're not interested in him.'

Sandra held out her hand for the photograph again.

'I dunno, Sammy is such a bastard,' she mumbled.

'How well did you know him?'

'I didn't. I kept well out of his way, but like I said, he was a sort of kingpin with these surfer guys. They like to get stoned or coked up.'

She looked at the photograph again.

'Yeah.' Then she passed it back up to Helen and took a drink from the bottle of water.

'What do you mean, yeah?' Helen asked.

'I seen him. Don't know him, but he used to be in the Smugglers. Got a real fancy car. Sammy was often with him. You know he's a poof, don't ya?'

'Sammy?'

'Yeah. These guys are all muscle and suntanned. They were sort of a clique, if you know what I mean. Acted like they was above everyone else and . . .' She sighed. 'Sammy used Errol 'cos of his size, like a henchman so nobody messed with him. That's all I know. It's the God's truth.'

Paul took the photograph from Helen.

'Do you know if this man, the blonde guy in the middle, was also a homosexual?'

Sandra shrugged and took a gulp of water. 'He was very friendly with Sammy so he could be one of 'em.'

'Did you ever see him use drugs?'

'Nah, I told you. I didn't get into any of that.'

'But Errol was involved—' Paul began, but he was interrupted.

'He's no fuckin' poof, he got me up the spout. I'm gettin' tired of all this. I'm gonna go and lie down.' Sandra hoisted herself out of the chair and gestured for them to get out. As they went into the hall she asked rather plaintively if it was true.

'What's true, Sandra?'

'That Errol's got fifteen other kids?'

'You should ask him. That's what we were told, but let him tell you himself.'

Sandra opened the front door.

'I'm sick of it all,' she said tiredly. 'Sick to death of people lying to me. You'd think by now I'd be old enough to know better.'

Paul walked out ahead of Helen, who remained a moment with Sandra.

'We really appreciate you taking the time to talk to us.'

'That's okay.'

'It looks as if you've had a few unpleasant callers . . . your door has been kicked in.'

'Yeah. When they come for Errol they almost kicked it right off its hinges. I stuck that board over my letterbox to stop getting the fucking junk mail.'

'Thank you again, love. I hope it all goes well with the birth. Just one more thing . . . you described a flashy car driven by the man in the photograph. Can you think what colour it was, soft top or hard top, modern or . . .'

'I dunno. It was low down with the roof off. Dunno what make it was, but it was silver-ish.'

As Helen left, Sandra hooked the safety chain across the door.

*

Paul was very quiet as they drove back to the station. Helen had suggested they stop off and get a bite to eat, but he had refused, saying they should get the new information back to the incident room.

'Okay by me,' Helen agreed. 'Do you think Sandra was straight with us?'

'You want my honest opinion?'

'Yes, of course.'

'I think that woman would lie her way out of anything. She's a slag and with two kids already, now about to have a third and all on the social services, living in that hovel of a flat.'

'Well, taking all that into consideration,' Helen smiled patiently, 'did you think she had more to tell us?'

'I dunno, but what we do know is that Mr Clean and everybody's best friend, Alan Rawlins, had another side to him.'

'A gay one.'

'For chrissakes, just because that slag says he knew Sammy Marsh doesn't mean that he was also sexually involved with him.'

'Maybe not, but it does give us an insight into the fact that he may have been using drugs with Marsh. It's just showing a different side to Alan, and one I think we're going to have to dig into.'

Anna sat in her office sifting through Alan's magazines and checking out the personal ads. A number had red rings around them as if they were of interest. They were mostly gay men seeking partners and a few were of a more explicit nature, but none of the bondage adverts were ringed. It meant they would now have to get in touch with all the advertisers who were possibly contacted by Alan Rawlins.

Brian Stanley was also going through the magazines and making similar notes. The pornographic DVDs were stacked to be checked out, and the homophobic or obscene remarks flying around the incident room as Brian constantly read out various sections were becoming tedious.

By the time Helen and Paul had caught up with the new developments and were able to add theirs, it was obvious that Alan Rawlins led a double life. Top priority was the need to trace Sammy Marsh, for which they would need the assistance of the Devon and Cornwall Drug Squad. Meanwhile, the computer taken from Alan's room was still being assessed by the Tech Support team. They had reported back that many files had recently been deleted, not that it mattered as they would still be able to gain access and reproduce whatever material was on them as they had the hard drive.

Anna called for a briefing update towards the end of the afternoon. Although they now had a lot of new material, plus the contacts to be sifted through, they were still no closer to identifying the victim. But they now knew that Alan Rawlins's double life was centred on his time in Cornwall. Anna realised they would have to go there, to search Sammy Marsh's flat, and his studio, and to start questioning everyone who might have known Alan Rawlins.

'First thing tomorrow we start the round of calls connected to the gay magazines' adverts. Also, I am certain that Alan had money stashed somewhere and it could be a considerable amount. We have the sales and receipts from his vehicle business and we can assume he rented a place in Cornwall so we need to check that out.'

Stanley did his finger gesture.

'You think that maybe he was in league with Sammy Marsh? From what we've gathered, Marsh was a drug dealer; what if Alan was also involved? We know that Marsh was a nasty piece of work; according to the Cornwall Drug Squad he's done a runner somewhere. As we still don't have the blood identified as Alan's in his flat, it could be someone else's – maybe even Marsh's.'

'He's got a criminal record so his DNA should be on the national database. Get Liz Hawley to check it out.'

Anna had even considered this herself, but they had been so snowed under with all the new developments, it had slipped her mind.

Helen asked if Anna believed Tina Brooks was aware of the double life Alan was leading.

'To be honest, I don't. That is not to say we shouldn't talk to her about it. So we line that up for tomorrow, and do a buccal swab for DNA. I also want to talk to Mr Rawlins again, just in case he removed other material from his son's room.'

Stanley had his finger in the air once more.

'Cash ... Do you know if Rawlins was making cash deals with his sale of cars? That would be a nice way to offload it, paying cash for drugs. I don't mean for his own use, but what if he went into business with Sammy Marsh?'

'It's possible, but we have not as yet uncovered this cash. We have no other bank account details or bank statements except for the ones we removed from his flat. From his receipts he had listed at least four hundred thousand over a period of five years, plus ... Paul, didn't the woman Sandra Fallow say he also drove a flash car in Cornwall?'

'Yeah. She was also very certain he had a relationship with Marsh; saw them together at the Smugglers café.'

Anna asked if the Tech Support had come through with anything, but was told they were still working.

'We might get lucky with the files and documents on his computer,' she said.

Stanley swung back in his desk chair.

'Yeah, probably more sicko gay stuff like his disgusting DVDs. I'm not gonna watch them – they turn my stomach. Paul, you might like to take a bunch home.'

Before Paul could rise to the bait Anna turned on Stanley.

'That's enough from you, but we do need to check these DVDs out.'

'I'll do it,' Helen said.

'No, we can all spend time on them, so split them up between you all – and that includes you, Brian, all right?'

There was a moan around the incident room.

'Listen up, everyone,' Anna snapped. 'A body was cut up in Tina Brooks's flat. Right now we have found no murder weapon and, in case you are unaware of it, no body. It has to have been dumped somewhere and this has to also be a priority.'

'We got a negative result from Forensics on her car. She was asking to get it back or said could she charge us for a rental,' Helen reported.

Stanley gave a wide-armed gesture.

'She's a cheeky cow, but do we release her car back to her or not?'

'Yes, as long as Forensics have finished with it.'

Anna checked her watch and then turned to look at the incident board. It was a display of names and contacts, arrows linking one person to another with Cornwall underlined.

'Tomorrow I'll arrange for a trip to Cornwall, but in the

meantime we'll see what the Newquay police can give us to trace where Alan Rawlins lived whilst he was there. As yet we have no address.' She scanned the board again. 'How could he hide his double life and give no addresses of rented flats or hotels, even?'

'We've underestimated him,' Paul said quietly.

'You can say that again.'

Paul stared at the board. 'Maybe he used another name when he was there?'

'Maybe he did, but we don't even have details of how often he went there. Was it once, twice or three times a year – or just a couple of weeks in the summer?'

'I'll check with the garage he worked in and see what holidays he took, going back a few years.'

'Good, yes – do that, Paul.'

'What about Tina? She must have been aware of how often he went so I'll also check with her.'

'No, I'll do that first thing tomorrow, and I'll also call in on Mr Rawlins. I'll check with him about Alan's holidays, hotels, guest houses et cetera.'

Anna instructed the team to break for the evening. She made a point of picking up three porno DVDs for herself to peruse and then she asked Brian to come into her office.

He already had his overcoat on when he came to see her. He held up three DVDs.

'The wife's gonna be worried about me watching these.'

'For goodness sake, Brian, grow up and stop giving the snide sexual remarks to Paul. It's not funny and quite clearly upsets him. You cut it out. I won't have it, understand me?'

'I didn't know he was a shirt-lifter.'

'For chrissakes, it's childish homophobic remarks like that which—'

'It's the truth. I didn't know he was homosexual and if he can't take a joke about it . . .'

'It's nothing to joke about. It's his private life, so consider this an official warning, and from now on just watch what you say.'

'Yes, ma'am.'

'I mean it, Brian.'

'I will curb my tongue. And besides, with the way this case is going I think he's going to be an asset.'

He gave a straight-faced small nod and she waved her hand for him to get out. He held up the porno DVDs.

'I can't wait to get home.' He turned to leave the room.

'One other thing, Brian. Any luck with the CCTV from Asda?'

'The manager phoned and said he thinks the system was down the day we're interested in, so . . .'

'Less talk more action, Brian. Go and see him personally and check it for yourself.'

'Yes, ma'am.'

After he had left she leaned her head in her hands, resting her elbows on the desk, before eventually sitting back and picking up the phone to talk to Langton. She gave him a brief rundown of all the new information and said they would open the budget because she felt they would need a trip to Cornwall and doubted that it could be accomplished in just one day.

'Well, let me think about it. That poofter kept it well under wraps, didn't he?'

She couldn't believe it. He was almost as homophobic as Brian Stanley.

'Yes, he kept this other life very secret.'

'You think that it was maybe some kind of queer-bashing scenario that went on in his flat?'

'I think it was something a lot more subversive than just—'

Langton interrupted her. 'They do get nasty, you know – handbags at dawn and all that.'

'For God's sake, I have had enough snide crude remarks from Brian Stanley without *you* joining in! If you must know, we are now looking into the possibility of a drug connection.'

'Ah well, watch you don't step on too many toes. If it's drug-related, bring in the Drug Units. Keep them abreast of your investigation and don't forget to take your bucket and spade.'

'You are very witty this evening.'

'Am I?'

'Do I get that you are okaying the trip to Cornwall?'

'Mulling it over. You need to get to grips with tracing the dismembered body. Someone had to cut it up and remove it, and whoever that someone was had to know what they were doing. They had to have gone to that flat well-prepared. There was no sign of a break-in, right?'

'Correct.'

'Right now you have no sign of a suspect – is that also correct?'

'Not exactly. I am still keeping Tina Brooks in the frame. It was a bloodbath in that flat of hers, but I am just not certain of the timeframe. She didn't admit that Alan was missing for two weeks, and even then nobody got onto it at once, so it's possible if she was involved she had a lot of time to clean up. Without a body we don't have a time of death.'

'Can't they give you one from the congealed blood?'

'No. It's a central-heated flat. The blood could have been there for a week or a month. All we have is the date of the last sighting of Alan Rawlins in London; we don't know if that was the last time he was alive. As we now have him leading a double life, he could have gone anywhere.'

'Jigsaw, isn't it?'

'Yes, but I am getting the pieces. It's always more difficult finding the ones in the middle, don't you think?'

'No. Personally, when I last did a jigsaw – when I was around ten – I enjoyed getting the frame like blue sky and the corners sorted, but then I would get impatient. In fact, my mother once caught me using scissors to make a piece fit.'

'Well, I can't cut any on this. It's painstaking, but we are moving.'

She found it strange that she was having this bantering conversation with him. In fact, he seemed loath to get off the phone.

'We should have dinner one night,' he said.

She shook her head. Here it was again, the proposed dinner.

'Yes, we should. Maybe when I get back from Cornwall. Hopefully we'll have more pieces by then.'

'Okay. Keep me updated.'

He hung up. She looked at the receiver in her hand and then dropped it back into place before gathering her things and turning off the office lights. On the way home in her Mini, she couldn't stop yawning. Rather than watch the DVDs or skim through them, she decided to go straight to bed. She set her alarm for 5 a.m. and after a shower she got under the duvet and drew it up to her chin. Then the unexpected happened. She wasn't even thinking about Ken or his death when a black cloud engulfed her. She sobbed, not really understanding where the darkness had come from, and cried his name over and over again.

'Grief has ways of creeping up on you when you least expect it,' Langton had told her. She remembered him saying it – she couldn't recall when, but it meant that he had felt the same way. Anna had been so preoccupied recently with her case that she hardly gave a thought to what she had been through – the murder of her beloved Ken. It was as if he was demanding that she didn't forget, and had reached out and touched a spring that opened her emotions and let them run out of control. She cried herself to sleep.

Chapter Nine

Anna was at Tina Brooks's salon at nine o'clock. She was surprised to see quite a number of customers there already. Tina was expecting her and was acting as the receptionist, rolling her eyes as she said Felicity was late as usual.

'You look busy,' Anna commented.

'Early-bird offers – it's half-price between eight-thirty and ten-thirty, but that doesn't include any beauty treatments, just wash and blowdry. I get the women going into work, as you can see.' She gestured towards the hairdressing section and then turned back to Anna.

'What's this about? I had a sleepless night wondering if it was bad news.'

'I'm sorry, I just called to arrange for us to have a talk. There have been some developments. I also need to take a buccal swab for DNA testing, basically for elimination purposes.'

'Really? Well, do what you have to do.'

Tina was wearing her salon robe, but had obviously had her hair done, and her make-up was flawless. She looked even prettier than before.

'I like your hair,' Anna said, smiling.

'I've had it straightened and had some highlights put through it.'

'Do you have to stay on the desk? Only I'd like to talk to you in private.'

Tina turned and yelled for one of the juniors to look after the desk and then gestured for Anna to follow her through to the staff cubicle.

Anna was surprised how willingly Tina allowed her to take a buccal swab from her mouth. As Anna placed the small saliva stick into a plastic evidence bag, Tina poured herself a cup of coffee. Anna then took out her notebook. She would have preferred a less public place, as the cubicle had no door, and the noise of the salon dryers and music was very intrusive.

'So ... don't keep me in suspense,' Tina said, sitting opposite Anna.

'Well, let me first tell you that we have not as yet discovered the whereabouts of Alan, and we are obviously treating this as a murder because of the evidence discovered in your flat.'

'I don't understand.' Tina leaned forward.

'The blood pooling has not yet been verified as Alan's.'

'What?'

'We are looking into the possibility that it could be someone else's. To prove it is Alan's blood we need his DNA and so far we have been unable to obtain any.'

'I don't believe this. Are you telling me that it wasn't Alan?'

'No, I am saying we have no positive proof that it was him.'

Tina closed her eyes.

'There is a possibility that Alan might have been with someone else and—'

'Another woman, you mean?'

Anna continued to be as diplomatic as possible without revealing that Alan was not the biological son of his parents. She showed Tina the photograph of the surfers, asking if she recognised anyone, and without hesitation Tina identified Alan, but did not know anyone else.

'How often did Alan go to Cornwall? He was a very keen surfer, wasn't he?'

Tina sipped her coffee. She obviously recalled the last time he had been away because she had told Anna about it previously.

'Did he go on a regular basis?'

'I suppose so. Well, not in the winter, but often if I had a hair competition he would go off then.'

'Did you ever accompany him?'

'No. I can't swim.'

'Did you know of any hotel Alan would have stayed in?'

'No, I think he said he stayed with friends.'

'Would it be possible that he also owned or rented a home there?'

'In Cornwall?'

'Yes.'

Tina was nonplussed, saying she doubted it and he had never mentioned it to her.

'But he did go frequently?'

'Yes, I suppose so, but I don't call a few times a year frequent, and like I said it was usually when I was away for competitions.'

'How long would you be away for these competitions?'

Tina said that it would depend. The big ones she'd spend a few days at as they sometimes ran on for that length of time, so she would travel to the venue and book into a hotel.

'So that would be what – five days?'

'Yeah, or maybe less, but I never wanted to stay that long. Liverpool and Birmingham were not that great, but the Blackpool one I'd take Donna with me and we'd have a week out.'

'Could you give me these dates?'

Tina sighed and said it would take a while, but she had a calendar somewhere. She then asked why Anna was so interested in Cornwall and in her hairdressing competitions.

'We are trying to discover how many times Alan was in Cornwall so we can trace his friends there.'

'You think he had a place there, do you?'

'Yes, it is possible, but we are not exactly sure of the location. We found his surfboards and wetsuit at his father's home.'

'Yeah, we didn't have any room and he was obsessive about his boards, wouldn't let them stay in the garage at the flats. He sometimes had a couple more at his work-place. Oh, by the way, can I have my car back?'

'Yes, you can. Tina, you said a "couple more" at the garage where he worked but we only found one there. Do you think he had more?'

'No idea. When can I move back into the flat?' She was beginning to sound very impatient.

'I'll ask the forensic team if they have finished.'

'It's a real inconvenience, this. I've got to stay at Donna's and all my clothes and stuff are still in the flat. Am I allowed to go and get a few more things to wear? I only took a small overnight bag with me to stay at Donna's.'

'Yes, I'll see they allow you to do that. There is some-thing else, Tina, but first I have to ask you this. Did you, after Alan went missing, ever entertain anyone else?'

'What do you mean?'

'We found items in the bed.'

'What?'

'We believe the bedding we took from your flat had been changed due to the fact there was no blood on it.'

'I don't understand.'

'It's probable that the bedlinen was changed after the violence that took place, and I am asking you if you brought anyone to the bedroom and had sex with them.'

'You must be fucking joking! Of course I didn't have someone in bed with me.'

'We found a hair and semen stains, Tina. The hair could be yours, or someone else's.'

Tina was adamant that she had slept alone, that she had never brought anyone back to the flat. Suddenly she pulled some hairs from her head.

'Here, take it, take it and test it! Christ, I feel sick – it makes me feel sick.'

If Tina was guilty of murder she was an exceptional actress, yet Anna was sure she had to know a lot more than she was admitting.

'When we found Alan's surfboards and wetsuit . . .'

Tina got up and helped herself to another coffee.

'We found other items that I need to discuss with you. Did you ever consider that Alan was homosexual?'

Tina turned, surprised. 'What? WHAT?'

'The items were of a very explicit sexual nature. There were DVDs all containing gay sex, and various magazines which had . . . contact ads – you know, and—'

'You are trying to say you think Alan was *gay*?'

'As I said, we have found pornographic literature and DVDs. We have also heard from a couple of witnesses that Alan mixed with a number of homosexual men whilst in Cornwall.'

Tina blinked and shook her head.

'You've got it wrong. There is no way! I would know, believe you me. Being in hairdressing, I'm surrounded by gays and especially at the competitions. Alan was not like one of them, so whoever you are talking to are off their heads.'

'So you and Alan had a heterosexual relationship?'

'You mean did we have sex?'

'Yes.'

'Listen, I've been around – I'm not making myself out to be a slapper, but I've had a few guys in my time – and I am telling you, Alan was straight. We had a good sex-life, even more so when I had got my hands on him. He was very shy and reserved to start with, but like I said I've had my experiences and there was no way I'd stand for a platonic relationship, no way at all.'

'But you mentioned that you thought he might have another woman. Why was that?'

Tina shrugged and fell silent. Anna persisted.

'You said that he might have gone missing and left you for another woman. Why did you think that?'

'Well, it had gone off a bit. I always had to instigate it and he hadn't been that affectionate with me for a few months, so what else was I to think? We were planning on getting married so we were having sex on a regular basis. It was just he wasn't . . . nice to me.'

'Nice?'

'Yeah. He was a bit short and abrupt, like he had something on his mind. I even asked him outright once if there was someone else and he swore to me there wasn't, said he was just tired as he was working hard at the garage.'

'Did you suspect when he said he was working late that he was seeing someone else?'

'Yeah, yeah I did, because like I said he was a bit off with me, and from being very close it worried me.'

'Do you think Alan could have been leading a double life?'

'With someone else?'

'Yes.'

'No, because we were always together. It was just sort of recent and I even wondered if me planning all the wedding invites was getting to him, but he encouraged me and said I should start looking for a wedding gown.'

'Did you ever overhear any unusual phone calls?'

'No.'

'Did you ever see him with anyone else?'

'No. I used to check his mobile – I'm not stupid, I wanted to see if there were any text messages – but he hardly ever used it, and then it was mostly to call me. You've got his phone – you took it, didn't you?'

'Yes. Could he have had another one?'

'I dunno. I doubt it. He was so careful about spending money because we were saving for a flat.'

'You never saw him with another man, maybe?'

'Back on that, are you? Listen to me: Alan was straight. He was a very gentle guy as well – you know, hated to get into a row or any confrontation. That was another reason I thought he might have run off – because he was having cold feet about the wedding.'

'What if I was to tell you we also found that Alan had earned a considerable amount of money from the sale of his reconditioned cars?' Anna said next.

Tina's eyes narrowed.

'We have receipts for the sale of an AC Cobra, a Ferrari and some other very high-end vehicles.'

'How much?'

'It's considerable, and it's possible there could have been a lot more as we only have the details from the receipts we found.'

'How much?' Tina repeated.

'Four hundred and odd thousand.'

'*What?*'

'I know his father helped finance the purchase of the cars . . .'

'Yeah yeah, and Alan paid him back with interest. How much did you say? FOUR HUNDRED THOU-SAND . . . no – no fucking way. I would have known how much he got. How far back are you going with these motors?'

'Five or six years.'

'Then that is crap. He saved his wages – we had a joint bank account – and I am telling you straight up that Alan never made that kind of money. If you want to know why *I* kept the accounts, it was so I always knew what he was spending.'

'Did you know he used his bedroom at his family home as an office?'

'He was living with *me*. He only stayed over there a few times because his mother was ill.'

'Nevertheless, that is where we found out about the money and that he had a possible double life.'

Tina hurled her coffee mug against the wall. It shattered and sprayed coffee over the floor and the sink unit.

'I don't know what you are trying to do to me – get me so riled up I'll admit I killed him? If that's your plan, it's not gonna work. Now you get out of here.'

Anna stood up and wiped a coffee spill from her shoulder.

'I am just telling you the truth, Tina.'

'I DON'T WANT TO HEAR ANY MORE!'

Tina pushed Anna and looked as if she would punch her. Her face was taut with rage and her fists were clenched.

'I loved him. I think you are just a sick woman. If he was murdered, then you should be finding out who did it, not trying to get me upset. I never did it – now you just get out, go on, get out and leave me alone.'

Anna bent to pick up her briefcase and acted swiftly as she saw Tina moving towards her before letting fly with a punch. Anna used her briefcase to take the blow and it almost knocked her off her feet. It was at this moment that Donna and Felicity hurried in to see what all the noise was about.

'Get that bitch out. GET HER OUT OF HERE!' Tina screamed.

As Anna passed between the two women, Tina fell to her knees sobbing, with Donna trying to comfort her.

'Have they found him?' Felicity asked nervously.

'No. Excuse me.' Anna left hurriedly. She had considered arresting Tina for assault, but thought better of it as she had caused the aggressive reaction.

By the time Anna got into her car she had calmed down. The interaction with Tina had not given any further insight into Alan Rawlins's double life. What it had done, however, was show just how vicious Tina could become, and also how strong she was. There was even a dent left in Anna's briefcase to prove it.

Anna drove straight to Liz's lab over at Lambeth and deposited the buccal swab for her to test on the one hair discovered in the bed. She also left a note saying it was very urgent she get a response as soon as possible.

*

Brian Stanley had a stiff neck from holding the phone beneath his chin as he made call after call to check out the circled adverts in the magazines. He had made twenty with no result, but eventually made contact with a Tony Ardigo who had run an advert asking for *studious partners and healthy physical guys with interest in sport and exercise.*

Brian asked him if he would be prepared to assist their enquiry as they believed a man who had answered the advert was missing. Mr Ardigo admitted that he had met someone fitting the description of Alan Rawlins, but he was called something else. They had only met the once and it was not a satisfactory occasion. Mr Ardigo did, however, agree to come into the station.

Brian replaced the receiver and looked over to Helen.

'I got a hit. Guy said he'll come in and talk to us. We might have the other name our victim was using.'

'Was it Daniel Matthews?'

'Yeah. You got the same?'

'Yes, twice, but they refused to come in. They each reported one meeting only that didn't work out.'

Brian crossed to the incident board.

'Hang on, hang on . . . Daniel Matthews, Dan . . . we've got a Daniel Matthews up here who was interviewed by Travis. His name was in Alan Rawlins's address book – an old schoolfriend.'

Helen joined him. 'Well, he was also gay – right?' she said. 'Maybe the magazines belonged to him?'

'One way to find out. Let's call him.'

'Hold it,' Paul said to them from his desk. 'I've got a hit as well. Same scenario but the guy was not called Alan Rawlins – he said his name was Julian Vickers.'

Paul came over and they all looked at the name of the other old friend of Alan's who ran the deli.

'What do you think he was doing, just throwing up the names of his pals, or are they all shirt-lifters?'

Paul ignored Brian's remark. Instead, he walked back to his desk, saying over his shoulder, 'He was just using their names, Brian, and it looks like they were all one-night stands. If the magazines were in Rawlins's house and all the adverts had been ringed by him, *he* was using them.'

Helen sighed and returned to her desk. 'We'll have to check it out with them.'

'I'm getting a stiff neck,' Brian complained, but he too went back to his desk to start making the calls.

Anna had arrived outside the Rawlinses' house when Paul called her with the update on the personal ads. She listened, weighing up the information, and told him that she too felt that Alan Rawlins was just using his friends' names. She would, however, be interested to sit in on the interview with Mr Ardigo to learn how Alan Rawlins behaved. She was certain that Alan used a different name as well when he was in Cornwall, and asked Paul to switch to trying to find out where he stayed. If Alan Rawlins was a keen and capable surfer he would probably have stayed in or around Newquay, as it was the home of British surfing.

Anna also suggested they get back to the car-wash surfer Sal and ask him for some help regarding the possible locations. Better still would be if they asked him to come into the station. She also wanted Paul to contact Joe Smedley, the head mechanic at Metcalf Auto, to ask about holidays taken by Alan Rawlins. At least if they had dates when he might have been in Cornwall, it would narrow down their search.

*

Anna had to wait a while before Edward Rawlins answered the door. He was wearing an old cardigan with a collarless shirt, creased cord trousers and carpet slippers.

'Have you any news?' he asked immediately.

'No, but we need to talk.'

He nodded and opened the door wider for her to follow him inside. Anna didn't waste time with pleasantries; instead, she got straight to the point.

'Mr Rawlins, I believe you went into Alan's room before you gave me access to it. I also believe that you removed—'

'I did.'

'You did what, sir?'

'I threw them out. They were disgusting.'

'I know what you found and we didn't need your permission to remove a black bin liner filled with gay pornography magazines, along with some very explicit homosexual DVDs.'

'Yes, I admit it.'

'Were you aware that your son was homosexual?'

'Of course not.'

'Was he?'

'Apparently. Why otherwise have those revolting things locked in a drawer?'

'What else did you find, Mr Rawlins?'

'That was enough.'

'What about bank statements, even cash?'

'I didn't find anything else.'

Anna sighed and then approached the subject of the amount of money from the sale of the reconditioned cars.

'Alan gave me back my initial loan with interest, nothing more. I had no idea of exactly how much he was making when he sold the vehicles.'

'But you must be aware now. You must have looked through his financial papers?'

'I didn't have the time.'

'So you are saying you were unaware of the amount Alan must have made?'

'That was his business, his sideline, not mine. Whatever he did with the money was entirely up to him.'

'But it is a considerable amount, isn't it? And I have found no tax returns detailing this money that I think came from cash transactions.'

'I have nothing to say. Whether or not he spent the money or banked it, he never mentioned anything to me.'

'We are now of the belief that Alan led a double life, possibly owning property in Cornwall. He might also have used a different name.'

'I have no idea where he stayed. All I know is he went surfing there frequently during the summer. Whether or not he used his own name or someone else's I'm unable to say.'

'You have decided to put your wife Kathleen into a care home?'

'Yes, that is correct.'

'But when I previously talked to you, you were concerned about the expense. Has that now changed?'

'Let us say *I* have. It is a decision that I have made.'

'What about the finances?'

'I have some savings, and I really don't think this is any of your business.'

'It is, if you found a substantial amount of cash hidden in your son's room.'

'I did not. I also own this house outright so that is how I will fund my wife's nursing-home expenses.'

He was very tense, sitting on the edge of a chair, his face pinched and angry. He suddenly stood up.

'I don't wish to talk to you any more. I have given you every assistance in tracing my son. I am still desperate to know if he is dead or alive.'

'We are endeavouring to do everything possible to find out the truth, Mr Rawlins.'

'The truth?' he snapped and had to dig his hands into his pockets as they were shaking so much.

'Let me tell you what the truth has so far done to me. I discover that my wife of thirty-five years lied to me, kept secrets from me about my son. The truth is, he is not my child. The boy I doted on and was so proud of has either been murdered or has been involved in some terrible crime. His secrets are as heartbreaking as my wife's.'

Anna stood up. She was almost the same height as he was. The dapper little man for whom she had felt such compassion appeared to be changing in front of her. His anger was such that he was having difficulty containing it and his voice was strangled in his throat.

'I want it to be *my* time now. I hate her, and her son disgusts me – that's what the truth has done to me, Detective Travis! I hope you never find him because I don't want to ever see him again. And now I would like you to leave.'

Anna nodded and went to the door. She hesitated.

'You know, whatever your son's sexual preference was or is, it's not a crime, and perhaps he only wished to keep it secret from you because he didn't want you to—'

Edward Rawlins interrupted her. 'Please don't talk down to me, don't interpret what I should or shouldn't feel about what I have discovered. I loved him. He was the light of my life, but it was all lies.' Tears trickled down his cheeks.

'Maybe the lies were all to protect you, Mr Rawlins.'

It was awful as he couldn't stop himself from crying.

Taking out a handkerchief he wiped his face, but the tears kept flowing. Anna walked out and he followed her, blowing his nose.

'Is that you, Alan?' came a shrill voice from upstairs.

Mr Rawlins ignored his wife as he opened the front door.

'She doted on him. I used to find it hard sometimes. When he was young it was as if he had taken over her life. She had so little time for me. It was always the two of them giggling and laughing together like two children, and it wasn't until he became a teenager that he really ever turned to me. She used to get so jealous. If we went to a cricket match together she acted as if I was trying to take him away from her. I suppose in retrospect I should have known.'

'Thank you for seeing me, Mr Rawlins.'

'Secrets ... secrets,' he hissed as he closed the door behind her.

Anna suspected that Mr Rawlins had found the cash, but it would be hard to prove. She was glad to be away from the pain-wracked angry little man as she headed back to the station. It had not been a successful morning.

Chapter Ten

No sooner had Anna taken off her coat in her office than she was called to say that Mr Anthony Ardigo was waiting in reception.

'It's the bloke that put in the advert,' Paul reminded her. Anna told him to take Ardigo into an interview room and she'd be there in a moment. She didn't waste time. Passing through the incident room she gave Brian a brief outline of the meetings with both Tina and Mr Rawlins. They had not been productive.

'Well, I'm getting into all these hotels and surfing beaches in Cornwall. I've run God knows how many checks, but so far there's no connection with Rawlins. As we now know that he used his friends' names, I'm trying those as well.'

'Did you get anything from Joe Smedley regarding Rawlins's holiday times?'

Helen looked over from her desk. 'I'm on that, and we've got a list from two years back so we're using the dates as we contact letting agencies . . .'

'Good, good – keep at it. Also, check with Smedley how many surfboards Alan kept at his place of work, and call Liz at the forensic lab to see if she has a result on the buccal swab I took in earlier.'

Anna headed for the interview rooms down on the floor below. Reaching the first one she paused as she heard Paul laughing. Looking through the window in the door she could see Paul leaning on the table chatting to a dark-haired, handsome Italian-looking man. She walked in and Paul immediately straightened up and introduced her to Ardigo. The latter shook her hand as she thanked him for coming in to see them.

'You look Italian,' she remarked.

'On my father's side, my mother is English. I've been brought up here.'

She sat down. 'Has Detective Simms told you the reason we wished to talk to you?'

'Yes. It's about the contact ad in a magazine, but I've told him it was a good while ago, at least ten months.'

'You were contacted from the advert by—'

Ardigo interrupted her. He seemed very eager to talk. 'He called himself Dan Matthews, but when he was described to me, I am sure it was this person called Alan Rawlins.'

'You describe him to me,' she asked, taking out her notebook.

'He was tall, six feet or over, blonde, very blue pene-trating eyes, and was physically in great shape. He was also suntanned, and I was asked by Detective Simms if he ever mentioned surfing to me, which he did.'

'If I recall, the advert asked—'

Again she was interrupted. 'I like athletic types because I'm a fanatical skier. I work for a dry-ski company as an instructor.'

'Tell me about this person you think was Alan Rawlins.'

'Well, he contacted me; I gave him my mobile number, not my home phone. We arranged to meet in a wine bar in Soho, and we had a few drinks.'

'Was he a drinker?'

'No, he just had a Coke, I think, but we chatted about this and that and he asked me what I did for a living, sort of sizing me up. After a while, because we really got along, I suggested he come back to my place. He agreed and we got a taxi.'

Anna glanced at Paul, asking if they had the address and contact numbers and he nodded.

'Please go on, Mr Ardigo.'

'I found him very attractive. He was quiet – shy, almost – and I think I had another couple of drinks, but he just asked for water. The next minute, he started to strip off. I said something like we should maybe get to know each other a bit more, but he said that we both knew what we met up for, or words to that effect, and . . .'

'And?'

'I said to him that I was really interested in forming a relationship with someone, and that I wasn't into casual sex. I know I put the advert in, but it was the first time I'd done it and I wasn't sure how it worked. But he said that wasn't what he was interested in – he didn't want a relationship. Then he asked if I wanted money.'

Ardigo reached for a bottle of water and unscrewed the cap.

'I certainly wasn't in it for money! It felt as though he thought I was some kind of rent boy. It really rattled me, and I told him again that I felt it was more important for me to get to know him. He then gripped my face in his hand and kissed me. It was a hard kiss and I tried to push him off, but he wouldn't let go of me.'

He drank some water and sat staring down at the tabletop.

'I let him do what he wanted. I just went along with it

because he scared me. He was like a different person from the one in the bar. To be honest, I think he would have really hurt me if I'd tried to stop him.'

Anna glanced at Paul and then looked back to Ardigo.

'Did he rape you?'

'No, it wasn't exactly rape. When he'd finished, he walked back into the room where he'd taken his clothes off.'

'Wait a moment . . . you had sex with him in your bed-room?'

'Yes. Then like I said, he just walked out. I think he went into my bathroom, but I stayed in the bed, and then he left. I waited God knows how long before I got up and went into my sitting room. He'd left a fifty-pound note on my coffee table.'

'We really appreciate you agreeing to see us, Mr Ardigo, and I am sure it must be very difficult for you,' Anna reassured him.

'As soon as I got the phone call, it made me angry all over again. You know, the way he had treated me – I just wanted it on record. It taught me a hard lesson, and as it turned out, it was actually a positive thing because I was pretty shaken up the next day. One of the guys I work with could see I was anxious and I blurted it all out to him, and he admitted that he was gay so we're now together.'

'That's good. When you say you were anxious . . .'

'Bit more than that. I had a lot of bruises and had to wear a scarf round my neck.'

'Bruises around your *neck*?' Paul asked.

'Yeah, from when he almost strangled me. That's another reason why I wanted to come in; the next guy could get killed.'

After thanking Mr Ardigo for giving his statement, Anna asked Paul to show him down to the reception then come to see her in her office.

As Anna passed through the incident room she asked Brian to see if Sal, the owner of the car wash, would agree to an interview.

'I've called a couple of times already – he's not around,' Brian said.

'I want him to give us more details of the surfing beaches and locations.'

'I'll keep on trying.'

'Thank you.'

Anna sat behind her desk mulling over the interview with Anthony Ardigo. Yet again they had another insight into Alan Rawlins and it wasn't a pleasant one. Paul tapped on her door and walked in.

'That was interesting,' he said.

'Yes. What were you two laughing about before I came into the room?'

'He was telling me how hard it had been for him to come out . . . Italian father, very macho guy . . . and I said that I could understand.'

'I see. So you told him that you were homosexual?'

'Yeah. It was good because it opened him up – in the literal sense.' Paul laughed.

'Mind if I give you some advice?' Anna said icily. 'Your sexual preferences are your business. If you find it necessary to make sure it is out in the open, that again is your business, but you should retain a separation from your private life as a detective. I am not asking you to do anything other than maintain a professional distance. I don't think it's advisable to elaborate on your private predilections when interviewing a possible suspect.'

'But he wasn't a suspect, for chrissakes, and he was very nervous.'

'Put him at his ease – that's your job, to get a result. And let me tell you, Paul, everyone we interview could be a suspect until we clear them of suspicion.'

'Okay, I'm sorry.'

'What I don't want is the "gay" detective slur against you because you are very competent and a good officer – that's what should be relevant. That's all. You can go.'

Paul sheepishly walked out. She didn't actually know anything about Paul's private life, whether he lived with a partner or not, and she didn't particularly want to know. All that mattered to her was that he was a valuable member of her team.

Meanwhile the team had worked hard on piecing together the date byline. The information was listed on the board. The holiday periods Rawlins had whilst working with Joe Smedley at the garage were matched with the dates that Tina had given for her hairdressing competitions. Helen had contacted the salon to ask for the details as Tina had not given them to Anna. Donna told her that Tina was out making a call, but she could give the dates, since she had been with Tina on some of them and knew exactly how long they would have been away. It varied from two days to five.

Anna was certain that Alan Rawlins was able to lead a double life because there were so many days when Tina had been away from their flat. His holidays from the garage were always in the summertime. Joe Smedley had said Alan would take no time off for Bank Holidays or over the Christmas period, but liked to have as much time as possible clumped together for his summer sojourns. It had taken considerable effort going through the records and calculating that June, July, and often August were the times Alan Rawlins was absent.

Late that afternoon Silas Douglas had returned Brian's calls and agreed to come into the station the following morning. It had been a frustrating day as more and more information was collected. The team were still very keen to get the results from the Tech Support unit about the hard drive taken from Rawlins's computer. Tech Support were dragging their heels and so Anna got onto them and tore a strip off their Head of Department, pointing out it was imperative they get the information as soon as possible; their excuse that they had a backlog of work didn't wash with her. She angrily insisted that as this was a murder enquiry they should put her at the top of their list.

Langton called just as she was about to leave for the day. She gave him a brief rundown of the developments and he thankfully listened without interruption. He seemed distant, almost abrupt as he finished the call, saying he had someone waiting on his other line. She left the station shortly after, while both Paul and Brian were still working as the jigsaw grew.

Langton drove into the station just after 7 p.m. and went straight up to the incident room. He'd missed Anna, but Brian Stanley was still there. He was about to leave, but Langton asked him to stay behind as he wanted him to talk him through the investigation to date. It was not that unusual. He was, after all, the Chief Superintendent overseeing the entire Murder Squad. He made Brian feel slightly nervous as he fired off question after question and constantly made notes while muttering to himself.

'How has the search gone trying to find the body?'

'We've had a team looking into it, but we've no trace.'

'And no positive identification of the victim?'

'Correct.'

'This woman, Tina – has she moved back into her flat?'

'I believe it's on the cards. The scientists are out of there and the SOCOs have completed their work as well. I know she asked the Gov if she could go and collect more clothes.'

Langton paused by the forensic reports from Liz Hawley. 'Do we know if they could get a toxicology result from the blood pooling beside the bed?'

'No. The lab said it would be unreliable as bleach was used to try and clean it up, and they couldn't even tell us how long it had been there,' Brian informed him.

'Mmm ... It's been about eight to nine weeks, right – from the time Alan was last seen.'

'Yes, but we don't know whose blood it is.'

Langton looked at the photographs taken from the Luminol tests. He tapped the pictures.

'Fucking bloodbath in there and you've no body parts turning up?'

'No, sir.'

'If Tina Brooks is to be believed, then whoever did the murder had less than a day to clean up. If she's lying, and she was part of it, then she and any accomplice, had at least two weeks to get rid of the evidence.'

'Yes, sir.'

'No witness saw anything suspicious?'

'No. We've questioned all the residents and the near neighbours.'

'This Tina woman's car was clean, right?'

'Yes, sir. She's requested it to be returned.'

'What tests have been done with the semen stains and the hair found in the bed?'

'Still ongoing with the hair, but the semen isn't a match.'

'What – the semen DNA doesn't match the blood DNA?'

'Correct.'

'So someone else, another male, slept in the same bed as the victim.'

'Right. Our problem is that we don't have a positive DNA profile for Alan Rawlins so we have been unable to ascertain if the blood was his or if the items from the clean bedlinen were his.'

'Which would mean either Rawlins was the victim or he killed someone and then did a runner?'

'That's what we are considering.'

Langton sighed and moved along the board, looking at the details written up about the gay DVDs and pornographic magazines. He shook his head and moved on to the latest entries.

'So we suspect that Alan Rawlins led a double life. He used his friends' names when answering sex adverts, and this guy Ardigo came in and admitted that he'd almost been strangled?'

'Yes. We got that result today.'

Langton snapped his notebook closed, saying, 'Fucking Tech Support need a firecracker up their arse.'

'I think the boss gave them one.'

Langton laughed. 'I hope she did, because this is looking like a cold case if it goes on any longer. No movement in the joint bank accounts, but if he had access to all this cash he could be anywhere by now.'

'We're hoping to get a result from Cornwall and to trace his whereabouts from there.'

'You're hoping. Jesus Christ, I'll get on to the people there, and this Sammy Marsh – he's got a record, right? Anyone asked if they have *his* DNA on the database?'

'I think so. We're waiting for Liz Hawley to get back to us.'

Langton stared at Brian with a cold glint in his eye and snapped that it was not their job to think, but to get facts. He then walked out leaving Brian, already tired from a long day of making call after call, to go to his desk and leave himself a memo to double-check Sammy Marsh's record in the morning.

The following day when Anna drove into the station, Brian was just parking his car, and so they walked in together. She stopped abruptly when he said he'd not left until late the previous evening due to Langton's unscheduled visit.

'He came here?' she asked.

'Yeah. Bad-tempered cuss, isn't he? He went over every inch of the board. Said we had to concentrate on Sammy Marsh. I told him that Marsh is missing or on the run. Anyway, he wants us to run a check to see if there was a DNA sample taken after Marsh's arrest.'

Anna spent the morning, a working lunch and most of the afternoon checking over the case-files, all the statements taken and information they had so far received during the investigation. She wrote down copious notes as she went through the mounting paperwork, raising actions where necessary for the team to complete. The initial Misper investigation into the disappearance of Alan Rawlins had, somewhat understandably, been poor as he was not considered a serious or high-priority case. Indeed, she herself had at first thought he had gone walkabout of his own accord, but now had to make sure that every piece of information and possible lead was thoroughly scrutinised and followed up.

By late afternoon, Anna was still thinking about Langton. Why had he come in to oversee the board when she had spoken to him last thing yesterday and had spent a long time giving him all the details already? It felt as if he was sitting on her shoulder, and she didn't like it; it made her feel inadequate.

Her thoughts were interrupted by the roar of a Harley arriving in the station car park. She looked from the window as Silas Douglas locked up his bike. Anna called out to Paul to go to reception to meet him and take him into an interview room.

Silas was wearing biker's leathers with a lot of fringe and he carried his black helmet under his arm. He was even bigger than Paul remembered and towered above him. Added to the creaking of his leathers was the thud of his studded boots as they headed down the corridor.

'Do you want a coffee?' Paul asked.

'No thanks, but a bottle of water would be good.'

He unwound a white neckerchief that he had used to draw over his mouth and sat with his legs apart undoing his fringed jacket. He had a cotton navy-blue scarf with skeleton heads tied round his head in gypsy fashion. His pigtail was tucked into the jacket.

'Will this take long,' he asked, 'only I'm planning to go to the Isle of Man for a drag race.'

Anna arrived and introduced herself and Silas rose to his feet, head and shoulders above her, putting out his hand to shake hers.

'Thank you for coming in,' she said, sitting down opposite him.

'The bloke who phoned me asked me to draw up a list
of the best surfing beaches. He could have got them off
the internet, but what I've done is sort of earmark the top
slots for experienced surfers and middle-of-the-road types.'

Sal Douglas dug into a pocket and took out a printed
sheet of paper.

'Now the top surfers would usually hit the north
beaches, as tides are stronger there. Amateurs go for the
more sheltered ones. Top of the list has to be Newquay
Bay. It's got three big sandy beaches – bit overcrowded in
the summer, of course – but it's the most famous beach in
the UK for surfers. All the competitions are held there.
Then there's Crantock Bay and Holywell where the surf's
best at low tide.'

Douglas concluded his descriptions of the surfing
beaches by looking at Anna, and saying with a grin, 'This
guy that's missing – he could be anywhere between Land's
End or East Devon if he's serious.'

'Did you make a customised board for him?'

'It's hard to say. I've been doing this for years, so Christ
knows how many boards I've sold. I've got a small stake in
a shop in Newquay Esplanade and I supply them as well.
I also sell direct on the beaches from the back of a van.'

Anna placed down the photograph taken of the boards
found in Alan Rawlins's parents' home.

'Take a look at this . . . it might jog your memory.'

Silas picked it up in his huge hands.

'Well, right off I can tell you that this is not what I'd call
top of the range. This is more an intermediate's board.
I was shown another photo and that was one of my old
hire boards.'

Anna placed down the photograph of Alan Rawlins carrying a board. 'This?'

'Yeah, that's the one, but as I said before, I couldn't tell you anything about the bloke holding it. I don't ever recall making a customised board for him. He could have bought a second-hand one off me, but I'm not the only board-dealer out there making money. Kids who buy my intermediate or beginners' boards eventually sell them on, plus the hire ones get nicked if people don't keep an eye on them when they're off the water. The surfers come from all over the world to Cornwall.'

'He drove a silver sports car, drophead ...'

Silas puffed out his cheeks. 'Again, these guys all have sports cars. You know, it's a big seasonal thing, guys in their hundreds pulling the chicks, driving around in their flash motors. It's part-surfing, part-sexual conquests.' He laughed.

'This man is homosexual.'

Silas shrugged. 'We get all sorts and true, there is a clique of the gay dudes. They tend to stick together, but I personally don't have any time for them. To me, it's a God-given shame. Great bodies and the women drooling, and they bat for the other side.'

'What can you tell me about the Smugglers café.'

'Not much more than I already have. It comes and goes in popularity. One season it's not the place to be seen at, next it's thriving. It's cheap. They do hamburgers and chips and it jumps a bit at night, but the cops have been coming down on them for building fires on the beaches. Can't hear yourself talk in there; the music is throbbing out, which also gets complaints.'

'You knew Sammy Marsh?'

'The photographer, yeah everybody knows him. He took that picture I gave Detective Simms and the lady officer.'

'You told them that he did a moonlight flit to Florida. Do you know why?'

'Not really no, but I'll be straight with you, Sammy was a bit of a ducker and diver, regular Mr Tambourine man, moving from beach to beach knocking out good weed. He'd sort of cornered the market as everyone does a joint down there, kind of goes with the sport and I used to buy off him as well.'

Sal smiled and shrugged his massive shoulders.

'He used to have this big Rasta looking out for him. Sometimes it could get a bit hairy and Sammy didn't like competition, I know that.'

'How do you mean?'

'Well, I don't know all the facts, but some kids were all sharing a farmhouse, a good way out from Newquay, and they were growing their own cannabis plants. Had several greenhouses – lights – the lot. They were underselling Sammy and he didn't like it. He got unpleasant, warned them off, and in the end I think they started working for him. I dunno . . .'

'Was he violent?'

'Sammy?'

'Yes.'

Silas gestured with his hand to about his shoulder level sitting down. 'He was only this big. Like I said, this Jamaican dude, Errol, was his heavy arm, but he also had a few other bodyguards.'

Paul produced Errol Dante's mugshot. 'Was one of them this man?'

Silas looked and nodded. 'Yeah that's Errol, but I haven't seen him for a while and nor have I seen Sammy since he went to Florida. I'm only there come the summer months.'

There appeared to be little else that Silas could help

them with and so he was thanked for coming in and left the station.

Anna watched from her office window as Silas, 'call me Sal', replaced his helmet, having drawn up the white scarf to cover his mouth. He fired up his Harley and almost collided with Langton, driving his beat-up old Rover. She was glad she had seen him as it gave her a few moments to gather her thoughts on how she would approach the fact that he'd been 'busy' the night before. She expected him to come in to see her straight away, but when he didn't she eased up the blinds of the window looking into the incident room. He was standing beside Paul, who was writing up on the board the information from Silas Douglas. Quickly flicking the blind closed as Langton turned towards her, she hurried to sit at her desk.

He did sort of knock, but it was only a tap and the door opened as he strode in.

'You free for an early dinner tonight?'

Taken by surprise, she blinked and then nodded.

'Good. There's a small Italian round the corner, we can walk to it. Say in ten minutes?'

'Fine. Do I see you there or ...?'

'No, we'll walk over there together. I just want to catch up on a couple of things.'

'I would have thought you caught up enough last night.'

He hesitated, swinging the door open. No matter how long she had known him, he could still make her hairs stand up on end when he gave her that cold, arrogant look.

'Just doing my job, sweetheart. Ten minutes.'

He closed the door and she could have kicked herself for bringing it up. She had always hated it when he called her 'sweetheart' – now even more so. She also reckoned that the promise of a dinner between them wasn't what he intended by this evening's date. Instinct told her he was going to use it for another reason.

As Anna made her way to the ladies cloakroom to comb her hair and freshen up, Langton was in deep conversation with Brian Stanley in the incident room. Exactly ten minutes later, he was waiting for Anna in the corridor.

'Let's go,' he said briskly.

'Do you mind if I just tell the team I'm off?'

'Already told them.' He took her elbow and guided her out. It didn't feel right. It felt as if he was pushing her.

They hardly spoke during the short walk to the restaurant and he no longer held her arm, but walked quickly. As always she had to speed up to keep up with him.

Sole Mio was a small restaurant furnished with checked tablecloths and candles stuck into wine bottles. The owner greeted Langton like an old friend and asked if he'd like his usual table. As it was virtually empty being so early, they had a choice, but Langton went to a small booth at the side and eased himself in, leaving Anna to sit opposite. He picked up the menu, glanced at it briefly and suggested that she have the house special.

Anna hid herself behind the menu. She was feeling very nervous and unable to read. Langton took out his reading glasses to look over the wine list.

'I'll have the sea-food spaghetti,' she told Langton as he signalled for the waiter. He ordered the food, asked for a bottle of Chianti and then removed his glasses, tucking them into his pocket. He then spread out his cutlery, leaving a larger space in front of him.

'Anna,' he said quietly.

She glanced up and gave a shaky smile.

'How you doing?'

'Fine, thank you.'

'Remember I once told you that I'd worked with your father? I'm going back quite a long time now – fifteen years or more ... Anyway, I got my first murder enquiry as a DCI. Jack wasn't on the case with me, but I'd just been working alongside him learning the ropes so to speak.'

He paused as the waiter showed them the bottle of wine and then uncorked it and poured a drop for Langton to taste. He swirled it around the glass and then drank it.

'Lovely, thank you. Just leave the bottle on the table.'

The waiter poured a glass for each of them and did as requested.

'The case was a murder enquiry, obviously. The victim was a twenty-two-year-old waitress – a single mother with a little girl aged three. She was found in an alleyway not far from where she worked; her throat had been cut and she was almost decapitated. She was or had been a very pretty woman, but the unusual thing about the case was, she had not been raped and her handbag, with her wages in, was still beneath her body. So robbery was not the motive and we could find no one who had a bad word to say against her. The first suspect we looked at was her ex-boyfriend. He was a pleasant enough guy and—'

Anna interrupted. 'Why are you telling me this?'

'Just listen, will you?'

He sat back as his starter was brought to the table, a shrimp salad.

'Did you order a starter?' he asked Anna.

'No, just the sea-food pasta.'

'Do you want that brought now, or will you wait until my main course is here?'

'I'll wait.' She took some bread and buttered it, watching as he ate at his usual fast pace, jabbing at the salad with his fork.

'Okay, where was I . . . the boyfriend was not the father of her little girl, so I traced him, a Spanish waiter, and I discovered that he had quite a history of petty crime. He'd also legged it to Marbella so I went over there and questioned him, and he gave me three or four names of men he knew my victim had been seeing. I came back and I tracked down all four of them, questioned each one, and they gave me two more names. Seemed my innocent little single mother had quite a sexual appetite.' He took some bread and wiped around the salad bowl, then picked up his wine glass and sipped before placing it carefully down beside his plate.

'I schlepped from one end of the country to the other. Was into the case four weeks when the parents admitted they had kicked her out when they discovered she was pregnant. I had a slew of ex-boyfriends, plus women who had known the victim, but what I was still trying to uncover was a motive. Who, out of all these people I'd interviewed, would have sliced her throat and left her dying in this back alley? I checked into her bank accounts, all the boyfriends' bank accounts; she had a pittance of a savings, so after another two weeks the case was getting cold. I had nothing.'

Langton stopped speaking as his starter plate was removed and he began to twist his napkin.

'I was having a drink and Jack Travis came into the bar. He asked how it was all going. This was my first solo DCI case, right, and I wanted to make an impression. I said to him, "I've fucking turned over every possible stone and got zilch."'

Their main courses arrived so he remained silent until the waiter had left, pouring more wine for himself and topping up Anna's glass. She waited, toying with her pasta. Langton had a Saltimbocca alla Romana with vegetables and again ate hungrily before he continued.

'Your dad listened. I'd had a few beers and then he asked if I minded if he gave me some advice.'

Langton held up his hand and pointed his index finger.

'He said that one – in a murder enquiry, always look close to home. Someone had hated my victim enough to slash her throat – not to take her money, not to rape her – but just slash her and walk away.'

He ate another mouthful and then held up his hand again.

'Two – the motive was hatred. It wasn't robbery, it wasn't sexual. It had to be someone who knew her, knew what time she left her job, knew she walked up that alley as a short-cut to the bus stop.'

He ate more, chewing his meat, and gestured towards her plate as she'd hardly touched a morsel.

'Is that all right?'

'It's fine.' She took a mouthful, but the food felt greasy and she could hardly swallow. Langton repeating her father's words had made her feel very emotional.

'Three – by looking at the kill, it had to be someone close to her. She had no defence wounds, no struggle, no blood or skin under her fingernails, which meant she faced her killer and wasn't afraid of him.'

Again he paused to eat. Anna just moved her pasta around the plate.

'Four – he said I should return to anyone close, partic-ularly the ex-boyfriend. Next day I brought him in again and after two hours of interrogation he gave it up. He admitted to the murder. He said she had kicked him out. By this time he had grown to love her little girl and wanted to marry her, but she had rejected him.'

Langton drained his glass. He then stared hard at Anna, wiping his lips with his napkin and tossing it down.

'You want to know why I am telling you all this?'

She nodded, pushing her food aside.

'Anna, you are bringing in how many fucking links and suspects? You've got a board that looks like the train timetable at Euston station, with links and arrows and possible connections. You've got homosexual contacts from magazines; you've got a whole slew of suspects connected to drugs in Cornwall. You keep opening up avenues of probable suspicions when what you have is a bloodbath at that flat Alan Rawlins lived in. You've got no body, you've got evidence that another male slept in that same bed where you believe the murder took place, a victim you have yet to even bloody identify.'

'I am aware of that,' she said stiffly.

'You can't keep chasing all these probable connections. You have to get to grips with this Tina Brooks woman. She's lived with him, but she only admitted he was missing after his father reported it. She could have disposed of the body with help maybe, so I'll give you that, but the whole reason I am talking to you is because I think you have started to open up a can of worms that may wriggle and look suspicious, but you haven't hit close to home. It doesn't matter if Alan Rawlins led a double life, that he was homosexual with a nasty streak to him. The basic facts are that someone was brutally murdered in that flat. Tina has to be your prime suspect and all this surfing stuff, this drug dealer Sammy Marsh, is making the enquiry look like a trainwreck.'

'I don't know if it was Alan Rawlins who was murdered in that flat.'

'But *she* must bloody know what went on – she lived there! I don't want to make you lose confidence, but what I do want you to do is put the pressure on Tina Brooks. Going off to Cornwall is *not* going to bring in a result, Anna. So what if Alan surfed with a gay troupe of guys? So what if he led this other life? The basic facts are it is very probable he was murdered inside his own flat, his body dismembered and then dumped. The answer is close to home, Anna, believe me. I want you to think like your dad, think how he guided me, because right now I am sorry to say it, but you have let this case run right off the rails.'

She had to cough to clear her throat. It felt terribly constricted.

'How long have I got?'

He sighed, rubbing his face tiredly.

'Listen, I am not about to pull the enquiry. All I'm asking you to do is to focus on the basic facts. Remember, I am telling you this because I did the exact same thing and it was Jack, your father, who pointed me in the right direction.'

Anna sipped her wine. He went to top up her glass again, but she shook her head.

'No, thank you.' She chose her next words very carefully. 'I would like to discuss this with you tomorrow.'

'Why not now?'

'Because I need to digest everything you've said to me, then I'd like to talk it over with you.'

She got up and he gestured to the ladies cloakroom, thinking she wished to use it, but she picked up her bag.

'I'm leaving now. If it's preferable I will come to your office, or shall we say nine o'clock here at the station?'

'I'll come to you.'

'Thank you, and thank you for dinner.'

Langton watched her walking out, unsure if he should go after her or not. Her expression had been unreadable even for him. He didn't think he had been too hard on her, on the contrary. He would, if it had been anyone else, have expressed his concerns over the way the case was being handled in front of the entire team. He would also have replaced her with another DCI. Maybe she should learn the hard way. Instead he had taken her out for dinner and tried to be as diplomatic as possible. He truthfully felt her murder enquiry was a mess of over-investigation, wasting valuable time.

He signalled for the waiter to remove their plates and then ordered a double brandy, deciding that in the morning he would call a briefing. Anna must by now be aware of his misgivings and realise that it could not continue.

'Was there something wrong with the sea-food pasta, sir?' the waiter asked.

Langton shook his head as his brandy was placed in front of him.

'No. She just wasn't hungry.'

Anna went straight back to her office and spent a long time on her computer looking over the file of the old case that Langton had referred to. Eventually she'd had enough and left for home. She had fought to keep control of her emotions, refusing to allow Langton to see how deeply his criticism had affected her. But by the time she'd returned to her flat and was getting into bed, the flood-gates opened; she couldn't stop crying. She felt that by using her father as part of his review of her work, Langton had betrayed her.

Sleep didn't come easily as she finally calmed down enough to digest everything Langton had spoken about. Intuitively she knew that the meeting with him in the morning would be make or break time, but somehow the old fighting instincts she used to have lay dormant. She had never felt so alone and so lacking in self-confidence.

Chapter Eleven

Anna was up and blowdrying her hair at six. She chose her wardrobe carefully, not that she ever had much choice as the row of similar black suits and white shirts were like her own uniform. But this morning she dressed in her most expensive ones and wore high heels. She even put more make-up on than usual, and whether or not it was for Langton's appraisal, it made her feel better.

She left early for the station, wanting to have an overall grasp of the case, and once there, took all the files into her office and sat behind her desk, checking and cross-referencing all the data. Instead of her confidence being severely damaged, she now felt the reverse. She rang through to the incident room to say that she wanted to be informed as soon as Detective Chief Superintendent Langton made an appearance, and for coffee to be brought into her office.

Paul tapped on her door and she waited a moment before telling him he could come in.

'Yes?' she said briskly.

'The report from the Tech Support team has arrived.'

'Good or bad news?' she asked.

'I've not had time to read it. It's quite dense and I've a copy here for you.'

She put out her hand. 'Thank you.'

He hovered and then asked if everything was all right. She glanced up as she began to read the report.

'Everything is fine, Paul. Why do you ask?'

'Well, I've heard that Langton's coming in. Brian Stanley seems to think something is up.'

'It is. We are going over budget. Have we had any feedback from checking out the hotels and estate agents in Cornwall?'

'Not as yet. We're onto that this morning.'

'Good. That's it – you can go.'

Paul closed the door and returned to the incident room. Something was up and the entire team could feel it. Anna's manner that morning had been brittle and they had all noticed how much of an effort she had made with her appearance. Not that she ever looked scruffy or even untidy, but of late she had worn her hair snatched back in a band and no make-up. Now she looked 'glossy' as Helen had described her – as if she was getting ready to do battle.

Brian did his irritating hand up in the air gesture, with his index finger pointing to the ceiling.

'We got a hit. There's a property owned by a Daniel Matthews in Newquay. He's the woofter friend of Alan Rawlins – right?'

Paul and Helen went to his desk.

'I was onto the estate agents. This property was on the books of Kimberley's, May Whetter and Grose, and also with a company called Lillicrap Chilcott. They're independent estate agents and they specialise in the sale of houses with a sea view. They've got agents in St Austell and Fowey, and it was a subsidiary agent who arranged the sale eight months ago – cash deal. It sold for four hundred and fifty grand. Place was unbelievably cheap for the location as it was a bit run down and needed a lot of work done on it. The buyer forked out an extra fifty-thousand cash for the agent to get the work done ASAP. With the renovation now complete it's worth nearly seven hundred thousand.

Paul looked at Anna's closed office blinds as he returned to his desk to place a call to Daniel Matthews, the graphic artist they had interviewed very early in the enquiry.

'He must have bloody known about the place and been lying through his teeth,' Paul muttered.

But Daniel Matthews denied any knowledge of a property in Cornwall and said that there had to be some mistake. He also denied ever being there or ever having any discussion with Alan Rawlins regarding ownership. Paul looked over to Brian.

'You got a phone number for this place?'

'Yep. You want me to ring? The agents said someone was living there.'

'Maybe talk it over with the Gov – see what she thinks. Don't want to tip him off.'

Anna was concentrating on the Tech Support report on the hard drive from Alan Rawlins's computer. Paul tapped, but didn't wait for her to answer. He barged in, saying, 'We've traced a property sold for cash to someone calling himself Daniel Matthews – the friend of Alan Rawlins whom we interviewed.'

'"Calling himself" – what do you mean?'

'I've just talked to him and he denies any knowledge of owning it or ever even going to Cornwall. Brian's checked and there is someone living there. Do we contact them or not?'

'No. Make no contact. Not until I give the word. And Paul, could you not just barge into my office.'

'I'm sorry, it's just good news and I wanted to tell you.'

'Enthusiasm is terrific, Paul, but in future wait. All right, how much was the property sold for?'

'Four hundred and fifty grand cash, plus an extra fifty K for renovation work.'

'Lot of money. Will you now concentrate on the Tech Support information? I want everyone up to speed on it for a briefing later this morning. Also, wait a minute.'

Anna reached for a file and thumbed through it.

'It's a report made by Helen. This was to do with me wanting to get the dates when Tina Brooks went on the hairdressing competition forays.' Anna skimmed down the page and looked up. 'Okay, this is it. She spoke to Donna because she said Tina had gone out to make a call. Did she mean out of the salon? We've so far not been able to make any connection between Tina and anyone else she could be involved with, which for me would be the neighbour Michael Phillips. Can you ask her to re-check with Donna exactly what she meant?'

'Yep. Anything else?'

'No, thank you.'

Paul immediately went to talk to Helen. She had not given it much thought and shrugged, saying that Donna probably meant that Tina had simply gone out of the salon, but she would double-check.

Helen then nodded over to Anna's office. 'What's going on?'

'Bloody hell!' Brian Stanley blurted out. 'Any of you up to speed on what the Tech Support got off Alan Rawlins's hard drive? Fifty-eight homosexual contact websites, and I'm only on page three . . . The guy was into some sex toys, I can tell you. Have you read it yet, Paul?'

Paul glanced in Brian's direction and returned to his desk.

'Not as yet,' he replied coolly, 'and the Gov says no contact is to be made with the property in Cornwall. She wants to keep the element of surprise, so maybe you should get back onto the estate agents to ask them not to make any approach to whoever is living there.'

'Does she think it could be Alan Rawlins?'

'I dunno. But I think we are up for a trip to Cornwall.'

Unseen by any one of them, Langton was standing in the entrance to the incident room listening to their conversation. As he approached the team, Helen quickly put in a call to Anna and then asked if Langton wanted a coffee as DCI Travis was expecting him.

'Yes, and a bacon toasted sandwich, no tomatoes.'

'Yes, sir.'

Helen hurried out as Langton made his way to Anna's office. She was ready and waiting standing beside her desk. He didn't knock, but walked straight in.

'Good morning,' she said brightly.

'Morning. Your team reckon it's seaside-time. I overheard that you still want to go to Cornwall.'

'I think it might be necessary.' Anna went and sat behind her desk.

'So you've not discussed with them what we talked about last night?'

'Not yet, no. I wanted to talk to you first.'

He sat down in front of her desk and gave an openhanded gesture. 'I'm ready when you are.'

'Let's just wait for coffee to be brought in so we won't get disturbed. It's been quite a busy morning already as we received the tech report from the hard drive off Alan Rawlins's computer. Makes very interesting reading.'

'Don't tell me it throws up yet more suspects to be interviewed?'

'I think his father attempted to delete a lot of the files, but they were able to retrieve them.'

Helen tapped and carried in a tray of coffee and the toasted sandwich, which she placed on the table between Langton and Anna.

'Did you call the hair salon?' Anna asked.

'I did, but Donna isn't in until eleven.'

Helen left as Anna passed over his toasted sandwich.

'Not had breakfast?' she asked.

'Nope. What about you?' He took a bite and cocked his head to one side. 'You look very pretty. You've done something to your hair.'

'Washed it.' She picked up her coffee and sipped.

Langton said nothing as he finished his sandwich, eating at his usual rate of knots.

'About last night,' Anna said tentatively.

'Yes?'

'I do not agree with you regarding the way I have been handling this investigation. For one, you brought up the case my father advised you on because you had tunnel vision and followed the wrong line of enquiry. He told you to focus the investigation and interview all known previous contacts of your victim; the culprit, in his estimation, was close to home and probably her ex-boyfriend. Which proved to be correct.'

Langton nodded, wondering where she was going with her carefully chosen words. She was very tense – he could feel it.

'I think you brought up this old case you worked on because you believe that I am going in the wrong direction by widening the trace and interview of Rawlins's contacts to such a degree that it is removing suspicion from Tina Brooks, who *you* believe should be the prime suspect.'

'Correct.'

'In your case, James, you had a body. I don't. I have blood pooling and we have been unable to get a positive DNA result so my victim remains unidentified. As far as I can ascertain, the only similarities with your case were that your victim went from being a nice young woman with a small child to you uncovering that she did have quite a voracious sexual appetite. So she led a somewhat double life, changing sexual partners frequently.'

She sipped her coffee. He stared at her, refusing to interrupt, but becoming irritated by her appraisal of his old case.

'My investigation is only similar in that one aspect. To all intent and purpose, when we first looked at Alan Rawlins as a missing person, no one had a bad word to say against him. He was a handsome, dedicated, hard-working and caring man. He was consistently described as shy, introverted and a man who loathed confrontation of any kind. It appeared that this gentle, decent and respected man had no enemies and it was possible that his girlfriend, Tina Brooks, had killed him in some kind of rage. The blood distribution was so extensive that even without a body, it was deemed by forensic experts unlikely that anyone could have survived the attack. It is also suspected by Forensics that the victim was dismembered, and again this is supported by the blood spattering and various blood samples taken from the victim's bathroom.'

Langton sighed and crossed his legs.

'I'm sorry to take so much time, but I think this all needs to be said because you implied that I was not managing the investigation, but allowing it to spiral out of control.'

'Correct,' he said. To make even more of a point he glanced at his watch.

'I have subsequently discovered that my possible victim, Alan Rawlins, led a double life. He was a liar, he was also homosexual and favoured what can only be described as sado-masochistic one-night stands from men he contacted through the internet or erotic male magazines. He was able to continue this double life by leaving London whenever the opportunity arose to spend time in Cornwall. He was very athletic and an experienced surfer. We now have information that he also accumulated a considerable amount of money, cash payments for vintage cars he customised and sold. We believe he has purchased, for cash and using the name of his old schoolfriend, a sea view property in Cornwall worth over half a million. He also used schoolfriends' names when he paid for sex. He was able to hide this double life from his girlfriend also. She believed they were to be married, they had a joint bank account for seventy thousand pounds and he had only a small life-insurance policy for fifty thousand. Alan Rawlins lied to Tina Brooks, who had no knowledge of his homosexuality nor that he had substantial cash savings.'

Langton looked on with surprise as Anna opened her desk drawer and took out a packet of cigarettes; she opened it, but then before taking one out she tossed the pack down. He had never seen her smoke. In fact, he didn't even know that she did.

'From the files on his computer we have learned that Alan Rawlins was also making more money, again in cash, and he was also paying out large chunks of money whilst living in Cornwall. These are in payments of five to ten thousand pounds and on a regular basis. I think that he was possibly involved in dealing in drugs and the purchase of the house and other cash transactions are a means of laundering the money.'

Langton closed his eyes and shook his head.

'Also missing is a known drug dealer called Sammy Marsh. He's got a police record so it's hoped we may get a DNA match from his profile to ascertain if *he* is actually the victim we first believed to be Alan Rawlins. We have semen and a single strand of reddish-coloured hair recovered from the bedlinen at Tina Brooks's flat. As yet we have not had confirmation that the hair belonged to Tina, but I'm waiting for the forensic team to get back to me as I personally took a buccal swab test from her. We have been unable to find a razor, hairbrush or toothbrush that belonged to Alan Rawlins to test for his DNA. It would appear that he was more than aware of forensic testing, as his computer files show extensive research into forensic science. Also, the internet search history, believe it or not, shows he has been looking at numerous cases of people changing their identity. These cases range from the UK to the USA. Alan Rawlins, I now believe, planned his disappearance.'

Langton took a deep breath.

'James, he planned it and perhaps whoever died in that flat is either this Sammy Marsh or the person he has changed identities with. What Alan Rawlins didn't believe was that his hidden life would be uncovered. He must have been planning this for some considerable time and I think we might be able to prove it by checking out the person living in his property in Cornwall.'

Langton rested his elbows on his knees, looking at the floor. Anna waited for him to speak, but he kept his head down.

'I need to go to Cornwall,' she insisted. 'I totally refute

your insinuations that I have allowed this case to run out of control. I *am* in control and I have *not* got tunnel vision. I think the detective work done by myself and my team cannot be faulted. It may appear extensive, but we are still on budget and—'

'Shush, shush,' he said softly, still looking down. Eventually he sat upright and stretched his legs out in front of him, then began to speak.

'Tina Brooks lived in that flat and she agreed to her boyfriend or fiancé being reported missing after two weeks, after he was last seen leaving work early because he had a migraine. She says she left him in bed and when she returned from her work he was not there. He hasn't reappeared since. You have had almost two weeks whilst you handle the investigation into whether or not he is murdered. You come to the conclusion that he has met with foul play because carpet has been cut from beneath the sitting-room sofa and then used as an insert to replace a damaged area beside the bed. This, you believe, was obviously done to conceal heavy blood-staining.'

'Yes, I know that, but—'

'Don't interrupt me,' he snapped. 'You also discover as yet unidentified semen and head hair from a sheet that may have replaced the original one, which would have undoubtedly had bloodstains on it. You subsequently discover further blood pooling and blood-spattering in the bathroom that was cleaned with bleach you know was bought by Tina Brooks. You also know she ordered a roll of new carpet, her excuse being that the landlord would keep the initial deposit if he discovered any damage to the old one.'

Anna sat listening tight-lipped.

'You have a young man living right next door – a suspect, who has refused to give you a DNA sample –
correct?'

'Yes.'

'You have so far been unable to make a connection
between these two – Tina and what's his name?'

'Michael Phillips.'

'You have her landline records and her mobile ones and
there has been no contact between the two of them – correct?'

'Yes.'

He stood up and rubbed at his old injured knee.

'You believe that Tina Brooks was unaware of her
boyfriend's predilection for homosexual one-night stands.
She never went to Cornwall, she claims she has no knowledge of Alan Rawlins's other life. They planned to marry
and she did wonder if there was perhaps another woman
as . . .'

Langton paced the office. No matter how irritated
Anna was by him, she still had to be impressed by his
retentive memory.

'I think she said he had become distant and tetchy with
her, and she wondered if she had been pressing too hard
for wedding dates and so on. Yes?'

'Yes.'

He sat down again. 'I don't believe it. I think she's a liar.
You want a motive? What if she discovered what her
boyfriend was up to? Found out he was leading this
double life and added to that was awash with money?'

'Money she couldn't or wouldn't be able to get her
hands on,' Anna said, getting very edgy.

'Believe me, people have killed for a lot less than what
she's got in their joint bank account, but your motive is

261

there: betrayal and rage. She is also, according to one of your reports, very strong. She works out in the local gym and she flew at you – right?'

'Yes.'

'Think about it, Anna. She was the last person to see him alive, and unless you have proof that she did not return to that flat, and did not, as she claimed, come back the same night he left work with a migraine, but stayed away for a week or two weeks even, *someone* picked up that blood-drenched bedding, *someone* replaced the blood-soaked carpet, *someone* used bleach to clean that flat or attempt to clean it up. *Someone* had to carve up the body and remove it, and you believe that she is Miss Innocent? Clean linen was put on the bed, Anna; someone had sex in that freshly made bed. Who else is living there?'

Anna swallowed and looked down at the mass of files and statements on her desk.

'Now you are bringing up Christ knows how much evidence that opens up this double life Alan Rawlins lived. How many drug dealers are you going to question? How many surfers, estate agents and ex-boyfriends, when what you have is your prime suspect throwing a punch at you. You have to crack her open, Anna, you have to find the key that'll make her tell you the truth because in my estimation she has been lying and leading you by the fucking nose.'

Anna said nothing. Langton glanced at his watch again.

'I have to go. Break her, Anna, break that flash neighbour of hers too and find out if he's involved or not. In the meantime, just drop this Cornwall escapade. It's proof of only one thing: that Alan Rawlins was a man scared to get out of the closet and who hid his homosexuality.'

'It's more than that,' she said churlishly.

'No, it isn't. Better still, Anna, try and find the fucking body. It has to be somewhere, it has to have been dumped somewhere.'

'I don't agree with you.'

'What?'

She stood up to face him. 'I said, I don't agree with you. I will focus on Tina as you have suggested and the neighbour, but if I don't get a result I want to go to Cornwall.'

'Christ,' he muttered.

'I agree with much of what you have said with regard to Tina, but at the same time I think that there is another scenario that I want to look into.'

Langton rubbed his head. 'Anna, if Alan *was* planning to do a runner, planning to change his identity, why leave his computer with the hard drive for you to find?'

'I think he planned it, but then something happened and he couldn't or didn't have the time to carry it through in the way he had wanted. And added to this, I don't believe that Alan knew he was not the biological son.'

'All right, all right. Go another round with Tina, put the pressure on her. It has to be done that way because as it stands this is circumstantial evidence. That said, it's pretty thickly laid on and a jury would find it hard to believe that she lived in the flat at Newton Court and didn't have any-thing to do with the murder. So you have to break her into admitting what part she played. See what you can get in the next two days. Then let's have another talk and I will decide whether or not it is necessary for you to go to Cornwall.'

'What if whoever is living in this property gets tipped off? You know we've had to go through numerous estate agents, and as it was a cash deal, they could have had a kickback and might make contact.'

'All right, go to fucking Cornwall! But you've only got until the end of this week. You have to get a result – understand me?'

'I think you've made it abundantly clear.'

'Don't get sarcastic with me, Anna. I've got a job to do and this isn't in any way personal, so don't make it out to be anything but my professional take on the way you are handling this enquiry.'

She wouldn't back down. 'I think I have handled it to the best of my ability. If you want to replace me . . .?'

He turned on her angrily. 'Don't think it's not on the cards – and you *can* take that personally because I want you to succeed. I believe in you and I am trusting you to do as I have asked.'

'Thank you.'

He gazed at her with her chin up and that stubborn glare, and he had never seen her looking so attractive. The window behind her desk gave a light to her red hair and made her eyes bluer than blue.

'Thank you, too,' he said softly, walking out and closing the door quietly behind him.

Anna slowly sank into her desk chair, opened her cigarette pack and lit up. Her hand was shaking. In case she set the smoke alarm off in her office, she opened the window. Puffing on her cigarette, she observed Langton crossing the station yard below towards his erratically parked old Rover, which was never locked. He yanked the driver's door open, and then for some reason he paused and turned to look up at her window, smiled and gave her a small salute. She watched as he drove out.

She hated the taste left in her mouth after smoking, she thought as she stubbed out the cigarette on the sill before closing the window. She would do exactly as he had requested. She would go in to tell the team that they would arrest Tina Brooks before they travelled to Cornwall.

First, however, she had to sort out all the files that littered her desk. She'd just begun on the task when Helen rang to ask if she could see her for a moment. Anna opened the door, saying, 'I was just coming to speak to you all.'

'I wanted to apologise about something I had over-looked – my call to Donna at the hair salon. I didn't think, but now in retrospect I should have paid more attention. You were right.'

'Right about what?'

'I spoke to Donna again. I didn't want to make it too obvious, but I just said that when I had last talked to her about the competition dates, she'd mentioned that Tina was not in the salon as she'd gone out to make a call.'

'Yes, and . . .?'

'I asked her if Tina was actually out of the salon.'

'What did she say?'

'That Tina used a pay-phone. The girls never really knew why she didn't simply use the desk phone or even her own mobile.'

'Did she tell them she was using a pay-phone?'

'Not in so many words, but she would often take some of the change left for tips, which irritated the juniors.' Helen crossed to Anna's desk and laid out a computer printout of a map. 'This is the area around the salon. There are no public telephone booths close by, but there is a pay-phone in a pub on a corner within yards of the salon, and there's also one in a café across the street. There's two more further along, and . . .'

Anna studied the map. 'Get Paul to come in, would you?' she asked, stacking more files from her desk.

'Knock, knock, who's there?' Paul said from the door-way.

'Very witty. Shut the door. I want you to do something.'

Closing the door, Paul glanced at the map, saying, 'Maybe the reason we could never discover if Tina was contacting anyone outside her work is because of—'

'I'm ahead of you,' Anna said, standing beside him.

'It's going to take a bloody long time if we want any calls accessed from these pay-phones,' Paul complained, 'because she could be using any one of them.'

'Plus we don't know what number she will be phoning. So I want you to do some surveillance. You get over to the salon and wait.'

'But it could take all day before she makes a call!'

'I don't think so. If she is contacting someone who is connected to the murder, she's bound to ring them. And as soon as we know which pay-phone she's using we'll get the number accessed.'

Paul gave her a sidelong glance as she folded the map.

'Right – get moving,' Anna told him, 'and ask Brian to come in and see me. When you are in position, let me know.'

A few moments later, Brian came into her office.

'I want Daniel Matthews brought in for questioning,' Anna told him.

Brian hesitated. 'Sorry, I've got a slew of names on the board. Who is he?'

'The graphic-artist friend of Alan Rawlins, whose name he used to purchase the house in Cornwall.'

'Christ, yes, of course. Sorry.' Then: 'Everything all right? Only I noticed the Boss was in with you for a lengthy session.'

'Everything is fine, thank you, Brian.'

'Is a trip to Cornwall on the cards then?'

'Yes, it is,' she said tetchily as Brian left.

Sitting at her desk she was able to watch through the blinds as Brian started talking with Helen. She was certain that he had also spoken to Langton. It made her feel uneasy that the team didn't think of her as being in charge of the case. She knew she would have to give a briefing and bring back their confidence in her.

Paul left his car at the local supermarket and walked the short distance to Tina's hair salon. He rang through to Anna to say he was in position near the salon and that he'd remain on foot as the pay-phones were all within walking distance. Anna then put in a call to talk to Tina.

'I'm really busy at the moment, Detective Travis. I'm giving a treatment to a client.'

'This shouldn't take long, Tina. I just wanted to run a few things by you that we have uncovered. We now know that Alan Rawlins purchased a substantial property in Cornwall – a cash buy for over four hundred thousand pounds. We have also been able to access some files from his computer. It appears that he has further substantial amounts of money. He was making payouts on quite a regular basis, amounts between five to ten thousand pounds.'

As she spoke, Tina constantly gasped, repeating that she couldn't believe it.

'I will need to discuss these new developments with you, but I wanted to know as soon as possible if you were aware—'

'I never knew anything about it,' Tina interrupted her. 'It just doesn't make any sense to me and I can't help you at all. It's all news to me.' Her voice was shrill and then she started to cry.

'I'm sorry if this is distressing for you.'

'I can't talk to you – there's customers here. I've got to go.'

Anna replaced the receiver and her phone rang immediately. It was Brian to say that he had contacted Daniel Matthews, who was at home, so they were going to pick him up and bring him in. Then line two bleeped and Anna had to cut off Brian to answer. It was Paul. Tina had left the salon two minutes ago and he was tailing her.

'Good. As soon as you know the location I'll get onto Tech Support and you can return to the station.'

She smiled, pleased with herself, but the good feeling didn't last long. Had she been so off-kilter as Langton had suggested that she had sent the murder enquiry into areas that were not even relevant? She got up and straightened her jacket. If she had, she was going to have to apologise, but the old adage that Langton always used to use: 'What's your gut feeling?' made her think again, because *her* gut feeling was that the case was on course.

As everyone waited for Paul to get in touch, the tension grew. By now Anna had filled the team in on the importance of discovering who Tina was in contact with, and that it had to be someone she didn't want anyone at the salon to know about. Fifteen minutes ticked by and still nothing. Then Paul rang in to say that Tina had done a walkabout before she went into the local pub. She did, however, make two calls – one after the other. She spent no more than a few seconds on one and five minutes on the other.

By the time Paul had returned to the station they had accessed the numbers and the buzz was on. The first call had been to Michael Phillips's office and the second was to his company mobile. This had not been checked by the team as they only had access to his personal mobile. Just as the buzz started that they were moving forward, Anna got bad news.

Liz called from the forensic lab. She explained that they had been unable to match the single strand of hair taken from Tina Brooks's bed with her DNA. The one strand was in very poor condition, with no root attached. It also had bleach, or hair-dye on it which made the job even more difficult.

'But it could possibly be Tina's?' Anna persisted.

'I honestly can't say.'

'She's a hairdresser and she uses hair-dye.'

'But that really won't help me. If it was ever brought up in court, I would have to deny that my tests were conclusive.'

Anna thanked Liz, very disappointed.

Brian Stanley had brought in Daniel Matthews for questioning. Before Anna went to interview him she gave a briefing to the team. The link she had been hoping for between Tina and Michael Phillips was now confirmed. She made no mention of the call from Forensics. She wanted Tina arrested at the same time Michael Phillips was to be brought in. The latter would be told he was assisting police enquiries, but Tina was to be unnerved. Anna stipulated that she was to be arrested for the murder of Alan Rawlins and handcuffed.

Chapter Twelve

Daniel Matthews was sitting waiting in interview room two. He had been given a coffee and was asked if he required a solicitor. He repeated over and over that he had done nothing wrong, so he wouldn't need anyone to be with him. He seemed very agitated, however, and his skinny frame was hunched up as he asked for water.

It was over an hour before Anna and Paul went in to talk to him. Anna had told Paul that he was to open up the interview but then remain silent, as she wanted to head up the questioning, until she gave him a signal to do otherwise.

'I don't understand why I've been brought here. I told you everything I know about Alan and I've not got anything else to add,' Daniel protested.

'We really appreciate you coming in to help our enquiry,' Paul said as he opened his notebook, flipping back the pages to read his notes from their previous interview. He then waited for Anna to take over.

'Are you aware, Daniel,' Anna began, 'that your name is on the deeds of a very substantial property in Cornwall?'

'I told you earlier – I don't know anything about it.'

'We believe that Alan Rawlins purchased this property and we need to know if you are—'

'I said, I don't know anything about it!'

'But were you aware that Alan Rawlins used your name?'

'No.'

'Did you ever sign any documents appertaining to this property?'

'No.'

'Have you ever been to Cornwall?'

'No.'

'Did you know that Alan Rawlins was homosexual?'

Daniel flushed and Paul picked up on this.

'Tell me about how you knew.'

'What do you mean?'

'You have admitted that you are gay and that you were friends for a long time. You came out to him in confidence. Did he ever do the same to you?'

'We were friends, that's all, nothing more. I don't know why I am here.'

'You are here, Mr Matthews, because your friend Alan Rawlins has been missing for some considerable time and it is very probable that he has been murdered.'

'Oh my God.'

'We have found some very strong evidence that makes us believe he was killed inside his own flat.'

'I don't know what to say.'

'You just have to tell us the truth. You maintained that you had not seen Alan for some considerable time – in fact, four months before he was presumed missing. Do you want to change that statement?'

'No, it's the truth.' Daniel paused and took off his glasses.

'Just take us through the last time you met with Alan Rawlins,' Anna interjected.

Matthews was polishing his glasses with a handkerchief, rubbing at the lenses.

'He just dropped by to see me. We had a pizza, I think, and then he left. It was ages ago. Previously I'd not seen him for some time. He got engaged and we didn't meet up as frequently as we used to do, just as I explained to you before. Oh ... I did see him again – I'd forgotten, sorry. It was before that – maybe a month before.'

He replaced his glasses and continued to address Anna.

'He asked me to sign his Will – that's what he came round for. He wanted me to be a signatory on his Will because he said if anything ever happened to him, he'd want me to be executor.'

'Did you read the Will?'

'No. He just showed me where I had to sign.'

'Do you recall the solicitor's name?'

'No, I didn't see the top page. I just signed at the bottom where he indicated and then he left.'

'Didn't you find that odd?'

'What?'

'That he wanted you to sign his Will?'

'Not really. He said that he was planning on getting married and might be moving away, and then with all his surfing he said there could be an accident and he wanted Tina taken care of.'

'Did he seem concerned in any way or worried about anything?'

'No.'

Anna was becoming frustrated with Daniel's obvious lies. 'Mr Matthews, you openly admit to being homosexual and we now know that Alan Rawlins was bisexual. You must have been a very close friend for him to want you to be executor of his Will.'

'We have been close friends since school. Alan always looked out for me. I used to get bullied and he was the one person who wouldn't let them carry on messing me around. I was always skinny, always a bit effeminate – it was just the way I was – and to have Alan as my friend made my time at school bearable. I owe him a lot.'

'Did you owe him enough to sign a document that you were told was a Will, but could also have been ownership of a very valuable property?' Anna asked in a loud voice.

'I told you, I didn't look at it. If you must know, I'd have signed anything for him if he'd wanted me to.'

'So you cared for him a lot?'

'Yes, I did and do, and it was only because of his relationship with Tina that we didn't see each other as much.'

'You didn't like her?'

'No, but if it made him happy then I just had to accept it.'

'It's not because you thought she was wrong for Alan that you disliked her, is it? You've never accepted her because you're jealous. She had the one thing you've always wanted for yourself. You loved Alan.'

'Yes, I loved him but not like you're trying to make out.'

'So you never had a sexual relationship with him?'

'No.' He took off his glasses again and began polishing the lenses once more, blinking rapidly.

'I think you are lying.'

'You can think what you want,' Daniel Matthews said waspishly.

'Why lie about it?'

'I hero-worshipped him, if you want the truth. I'd have done anything for him.'

Anna nodded to Paul to indicate he was to take over the questioning.

'What other things *did* you do for him, Daniel?'

'I did his washing for him sometimes.'

'His *washing*?'

'Yes. When he'd been away I'd take his laundry and wash and iron it for him.'

'So this would be when he returned from Cornwall?'

'Wherever, but I hadn't done it recently.'

'Did you do drugs with him?'

'*No.* I just don't understand what you are trying to get me to say. You want me to admit I had a sexual relationship with him, but I didn't – in my dreams maybe, but Alan was always straight and . . .'

His eyes filled with tears and he took off his glasses yet again.

'I find this very distressing because I just can't come to terms with the fact that you say he might be dead. If he is, then that's the reason why he's not contacted me for so long.'

'This washing you did for him . . . why do you think he brought it to you rather than take it back to his own flat?'

'He was very particular. He said *she* couldn't iron.'

'So when you'd done his laundry, did he have a suitcase or a bag to take it home?'

'He had a laundry bag and I'd fold it all into that.'

'What type of clothes did he bring to you?'

Daniel sighed and described T-shirts, jeans and underwear. He mentioned that Alan would sometimes keep the items at his flat for collection. He would then call in to pick them up and take them back to his own flat.

Anna jotted down that this was yet another part of Alan Rawlins's double life. These were probably the clothes he wore when away from home. She also believed that the so-called Will Alan Rawlins had asked Daniel to sign was some kind of document appertaining to the purchase of the property in Cornwall reverting the ownership back to himself. Anna again interjected.

'Did you know that Alan Rawlins used contact magazines for dates with gay men?'

Daniel looked astonished.

'He often used his schoolfriends' names to hide his own identity. He used your name, Daniel.'

Daniel stared at Anna in disbelief.

Anna closed her notebook, and gave Paul a small nudge to his knee beneath the table. Paul cleared his throat.

'Listen to me, Daniel. You may think that we are questioning you in an attempt to blacken Alan's name, but the truth is we are trying to find out if someone brutally murdered him. We found extensive blood pooling beside his bed at Newton Court. Our forensic expert believes that whoever the victim was, they would not have survived such an injury. The blood seeped down under the floorboards below into a deep pool, where it congealed. Added to this we have also discovered further bloodstains in the bathroom of the flat he shared with Tina. We can only surmise, because we have found no body, that the victim was dismembered in the bathtub and the body parts dumped. All we are attempting to do is get to the truth, discover anything that can help us trace whoever did this murder, and find the killer. Whatever secrets you had between you both might help us. You can't protect him, but what you might be able to do is give us something that'll help solve this terrible crime and lay him to rest.'

Paul had kept his voice low and gentle, holding Daniel's frightened eyes with his own. Anna now remained silent, watching as Paul reached over and took the young man's hand.

'He protected you from bullies at school; you say you owe him, you hero-worshipped him – then do this for him, Daniel. If you have anything that might help us, now is the time to be honest. Help us get to the truth and find out who killed him.'

Anna was impressed. Paul didn't release Daniel's hand, but continued to hold it tightly.

'If you feel that you might say something that could implicate you, then we can arrange for a solicitor to be present. We'll protect you. All we want is for you to help us.'

Daniel's voice dropped to almost a whisper. 'He made me promise never to tell anyone.'

'You kept that promise, I know you did, but now it is time to tell me what you know.'

Daniel sighed and slowly withdrew his hand from Paul's to wipe away his tears.

'I loved him. It seems as if I have loved him for my whole life. My father was very violent – well, it appeared that way to me. He just couldn't come to terms with his only son being gay. He threw me out of the house and I went to stay with Alan's family. They took me in and his mother was so lovely and different to mine.'

Anna, impatient for Paul to get to the truth, bit her lip knowing that any interruption might undo the bond that Paul was forming. Daniel took a deep breath and leaned back in his chair, Anna knew that at last he was about to unburden himself to Paul.

'I went to college and got a place of my own. As much as I detested my parents, I did have an allowance and they also left me well off so I used to give Alan money. I also paid a substantial amount for his cars as his father didn't have enough to finance their purchase. We were very close and he always knew how much I loved him. In retrospect, I always sort of knew that he used me. It wasn't just laundry; he'd ask me to cover for him when he went to auctions, and he had a number of garages where he would leave the cars until he was ready to work on them.'

'Did he give you a cut of the money when he sold these cars?'

'Sometimes, but usually he'd only give back what I'd put in. He was very secretive about what he actually made from the sales. In fact, he was almost obsessive about money. I saw his personality change about four years ago. I think by this time he was living with a girl called Alison and we had a couple of dinners, but I wasn't seeing that much of him. He was as obsessive about surfing as he was about his cars. He was working out and I think he was using steroids. He could be very quick-tempered, and that was when I found out he was seeing Tina on the side. I said to him that Alison was a really nice person and he dismissed her as being a waste of space. I can't remember the exact words we had, but Tina had started to put highlights in his hair to make it more blonde and I said something stupid.'

Daniel went silent. Paul reached out and patted his hand.

'Go on, what happened?'

'I said something like he should be careful in case someone might think he was gay, and . . . he almost killed me. He was terrifying and wouldn't stop no matter how much I screamed, punching me and squeezing my throat.'

Daniel was hardly audible as he sobbed that he was raped, and how the next morning Alan had begged for forgiveness, saying that he hadn't meant to hurt him, that Dan was his best friend and that he loved him more than Tina, more than anyone else.

'It was after that we separated. Months would go by and I'd not see or hear from him, and then he would turn up with his bag of dirty washing. Sometimes I was scared not to do it. He would leave it for weeks on end with me. Then he came round to tell me he had made out this Will and that he wanted me to be the executor of it, just in case anything happened to him. I joked with him, saying that I knew he could take care of himself, but he got very serious and said he was doing some business with people he didn't trust.'

'In Cornwall?'

'Yes. He said he was making a lot of money and intended going to live in Florida eventually; that he planned to leave Tina as he couldn't stand her.'

'What business do you think he meant when he said he was making a lot of money?' Anna intervened, and Daniel flinched as if he had forgotten she was in the room.

'I don't know. I didn't dare ask him.'

'You think it was drugs?'

Daniel hesitated and then nodded. He explained that he had found a number of packets in his laundry bag. It was cocaine. Alan had joked that he was laundering them for him and took them back.

'I never saw him again. I didn't know where he was until I was interviewed and told that he was missing. I didn't say anything because I just thought that he had done what he said he was going to do – go off to Florida.'

Daniel sighed as if relieved it was over. He looked at Paul.

'I'm sorry – I should have told you all this before.'

'Yes, you should,' Anna snapped as she stood up. It never ceased to amaze her how well some people lied. She had not suspected that Daniel was one of them.

Daniel Matthews was allowed to leave the station and Anna congratulated Paul, because she doubted if she would have got Dan to open up and tell her the truth. They broke for an hour to prepare for the arrival of Tina and Michael Phillips.

Tina was being held in the cells down on the ground floor. Michael Phillips was in interview room one. They had been kept separate and Tina had demanded that her lawyer be present. As Jonathan Hyde could not come to the station for two hours and would then no doubt wish to have a discussion regarding the new evidence against his client, Anna decided that Michael Phillips would be questioned first.

'Do you want legal representation, Mr Phillips?' Anna asked as she entered the interview room.

'I'd like to know what I've been brought in here for.'

'You have agreed to be interviewed with regard to a murder enquiry. You do not have to say anything, but it may harm your defence if you do not mention when questioned something—'

'Wow – just wait a minute. You can't still believe I have anything to do with this man's disappearance. It's preposterous!'

Phillips was very well-dressed in a smart suit, expensive shirt and tie, which he began to loosen.

'We are investigating the disappearance and possible murder of Alan Rawlins.'

'I've been questioned about this before, for chrissakes. I didn't know him, I just happen to live next door.'

'You also refused to give a DNA sample.'

'Yes, I did. Why should I give one? I have nothing

whatsoever to do with this. It's a total invasion of my privacy, and don't think I don't know what will happen. You'll keep my profile on some DNA database and I am not agreeing to it, full stop.'

'Then you can understand why we wish to question you further as your refusal is suspicious.'

'No, it isn't. I had nothing whatsoever to do with this man and you are just forcing me to do something that I have every right to refuse. I know the law and you are not charging me with anything because I have not done anything wrong.'

'We are aware that Miss Tina Brooks called you this morning at your office and on your mobile phone.'

Phillips gave a resigned sigh. If he was taken aback by the fact that they knew about it, he showed no reaction.

'Could you tell us why you have previously denied knowing Miss Brooks?'

Anna was interrupted as Phillips slapped the table.

'I'm her neighbour – right? I live in the flat opposite hers and it's obvious that I have had to be aware of what has been going on. So although I said to you previously that I was friends with neither her nor her boyfriend, we have since begun talking to each other – and there's no law against that.'

'What exactly do you think has been going on in the flat opposite to yours, Mr Phillips?'

He sighed again in exasperation. 'Her boyfriend, Alan Rawlins, went missing, that's all I know.'

'Miss Brooks didn't tell you about the blood pooling beside her bed or the blood traces in her bathroom?'

He ran his fingers through his silky hair. 'No she didn't.'

'I think, Mr Phillips, you are lying as Miss Brooks has not been resident at her flat due to police procedure. So just how long have you been on friendly terms with her?'

'Christ, not long. I met her in the hall and she told me she was taking some clothes from her flat as she was staying with a girlfriend. She said that something bad had happened in there, but she never went into any details, and said that was the reason she'd not been living there for a while.'

'So at what point did you exchange phone numbers?'

He shrugged. 'I've just told you – a couple of days ago. Listen, I was obviously interested in what was going down in there, even more so after I'd been interviewed. Anyway, we got talking and she came into my place for a drink. She was in a very nervous state. I gave her a brandy, we talked and I said if there was anything I could do at any time, she could call me.'

'You do know that as we know your phone number we can check just how often and how long you and Miss Brooks have been in contact with each other for.'

Again he shrugged. 'It's just over the past few days, and to be honest, I've started to regret inviting her in. She's called me a few times.'

'Have you and Miss Brooks had an intimate relationship?'

'I just told you we've only really been talking to each other recently.'

'Have you had sex with Miss Brooks?'

'I don't think that is any of your business. I am really finding it exceedingly disturbing that you have even brought me in to question me again, after I have already given you an interview and I have nothing further to add.'

Anna stood up and gathered her papers.

'I suggest you get representation, Mr Phillips. If you are

withholding evidence you could find yourself charged with perverting the course of justice.'

'What fucking evidence do you think I have?'

'Don't swear at me, Mr Phillips. I am requesting that you give a DNA sample and if you continue to refuse I could arrest you and it would then be taken legally by force if you resist.'

'I am not withholding any evidence, but I do want to have legal representation.' Anna told Phillips that he was to remain in the interview room while they organised for a solicitor to be present.

'I'm supposed to be at work,' he said furiously. 'How long will this take?'

'As long as necessary.'

Anna walked out and Paul followed. She was tight-lipped with anger and disliked the arrogant Michael Phillips even more.

'You know we don't have anything on him,' Paul said as they headed along the corridor.

'Not yet we don't. Let's see if Tina matches his story about when they met. In the meantime, arrange for the duty solicitor to come in and talk to him. I think he is refusing the blood test because if we get a DNA match with the evidence taken from her bedsheet, it will show he was certainly seeing her for a lot longer than just the past few days.'

Anna stopped at a water fountain. Her mouth felt dry but she was impatient to continue. However, they had to wait for Jonathan Hyde for over two hours, and until he was at the station Tina remained in the cells. Paul checked on her twice. At first she had been very angry and abusive, but the longer she remained in the cell the quieter she became.

Jonathan Hyde eventually arrived, and although he apologised profusely about taking so long, his manner was not in any way apologetic, but abrasive. Anna told him of their findings to date as he made copious notes in a leather-bound notebook. He occasionally held up his Mont Blanc pen for Anna to repeat herself, and had an irritating habit of directing the pen towards her to continue. Eventually he closed his notebook, replaced the cap on his pen and suggested they get on with it.

'You will obviously wish to have a private meeting with your client,' Anna said.

'Obviously.'

'I'll get her brought up from the cells.'

Anna asked Helen to escort Tina Brooks to interview room two.

'Would you like a coffee, Mr Hyde?'

'No, thank you. Perhaps some water?'

Anna opened the interview-room door and Hyde went in, placing his Gucci briefcase on the table. She watched him remove his leather-bound notebook, set his pen down beside it and take out a handkerchief and wipe the table in front of him. She closed the door quietly and turned into the corridor to find Tina approaching, accompanied by Helen.

'That cell stinks, it's disgusting!' Tina said, glaring at Anna as Helen led her into the interview room. As Helen closed the door, Tina was complaining about being kept waiting for hours. Hyde's dulcet upper-crust tones were heard apologising, explaining that the delay was due to his representing another client in court.

Helen walked back along the corridor with Anna. 'Nasty piece of work, isn't she?'

Anna nodded, not wishing to get into how she felt about Tina.

'Could you manage to get some lunch brought up to my office?' she asked.

'Canteen might be closed, it's almost three.'

'Just a sandwich and coffee will do. Thank you.'

By now Anna had a headache. She was just taking a couple of aspirin when Paul called through to say that the duty solicitor was now with Michael Phillips, and had also asked to see her. Sighing, she asked for Paul to give her fifteen minutes and by the time Helen had brought her lunch she was feeling a little better. Still the headache persisted so she took two more aspirin before she agreed to speak with Rhaji Simonie, now representing Michael Phillips.

'Hello again,' he said, smiling as he entered her office. Anna stood up to shake his hand, having no recall of ever meeting him previously. He was very young, with tawny skin and gleaming black hair combed straight back from his angular face.

'Well, I've talked with Mr Phillips, or should I say he talked at me, and I think we need to establish a few things.'

He sat down, opening a very beaten-up bulging leather briefcase, and rooted around to bring out some loose pages. He then had another search around and Anna offered him a sharpened pencil from a jar on her desk. He shook his head, patting his jacket pockets and finally smiled as he took out a biro. He clicked it open and closed as he looked over his scrawled notes.

'Right, my client is not officially under arrest but had agreed to come here voluntarily to assist your enquiry. You have previously interviewed him at his place of work requesting information with regard to the disappearance of someone called Alan Rawlins.' He glanced up at Anna and gave her yet another wide smile. She was impatient, and his irritating click-clicking of his biro didn't help.

'Mr Simonie, your client is the neighbour who lives in the flat opposite.'

'Yes, yes, to a Miss Tina Brooks. He claims that he had no contact with the missing chap and that he has only recently become friendly with Miss Brooks.'

'Your client has refused to give a DNA sample.'

'Yes, yes, I am aware of that, and as he has not been formally arrested that is his prerogative.'

'The reason why I have requested Mr Phillips to assist us is to basically eliminate him from my enquiry. It is far more serious than whether or not he knew Mr Rawlins. We know that it is possible Alan Rawlins was murdered in Miss Brooks's flat and we have recovered DNA evidence from the bedding in Miss Brooks's bedroom.'

'Wait – just let me make a note . . .'

'I don't have very much time, Mr Simonie. Basically, if your client's DNA does not match the evidence we have then he could be eliminated as a suspect.'

'Hang on a second, I don't quite follow . . . you have DNA from bedlinen that is connected to the possible murder of er . . . well, do you have a positive identification of who the victim is?'

'No, we do not. But let me explain. We have substantial blood pooling beside the bed, blood on the edge of the mattress, and the bedlinen was freshly laundered and obviously replaced the bloodstained set. Are you following me?'

'Yes, yes, just jotting it all down.'

She watched him scribble away and sighed.

'It is obvious, Mr Simonie, why we suspect that your client may have been involved with Miss Brooks for a considerably longer time than he has admitted. He could therefore be . . .'

'In cahoots with her?'

'Yes.'

'Is Miss Brooks a suspect in the murder of persons unknown?'

'Yes.'

'Ah, the plot thickens. Could you give me an indication of why you believe she is connected to the murder of whoever bled on the bed?'

'There was blood on the floor and in the bathroom, leaving us to suspect that a body was dismembered inside Miss Brooks's flat.'

'Bloody hell! Right – and my client has denied knowing anything about this awful situation, correct?'

'Yes.'

'But you believe him to be connected?'

'You tell me, why does your client refuse to assist us? By not giving a DNA sample it is reasonable to suspect his involvement.'

'No, no, no, I disagree. My client does not realise the seriousness of why you have been questioning him. If, however, you have evidence that proves him to be connected . . .'

Anna sighed and shook her head.

'Mr Simonie, it is a very simple request. He has lied, he has denied knowing Miss Brooks or having any kind of relationship with her, yet we have a series of phone calls between them.'

'These calls, how did you get them?'

Anna tensed up and explained that they had acquired them after Miss Brooks had left her salon to place calls to Mr Phillips, first at his office and then to a mobile phone.

'Ah yes, but these calls have only recently taken place. He admits that he has become friendlier with Miss Brooks, but this has only occurred over the past few days.

Miss Brooks was in his apartment for one occasion only and not since. Do you have any evidence that disproves this?'

'He can resolve the situation by agreeing to give a DNA sample,' she snapped, exasperated by Simonie.

'Do you see his predicament?'

'What?'

'Well, it's obvious, isn't it?'

'The only thing obvious to me is that your client's continued refusal to assist my investigation is because he is withholding evidence.'

'My client is guilty of nothing, Detective Travis. His refusal to comply with your request for a DNA sample is, as I have already stated, his prerogative – unless, of course, you have evidence that proves he is connected to your murder investigation. As his legal representative I will also refuse to encourage my client to—'

Anna stood up, angrily suggested that he leave and crossed to open her door to usher him out.

'If we find that your client is lying and perverting the course of justice, he will be arrested and charged. You may take him out of the station.'

Simonie stuffed his loose papers back into his briefcase and, clicking his pen, walked towards her.

'I will inform my client he is free to go. Thank you so much.'

She wanted to slam the door behind him, but she restrained herself and closed it firmly before kicking out at the chair he had just vacated. Then she rang through to Brian Stanley.

'Brian, have you got the results on Michael Phillips's mobile and office calls yet?'

'I think that's already in progress,' he said.

'I asked you personally to do it and I need them urgently. See how far they go back, then let me know the dates ASAP.' She banged the receiver back and drained the dregs of her cold cup of coffee.

Fifteen minutes later she was heading down the corridor to the interview room as Mr Hyde had finished talking to his client.

By now, Michael Phillips had left with the irritating Rhaji Simonie, who may have been wet behind the ears, but had won round one. Anna had no doubt that she would be seeing him again.

Chapter Thirteen

Tina Brooks was very subdued. She sat with her head bent down and her hands clasped in her lap. Anna seated herself opposite Hyde, who had moved his chair as far from his client as possible. His legs were crossed beside the table rather than beneath it. In front of him he had his leather-bound notebook open and his pen placed beside it. Paul had the stack of case-files beside him, leaving Anna space to have her notes in front of her. Quietly she cautioned Tina and reminded her that she was under arrest on suspicion of murder.

Hyde coughed, clearing his throat.

'Let's begin with clarifying that my client is suspected of murdering someone as yet unidentified. The possibility that the victim was Alan Rawlins, with whom she cohabitated in flat two Newton Court, Hounslow, has as yet not been proven. So there is also the possibility that the victim was in fact killed *by* Mr Rawlins, who has since absconded after disposing of the body.'

Anna met his cold flinty eyes and nodded.

'So taking on board this rather confusing scenario, let us now discuss why my client is here.'

Anna looked directly at Tina.

'Your client, Mr Hyde, is under suspicion of murder.

Miss Brooks, could you please describe the last time you saw Alan Rawlins.'

Tina kept her head down as she replied.

'I got a call at about ten in the morning. Alan said he was feeling ill and that it was probably a migraine. He had driven into work, but I agreed to pick him up and take him back to the flat in case anything happened while he was driving. He said he was really feeling bad and went straight to bed. I closed the curtains, made him a flask of tea and I went into work.'

'And that was the last time you saw him?'

'Yes, it was. I did call home later, but I didn't get an answer so I presumed he was sleeping.'

'How frequently did Mr Rawlins have these migraines?'

'Not often, but he had one or two before that I can remember, and he always slept them off.'

'Taking no medication for them?'

'Not all the time, no.'

'What time did you return to the flat?'

'It was after I finished work – maybe six or quarter to seven.'

Anna flicked through her notebook.

'Take me through what happened when you got home.'

'Alan wasn't there. He had been working a few nights until late so I presumed he must have felt better and gone back to the garage. I rang them, but no one answered. Well, they wouldn't because he would have been outside where he worked on his own car.'

'Go on.'

'How do you mean?'

'When he didn't come home, what did you do?'

'Oh, I see. I went to bed.'

'In your bedroom?'

'Yes.'

'Okay, so what happened the next day?'

'I went to work and I did phone home again, but there was no reply. I began to think that Alan had left me. He had been very distant with me for a while, non-communicative, and I started to think he had someone else. I rang his work again and they told me he hadn't turned up there either.'

Anna watched the way Tina was acting, demure and upset. She constantly glanced towards Hyde, never looking at Anna.

'I really believed he'd left me for another woman. His father phoned wanting to talk to him, and I asked him if *he* had seen Alan and he said he hadn't.'

'You remained alone in your flat?'

'Yes. It was horrible because I didn't know what was going on. He had never done this before, but I still thought he had maybe taken off with another woman or gone to Cornwall. He often went there whenever he had spare time.'

'Without telling you?'

'Yes.'

'But also not informing his boss at the garage?'

'I don't know – maybe he did tell him. Mr Smedley never mentioned it when I called, but that was sort of why I felt suspicious – you know, that maybe Alan had told him and asked him not to tell me.'

'How long was it before you became concerned about Alan's disappearance?'

'Well, it may sound awful, but not until about a fortnight had elapsed. This was because his father kept on calling me as he expected Alan to make contact as they were going to go to the cinema. Well, that's what he told me. He then said he was going to report him missing so I agreed and that's what we did.'

Anna paused, flicking the pages of her notebook back and forth.

'During all this time you slept in the flat?'

'Yes.'

'Was there anyone else sleeping there?'

'No.'

'Do you have a cleaner?'

'No.'

'So did you change the bedlinen on your bed?'

'I can't really remember, but yes, I suppose I did. I usually change the bed every Monday and take the used stuff to the launderette for a service wash.'

'We have been to the laundry you use and they have no record of you bringing in anything for the period of time when Alan Rawlins was missing. How do you explain that?'

'I dunno. I said every Monday, but sometimes I'd skip a week or so if we'd been away.'

'But you weren't away, so what did you do with the sheets left on the bed when Alan was at home with a migraine?'

'I can't remember.'

'You can't remember?'

'I just said so.'

Paul passed over the photographs taken at the scene of crime. They showed the blood pooling, under the floorboards and the removed segment of carpet. Anna handed them across to Tina.

'As you can see, we discovered dense blood pooling beside your bed.'

Tina stared at the photographs.

Next, Paul produced the print of the staining to the edge of the mattress.

'This bloodstain was on your mattress.'

Again, Tina just stared at the photograph.

'We also know that you purchased four large containers of bleach and carpet cleaner, but we found only one container of bleach in your flat. Forensics have ascertained that bleach was used in an attempt to clean up. The blood must have soaked through the original carpet, through the underlay and down onto and under the floorboards.'

Paul got out the forensic shots. Again Tina stared at them, but remained silent. She turned to hand them to her lawyer, but he shook his head, having already been shown them.

'Do you have anything to say about the findings, Tina?'

'No.'

Anna nodded to Paul as she explained the use of Luminol in the bathroom and hallway.

'As you can see, although there had been an attempt to clean the bathroom and the surrounding areas, we were able to uncover further blood-staining.'

Tina chewed at her lips. Again she turned to her lawyer, almost as if *he* could give her an explanation, but he said that he was already privy to the photographs.

'We have, as you know, been unable to identify the blood recovered as that of Alan Rawlins, but it stands to reason that as he has been missing for over nine weeks now it is very possibly his,' Anna went on. 'And that he was murdered in the bedroom then carried into the bathroom, due to the amount of blood-stains discovered in both rooms.'

'I don't understand any of this,' Tina said, and placed her hands over the offending photographs.

'It's very difficult for *us* to understand, Tina, especially as you claim that the last time you saw Alan Rawlins was—'

'I'm telling you the truth!' Tina burst out. 'I don't know anything about this, I really don't. I am telling you the truth!'

'But if you changed the bedlinen, you must have been able to see *this*.' Anna snatched the photograph of the blood pooling by the bed and slapped it down in front of Tina. 'You *must* have known about it! How else did that section of carpet get to be in place over the stain?'

'I told you – Alan spilled wine, and he must have done it.'

'When did he do it?'

'I don't know, maybe the same day he had a migraine.'

'Really? And yet Forensics have been unable to discover any wine stain left on the underlay in the living room or the piece of carpet in the bedroom.'

'Well, I *saw* him spill wine and he was upset because it was a big stain and he cleaned it up.'

'You recall the spillage as a reason for the carpet being cut by Alan, correct?'

'Yes, that's right.'

'Whether or not there was a stain, the sofa was moved across it. We know that the section cut out was wide and long enough to cover the exact area of the bloodstain beside your bed.'

'Alan must have done it,' Tina repeated.

'When did he do this?'

'I don't know exactly.'

'I think you do know, Tina, because I think you cut that section of carpet and you thought it would not be noticed. You cut the exact size of carpet needed to hide the bloodstain; you then moved the sofa over the missing section in your lounge and returned to—'

'I DID NOT.'

'Why did you subsequently order a new roll of carpet, Tina?'

Jonathan Hyde leaned forward, frowning. 'I was not told about this. What carpet are you now referring to?'

Anna explained that whilst she was at his client's flat the caretaker had taken possession of a new roll of carpet that Tina had ordered. Tina looked at Hyde rather than Anna as she explained.

'I'd ordered it weeks ago 'cos I couldn't clean off the fucking wine and other food and drink stains in the lounge. When the landlord comes round to check before we leave, we gotta have everything as it was when we moved in. He says he's been done before and wants the flat to be left as we first saw it. I told you this; I said all this to you! We had to leave a big deposit.'

Paul passed Anna a receipt in a plastic cover.

'This is a receipt from Wall-to-Wall, a carpet warehouse. As you can see, the order was placed *after* Alan Rawlins disappeared.' Anna pushed it across the table to Hyde.

Tina didn't even glance at it, but continued, 'I wanted it done because I'm not plannin' on staying. That place has got too many bad memories for me.'

'Are these the bad memories, Tina, the bloodsoaked carpet?'

'No, I didn't mean them! I meant because of Alan leaving.'

Anna gathered the photographs up as Hyde carefully checked the receipt and the agreed delivery date. He passed it back to Paul, making a note in his notebook.

Paul looked to Anna, who leaned over and whispered to him. He opened another file and took out a report.

297

'We discovered further forensic evidence from the sheet and pillowcase on your bed, Tina. We have semen stains that don't match the blood DNA, and hair that is not Alan's as it's seven inches long. From recent photographs of Mr Rawlins we can see that his hair is cut short. Can you explain how this evidence came to be there?'

'No, I can't.'

'You have claimed today that you and only you stayed at the flat – no one else – but this is a lie. You are lying, aren't you, Tina?'

'I am telling you the truth.' She turned to Hyde and tapped his arm. 'For fuck's sake, why don't you say something and stop all this because I am telling the truth. I never had nobody sleeping with me. I was there on me own.' Her accent was slipping more towards cockney as she grew increasingly upset.

'Miss Brooks, the officers are required to put the evidence in their case to you, and you do not have to answer unless you want to. I assure you I am more than aware of Detective Travis's accusations, but this is your opportunity to tell them your version of events . . .'

'It's the truth! I mean, I never hurt Alan and she's been telling me that he had this other life – right? Or was that you trying to make me implicate myself?'

Anna pursed her lips, saying, 'We have uncovered records of substantial amounts of money that Alan had acquired, also a property in Cornwal—'

Tina interrupted her again. 'I don't know nothing about any money or what you said about him being a queer. I've been telling you the honest-to-God truth.'

'Then please explain to me, if you still insist that you and you alone slept in your flat after Alan's disappearance, why we have evidence that indicates another man was in your bed.'

'One moment.' Hyde tapped the table with his fountain pen. 'You have as yet been unable to identify whose blood was discovered beside the bed or who left the evidence found on the bedlinen, correct?'

'Yes, that is correct. We have been unable to acquire DNA from Alan Rawlins for a direct comparison.'

'Then surely it is possible that the evidence uncovered from the bedside plus whatever DNA has been found on the bedlinen, could well belong to someone other than Alan Rawlins?'

'That is possible,' Anna said curtly.

'Then isn't it also possible that Alan Rawlins not only murdered someone else, but changed all the bedlinen and cleaned the flat? He would have had the entire day whilst my client was at work.'

'YES!' Tina half-rose from her chair.

'Please remain seated, Miss Brooks.'

Tina sat back in her chair with a smug look on her face. She jabbed the air with her finger.

'He could have removed the carpet, he could have shoved the bed over the bloodstain. I wasn't thinking when I got back from the salon that we'd got different bedding on – right? That fucking semen stain you say you got could be his, right? Well, am I right?'

'Just stay quiet, please, Miss Brooks,' Hyde said coolly.

'But that makes sense, don't it? And it's just coincidence that I ordered the new roll of carpet. I've been telling the fucking truth since I've come here.'

Jonathan Hyde closed his notebook, pocketed his pen and gave half a smile.

'I think, Detective Travis, that until you are able to

identify who the victim is, you really have no option but to release my client.'

Anna knew she was cornered and said that Tina should remain available as they might well need to question her again.

'Is that it, then?' Tina said, smiling.

'Just one more thing. You have denied knowing Michael Phillips?'

Hyde looked up enquiringly.

'Miss Brooks's neighbour,' Anna explained. 'Do you still maintain that you do not know him?'

'I didn't, but I do now. I met him coming in one night recently and I was so upset. I wanted some change of clothes, remember I asked you for permission. He was going into his flat and I was trying to get my key out to go into my place. He asked if I was all right and I just broke down crying. He was ever so nice. He asked me in for a brandy and since then we've become friendlier. We exchanged numbers and he said if I needed anything, to call him.'

'When did you last call him?'

'From the pub before you arrested me.'

'What did you talk about?'

'All the stress this is causing me. He was like I just said, very kind, and if you want the honest truth, I fancied him. I need someone, for God's sake!'

It was a depressed Anna who released Tina and then returned to the incident room to give the team the update. Thanks to Langton's belief that the evidence from the flat strongly implicated Tina, she had gone along with his request to put pressure on the woman, but all along she had known they were skating on thin ice.

*

Brian Stanley still had no confirmation that Tina and Michael Phillips had been in close contact for longer than she or he had admitted. At the briefing, Anna stressed the importance of identifying the victim and the semen from the bedlinen. She only now gave them the information that the hair was not going to be significant. Liz Hawley had informed them that Sammy Marsh's DNA had been taken on a mouth swab when he was arrested for drugs offences a number of years ago but, for reasons she was still trying to discover, it did not appear to have been uploaded onto the national database. Sammy was still only a tentative link to Alan Rawlins, and without any evidence it was also possible it was nothing more than a coincidence.

'So a trip to Cornwall is still on the cards is it?' Brian asked.

Anna nodded, although she would first have to get it passed by Langton, and she was not looking forward to giving him the details of her interview with Tina Brooks.

As the team broke up for the night, Anna sat in her office mulling over the uneventful day's work. She jotted down notes to look into the following morning, loath to pick up the phone to Langton. Just as she was about to call him, Paul rang through to say that Joe Smedley, the head mechanic at Metcalf Auto, was on line two.

'What does he want?'

'He's had a break-in, happened last night. He reported it to the local cop shop, but then reckoned we might be interested.'

'Put him through.'

'Detective Travis?'

'Speaking.'

'I had a break-in last night. It must have happened very

late as we was working here up until after nine. It wasn't in the main part of the garage, but in the workshops attached, and they're not alarmed, just got a padlock on the roll-up.'

'Was anything stolen?'

'That's what is odd. Nothin's gone that I could tell you 'cos it was where Alan kept the Merc he was doin' up, so there weren't much room for anythin' else. Some bastard has ripped the Merc's seats – good quality leather, they were – and the door panels have been torn out. The boot was open and scratched to hell and it had just been resprayed. So it's a lot of damage. I mean, it don't hurt me because it wasn't my vehicle, and to be honest I was gonna call his girlfriend as I dunno what anyone wants to do with the car and I will need the space.'

'Thank you for calling, Mr Smedley. If you are there now, could you wait as I'd like to have a look at what was done.'

'Okay. I'll be here until eight tonight.'

Anna replaced the receiver. She could legitimately put off calling Langton. With Brian in tow, rather disgruntled as he was ready to leave for the evening, she drove to Metcalf Auto repair garage.

The padlock had been broken. As Smedley had said, the workshop was not alarmed, but both padlock and chain were heavy-duty.

'Hadda come with bolt-cutters, and like I told you, nothing else was broken into – just this lock-up.'

Smedley was still wearing greasy oil-streaked overalls and his hands were black with engine oil. He eased up the gate, which swung out and then slid up under the roof of the workshop.

'I never charged Al for storing his vehicles in here, only for whatever equipment he needed. The paint-spraying was done round the back and he'd use the hydraulic lift to check the under-carriages, but always when it was convenient. We've also had delivery of a new soft top, which is over in the main garage.'

They stood in a row looking into the garage. The 280SL's seats had, as Smedley described, been hacked, slashed and the stuffing dragged out. Both doors had the panels hammered out, and even the dashboard looked as if someone had attacked it with an axe. The glove compartment door was broken and hanging on its hinges. The boot had deep indentations as it had been locked when it was prised open.

'It's a crying shame,' Joe mourned. 'Al loves this car and it was just about ready to sell.'

Anna and Brian walked around the damaged vehicle. At the rear of the garage was a tools locker that had been forced open and the contents were strewn around the floor.

'What do you think they were looking for?' Anna said quietly to Brian.

'Christ only knows. Only time I've seen a car broken up like this was when I was with the Drug Squad. It had cocaine stacked between the panels in the door. Mind you, that wasn't a vintage car like this one. This is a real damage job and it must have created a lot of noise.'

'Did anyone complain about hearing a noise or see anything?' Anna asked.

Smedley shook his head. 'There's no housing close to the yard, and besides, there's often a lot of noise from us. I dunno even if it's insured.'

'Did the locals dust for prints?' asked Brian, still inspecting the damaged vehicle.

'I don't think so. A couple of uniforms came and looked over it, and they thought it might be drunk kids, vandals or whatever.'

Anna suggested to Brian they get SOCO to dust and see if they came up with any prints, although she doubted it. Probably whoever did the damage wore gloves.

'How many cars did you see Alan Rawlins work on in here?'

'Quite a few. He's worked here for years and always had one or another on the go. They made a nice little earner for him and they were always top-of-the-range vintage. He was also obsessive, you know? Hadda be perfect. I've seen him do a complete respray, and to me it was perfect, but not to him. He's also had a couple of motor bikes he customised with a little thin guy, pal of his – a graphic designer – and they did a lovely job between them.'

Anna suggested they close up the garage and asked for Smedley to allow their SOCO officers to dust for prints.

'How long do I have to keep it here?' he asked.

'We'll be as fast as possible and then I'm not sure what will be done or who now owns it.'

'So you still got no trace of him then?'

'No.'

'Bloody weird – doesn't make sense.'

As Smedley locked up with a new padlock, Anna asked if she could have a quick chat to him, but Brian was eager to take off home. 'It's all right, Brian,' she told him. 'This won't need the two of us. You go.'

Smedley took Anna into his small office and offered to make her a cup of tea, but judging from his filthy hands she didn't think she'd care for one.

'Can I just ask you again, Joe – the morning Alan

Rawlins left, the last time you saw him ... just take me through it.'

'Well, I've not got anythin' more to add. He come in early as always – he was always the first here, last to go. He'd often work on his own vehicles before we got here and before he started on scheduled work. He was a bloody good mechanic, very thorough ...' He scratched at his beard and then his chest, trying to come up with something else.

'He said he was unwell, had a migraine?' Anna prompted.

'Yeah, that's right. He was wearing his overalls, we had a car up on the ramps and he was scheduled to look at it. I was in here sorting through some bills and receipts. I saw him when I drove up as his Merc was out on the forecourt. I said to him it was looking in great shape and he said something about he was just waiting for the soft top to be delivered. That must have cost a lot, 'cos the one the Merc came with was worn and torn. There's a company that supply them that he's used before.'

'How did he seem when you saw him?'

'The usual. He was quite a shy bloke, didn't talk much, but he was smiling and then I saw him drive the Merc into the lock-up.'

'So when did he come in to say he was feeling unwell?'

'Not long after. It was about ten-fifteen. He was very pale and his hands were clenched. He said he needed to call Tina because he was feeling sick and said he had a headache.'

'Had he ever taken time off for headaches?'

'Maybe once before, don't really remember. I joked with him that he should watch himself, it might be swine flu. Then he used my phone in here.'

'Did you hear the conversation?'

'Nope. I was called out – don't remember what for, but when I came back he said that Tina would be collecting him and taking him home.'

'How long after that did Tina drive up?'

'Not long. He was on the forecourt pacing up and down waiting. He got in and they drove off.'

'And it was Tina?'

'Yeah. She waved over as they drove out.'

'Thank you.' Anna stood up as Smedley opened a drawer.

'I was asked about when Al took holidays,' he said. 'Did you get the details?'

'Yes, thank you.'

'He'd come back all tanned and his hair lightened by the sun – good-lookin' fella.'

'He was bisexual.'

Smedley did a classic jaw-drop and then chuckled. 'You pullin' me leg? Living with a hot tottie like Tina Brooks? No way.'

'So you never had any indication that he was gay or rather, bisexual?'

'Al?'

'Yes.'

'You serious?'

'Yes.'

Smedley seemed to take it personally, shaking his head and scratching at his beard.

'If he was, he kept that under his bonnet, not that I have anythin' against them, but you surprise me. My wife'll not believe it, as he was a good-lookin' guy and strong as an ox.'

They walked out onto the forecourt and headed towards Anna's Mini.

'You got me flummoxed,' Joe went on in disbelief. 'We did used to joke about him always scrubbing at his hands – liked to be clean before he went home. And a lot of the blokes here wouldn't mind having Tina as their girlfriend; she's a lovely-lookin' woman.'

'Yes, she is,' Anna agreed as she unlocked her door.

Smedley stood watching her driving out, still scratching at his beard and his hairy chest.

Anna didn't go home, but returned to the station. It was eerie, walking through the semi-darkened incident room, as only the night-duty officers were there. She stood for a long time looking over the incident board and then at the lists of estate agents contacted in Cornwall. They had now acquired a photograph of the property Alan had bought. It was a medium-sized detached house with views over the beach, and a wide paved patio with umbrellas and outdoor furniture. There was a barbecue and glass sliding doors opening into a sunken lounge. It had three bedrooms, an en-suite bathroom and a high-tech kitchen with a breakfast bar. It also had a double garage and a gated entrance with a tiered rock garden.

Anna headed into her office, switching on only her desk lamp as she sat down in her chair. She dreaded making the call, but she knew she had put it off long enough. Her hand was reaching for the phone when her door opened and Langton walked in.

'I was just about to call you,' she said.

'Don't you have a home to go to, Travis?' He drew out a chair, put his coat over the back of it and sat in front of her.

'The same could be said of you.'

'I know. Been up to my eyeballs. I'm tired out and my knee's killing me. What happened today?'

'Sadly, not a lot.'

Langton stood up and rubbed his knee, then leaned forward, placing both hands on Anna's desk.

'You've yet to prove me wrong because without a body you are still running on empty. Even more so as you still have not identified your victim.'

'It's not for want of trying.' She had stood up to face him across her desk.

'You try harder, sweetheart, otherwise I am going to have to say time is up, and I still maintain that someone close to home, by home I mean the flat where the murder happened – someone knows something.'

'Give me a clue then, because I have interviewed every tenant, the neighbours across the street and to the side of the block of flats. I've interviewed the caretaker, and nobody saw anything. I have no witness.'

'There is always a witness, remember that. How did the body get moved?'

'I don't know.' She felt like shouting it at him.

'If it was carved up, it still took time – it'd be heavy, and if you no longer have Tina as a suspect . . .'

'I never said that.'

'Right. If you are still suspicious of her, could she have moved it out single-handed?'

'I am still not losing Michael Phillips as a suspect or a possible accomplice.'

Langton picked up his coat from the back of the chair.

'Body's got to be somewhere. If she maintains she returned to the flat after work it means the body was cut up or had to have been moved in broad daylight.'

'I know, I know . . .'

'But do you know why I am consenting to your trip to Cornwall?'

'Because you agree with me that Alan Rawlins could be alive.'

'No, I don't agree with you, Anna, but the drug link now has to be treated as a motive. The wrecking of his Mercedes, it's not malicious, not a vengeful act, it was done by someone looking for something and that is either drugs or money.'

'I had thought of that, but again there's no witness – nobody saw or heard anything – and yet it looked as if whoever did it was using a sledgehammer.'

Langton paused, shrugging into his coat.

'Don't take any risks, Anna. You uncover something that could be a threat to you, make sure you have back-up and contact the Drug Squad down there. Understand?'

'I will.'

She walked towards him to see him out and he took her totally off-guard, cupping her face in his hands and kissing her forehead. Then he opened the door, and turning back he smiled.

'I watched you through the blinds. The lamplight made a halo around that lovely head of yours. See what you can produce from Cornwall. Let's hope it's not a wild-goose chase.'

'Yes, sir. If Alan Rawlins is alive, I'll track him down.'

He was about to say something, but then changed his mind. He had not forgotten, and probably never would, the loss of his prime suspect in the drug-related murder enquiry they had both worked on. Anthony Fitzpatrick had outwitted him, escaped arrest and was still at large. Langton did not consider with the new evidence that Alan Rawlins was anywhere in the same league as Fitzpatrick, nevertheless if he was involved in a drug-dealing racket it meant he would have contacts. Rawlins also had financial resources. He could, as Anna had suspected, have flown the coop to Florida. Fitzpatrick had managed to escape arrest after a series of murders; he was only able to do so because of his wealth.

When Langton left Anna he had grave concerns, primarily for her safety. In the morning he would begin to make certain enquiries himself.

By the time Anna got home it was after ten. Apart from the half-finished sandwich at lunch, she hadn't had anything else to eat, but she didn't have the energy to cook anything bar a couple of slices of toast. She took a mug of tea and sat on her bed. As she dipped the toast into the tea she thought about what she would need to pack for the following day. Langton had given the go-ahead for herself and one other officer to travel to Cornwall, although he had said air flights were out of the question due to budget shortages. He suggested she get the train to Newquay and arrange for the local station to provide a squad car for them to use. If it was necessary, they could stay a couple of nights in a B&B that the locals knew or used.

Anna decided that a five-hour train journey with Brian Stanley would do too much head damage, so she would be accompanied by Paul. Langton had even suggested that Paul would be the best choice as he was homosexual. When she had given him an admonishing glare he had simply laughed.

Anna drew the duvet up to her chin, snuggling down in her bed, but wondering what she might uncover in Cornwall kept her wide awake. She closed her eyes, recalling Langton's comments as he left. She realised that he had not admitted in as many words that her diligent enquiries had moved the case into a different league. It proved that she *had* been on the ball and not, as he had implied, over-investigating. Typically, Langton agreeing to the Cornwall visit was to her mind a step forward, and she was even more determined to prove herself right and Langton wrong about her digging up too many suspects.

She too remembered Anthony Fitzpatrick and what it had felt like to see the man they had hunted for so many months escape arrest. Forever lodged in her mind were the faces of the drug dealer's two small children looking out from the windows of the plane. Wherever they were, wherever Fitzpatrick was hiding out, there had been no sighting of him. It was, she knew, a testament to failure on Langton's part. She vowed to herself once again that if Alan Rawlins was alive, she would not let him escape arrest.

Chapter Fourteen

'I thought they'd have a restaurant,' Paul complained, as he had not had time for lunch. He and Anna were on the two o'clock train at Paddington, bound for Cornwall.

'I thought so too, but apparently they have a buffet cart they wheel through the compartments.'

The train had few passengers and they were virtually alone in their carriage.

'You know this stops off at a shedload of stations?' he whinged.

'Yes.'

'It's going to take about five hours.'

'Yes, I know.'

'Didn't the budget run to a plane – only that would have taken a fraction of the time?'

'I know that, Paul, but by the time we got to Gatwick airport and allowed two hours before the flight took off it'd still be around the same time.'

He was about to argue but thought better of it, knowing it had to be down to the budget.

Anna opened *The Times* and suggested they not discuss the case until later.

'Sure, why not. We've got five whole hours.' He sat back in his very comfortable seat and closed his eyes. Anna

313

read the paper, noticing as she turned a page that Paul was fast asleep. She put it aside and stared from the window. They had two days with a stopover in the B&B. She opened her briefcase and took out her notebook, intending to underline what she felt was a priority. But the rhythm of the train made her sleepy and she eventually dozed, resting her head on her arms on the table.

Back at the station, Langton was carefully going over everything on the incident board.

'This caretaker stroke janitor at Tina Brooks's block of flats – we have a contact number for him?' he asked Brian.

Brian nodded.

'I want to talk to him, today,' Langton went on. 'See if he's available. I also want access to Miss Brooks's flat, so arrange that at the same time. Unless, I suppose, he might have a master key. Check if he has.'

As Brian drove Langton to Newton Court, Langton grilled him about the break-in at Metcalf Auto garage.

'The guy who runs it mentioned that he had taken delivery of a soft top for the Merc. Do you know if DCI Travis had it taken in or checked out?'

'Not sure, Gov. I left her there so she might have looked at it.'

'We go there next, and I want a visit to the salon.'

'Right you are.' Brian drove them into the horseshoe drive of Newton Court. Standing at the front doors was Jonas Jones. He watched them park up and then went inside.

'Does he have a record?' Langton asked as they headed towards the reception.

'Petty theft, couple of prison terms, but nothing for ten years.'

Langton pushed open the doors and headed towards Jonas, who was using a duster-covered broom to sweep around the small entrance area.

'Good morning, Jonas, I am Detective Chief Superintendent Langton. You got a place we can have a little chat?'

'No. I only got a broom closet in the hall which is where I keep all the cleaning stuff. I just check the reception area and stairs.'

Langton nodded. 'You keep it nice and clean.'

'Thank you. That's what I'm paid for. When I run out of stuff I phone the landlord and he replaces the Brasso and floor polish. I used to have an electric floor-polisher, but that broke recently and so I do it by hand now.'

'You know Miss Tina Brooks?'

'Yes, sir. Well, not *know* her – just to say good morning to.'

'What about the other occupants?'

'It's about the same apart from Miss Jewell. She often makes me a cup of coffee so I've been inside her flat a few times.'

'Must have had a good chat about the missing bloke, Alan Rawlins?'

'Yeah, but like me she didn't know him and she's up on the top floor.'

Jonas sucked in his breath; he was minus a number of front teeth. He had iron-grey tight curls and his cheeks were sunken. His scrawny body looked as worn as his overalls.

'What was the gossip?' Langton asked, offering a cigarette.

'What?'

'What did you talk about?' Langton lit the cigarette for Jonas and himself.

'Oh, I see. Well, she was interviewed – like me, like all of us – and we talked about that and how we never knew the missing bloke. Just goes to show really, doesn't it? Living on top of each other like that and never talking.'

'Did you talk to him?'

'Not much.'

'What else do you do round here?'

'I also sweep up around the garages. I keep all the grounds tidy, cut the bit of grass. We got an empty garage 'cos Miss Jewell doesn't drive so that's where I keep the lawnmower and hedge-cutters.'

'What about the garbage, the bins?'

'Well, they put their rubbish in them during the week and on a Monday I wheel them out to the front for the binmen. They used to collect twice a week, but now it's just the once. After they've been emptied I put them round the back again. We've not got rubbish chutes or anything like that. The tenants take down their own rubbish and they've each got an allocated wheelie bin.'

'Take me round there, would you please, Jonas?' Langton asked.

Brian was fascinated, listening to Langton's easy banter with the caretaker, realising he had got a lot more out of him than Travis when she had interviewed him. The pair of them puffing on their cigarettes.

The neat row of big green wheelie bins each had a number on them. Langton tapped the one marked for flat number two.

'This is Tina Brooks's, right?' He lifted the lid and looked inside. There was one black bin liner in there. 'You ever get any foul smells from one of the bins?'

'Not really. I mean, I don't look inside. They always have a bit of a stink as it's only collected . . .'

'Once a week – yes, you said.' Langton closed the lid. 'You ever feel one or other to be very heavy? Unusually so?'

'No.'

'You ever find anything useful to take home with you?'

'No.'

They headed back to the reception. Langton tossed his cigarette butt aside. Jonas was smoking his down to the cork tip.

'You took an order of new carpet for Miss Brooks, didn't you?'

'Yes, sir, about a week ago. She was leaving one morning and she asked me to sign for it and take it in as she knew it was being delivered, but wasn't sure what time.'

'She give a tip for doing that?'

'Yes, sir, a tenner because I'd finished up my work and had to hang around waiting for the van, but it arrived at about ten so I didn't have to wait long.' Jonas flicked the last remains of the tobacco from the cork and pocketed it.

'You have keys to the flats?'

'Yes, sir. I have to have them for emergencies. We had a bath overflow one time a few years back and I had to open up and sort it out. They'd left a tap running – Mr and Mrs Maisell.'

'But you didn't deliver the carpet into Miss Brooks's flat when it arrived; it was left out here in reception, wasn't it?'

'That is correct, sir. Reason is I've got a bad back and I wasn't gonna make it worse. It was just here in the reception for when she got home.'

'So how did she move it?'

'I don't know. When I came to work again it had gone. I only work two mornings a week here.'

'I see. When you were cleaning around the garages, did you meet up with Alan Rawlins at all?'

'Er, yeah, I did a few times. He was either driving in or out. She kept her car in there, a VW, but sometimes he had one so he would park it directly outside her garage doors or he'd put his car in and hers would be left outside.'

'How did he seem to you?'

'He was polite, give me a good tip at Christmas, but I wouldn't say I ever had a whole conversation with him.'

'You ever see him with anyone else apart from Miss Brooks?'

'No.'

'How about the bloke from flat one, Mr Phillips?'

Jonas shrugged.

'Don't like him?' Langton asked.

'Well, he's got a very nice car, a Lotus, and a couple of times he asked me to give it a clean. I don't have a hose over that way so I'd give it a polish and I got a small battery hoover so I did the inside for him. He only gave me a fiver and he's not been here as long as the other tenants so I've never really had much to do with him. But like I said, I only did the car a couple of times.'

'Why don't you like him?'

'He'd have to pay more in a car wash, and when I done it the second time I said to him that it would cost him a tenner and he was just edgy with me, said he only had a fiver on him and he'd give me the rest when he next saw me. He never did.'

'Did Mr Phillips seem friendly with Miss Brooks?'

'I dunno. They leave for work when I'm here or they've already left and I don't do weekends. Then I'm gone by the time they come home. I know he drinks a bit – lot of empty bottles of wine and vodka in his bin.'

'Ah, so you *do* open them and check them out?'

'No, they were left in a carrier bag beside his bin. We've got recycling containers that they're supposed to put glass bottles and plastic into, but they can't always be bothered.'

'Single guy, was his bin full then?'

Jonas shrugged and said he couldn't remember.

Brian shifted his weight, becoming impatient. So far Jonas hadn't given them anything new and he wondered why Langton was spending so much time questioning him.

'Come on, Jonas, give it up. You pick through those wheelie bins, don't you, see if there's anything worth taking?'

'Sometimes, yeah — all right, I do. No harm in it 'cos they're for the rubbish tips and occasionally there's been something worth taking home.'

'Carpet? Did you find any sections of carpet in Miss Brooks's bin?'

'Yeah, but not worth taking as the piece was so small. I reckon when she lays the new one she'll give me the old one.'

'Anything else?'

'From hers?'

'Yes, from Miss Brooks's bin.'

'There was some clothes once, but I think they was old 'cos they was in a bin bag.'

Langton looked around casually as if the conversation was finished but then he turned back to Jonas.

'Men's or women's clothes?'

'Don't know. I didn't look real close but I know she has a lot of thick sort of bandages she tosses out.'

'Bandages? How do you mean?'

'Like wide elastic ones, but they're covered in gunge and not worth taking.'

'Gunge? Like blood?'

'No, green stuff. It smells a bit rancid, but like I said not worth taking.'

'The time you found the carpet, Jonas, what else was in the bin?'

'Bleach cartons – empty. The tenants never toss anything worth my while.'

Langton patted him on the shoulder, thanking him. He then asked to be let into Miss Brooks's flat. Jonas didn't hesitate but led them straight to the door and unlocked it. Only then did he ask if this was all right and if Miss Brooks had given her permission. Langton said he didn't need it as they had a search warrant. Jonas asked if he wanted him to stay as he had another block of flats he was due to clean.

'You go ahead, I'll lock up after we leave. And Jonas, thank you for your time. I really appreciate it.'

Jonas hurried back to his broom closet and stuffed his brush and dusters inside. He then got into his beaten-up old van and opened the glove compartment. Tucked inside was the touch-screen mobile phone he had found under the piece of carpet in Tina Brooks's bin. The battery was dead and he had planned to go to the market near him in Portobello Road to get a new SIM card. Now he thought he would just toss it. He reckoned it had been thrown out by mistake but he wasn't going to admit he'd got it in case he could be accused of stealing. He had no idea that it was actually Alan Rawlins's additional mobile used for his gay and business contacts.

Langton didn't say a word as he examined Tina's lounge. He moved the sofa aside and inspected the patch cut out from the carpet. He eased the sofa back into position and walked into the hallway, pushing open the bathroom door. Although there had been extensive cleaning after the forensic team had left, there was still a residue of their powders.

He glanced at Brian, muttering, 'Lazy sods not done a good clean-up, have they?'

He opened the bathroom cabinet that contained rows of hair solutions, hair-dye and shampoos. Moisturisers and face creams were lined up alongside soaps and bath oils. There was also a large can of mechanic's special soap, the only item obviously connected to Alan Rawlins. In the small drawer under the cabinet were bottles of nail varnish, a manicure set and bottles of vitamins and paracetamol tablets. There was only one battery-powered toothbrush and toothpaste, and in a jar were an array of very clean hairbrushes and combs. He knew they had not found any hairbrush or comb belonging to Alan Rawlins.

Brian stood watching as Langton walked back into the hall and checked the measurement scale markers left on the wall by the forensic team.

'She's moved back in, right? So she's not cleaned up either.'

Next he paused in the doorway of the bedroom and then crossed to kneel beside the bed. He had to push it with his shoulder to move it to show the second section of cut carpet. The bed was bare, with just the base remaining, no mattress or pillows. He lay down on it and had to lean quite far over to see the bloodstained area. He reckoned whoever was killed had to have had his head, neck and the top part of his shoulders over the side of the bed. Could whoever it was have been held down by someone maybe kneeling on his back?

Getting off the bed, Langton opened the wardrobe: there were a lot of dresses and evening clothes, shoes in their boxes, and on a shelf above, some flowery hats.

'Where is she sleeping?' Langton asked.

'There's a box room next door.'

Langton followed Brian. The small box room had a single bed, which was made up and a duvet cover thrown to one side. There was also the roll of new carpet. Langton lifted it a fraction and found it was, as Jonas had said, heavy. The roll was probably intended to re-carpet the lounge. A fitted wardrobe contained a few clothes, but most of the space was taken up by a box of thick bandages in rolls, each roll fastened with a safety pin. Next to this was another box with containers of seaweed solution in large green cans. He took one out and read the label before replacing it.

'So she's sleeping in here.'

'Don't blame her,' grunted Brian, waiting in the doorway as the room was so small. He watched Langton lift the bedcovers to look beneath them and then as he checked through the drawers of a dresser.

'Nice underwear,' he murmured, sniffing a lace bra. 'Shalimar perfume, isn't it?'

'I wouldn't know.' Brian glanced at his watch.

'You in a hurry to go somewhere?'

'No, Gov, just wondered what time it was.'

Langton looked at the top of the dresser, which was filled with make-up and bottles of perfume. He opened one then replaced the top.

'Shalimar. I was right. Very distinctive smell, sort of old-fashioned, but very pungent.'

'If you say so. I've got a terrible sense of smell.'

'Right – let's see the kitchen.'

Brian had to stand and watch as Langton went through every drawer and cupboard, checking all the cans of food.

'I wouldn't say she was a good cook.' He was going through the freezer now. 'All frozen diet dinners. He was a fitness freak, wasn't he, Alan Rawlins? This doesn't look like the kind of stuff he would want to eat: lean cuisine, low-carb spaghetti and meatballs?'

'I expect she just cooks for herself now.'

'Yeah maybe.' He shut the freezer door and then looked into the fridge which contained yoghurts and fruit juices and half a tomato.

'Any carving knives missing?' he asked.

'Nope. There's a block on the side there, and all the knives are in their slots.'

'What about tools – any tools in the flat?'

'Didn't find any.'

Langton opened a closet that contained bleach and cleaning fluids. He dragged out a cardboard box of screws, nails, light bulbs and screwdrivers.

'Odd? No hammer.'

'Forensics took it but didn't find anything on it.'

'Shame.' Langton replaced the box and went to close the door, but swung it open again as he noticed an apron and a plastic overall with *Tina's Salon* printed on them. The apron looked as if it had never been used, but the overall was stained and smelled of bleach.

'One more look into the lounge, then that's it.'

Brian nodded, following behind. Langton squatted down in front of a small bookcase. He carefully checked one title after another. On the top row were mostly chick-lit novels, Martina Cole paperbacks and eight Danielle Steel novels. There were a few books on racing cars, vintage cars and motor-racing manuals. There were also numerous true crime books and one about the latest developments in forensic science. He thumbed through every page of this one. The book did not appear to have been well-read; no corners were turned down, nothing was underlined, and the chapters detailing DNA evidence appeared to be unmarked.

Langton replaced it.

'Hard to get my head around the fact that Alan Rawlins even lived here. We got his clothes, right – but no shoes. No shaving equipment, no toothbrush, and they found no brush or comb used by him.'

'That is correct.'

'You get anything from his work locker?'

'Nope.'

'Anything from the garage out back?'

'Nope. Are you thinking he packed up some of his clothes and stuff and pissed off?'

Langton sighed, shaking his head.

'Or somebody else packed it for him to look like he pissed off,' he said grimly, crossing to the small side table close to the large flatscreen TV.

Brian rolled his eyes. He knew the SOCO and lab teams had gone over the flat in detail and he felt this was all a waste of time.

'Maybe whoever killed him had time to give his possessions a good clear-out,' he suggested. 'If Alan was murdered shortly after Tina says she left for work, the killer or killers would have had five or six hours to clean up.'

'Thank you for that insight, Brian. You have any idea how long it would take to carve up a body, wipe the place down, make up the bed again?'

'And maybe have sex as well?'

'Yeah – and remove anything that would give us a DNA link to Alan Rawlins.'

Langton began reading all the letters and bank statements in the side table drawer.

'She's very neat and methodical. The tax is up to date, VAT is up to date, but there's nothing of his in here. His address book was taken in, wasn't it? But there's nothing relating to him in the diary, just her appointments and gym sessions listed. Often she's not filled in days; sometimes we've got a whole week with nothing written. There's car licence and insurance, house insurance . . .'

Brian stifled a yawn. 'His life was insured for fifty grand and we've not found any evidence that this was upped or changed by Tina,' he said, but Langton paid him no attention.

'She's the main beneficiary,' Brian went on. 'They had a joint bank account, which his wages and hers went straight into, and it looks like she then withdrew cash for them both. They've got just over seventy thousand saved.'

Langton nodded, replacing papers as he sifted through the drawers. He took in the room: the awful bland pictures on the walls, the beige on beige furniture. It was boring and featureless – yet two young people lived in the flat. Even though it was a rented one, it nevertheless had little of the personality of either Alan or Tina.

'They were planning on getting married. She told Travis that he had suggested she look for a wedding dress,' Brian remarked.

'What?'

Brian repeated his comment, adding sarcastically that Tina maintained she was unaware of her boyfriend's sexual activities elsewhere. Langton remembered when he had been with Anna, holding her in his arms as he told her about the death of her fiancé. The bridal magazines, the way she had cut out pictures of the wedding dress she was contemplating wearing. There was nothing similar inside this flat to indicate that Tina was thinking of getting married, and nothing connected to surfing or Alan's so-called other life. Could he have been that secretive?

'Photographs?' he said to himself. 'Where are they?' He gave a wide open-handed gesture.

Brian shrugged. 'I think they did take in some kind of an album, but that was why we had a problem with Alan. To get him ID'd we've been using a surfing photo DCI Travis took from his parents' home.'

Langton stood up, looking around the room.

'Doesn't make bloody sense. I mean, we can tell she lives here because of her make-up and hair shampoos, but what about him?'

'DCI Travis reckons his life will be in Cornwall. They'll be looking at the property there. Added to that he used his bedroom at his parents' home.'

'I know that,' Langton snapped, walking out. 'I'm through here, but I have got to talk to Tina.' As Brian hurried to catch up with him, Langton added grimly, 'You know why? Because this place doesn't make any sense.'

'Well, if they were planning on moving out to buy their own property, why bother doing anything with a rented flat?'

Langton paused on his way towards the patrol car, and turned back, saying, 'I want to see the garage she uses.'

'We don't have a key,' Brian said, exasperated. But it turned out that they didn't need one as the garage was unlocked.

'They took her car in, didn't they?'

'Yes. It was released back to Miss Brooks a few days ago.'

Langton looked around the empty garage. Like the flat, it was devoid of anything personal; there were just some car-cleaning products left in a cardboard box and a small cabinet at the back of the garage that had been checked out.

Langton looked over the odd tools. Again, these were in a neatly arranged order on a small bench. There was a tyre-pressure pump, petrol can, cans of oil and two small paint cans for white and cream bodywork. He sighed, beginning to understand more and more why Anna had broadened her investigation.

Anna woke with a start as Paul tapped her arm, to find that the trolley with food and drink was rattling towards them. They chose coffee and sandwiches and some fresh fruit.

'I was fast asleep,' Anna admitted, opening the wrapping.

'Me too. At least these are fresh.' He took a mouthful of his sandwich.

'How much longer?' Anna asked, biting into her ham and salad sandwich.

'Another three hours,' Paul said without looking at his watch.

'Three hours . . .' She sighed.

'Did we ever check if Alan Rawlins went by plane? They'd have a record of it at the airport if he did. He had to be a bloody frequent flyer because I'm sure he wouldn't be schlepping back and forth so often by train.'

'Unless he drove himself,' she said, chewing.

Paul took out his mobile and called into the incident room to speak to Brian Stanley, but was told he was out with Langton. Helen gave him the latest updates; they had found no vehicle licence or insurance on any other vehicle apart from Tina's VW. Paul asked them to run a check with DVLA on anything with Alan Rawlins's name and then to try the other names they knew he used. Anna looked over as Paul ended the call.

'Brian's out with Langton,' he told her.

'What?'

'That's all that Helen knew. They've been gone all morning.'

'Call him.'

'Langton?'

'No, Brian Stanley. Find out what they're doing, or more to the point, what Langton is nosing around for.'

When Brian saw that it was Paul who was ringing his mobile he didn't pick up, as he and Langton had just arrived at Tina's salon.

Langton breezed inside, where Felicity, on the desk as usual, said that Tina was not available as she was giving a treatment. Langton smiled and introduced himself, saying that he was not a client and he could wait until it was convenient for Tina to talk to him.

'Is there a place we can sit,' he read the name on her salon gown, 'Felicity? And perhaps you could inform Miss Brooks I am here, and I wouldn't mind a cup of coffee.'

'Oh, I suppose you can sit in the staff section. There's a coffee percolator in there. Hang on.' She turned from her desk and called out for Donna, who was cutting a client's hair. She yelled back that she was busy.

'Just direct me – no need to get anyone,' Langton said pleasantly.

Donna came up to the reception desk with the scissors in her hand, saying, 'What is it?'

Langton looked at Donna's name on her gown.

'Good Afternoon, Donna. I am Detective Chief Super-intendant Langton and this is Detective—'

Donna interrupted him. 'Tina's with a client.'

'We know that, Donna, and Felicity here suggested we wait in the staff section.'

'Is Tina expecting you?'

'I don't believe she is, but we can wait.'

Donna looked pensive and then shrugged. 'Come on through then.'

Kiara was working at a small table with a client having nail extensions. She glanced up as they passed her. The small sectioned-off area used for the staff was an untidy mess of hairdressing magazines and a mound of wet towels. A junior was in there eating a bun but Donna told her to get back into the salon.

'I'm supposed to be washing the towels,' the girl said, stuffing the last of the bun into her mouth.

'You're also supposed to be sweeping up the hair. I'll take these through to the washing machines.' Donna gathered up the towels and tried to clear a space for Langton and Brian to sit, muttering, 'Sorry about the mess in here. We've been very busy today.'

Langton stepped aside to allow her to pass by.

'The washers and dryers are out in the back. Help yourself to coffee.'

'I will, thank you.'

Langton noticed an array of used mugs and rinsed one out in the sink before he poured himself a cup of rather stewed black coffee.

'You want one?' he asked Brian.

'No, thanks. The nail stuff they use here stinks and makes me feel sick.'

Langton picked out a biscuit from an open tin and then cleared a stack of magazines before he sat down.

'Business looks thriving,' he remarked.

'Yeah, its running costs are high though. We had all her accounts checked out. She doesn't own the premises, but rents them so she has to have a good turnover to make ends meet.'

Langton seemed totally relaxed now, flicking through one of the magazines. After a moment he tossed it aside and picked up a laminated salon price-list left on a chair.

'Thinking of having a trim?' Brian joked.

'Hair extensions, nail extensions, colouring and perms, cuts and blowdries, beauty treatments, pedicures, mani-cures, massage, laser hair removal, seaweed wraps . . .'

He looked up at Brian. 'What's a seaweed wrap?'

'No idea. Doesn't this smell get to you? Reminds me of when I was a kid. My mother took me with her when she had her hair permed. She used to have these funny little rollers all over her head – it took ages and they slapped on this stuff that smelled of paint stripper, and after hours of sitting in this small cubicle she'd come out with tight curls all over her head.'

'How fascinating,' Langton said sarcastically.

Donna returned. 'A client wants a coffee – is it still hot?'

'Warmish,' he said, watching as she rinsed out a mug and poured the remainder of the coffee into it.

'I'll come back and make a fresh pot.'

Langton nodded. Brian now sat down and started to read a magazine. They both turned as Kiara, the girl doing the nail extensions, walked in.

'Have you found him?' she asked.

'No. How well did you know Alan Rawlins?'

'I didn't. None of us really had anything to do with

him. He'd just come and sometimes collect Tina and wait for her in the car park. I told that to the lady who was asking questions before.'

'So you did.'

Kiara got some fresh coffee, lifted the percolator lid and poured in the water. She sighed with irritation when she saw all the used mugs.

'I dunno, the bloody juniors are supposed to keep this place tidy but they're always brain dead. We had to let one go last week 'cos she was nicking stuff.'

'How do you get on with Tina?'

Kiara washed the mugs and began to dry them on a dirty tea towel.

'She's my boss – I have to get on with her.'

Brian tapped Langton's elbow. 'You mind if I go out and get some fresh air? I'm feeling ill.'

Langton nodded and then smiled at Kiara, explaining, 'It's the stuff you use on the nail extensions.'

'Tell me about it. Sometimes I feel as high as a kite and it takes so long, especially if you've got a client who wants the old ones removed. Mind you, if you think nail extensions take time, try hair extensions – up to four hours a session.'

'Really?'

'Yeah. You got to glue the hair onto the client's bit by bit, then do the braiding. You want a fresh cup of coffee?'

'Yes, thank you.' He passed his mug to her. 'How long have you worked for Tina?'

'Two years, but I really want to work in a West End salon. This is in the sticks and we get so many pensioners on our cheap days. Not that I have anything against them, but that's why we keep some of those old dryers; we roller the old ladies up and stick them under.'

Kiara passed Langton a cup of coffee and then sat opposite him. She had the longest, shapeliest legs he'd seen in a long time, revealed by her wearing a tight mini-skirt and the salon robe which just covered her thighs. She was also wearing very long ginger hair extensions with small beads at the end.

'I like your hair.'

'Thanks. I do it myself.' She tossed her head, making the beads clink against each other. Then: 'Odd thing, isn't it?'

'I'm sorry?' He waited for her to explain.

'Well, this Alan business. We all have a natter about it. She was upset when it started – you know, when he first disappeared.'

'I suppose she would be, as they were going to get married.'

Kiara raised her eyes to the ceiling.

'Well, let's say she hoped. I don't mean she was desperate, but she'd been dumped a couple of times before, or that's what I was told. She kept him very much under wraps, worried in case he might fancy one of us.'

She giggled and then leaned towards him confidingly. 'She's older than she lets on – she's always having Botox. I dunno if she keeps on doing it. There's a bloke what comes in who's one of her clients so she gets it on the cheap.'

'What is a seaweed wrap, by the way?'

'Oh, that's one of her treatments. None of us girls are qualified beauticians. She always does all the treatments herself and has a regular stream of clients.'

'What is it, though? I mean, would she do it in her own flat?'

'Oh no, it's ever so messy. They've got to strip off, then

she smothers their body in the stuff; it smells like seaweed washed up on a beach, it's horrible, and then I think it's mixed with some kind of mud. Anyway, she has to lather it all over their body and then she wraps these bandages around them – quite tightly, I think – and then they sleep with a cooling mask on. When it dries it draws out the excess fluid and they can lose a few pounds off their entire body weight, especially the thighs. Then she unpeels the bandages, they shower and finally they get a body massage. That all costs about fifty quid.'

'You think she gives herself a wrap ever?'

'I dunno. She's got a great figure, I'll give her that – works out a lot so she don't look her age, and you've got to be strong 'cos most of the clients who want it are over-weight. One woman is at least seventeen stone and Tina's gotta lift them up and turn them over. I think it'd be dif-ficult to do it on yourself.'

'Maybe she gave Alan one?'

Kiara shrugged. 'He was good-looking. I think she gave him a few hair streaks 'cos he was ever so blonde. I know he used to use the sunbed at night. She does too, or she did, but with all the bad publicity about tanning beds we don't really use the one we've got any more.' She tossed her head again and laughed. 'I don't need one though.' She rubbed her brown-skinned arm.

Langton smiled. She was flirting with him.

'So he maybe came into the salon when you had all left?'

'I presume so. I never saw him in here and we're out like rats off a ship come six o'clock. She'd have us staying late and without extra pay, and did you get told about how she was always dipping into the juniors' tip box?'

'No, I didn't know.'

'Yeah. She's always moaning about having no change and taking a few pound coins. None of us like it. I mean, they get paid a pittance anyway.'

'She uses the coins for phone calls?'

'Yeah. Why she needs to be nippin' out when we got a phone here and she's got a mobile beats me, but then I suppose it's hard to have a private conversation at that pint-size desk of Felicity's, and she's always all ears.'

'Who do you think she was calling?'

'No idea. Alan maybe, but she'd not tell any of us. Very much above us all, she thinks she is. That's why some of us reckon he never disappeared.'

'How do you mean?'

'We think he just did a runner to get away from her. I know I would. She's got a terrible temper and—'

Donna appeared. 'Kiara, you've got a client waiting.'

Paul and Anna were going through lists of the best way to start their enquiries in Cornwall when his mobile rang. It was Brian. Anna, only able to hear one side of the conversation, was impatient to know what was going on.

'They're at Tina's salon. He's had to walk outside as the—'

'Give me the phone.' She held out her hand. 'Brian, what exactly are you doing?' She listened and her face tightened with anger. 'He's in the salon? Is he talking to Tina?'

Brian told her about the visit to Tina's flat. Furious, she gave him instructions to call back as soon as Langton had left the salon.

She passed the phone back to Paul, saying, 'I don't know what he thinks he's doing. Apparently he's been at the salon for over half an hour.'

'Maybe he's having a haircut.'

'Very funny. I don't like this nosing around – it makes me nervous.'

Paul's phone rang again. This time it was Helen saying they had no records of any other vehicles registered to Alan Rawlins or to any of his friends apart from the vehicles they personally owned. Helen had also been checking with flights from Gatwick and Stansted to Newquay and again had no result. He repeated all of this to Anna.

She folded her newspaper. The train journey felt like it was taking forever.

'It'll be almost dark when we get there,' she grumbled.

'Not long to go, couple more hours. You want me to see if the trolley is anywhere near our carriage?'

'Yes. I'll have another coffee.'

She stared out of the window, seething with anger. It felt as if Langton was checking her out. As she closed her eyes, she hoped there was nothing she had missed that he would uncover. It was as if he was sitting on her shoulder. Paranoia set in. Had Langton agreed to let her travel because it freed him up to oversee her investigation? She took out her mobile, deciding that she would call him herself, but then stopped. Instead, she rang Helen in the incident room and asked her to make sure that anything that came in from Langton went directly to her.

Helen agreed, and added that he had asked them to get the soft top ordered by Alan Rawlins brought into the station.

'Have you got it?' Anna knew she should also have checked it herself.

'Yes, it arrived ten minutes ago and it is exactly as described – a new soft top for a Mercedes 280SL.'

'Thanks, Helen.' She cut off the call. At least that was a dead lead, thank goodness.

Paul returned to his seat with the news that the trolley would be passing in a few minutes. The train would then be making a lot of stops as they got closer to Newquay.

'All the little out-of-the-way stations, but they said it'd only be another hour and a half.'

Anna closed her eyes. They would get the plane back, budget or not.

Donna was now sitting where Kiara had been. She'd helped herself to a coffee and was munching on biscuits. Langton had refused another cup and was now becoming a little impatient.

'What's she been telling you?' Donna eventually asked.

'Just describing how she does nail extensions.'

'I bet. She's a gossip, that one, and she and Tina have never got along, but to find someone who can do nails and hair extensions isn't easy round here. We've got a lot of black customers so that's why Tina keeps her on.'

'You just do haircuts, do you?'

'No, I do manicures and pedicures as well. Salon this size you gotta be jack-of-all-trades.'

'But you don't do the massage and beauty treatments?'

'No, that's Tina's department. She can do hair, and she's good, but she gets impatient with the client if they don't want what she wants. I've seen them go out crying 'cos she lopped off more than they wanted. She's also a good colourist, very professional. She was trained by L'Oréal and she still does competitions. We work them between us. I told that lady about how many we done, I sent in the dates – well, the ones I could remember. She wanted to know how long Tina and me are out from the salon.'

'This would be DCI Travis, yes?'

'Yeah, that's right. I'd love to have a go at her hair, give her a real sharp cut. It's a lovely colour, that red. Is it natural?'

'I believe so. Do you get on well with Tina?'

'Yes, I've worked for her for years. When I say we get along, it's my job and she's okay just so long as you don't get on the wrong side of her. She can fly off the handle.'

'Did you know Alan, her fiancé?'

'Only to say hello, never had much of a conversation with him. I think she used to get browned off with him going away all the time, but she always said she didn't go with him because she couldn't swim. We all reckoned it was because he didn't want her there.'

'They were engaged to be married?'

'Yes, so she said, but I dunno when they planned it. A few of us thought he might be getting cold feet.'

'Why do you say that?'

'Well, they were having a big row out in the car park one night and the next day she was like a bear with a sore behind having a go at every one of us. These past few days she's been making secret phone calls, hurrying out of the salon.'

'Taking the juniors' tips?'

'Yeah, that's right – who told you that?'

'I think someone mentioned it to DCI Travis.'

The girl put her hand over her mouth and grinned. 'Could have been me. I don't want to sling the dirt. Don't get me wrong, but he looked younger than her and she changed the colour of her hair, was always on a diet, working out, trying to look younger than she is.'

'Botox?'

Donna giggled again. 'Yeah. Once it must have hit a nerve by her eye 'cos it twitched for days.'

Donna almost fell off her chair as Tina stepped round the screen.

'Can you work with the junior, please, Donna. You are supposed to be training her, not sitting in here gossiping. Off you go!'

Donna scuttled out fast. Tina glared at Langton as he stood up to introduce himself.

'Don't bother – Felicity's told me who you are. Where's the other bloke?'

'He's outside, felt a bit sick with the smell of the—'

Tina brushed past him and picked up Donna and Kiara's dirty coffee mugs.

'Bloody girls can't wash up after themselves.' She dumped them into the sink, turning to rest against it. 'What do you want? This is now bordering on harassment.'

'Just to talk to you, Tina.'

'I'm all talked out with the police. I have no intentions of saying anything unless my lawyer is present.'

'That's a pity, Tina. I just wanted to iron a few things out. I'm overseeing the enquiry.'

'Really? Well, somebody should be.'

Langton sat back down. He was surprised at just how attractive she was, and taller than he'd expected. Her glossy reddish-brown hair fell to just below her shoulders, and her make-up was flawless.

'If you don't mind me saying so, you are a very good advert for your salon.'

'Flattery won't get you anywhere.' She poured what remained of the coffee and leaned back holding the cup between her hands – revealing long perfect fingernails with white tips.

'What's happened to that woman Travis?' she asked rudely.

'She's on her way to Cornwall to make enquiries.'

'I'd like to make some myself. I've never had much luck with men, but with Alan I really thought it was special, different. Just goes to show, doesn't it?'

'What does?'

'That he was a liar like the others. You'd think I'd have learned my lesson. The guy before Alan left owing me ten thousand quid. He was a carpenter and said he needed it to buy some equipment for a big job, and like an idiot I gave him a cheque. That was the last I saw of him.'

'Sounds like a habit.'

'What?'

'Men disappearing on you.'

'I know where he is – with his wife. He lied about that too.'

'I'm sorry, and amazed that anyone would leave someone as attractive as you.'

She rolled her eyes and then laughed. She had a deep sexy voice and her laugh was infectious.

'Looks aren't everything, although Alan certainly had them.' She sipped her coffee and pulled a face. 'It's cold.' She turned and tossed the coffee down the sink then stood with her back to Langton, her hands resting on the edge of the sink.

'It just doesn't seem real,' she said bleakly. 'First he's missing, then I'm accused of killing him, then I'm told he was homosexual and also stashing money away. What kind of fucking idiot am I?'

Langton got to his feet as Tina tossed her head back and ran her fingers through her curls.

'I've got to go back to work,' she mumbled.

'This must be very hard for you to deal with.' Langton moved closer.

'You can say that again, but you know I've been hurt a few times and I'm getting used to picking myself up and getting on with my life.'

Unexpectedly she started to cry, wafting her hands as if annoyed at herself. She plucked a tissue from a box beside the sink.

'Going to ruin my eye make-up,' she laughed shakily.

'I understand. I've been told you were planning on getting married.'

She sniffed as her eyes welled with tears again. She grabbed another tissue from the box.

'Yes. I even thought that maybe he'd got cold feet because I kept pushing for him to set the date. I was going to arrange it all. I've no parents so it was all going to be down to me.'

'You mind me asking you a personal question?'

She sniffed. 'Like what?'

'How old are you?'

She looked taken aback and then started to cry again. 'What's that got to do with anything?'

'It doesn't matter. I can always check.'

'I'm forty-two – all right!'

Whether it was admitting to her real age or not, more tears came down and she pressed her hand to her mouth.

'You don't look it,' Langton said gently.

'Yes, well, it takes a lot of work. I don't know what those gossiping little bitches have told you, but they don't know my age.'

'So Alan was a lot younger.'

'Yes . . . Shit, all I need now is for one of them to walk in and see me like this.' She sniffed and then pulled at her eyelashes which were coming away in a section. 'I use single lashes and they're all coming unstuck. I have to go upstairs.'

'I'd like to see where you do your treatments.'

Tina hesitated and then walked back round the screen. As she hadn't refused him, he followed her.

There was a narrow staircase at the rear of the salon by the back door and the washing machines. As Langton moved up the steps behind her he could see how shapely her legs were, with good muscle tone and tanned a golden brown.

'You've got a nice colour on your legs,' he observed as she moved aside a plastic strip curtain.

'Fake tan, I spray it on.'

He was surprised at the size of the room, as it was as big as most of the salon below. The ceiling was slanted and there were two massage tables and a covered self-tanning cubicle. A shower room was built into one side, with a toilet and washbasin. The floor was of stripped-pine boards. A row of lockers were lined up against the far wall. There was an exercise bike and an odd contraption in cream leather, which had a folding back and two long sections for legs.

'What's this?'

'It's for fatties who don't want to exercise. You sit back and the bit with your legs moves up and down and tightens the stomach muscles.'

Tina went into the bathroom, leaving the cubicle door open. Langton watched as she looked at herself in the mirror and began to reapply her make-up. Lined up on two shelves were a vast number of massage oils and big tins of the seaweed emulsion. Neatly placed beside them were stacks of rolled elastic bandages and spatulas in a jar.

Langton took in the content of the shelves.

'So this is what a wrap treatment is all about, is it?'

Tina leaned out. 'Yes. The stuff is mixed with water and I apply it over the body. The far table is the one I use as it creates a hell of a mess.'

'I noticed you had some in your flat.'

'Yes.'

'Do you give yourself treatments?'

'Christ, no. Alan used to use it sometimes on his thighs. He was very vain and he knew how to mix it and wrap the bandages around. Got to be careful they're not too tight.'

Tina walked out, brushing her hair as Langton turned, smiling.

'You've got a big space up here as well as the salon below,' he remarked.

'Yeah. This just used to be a loft and I did the conversion. Now the bastard landlord ups the rent, but I need the space for my treatments. I do all the massages up here and the leg waxing and bikini waxing.' Tina sighed. 'You know, I've worked hard all my life. Nobody ever gave me anything. My parents died when I was just a teenager so I've been on my own, so to speak.'

'Never married?'

She shrugged. 'Long time ago. It lasted a year and then he took off with my best friend, leaving me with debts up to my eyeballs. Bloody men!'

Langton glanced at his watch. 'You've been really nice, and thank you for giving me your time.'

'You want a massage?'

He laughed, shaking his head.

'I was joking,' Tina grinned. 'Can you see yourself out?'

'Yes, thanks a lot.'

'That's it, is it? You said you had a few things you wanted to iron out.'

'Not necessary now. I just wanted to meet you.'

'Now you have, what do you think? You're a hell of a lot nicer to talk to than that woman, but you know women have always had it in for me – jealous bitches, most of them. I have to put up with a lot of crap from the girls I employ. I used to have blokes, but they're even bitchier, little queens. And now? Christ, I was bloody living with one and I didn't even know!'

She watched him leave, moving the slatted curtain aside. Then she turned back to fix her hair. Staring at her reflection in the small cubicle mirror she felt like smashing the brush against it, cracking it, shattering it, but her sense of self-control got the better of her and she picked up her lip gloss to outline her lips, mouthing, 'Sons of bitches. Bastards.'

Brian was fast asleep in the patrol car, his mouth open. He jolted awake when Langton opened the passenger door.

'You all done?'

Langton slammed the door shut. 'Yeah, all done. Can you take me back to Scotland Yard?'

Brian put the car in gear and drove out of the car park.

'She's a piece of work,' Langton said quietly.

'You think she's been telling the truth?'

Langton stared out through the window. 'Hard to tell. I wouldn't like to tangle with her. How old do you think she is?'

'I dunno, I'm not good at guessing women's ages, but maybe thirty?'

'Forty-two. I think having to tell me her age made her more tearful than discussing Alan Rawlins's disappearance.'

'Bloody hell, she doesn't look it.'

'No, she doesn't, and she didn't like admitting it, but that doesn't make her guilty of beating her boyfriend to death.'

'I know DCI Travis has changed her opinion but do you think Rawlins is still alive?'

Langton sighed and shook his head. 'I don't know,' he said. 'Either way, we are going to have to come up with something. A fucking body would be a start.'

Chapter Fifteen

Helen looked over as Brian returned to the incident room, holding up her hand and tapping her watch.

'Don't have a go at me,' he grumbled. 'I've been with bloody Langton all afternoon. Any developments?'

'No, but I don't think the Gov liked you and Langton treading on her heels. She wants you to call her and tell her what went down.'

'Bugger all, that's what. Have they arrived in Cornwall yet?'

'Any time now. It's a long schlepp by train and . . .' Helen checked her watch again. 'Too late now, but the manager of the Asda store called re the CCTV.'

'Shit – I forgot all about that.'

Helen said that Anna had again asked if there was any CCTV footage from the time that Tina bought the containers of bleach. Brian slumped at his desk.

'What's so important?' he said wearily. 'We have the bloody receipt, so we know the date and time the bleach was bought.'

'Well, the manager said the interior CCTV *was* working but he'd only be there until six, so you've missed him. He said he will give us the hard drive for the CCTV footage we are interested in, but he wants a replacement.'

'You telling me they have cameras on every checkout till?'

'I don't know. You'll find out when you see the manager.'

Brian yawned and said he would go over there and collect it in the morning.

'You can get your groceries in at the same time,' Helen joked. 'There'll be a lot to go through so I don't mind helping you view it.'

'Okay, whatever. My stomach is playing me up. The ruddy hair salon had this stink of glue for false nails, got right on my chest.'

'You'd better call the Gov,' Helen insisted.

'Although I wasn't in there that long. Langton was – I didn't think he was ever coming out and I waited for him outside.'

'Just call her, will you?'

The train was pulling into their station as Anna received Brian's call. She listened as she climbed down from the compartment, leaving Paul to carry her overnight bag. By the time she caught up with him he was passing over their tickets to the ticket collector.

'What did he have to say?' Paul wanted to know.

'Not a lot. It seems Langton spent a long time in the hair salon chatting to the girls and eventually Tina.'

As they headed for the station's exit they could see a plain-clothes officer standing by a patrol car. He was short, overweight and yawning as they approached.

'This doesn't bode well for slick detective work,' Paul muttered.

They introduced themselves and DC Harry Took opened the rear passenger door, but Anna got into the front to sit beside him.

'I suppose the best way to start is to get you settled in to Mrs Morgan's,' the DC began. 'It's a nice clean place and she cooks up a good breakfast.'

'Is it far from the station?' Anna asked.

'The train station?'

'No, the police station.'

'Oh sorry. No, it's not far, but it's after six so I doubt anyone'll be there. Well, there will obviously be officers working late, but the ones allocated to assist your enquiry expect to get an early start. We reckoned you'd want to have something to eat, and my boss DCI Ed Williams has booked a table for seven-thirty at the Bear. Nice pub and a good menu, all home cooking on the premises.'

Anna thought he would never stop talking as he listed other restaurants that they should try. Eventually he turned into a residential area of three-storey townhouses with small front gardens and stopped outside one which had a *Vacancies* sign in the front window.

'This is it, ma'am. I'll be getting off now.'

Paul carried their bags out of the car as Anna tetchily asked how they were to get to the pub to meet DCI Williams. Harry swivelled his bulk round in his seat to point down the road.

'Right on the corner, fifty yards down.'

The bed and breakfast was spotlessly clean and Paul and Anna had rooms next to each other on the first floor. They didn't have en-suite bathrooms, but there was a wash-basin in both rooms and a shared bathroom and lava-tory on the same floor. Anna quickly unpacked the few things she had brought, hanging them up in the small single wardrobe that had a strong smell of mothballs. She put her underwear into a chest of drawers and laid out the contents of her vanity bag by the sink. She washed her face in cold water, cleaned her teeth, reapplied some make-up and ran a comb through her hair. It was by now almost eight as she tapped on Paul's door. He opened it up with a bath-towel strung around his waist.

'Sorry, I had a quick shower. You all ready to leave?'

'Yes. Knock on my door as soon as you are.'

'Right. You're not changing then?'

'No, Paul, I want to get on with this as soon as possible. We're not here on a ruddy vacation.'

It took Paul ten minutes before he was dressed, shaved and wearing a pair of jeans, a white T-shirt and a denim jacket. The landlady was a pleasant woman, handing them a key each and asking that if they were to come in late to be as quiet as possible.

'My husband and I have a room on the ground floor, but you are the only guests. Do you know what time you want breakfast?'

'Seven-thirty please, Mrs Morgan,' Anna said, pocketing the key.

'Will that be a full cooked breakfast or a continental?'

'Cooked for me,' Paul said immediately.

Anna asked for just coffee and toast.

'Have a nice evening.' Mrs Morgan smiled and then asked if they would like a newspaper.

'Thank you, but we'll leave straight after breakfast.'

'I've got you both down for two nights,' the woman said, her smile fading.

'Could we discuss this at breakfast?' Anna was eager to leave.

Mrs Morgan didn't seem that pleased, watching as they left, closing the door after them. It always annoyed her when guests changed their bookings, but luckily it was early in the season. If it hadn't been she would have told them straight away that they would have to pay for the two nights booked.

The pub was, as Harry Took had said, just a short walk, but it was colder than either of them had expected and the wind was really sharp.

'Christ, it's bloody cold, isn't it?' Paul complained, hunching up inside his denim jacket. Anna didn't reply, but she wished she'd brought a heavier coat. She was wearing her usual white shirt and black suit, and having had only a sandwich on the train, she felt really hungry.

The Bear pub was large with a big car park to the rear and a number of chairs and tables on a deck. The umbrellas were closed as the wind was really whipping up.

Inside, the place was spacious with a main bar, lines of stools and a snooker table to one side. A notice directed them towards a dining room with a big painted neon arrow. There appeared to be only a few local customers drinking, and a large plasma television screen was showing a football match, while two barmen were cleaning glasses and serving up sandwiches and hot dogs to a group of teenagers.

As Anna and Paul made their way to the dining room, all eyes were on them, not antagonistically, more simply out of interest.

The dining room was lined with booths, and four tables with bright red tablecloths were arranged down the centre of the room. Two waitresses were serving a few customers, but apart from them it was empty. Anna and Paul stood in the doorway, waiting to be seated.

'You see him?' Paul asked, looking around.

'Even if I did, I wouldn't know what he looks like.'

Nobody came to direct them to a table to be seated, although again they were of obvious interest to the diners, who avidly scrutinised them. Then a tall sandy-haired man stood up at the far end of the room and signalled for them to join him before disappearing back into the booth.

As they approached, Ed Williams eased himself out. He was at least six foot four, broad-shouldered, handsome in a rough way, and his thick sandy hair looked as if it was a crew cut growing out. He was wearing a brown tweed suit with a checked shirt and thick tie.

'DCI Travis?'

'Yes.' Anna shook his hand and introduced Paul. They all then slid into the booth. The table was low, making it difficult for someone of Williams's size to move in and out with ease. He sat opposite them, with his legs taking up so much of the space that he was almost sideways on.

He had a briefcase open on the table and an uncorked bottle of red wine. He had also moved the cutlery aside to be able to take out files and notebooks, but now he quickly replaced everything and snapped the case closed.

A waitress appeared with menus, passing them to Anna and Paul, but not to Williams. He said that he knew the menu backwards and asked if they would like wine. Without really waiting for either to say yes or no he poured for each of them.

'Cheers.'

The same waitress returned and asked if they would like to know the specials for the evening, and reeled off some Italian pasta, a risotto and sea-food platter, announcing the price of each dish before walking off again. Anna kept herself hidden by the menu, trying to assess Ed Williams as Paul said he was going for the sea-food platter with a chicken and sweetcorn soup to start. Williams nodded for the waitress to take their order, looking to Anna first.

'The risotto please, no starter.'

Paul gave his order and then Williams asked for his usual: a steak with salad and French fries.

'Am I the only one having a starter?' Paul said, embarrassed.

Back came the waitress with a red plastic basket of hot bread covered with a napkin, and a small dish of butter.

Williams offered the bread to Anna, but she shook her head. Paul took a big crispy hot chunk and slathered it with butter. Anna watched as Williams followed suit.

'You should try this,' he told her. 'They bake it on the premises and the butter is garlic and herb.'

'No, thank you.'

Anna wondered if it was par for the course that officers in Cornwall all had food on their minds.

'This is really gorgeous and the butter is mindblowing,' Paul said, slathering on even more.

'Go on, try some.' Williams offered Anna the plastic basket again.

'No, thank you.'

He dropped the basket back onto the red paper tablecloth.

'I've got a car arranged for you,' he told them. 'If you want a driver at all times it's up to you, but I thought maybe you'd like to take off and see—'

'We're not here to see the sights,' she said briskly, not meaning to sound like a school marm.

'I didn't think that you were, but sometimes it's good to get the feel of the place, and you've got a lot of areas to cover.'

He had very pale blue eyes and she picked up immediately that he hadn't liked her interruption.

'I've run off some maps for you. Focus on the main surfing beaches, hang-outs of the surfers, plus their rentals, hotels, hostels and B and Bs. The property you have enquired about is quite a drive from here.'

'We've been told that it is occupied.'

Williams nodded. He drank some wine.

'I had a covert look over it. There's a young guy living there who's about twenty-five and who drives an MG. We ran the licence plates and it's owned by a local garage so it's rented to the people at the house – a Mrs Chapman. There have been a couple of women seen going in: one young woman with grocery shopping and the other one a lot older. They are not locals, but we do have a local woman doing cleaning there twice a week.'

'You've spoken to her?'

'No. My instructions were to not give any indication that we were interested. She also works for another tenant in a property close by, so it is very easy to question her.'

'Could the guy be Alan Rawlins?' Paul asked.

'Well, I've seen the email pictures you've sent, so decide for yourself.'

He opened his briefcase and took out an envelope, removing some surveillance photographs which he passed to Anna. She looked through them and then shook her head, handing them to Paul for confirmation.

'Not him.'

'No.'

'Because it's early in the season, a lot of the hang-outs for regular surfers are closed,' Williams informed them. 'The all-year-rounders are still present and we've had some high waves this year that attracts them. We've also had storm warnings, a backlash of the hurricane, which also attracts the real hard professional surfers. They're all wetsuited up, obviously, but compared to the high season it's pretty quiet.'

The waitress served Paul his soup in a brown pottery pot with a lid with baked croutons on a separate plate. Williams asked for another bottle of the Beaujolais while he finished the first one, topping up their glasses.

'I have also arranged for a helicopter to give you an overview of the beaches and areas where your guy would hang out. It'll be at the airport at nine tomorrow morning.'

'Helicopter?' Anna repeated, unable to cover her concern.

'It's not going to dent anyone's budget. It's a training scheme we have organised with the Drug Squad officers, using dogs, which lets them get used to being up in the air for when there's a raid. Also, some of the canine team have been training their dogs to get used to the sounds and . . .' Williams came to a halt and lowered his voice. 'The reason I'm interested in giving you as much help as possible is because of Sammy Marsh.'

'Have you had any information about or sighting of him?'

'Nope, not so much as a whisper. He's a real piece of scum. He's been dealing for years. If we catch him and lock him up, he comes out with more contacts than before he went in. He was always a smalltime operator dealing mostly in weed and ecstasy tablets. He'd move from beach to beach selling to the young kids. I think – in fact, I know – he had access to a farm where they were growing the weed. The plants were inside an old barn with very sophisticated heating, hydroponic lighting and a drainage system, producing top-grade weed. It was busted four or five years ago.'

Again he withdrew photographs and passed them to Anna.

'The skunk as they call it was moving out on a bloody conveyor belt, being sent all over England. I know he was part of it, but he slipped out of the net and surfaced again a year later. This is Sammy.' He got out a mugshot for them to look at. Then another. 'This is also Sammy.'

Paul leaned closer to Anna to see the photographs. 'Looks like Johnny Depp.'

'Take a look at this one.'

Sammy Marsh was adept at changing his appearance. Williams kept on passing over one print after another, surveillance shots and mugshots. The man's hair went from shoulder-length to braids, to cut short, to a pig-tail with thin moustache and a small goatee beard. Some pictures even showed his hair dyed blonde.

'Right little chameleon, isn't he? He's only about five foot eight, always very slender, and in the summer he gets tanned. He wears top designer gear and drives flashy cars.'

More photographs showed how many cars Sammy had owned and driven: a Mercedes, Alfa Romeo, Ferrari, beach buggy and various motor bikes. In most of them he was smiling, posing with two or more gorgeous bikini-clad girls. In one of the prints, Sammy could be seen with a group of equally tanned and handsome men, their surf-boards stuck into the back seat of a Land Rover.

'Is one of these men Alan? Paul, what do you think?'

Paul shook his head and passed the photo back to Williams.

'Sammy's flat is still owned by him, isn't it?' Anna asked.

'Yes. Well, he rented a number of places, but he actually only owns one. Looks like he left in one hell of a hurry because there was food in the fridge, wet clothes in the washing machine and no sight of him for six months.'

'Any movement in his bank accounts?'

Williams laughed. 'Sammy will no doubt have accounts in God knows how many banks or countries, but he primarily dealt in cash. If he was to bank his earnings from drugs he'd have to prove how he was making enough to buy all those flash motors, never mind his flat. He also had heavies watching out for him, but even they have disappeared.'

Williams gathered up the photographs, put them in his briefcase and then took out a single sheet of paper.

'Here's a list of the names he used. He'd often keep his Christian name, but it's sometimes Sammy Miles, Sammy Myers, Sammy Lines . . . we found four passports in his flat all with different names – brilliant forgeries and they must have cost a packet.'

Anna sat back, watching Williams getting more tense and angry.

'Can I ask you something?' she said.

'That's what I am here for, Detective Travis.'

'Sammy, you have said, was smalltime, had numerous arrests for drug-dealing; he serves short sentences, then gets released and goes straight back to doing exactly what he had been doing before his imprisonment, right?'

'Correct. But he was mostly charged with possession. He was never caught with either money from drugs or actually dealing.'

'What about the photographs, the surveillance? If you knew he was up to his old tricks and from the photographs out in the open . . .'

'First off he moved from selling the skunk himself to using his heavies for dealing, collecting payment for him, breaking a few arms and issuing threats if the punters didn't pay up for their bag of shit. To be honest, with the government changing its mind two years ago and upping cannabis from Class C to B it looks like he decided to switch.'

'Switch?'

'Prison sentences for Class B are longer. Maybe he decided he might as well be hung for a sheep as a lamb so he started dealing Cat A drugs – heroin, cocaine and crack. He was under covert surveillance because the Drug Squad wanted to discover who the supplier was, and who was backing him financially because he didn't just focus on this area, he was moving from coast to coast. He also bought this.'

Out came a photograph of a high-powered speedboat. And again it was passed to Anna and then Paul.

'Paid for in cash from a local boat-builder, but the little bastard disappeared. That's still moored and no one has been near it.'

The waitress cleared Paul's soup bowl and returned with their main order. They remained silent until she left them to eat, saying in an expressionless voice, 'Enjoy your dinner.'

Anna was really hungry and tucked in straight away. Williams topped up their wine again and carved up his steak.

'This is delicious.' Anna grinned.

'Good food – that's why we use this place. Come high season though, it's packed with families and a load of screaming kids.'

For a while they were silent as they concentrated on eating before Anna said to Williams that she was a little bit confused. It appeared that the Drug Squad still did not have the names of the contacts that Sammy was now using to score the Category A drugs, but had decided to arrest him regardless.

Williams nodded and suggested they finish their meals before he showed them the reason.

'I don't think either Paul or I are squeamish enough to be put off our food, especially not after having only a sandwich on the train,' Anna offered.

Williams forked a large mouthful of steak into his mouth before yet again delving into his briefcase. He took out a brown manila envelope and opened it.

'Reported missing by her mother late last summer. She was washed up on the rocks aged sixteen – heroin overdose.'

Anna looked at the mortuary shot of the dead girl. Her wet hair plastered to her bloated face, her body covered in wounds from the jagged rocks. She passed it to Paul. However, Williams hadn't finished. He followed it with a second photograph of an equally young girl, her body found in a rented caravan. It was a heroin overdose and the needle still protruded from her arm.

'She doesn't look as if she was a regular user. She's not underweight and I don't see many track marks. She was fifteen years old.'

Williams produced yet another mortuary photograph of a young boy. His naked body showed the white skin on his buttocks and genitals, but the rest of his skin was a deep brown.

'Seventeen year old. All of them were here in Cornwall for the holidays. The boy worked the deckchairs on the beach. None of them were residents, but had been introduced to heroin whilst they were here. Nor did any of them have any previous drug-related arrests. They were simply kids from good families who became embroiled in the beach traffic scoring drugs.'

'Did you get direct evidence linking any of these victims to Sammy Marsh?'

'Just the first girl. She was in the photograph I showed you with the two other bikini-clad girls hanging around Sammy's jeep. Drug Squad joined forces with me and we did a lot of the legwork identifying them all. It was decided to pick up Sammy before he could sell any more of the gear, and he must have got wind of it because he disappeared.'

'But what evidence did the Drug Squad have that these kids scored from him?'

'We made an arrest of a young guy working at a bar. He'd ended up in hospital suffering from an overdose, but he survived, and we were able to get the remainder of the wrap he had bought. It was heroin, but it had been mixed with Christ only knows what. There were traces of ketamine and morphine, and it was very high quality and lethal, especially to someone who had never used before, so the first fix could kill.'

'So he gave up Sammy's name?' Paul asked. Unlike Anna he had found that the photographs of the victims had turned his stomach. He had hardly touched his food.

'Eventually he did, after a lot of persuasion as he was scared rigid that he would get beaten up by the heavies. Especially one bastard, Errol Dante, who acted like an enforcer.'

'We interviewed him,' Anna said sharply.

'Well, he did a runner before we could nab him, but apparently he'd stolen drugs from Sammy and . . .'

'Moved in with his girlfriend. He was dealing on the estate in Brixton where he lived and got busted for that. He and his girlfriend think that someone tipped off the London Drug Squad.'

'That would be Sammy, yet Errol is still refusing to give us any assistance,' Williams said grimly.

'Nor to help us,' Anna added.

'I'd say he was scared Sammy would cut off his legs.' Williams replaced the photographs and ate some more of his steak before he continued.

'We have a statement from a woman who lived in a caravan next to where Errol stayed with his girlfriend. She called the local police because of the row that was going on inside the caravan, saying she was certain she'd heard a gunshot. By the time they arrived, the place had been totally trashed, windows broken and every stick of furniture smashed. She was able to identify Errol Dante as the one living in the caravan and she described Sammy. She said he was first outside the trailer, banging on the door and screaming, then he eventually kicked the door open and went inside. She said he was hysterical and his face was twisted as if he was having some kind of fit, eyes bulging and so agitated that it looked as if he was frothing at the mouth.'

'How long after that did Sammy disappear?'

'Few days. He was sighted a couple of times, but then nothing. We know Errol went back to London, but all we had on him was that he'd trashed a caravan owned by Sammy. Previously he had been sleeping on Sammy's floor in his flat – at least, that's what we were told.'

He replaced the statement into the envelope and once again closed his briefcase. He finished his steak and glanced at Paul's half-eaten sea-food platter.

'Something wrong with that?'

'No, but the soup was very filling.'

Williams laughed and could see that Anna had now taken some bread and was cleaning around her plate with it.

'You want a dessert?' Williams asked, but they both declined.

Williams insisted he drive them back to their B&B in his unmarked patrol car when they left the pub. He had also insisted he pay for dinner. It was ten o'clock and Anna felt that although they had by now learned a lot of details about Sammy Marsh, they had no leads to Alan Rawlins. In fact, she felt that they had hardly touched on the reason why she and Paul were in Cornwall.

'I know it's late,' she said to Williams, 'but would you mind talking to me a bit more, maybe have coffee somewhere? It's just that we've been allocated so little time here and I don't want to waste it.'

Williams agreed to take them to the station, where he claimed the coffee was acceptable as the team had all clubbed together to get an espresso machine. As he drove he went into great lengths about the coffee machine, which could also make cappuccinos. Paul was in the back of the car with Williams's seat pressed so far back there was no leg room on one side, leaving him hunched against the passenger side. Unlike Anna, he felt exhausted. Thankfully it was not too long a drive.

The station was situated in a residential area, close to the railway station. As they pulled up, the car park was empty and it seemed to be very quiet. Even though it was dark, Anna could see that the building looked rather modern, but quite small in comparison to the station she had come from back in London.

Once inside, the station was as Harry Took had described, very empty apart from a couple of officers. The local uniformed police were located on the first floor, the Drug Squad were in a different building, and although the place on first view seemed modern, it was actually an awful sixties-built block.

Williams towering above Anna was very much the

gentleman, gently steering her by the elbow through a warren of corridors until they approached double doors leading into the incident room. Williams had to press in a code to gain entry. The lights were off and he switched them on from a panel by the side of the door, and holding it open, he gestured for Anna and Paul to walk in ahead of him. Even at his size Williams was very coordinated, moving quickly to light up the incident board before heading into a small kitchen annex to brew up some coffee.

Anna and Paul looked over the astonishing array of information in front of them. Many of the photographs they had seen in the pub were also pinned up here, along with witness statements and reports which cluttered almost every inch of the board. Then they noticed that a separate board had been brought in and placed beside the Cornwall investigation. There were the email contacts sent by Anna's team with photographs of Alan Rawlins, plus the photograph of the property they believed he owned. *Missing, Presumed Murdered* was written in large capital letters.

'Is Williams Drug Squad?'

Anna shook her head. He was obviously leading the enquiries into the dead teenagers.

'I like him,' she decided.

Paul agreed, liking Williams even more when he carried in a tray of mugs with steaming coffee, milk and sugar, indicating that they should help themselves to whatever they wanted.

'I see you've started to compile a board for my enquiry,' Anna remarked.

'Yep. Reason being, I am interested in the possibility that your man might have been caught up in the drug situation. We've sort of collaborated with the Drug Squad and we're working together. You'll meet everyone tomorrow.'

'I appreciate it,' Anna said, sipping the strong coffee.

Williams perched himself on a desk facing the boards.

'What's your gut feeling on this bloke Alan Rawlins?' he said.

It was strange to hear Williams ask the same question that Langton always asked, and Anna didn't say anything at first, continuing to sip her coffee. Then she sat beside him and gave a brief rundown of her enquiry to date, while Paul eased himself into another chair. She detailed the amount of money they'd established Alan Rawlins had accumulated and added that they'd found that he did know Sammy Marsh, so there was a possibility they were connected through the drug trade.

'He's also gay, right?' Williams asked.

'Apparently so, or bisexual. He was living with a woman called Tina Brooks and they were engaged to be married.'

Williams took a gulp of his coffee, staring towards what little information they had acquired from Anna's investigation on their board.

'Is she involved?'

'To be honest, I keep on looking at her as a prime suspect and then I back off.'

'The evidence found in the flat she shared with Rawlins puts her, in my mind, dead centre of the frame,' Williams said. 'She had to have known about the blood pooling, how could she not? Unless she has lied about going back to see the boyfriend. She said he had a migraine – right?'

'Yes. She's also been interviewed twice and we always get the same response. She denies knowing anything about it, denies knowing Rawlins was homosexual, denies being

362

aware of the amount of money we know he was hoarding and denies playing any part in his disappearance. Without a DNA sample for comparison we have been unable to confirm that the blood in her flat was in fact Rawlins's.'

'She ever come to Cornwall with him?'

'No. She says she couldn't swim so he always came alone.'

Williams drained his coffee and replaced the mug onto the tray.

'Well, we've got our work cut out for tomorrow, so let's call it quits for tonight and start afresh in the morning.'

Anna agreed, and Williams drove them back to the B&B. She liked the way he got out and walked with her and Paul to the front door.

He waited whilst Paul used his key to let them in before leaning closer to Anna and quietly asking her if she believed Alan Rawlins was still alive.

She hesitated and then nodded. But Williams didn't wait to discuss it further and returned to the car. He drove off as Anna waved goodbye and closed the front door.

'What did he say?' Paul asked as they moved quietly up the stairs.

'Nothing. Goodnight and see you at breakfast.'

Anna waited until she heard Paul finish in the communal bathroom before she went and ran a bath for herself. Lying in the deep hot water she closed her eyes, thinking about the evening and about Williams. She felt confident that they would uncover something that moved her case forward. She also began to think again about Tina Brooks. Could she have lied about returning to the flat the same night? The entire timeframe of the murder was based on her statements, as they could not determine when the blood pooling had been deposited. It meant they had no real time of death. The same applied to the reports of Alan becoming a missing person. This was not until two weeks after Rawlins had left work early with the migraine.

Anna sighed, trying to assimilate all the facts. If they didn't get a result from this trip to Cornwall, she knew Langton might well replace her or call off the investigation.

Chapter Sixteen

Anna woke early and repacked her things, but she doubted they would leave that night. She was finishing breakfast when Paul joined her at the small table laid for two. The other equally small tables were set with only a white cloth and a small plastic rose in a bottle.

'You sleep well?' she asked.

'Out like a light as soon as my head hit the pillow.' Paul poured himself coffee and Anna suggested he pack up just in case they did get the last train back to London, although they'd more than likely have to stay another night. They couldn't be sure until they'd seen what they could come up with during the day. His breakfast of eggs, bacon, sausage and fried bread was presented with a flourish by the land-lady, who also brought in a fresh pot of coffee. Anna asked if she could have a word about the possibility of staying on and whether they could leave their bags in their rooms.

'The rooms were booked for two nights.'

'Fine – well then, expect us when you see us.'

Leaving them to finish breakfast and obviously not happy with the uncertainty of not knowing if they were staying or not, she departed to her domain.

'Bit prickly, isn't she?' Paul remarked, eating like a starved man.

'It's her business, so who can blame her? I'll see you upstairs as I want to look over the maps Williams left.'

'Okay. When do we do the helicopter ride?'

'Williams said early this morning. No doubt he'll have the day organised, but we've a lot to get through. First port of call will be visiting the property Rawlins owns.'

Williams was parked outside the B&B waiting for them. It felt even colder today than the night before. He said he was a trifle concerned about the weather and that it might not be suitable for flying, but he hoped the wind would die down later in the morning. By the time they reached Alan's house, it was raining hard. The large gates to the property were open so they were able to drive up to the parking area. It was only nine-thirty and it didn't look as if anyone was at home.

'Maybe they're still in bed,' Anna said as she got out of the patrol car. The wind whipped around her and she hugged her jacket close as she walked up the path accompanied by Paul and Williams. It was just as the photographs had shown; the white umbrellas on the patio were tied straight, but the wind was tugging at them and the double garage doors were closed. Anna rang the doorbell and waited, while Williams stepped back to look up at the windows, catching the movement of a curtain inched aside.

'Somebody's home so ring again.'

Anna tried twice, keeping her hand on the bell until eventually she heard footsteps. The door was inched open and a blonde girl of about eighteen peered out.

'Yes?'

Anna showed her ID and asked to be let in as it was an urgent police matter. The girl stepped back and opened the door wider. She was wearing a short nightdress, was barefoot and her hair was tangled. She looked half-asleep. Anna did the introductions standing in the wide hallway with its stripped pine flooring, then asked if there was anyone else at home.

'They're in bed.'

Williams gestured to the girl to get them up and jerked his thumb towards an archway that led into a lounge.

'We'll wait in here, and Paul, you go on up with her. What's your name, sweetheart?'

'Kelly.'

'Okay, Kelly, get a move on, love. Who else is staying here?'

'My mum and my boyfriend. My dad's not here.'

Kelly hurried up the stairs followed by Paul as Williams walked through the archway into the lounge and sat on one of the very comfortable low sofas. The furnishing was stylish, but there were empty wine bottles left around and he picked up an ashtray to indicate to Anna that there were a number of roaches amongst the cigarette butts. Old newspapers were strewn about on the floor by the grate, where there were the remains of a fire.

'What do you want?' A woman was dragging on a dressing-gown. She still had pins in her hair. 'Is it to do with my husband? Has something happened?'

'You are . . .?'

'I'm Kelly's mother, Norma Chapman.'

Anna introduced herself and Williams again as Norma pulled out the hairgrips.

'We just need to ask you a few questions about this property, Mrs Chapman.'

Before she could answer Kelly returned with a young boy who looked so groggy he could have fallen over.

'Sit down. Who are you?'

'It's Kelly's boyfriend, Adrian Knowles; he's staying with us.' Mrs Chapman was now running her fingers through her hair in an attempt to make herself look presentable.

The three of them sat on a sofa. Anna drew up a wicker chair to sit opposite them. Williams remained seated. Paul stood behind Anna.

'Tell me how you came to be living here?' Anna asked.

'We've rented it for the next three years – my husband arranged it. He's away on business in Scotland at the moment.'

It didn't take long for Mrs Chapman to explain that her husband was working for a shipyard as a luxury yacht designer and he had arranged the rental through an estate agent. She was unsure about how the rent was paid, but believed it was by a banker's draft to the owner's account. She had never met the owner and she didn't think that her husband had either. She gave them her husband's mobile number and work number. She also mentioned that she had rented a car, and it was used by herself and her daughter. An MG.

Anna was disappointed, but proceeded to get out photographs of Alan Rawlins, asking the woman if she had ever met him. Mrs Chapman shook her head and passed them to her daughter, who also said she had never seen him.

'What about you, Adrian? Will you look at the photographs, please?'

Adrian was barely awake. He blinked and rubbed the sleep from his eyes and then shook his head.

Next they were shown a photograph of Sammy Marsh. Both women said they had not met him, but then Mrs Chapman hesitated. She looked to her daughter.

'Wasn't he the one that came round here?'

Kelly shrugged and passed the photo to Adrian.

'What about you, Adrian? Have you met him? He's a drug-dealer. I noticed a few roaches in the ashtray. Did you meet up with him at all?' asked Anna.

Mrs Chapman became very nervous. 'Just wait a minute, what's this about? I admit we've had a few joints, but that was because I have asthma and it helps me to sleep, but if you are here about—'

Anna interrupted her. 'I'm not interested in whether or not you use cannabis.'

'I use it to help me sleep!' The woman's voice was shrill.

'Did you score it from this man in the photograph?'

'No, but I think he might have been the man who called here. Adrian, didn't you see him?'

'No.'

Mrs Chapman grew even more agitated, taking back the photograph for another look.

'It was just after we moved in. We sold our place in St Ives and we're eventually going to buy somewhere, but my husband reckons we should wait for the prices to get lower so that's why we rented this house.'

'Tell me why you think you saw this man?'

'Well, I could be wrong. The reason I remember is because it was late at night. He asked about someone and I said we'd just moved in.'

'Do you recall the person he asked to see?'

'No, I'm sorry. Like I said, it was very late at night and I didn't even like opening the door. I also kept the chain on because there was something about him.'

'Was it this man?' Anna showed her another photograph of Sammy.

'I think so. He was very jumpy, I remember that, and it was only for a couple of minutes. Oh yes, something else –

we've got the gates at the bottom of the drive and he had to have known the code to open them. That's what I remember now.'

'But they were open when we drove up.'

'They are now because something's gone wrong with the mechanism and we've asked for it to be fixed. I think Kelly clipped them one time coming home.'

'I didn't.'

'Well, they've not worked since. But that was what sort of unnerved me about him; you know, that he knew the code to open them.'

Anna glanced towards Williams. He gave her a small shrug.

'If you scored from him, Adrian, admit it. We are trying to trace him in connection with a murder enquiry,' he told the youth.

'I never, I never.'

'Did you find any papers or documents left by the owner when you moved in?' Anna asked, looking to Mrs Chapman.

'No. It was spotless as the property had just been renovated. Most of the furniture was new and we had to agree to have the cleaner that the agents suggested, but we pay her. We need someone to look at the barbeque as it doesn't light up properly – the gas doesn't go through.'

'Can you just repeat to me exactly the method of paying the rent?'

'My husband deals with all that. I've never even seen the agreements.'

Anna stood up ready to leave, but Williams remained seated.

'Can you show us some identification, Mrs Chapman?' he asked. 'Passports, driving licence?'

Anna turned and looked at Paul as Mrs Chapman got up and left the lounge. Williams now addressed Adrian.

'Listen, son, I'm not coming after you, but if you scored your dope from Sammy Marsh I want to know about it.'

'Who?'

'This man.' He shoved the photograph under the boy's nose.

'No, I never met him. I got it from a bloke at the Smugglers café months ago.'

'He got a name?'

'Raj, that's all I know.'

'Young, old? Describe him.'

'He's Indian, used to work there when we first arrived, but he's not there now.'

Mrs Chapman returned with passports and handed them to Williams, which slightly annoyed Anna. He flicked through them and then passed them to Anna.

'Your husband's American?'

'Yes, from Kansas, but he's lived here for twenty years.'

Anna gave the passports back to her and asked if she would be kind enough to show her and Paul around the property. Williams said he would wait in the car.

Anna and Paul returned to the patrol car where Williams was waiting.

'Untidy woman – every room is a tip, but it looks like it cost a lot to modernise and furnish the place so they must be paying a considerable amount.'

'Not necessarily. On a fixed three years' rental they probably got a deal, but I'll check it out,' Williams promised. 'I think we need to chat to the cleaning lady, so we'll go to her place next.'

They drove in silence for a while and eventually Paul

asked from the back seat if they thought they had gained anything from the Chapmans' household that was of interest.

'Only the fact that Sammy was hammering on the door in a bit of a state and it's around the time he went missing six months ago,' Williams said abruptly.

'What about her husband being an American?' Anna asked.

'Doesn't pull my strings, Kansas. If he'd been Colombian I might have been interested. Anyway, I can check him out. In fact, I'll do it now.'

True to his word, Williams rang the station as they drove, asking them to contact Mr Chapman and arrange for them to see him as soon as possible.

He next asked his team if there was any news from the pilot regarding the helicopter trip, but there wasn't. The weather was still very blustery, the rain now lashing down.

Anna was frustrated. Williams being so dominant put her off her stroke and she considered asking for the car he had arranged so that she and Paul could work by themselves. Williams's priority was obviously tracking down Sammy Marsh whereas hers was Alan Rawlins. She felt that she would make more headway without him.

The small terraced house was on the outskirts of Newquay and Mrs Flowers, a robust woman in her late sixties, was expecting them. She ushered them into a small sitting room, where thankfully a fire was lit as Anna was now freezing. Anna didn't waste time, but began asking about the rental property.

'I'm there twice a week, should be three times but she

told me they didn't need me so I do what I can while I'm there. It's not the way he would like it as he's ever so particular.'

'When you say "he", Mrs Flowers, who are you referring to?'

'Mr Matthews. He's got a flat as well which I used to clean, but that's too far for me to go now.'

'Is this Mr Matthews?' Anna showed her the picture of Alan Rawlins.

'Yes. Lovely young man he is.'

Anna's pulse-rate jumped. 'When did you last see him?'

Mrs Flowers licked her lips and then got up to fetch a thick notebook.

'I can tell you exactly. He said he was here on a flying visit as he was not going to move into his new house, but rent it out. I've known him for quite a while now – about four years.' She sat thumbing through her book, then passed it over to Anna.

'It was seven months ago. He said he would arrange for me to keep an eye on the property. I've made notes for him of the damage. They've broken the gates, the kitchen is a real mess, and him being so particular everything was brand new. I can't shift the grease on the cooker and the microwave is always filthy. They never wipe around it after they've cooked in it.'

'Tell me about him.'

'Well, as I said he was a lovely chap. I often used to do his washing and ironing when he was down here.'

'Did you ever meet his fiancée?'

Mrs Flowers flushed and folded her arms.

'Her name is Tina Brooks.'

'Look, I don't like to gossip, but I didn't think he liked women.'

'Why do you say that?'

She flushed again and glanced at Williams.

'When Ed here was asking me about him, I told him that a few times Mr Matthews had guests – men – and he only had one bedroom.'

'Did you ever hear him being called a different name?'

'Who?'

'Mr Matthews.'

'No, but you know I just went in to clean, take his laundry back and forth. It was just a small place and he often wasn't there. He always left me my money, not like some of them, and when I last saw him he said if I did a good clean-up as he was leaving, he—'

'Wait a minute. Was this when you last saw him, when he told you he had rented out his house?'

'Yes, that's right.'

'So when you cleaned, did you find anything left by him?'

'No. He was very methodical. However, I did find . . .' She stood up and walked to the door. 'I never use the stuff myself, but my daughter-in-law when she stays has tried them out and says they're very good.'

Mrs Flowers returned with half-filled bottles of shampoo, conditioner and moisturiser and all had Tina's Salon labels on them.

'It's not as if I was stealing – he'd left them in his bathroom cabinet.'

Anna smiled, looking over the items.

'When he said he'd rented out this house he had here, did you find that odd?'

'Well, yes, I did. It had taken so long to be fixed up I presumed he was going to be living there himself. He had books of fabrics and magazines. I took some of those, but I've thrown them out.'

'Did he ever tell you where he was going to be living, if not at his house?'

'No.'

'Did he seem like his usual self on the last time you say he saw you? You said he told you it was a flying visit.'

Mrs Flowers shrugged. 'I put it down to the fact that he was renting out that lovely property. I mean, I never asked about his financial situation, but I reckoned it was because he was short of money.'

'How do you mean?'

'Well, for one he was in a terrible hurry, a bit agitated, and kept on looking at his mobile phone as if he was expecting a call.'

'Did he have any luggage with him, as if he was going away?'

'No, just his briefcase and a small overnight bag. He said he would be out of touch with me for a while and to liaise with the estate agents if anything went wrong at the house. He said they would handle everything.'

'And you've not heard from him since?'

'No, dear, not a pip.'

Back in the car, Anna leaned her head against the headrest.

'Not a pip,' she repeated.

'The time he was down here arranging the house coincides with him taking a holiday break from his work. It sounds to me as if he was planning on doing a runner,' said Paul from the back seat.

Anna made no reply, but simply stared ahead before addressing Williams. 'You interviewed her before, right?'

Williams nodded, explaining that Mrs Flowers had also at one time cleaned for Sammy, but he was always late paying her. He then said that it was possible Sammy had recommended Mrs Flowers to Alan Rawlins.

'Christ, he kept up using Daniel Matthews's name for years!' Paul exclaimed.

'Maybe he was planning to do a runner for that length of time,' Williams suggested.

Anna disagreed. 'Maybe he was planning to leave Tina and London to live here, but something changed his mind, and it had to have happened around the time he arranged to rent out his house.'

She looked out of the window. 'Where are we going now?'

'I thought you would like to have a coffee and meet the team at the station.'

'I would, but do you have access to Sammy Marsh's place? You said he'd upped and left it as well.'

'Yes, and legally, as he's wanted, it's still in our possession. You want to go there now?'

'Yes, if you don't mind.'

Williams gave her a sidelong glance and then put in a call for an officer to be at Sammy's flat with the keys.

It took almost three-quarters of an hour to get to the flat, which was in a modern block with small balconies overlooking the beach, and lock-up garages to one side. The place looked in very good order. Williams parked, and as they headed towards the entrance a patrol car drew up with DC Harry Took driving. He didn't get out, but dangled the keys out of the open window. Williams took them, and they headed into the apartment block.

'Sammy also had numerous rented flophouses, plus the caravan,' he told them, 'but he bought this place a few years ago. We've checked out all the other places and they've been let out since he disappeared – apart from the caravan obviously, because it was trashed.'

'So Mrs Flowers also cleaned for Sammy?' Anna mused.

'Apparently a few years ago she did, but like I said, he was always late paying her and the rentals were always left in a terrible state.'

Williams used an entry code that opened the glass-fronted reception door. There were eight flats and Sammy's was the large one on the top floor, which they reached via a small lift. Anna was impressed. It was all well decorated, and Williams observed it would have cost about four hundred grand, and was probably worth even more now. Most of the tenants were retired elderly couples who lived in the flats all year round, but a few moved out and rented their homes for the summer, to make some money.

Williams used two keys to open up the front door. There was no hallway; it opened into a huge lounge with spectacular views across the bay.

'It's pretty much left as we found it,' Williams said.

'How did you get the keys?'

'From the caretaker. He doesn't live on the premises so couldn't give us any details about who came and went.'

Anna looked around the tasteful room. There were huge floral-fabric sofas and matching armchairs, a glass-topped coffee table and a small bar close to the sliding doors to the balcony.

'Best place I've ever seen a drug-dealer live in,' she said.

'Yeah, compared with the other shit-holes. He had places all over the main beaches that he rented, mostly just bedsits. You can see from here, the boat is moored at the dock in front of the property.'

The boat was covered in a tarpaulin. It was amongst numerous others and yet the size of it was impressive.

'Cost two hundred grand and is very fast.'

Drawers had been left open in a fitted cabinet.

'You find anything of interest in there?' Anna asked.

'Nope. Lot of bills for his furniture, and wait until you see the kitchen – cost a fortune and looks like it was never used.'

They looked into the high-tech, very well-equipped kitchen. As Williams had said, it didn't look as if anyone had ever used it. New crockery filled the glass-fronted cabinets and some of the cutlery still had the prices attached.

'He must have come into a lot of cash to own a place like this,' Paul said, looking around.

'How many bedrooms?' Anna wondered.

'Just the one. Follow me.' Williams led them to one side of the immense lounge and pushed open a door. The room had white carpet, white walls, the bed was unmade and clothes were strewn around with the wardrobe doors left open. The clothes were mostly designer jeans and flash T-shirts, rows of trainers and boots with Cuban heels, and there was even a drawer dedicated to thick gold bracelets and chains.

'Left in a hurry, wouldn't you say?' Williams said as Anna fingered the heavy gold bracelets. There were a few empty boxes and a gold Rolex watch.

'You know how much these cost?' Paul asked, opening the case.

'We do, and ...' He turned as Anna was drawing the sheet away from the bed.

'Have Forensic checked out the bedlinen?' she asked.

Williams shook his head.

'We would like this done, if it's possible, to check for any DNA.'

'I can organise that, but basically we're only just beginning to consider that he might have been bumped off. If he hasn't been, I'd like to get my hands on him. I told you we found a few fake passports – good ones.'

They opened the bedside drawers, which were full of gay pornography and lubricants. There were also numerous DVDs with lurid titles. Paul entered the en-suite bathroom and after a moment he came out and gestured for Anna to join him.

There was a mirrored cabinet beside the huge Jacuzzi bath with gold dolphin-shaped taps and a glass screen around it. White towels were stacked on a shelf beside the bath and hung on gold rails. Paul had opened the cabinet to reveal fake tanning lotions, bubble bath, bath oils, shampoos and conditioners.

'What?' Anna asked, looking around the bathroom.

Paul held up the shampoo container. It was identical to the one shown to them by Mrs Flowers. Tina's Salon labels were on the shampoos, the conditioners and massage oils.

Anna turned to Williams. 'This is confirmation that Alan Rawlins knew your drug-dealer.'

Chapter Seventeen

Coffee was served with fresh pastries in the Newquay incident room. The pilot had called in to say that they could take a flight in the helicopter to get an aerial view of all the various beaches, and Paul couldn't wait to pass on the good news to Anna, who'd been busy ringing Helen.

'Good – although you might be on your own, Paul. I need to do a few enquiries and without Williams breathing down my neck.'

'Oh, right.' Paul was puzzled. He hadn't felt that Williams had been anything other than helpful.

Anna was introduced to everyone and accepted her coffee gratefully as four members of the Drug Squad also joined the team. With one eye on the wall clock she listened as they outlined their investigation into the whereabouts of Sammy Marsh. They were certain that over the past eighteen months, Sammy had joined forces with some heavy hitters. The boat, the flash apartment and his cars all flagged up that Sammy was moving from smalltime dealing along the coasts to large amounts of cocaine and heroin. The Senior Investigation Officer from the Drug Squad stood by a wall map of the beaches earmarked as Sammy's playground. He was a burly six-footer who introduced himself as Ted Brock and he had the same tough, no-nonsense attitude as Williams.

'Sammy has been well-known to us over a long period, but it is only in the last few weeks that we've had some factual evidence against him. The three teenagers all dying of heroin overdoses have been DCI Williams's priority, but obviously linked with us. We have now been able to learn that each one of the victims was supplied with drugs by Sammy or one of his henchmen. They scored the heroin from different locations, but it's taken time to get the poor kids formally identified. The Forensic Department have also ascertained that the heroin had been cut with ketamine and was very pure, so we'd back up DCI Williams to get Sammy charged with murder.'

'But if they scored the heroin themselves and injected themselves,' objected Anna, 'won't it be difficult to make such a charge?'

'It won't be if we can prove he dealt the heroin,' replied Brock.

'We have witnesses and we also have his fingerprints on the hypodermic needle,' Williams told her. 'By the time we got all the evidence together he had disappeared before we could arrest him.'

'Do you have any idea who Sammy was purchasing the drugs from?' Anna asked.

'Not yet,' Brock admitted.

'Have you had any sighting of Alan Rawlins over recent weeks?'

'No, but we have some surveillance shots. Your guy was caught with him on numerous occasions.'

'How long ago?'

Ted Brock gestured to the incident board which showed that the last sighting of Alan Rawlins was seven months ago.

'We've been trying to get him identified. When DCI Williams passed on your enquiries to us and the photograph of him, we thought we'd got a major breakthrough, but that was until we knew he had also disappeared. All we've come up with is that Rawlins went under various names and was a known associate of Sammy.'

Williams took over, pointing out the amounts of money they had calculated Sammy was splashing out.

'The pair of them were flush with cash.'

Anna came to stand beside Williams.

'Wait a minute,' she said. 'We know that Alan Rawlins was getting big money from the sale of vintage cars, and the cash was accumulated over a long period – not necessarily from the sale of drugs.'

'Unless he was financing Sammy.' Ted Brock drew a red arrow between the two suspects.

Anna shook her head. 'Not enough. Could I see the surveillance photographs, please?'

Ted Brock passed them to her and she sat with Paul thumbing through them. They were black and white and obviously taken over a quite lengthy period. There were shots of Alan Rawlins heading into Sammy's block of flats. Another was of him standing at the dock as Sammy was taking off the tarpaulin from his speedboat. Rawlins was wearing dark glasses and a baseball cap pulled low over his face. Two further pictures showed him in the passenger seat of Sammy's Ferrari, again wearing dark glasses and the same baseball cap. They had included an enlargement of the same picture and ringed in a red felt-tipped pen was Alan Rawlins's head. It was definitely him, Anna was certain of it. The date was two days before Mrs Flowers had said he called on her.

Anna looked up as Ted Brock listed the known hang-outs

for his team to revisit and a slew of names of people that he wanted questioned again.

'This guy Alan Rawlins could well be connected to the drug-dealing, so we spread the net.'

Anna began to feel as if the carpet was being tugged from beneath her feet. She raised her hand and Brock looked over.

'You mind if I give a few details about the reason I'm here, because if you do trace him, I want him.'

She stood up.

'I am here on a murder enquiry that could also involve your man Sammy Marsh.'

She spoke quickly and in brief explained her enquiry to date, describing their inability to get DNA evidence to identify if the blood belonged to Alan Rawlins or whether it was someone else who had been murdered in his London flat. The questions came thick and fast: why had she been unable to acquire the DNA to match with Rawlins, why had Tina Brooks not been arrested, and why had it taken her investigation so long to establish that Rawlins was in Cornwall and involved with Sammy Marsh? She answered every point, but found their manner antagonistic and sarcastic.

'We have only recently discovered that Rawlins used the names of his friends, Daniel Matthews and Julian Vickers, and we also found no passport and no evidence that he had property in Cornwall. This has taken a lot of time, and we did send an email days ago asking why Sammy Marsh's DNA wasn't put on the national database when your force first arrested him.'

'His mouth swab was rejected due to an administrative error,' Ted Brock snapped.

'What you really mean is whoever took the swab didn't

seal it or fill the form out correctly,' Anna retorted equally sharply. 'We have a head hair and semen stains from Alan Rawlins's bedsheet, perhaps you might also get evidence from Sammy Marsh's bedroom. If he is the victim we can get our Forensic Department to do a comparison. Both men were homosexual and it's possible the two of them were partners sexually as well as financially. I don't like the edgy feeling I am getting from all of you that insinuates my team has not been on top of our case – which began, in case you are not aware of it, as one of a reported missing person.'

'I'd say with blood swamping the guy's bedroom you would have an f'ing strong clue it was a murder.'

Anna was about to have another terse interaction with Ted Brock when Williams stepped in.

'That's enough. We're wasting time.'

'But for chrissakes sakes, how can that woman Tina Brooks *not* be involved? It doesn't make sense,' Brock protested.

'We've no body,' Anna said angrily.

'Well, we've got three bodies – of young teenagers. I think we have to take priority if we find this guy Alan Rawlins.'

'If!' Anna exclaimed, red-faced. But before she could say any more, Williams's phone rang. It was the pilot, informing them that the helicopter was standing by and if they wanted to use it, now was the time to do so, as if the weather got any worse they wouldn't be allowed to lift off.

Anna hurried across to speak to Paul, who had been out of the incident room for most of the arguments.

'You take off with them. I'm going to do some work here. Nice of you to back me up!'

'Come on! I left because I got a call from our guys.

Helen's run a check on the Chapman family and they're clean. The husband has no record and is, as she told us, working for a shipyard. The boyfriend also has no record. The estate agents have given details of a bank deposit transfer to the Cayman Islands. The rent goes direct to the bank – it's for two and a half thousand a month . . .'

Unseen by either of them, Williams had overheard.

'Checking up, are you? I could have told you that. We're trying to get more information regarding the Cayman Island deposit, but it looks like your suspect was taking flight.' He began to hand over fleece jackets and woollen hats for the helicopter flight.

'I won't need them,' Anna said. 'I meant to tell you, I hate flying especially in a helicopter so I'll take up your offer of a car and do some driving around here.'

Williams gave her a long steady gaze and then shrugged. 'Up to you.'

'How long will you be?'

'Hour or so, so we'll meet up back here. And maybe hang onto the fleece as it's cold out there.'

As the Drug Squad moved out with Williams and Paul, Anna took a closer look at their incident board. She noticed Harry Took helping himself to more of the coffee and pastries.

'Could I have you just for a second, Harry?'

'Sure,' he said, spitting crumbs out of his mouth as he joined her.

Anna pointed to the names of a couple of hotels. 'Why these particular hotels?'

Harry explained that Sammy Marsh had frequented one in Falmouth known for its restaurant, and they had also traced an ex-boyfriend there, who worked as a waiter.

'Is he still working there?'

386

'I don't know. The other one is a small hotel in the Rose peninsula area near Padstow. It's open all year round, has mostly elderly clients and overlooks a small cove. The body of victim one was washed up there.'

'You get anything from them?'

'No, just that we'd missed Sammy by a few days.'

'Do you know if Alan Rawlins ever used either of these hotels?'

'Nope, but then we've only just got all the information on him.'

Anna jotted down the locations and took a seat at an empty desk to study a map of the area. She checked the time, deciding that finding the hotels would be her starting-point. Picking up the fleece jacket, she was about to head out when Harry asked if she needed him to drive.

'No thanks, but I need the keys to the vehicle DCI Williams has arranged for me.'

Harry brought her the keys and said the car was parked outside in the station car park.

'You take care. Some of the roads are very narrow.'

'I will, thank you, and I'm on my mobile if anyone needs to contact me.'

Meanwhile Paul was seated in the helicopter with Williams, who used the radio-controlled microphone to talk to his guest through the headphones.

'We're going to start by flying north and then go south down the coast to Land's End. You'll get a good bird's-eye view of all the beaches and different locations used by Sammy and his henchmen.'

As they left Newquay, Paul's stomach lurched. Although it was no longer raining there was quite a wind kicking up.

'As you can see below, the reason why Newquay is a focal point for surfers is because we've got beaches facing in all directions. That means there's a good spread of the different types of surf, for beginners to professionals. We get some really excellent breaks.'

Williams kept up a running commentary, pinpointing the known locations and where two bodies had been washed up. They flew over Sammy's apartment and Paul could see way below his speedboat bobbing around in the swell.

Anna used the route-finder to drive out of Newquay heading for Falmouth. It was unseasonably cold, but the sun came out and now that she was alone she began to relax. She knew it might be a fruitless drive, but it was possible that the same waiter might also have known Alan Rawlins.

Williams received a text message from Harry Took that he had released a car for DCI Travis, who was driving to Falmouth to the hotels named on the incident board. Williams laughed and turned back to Paul.

'Your Anna Travis doesn't like flying? But I can tell you she's on a wasted trip whereas this would have been beneficial because she would be able to understand the number of locations we've had to check out.'

As they headed for Bude, Williams pointed out the various beaches used by the surfers: Duckpool, Sandymouth, Northcott Mouth, Crooklets. They swooped down low over Widemouth Bay, Crackington Haven and Trebarwith Strand. The constant motion as they flew lower with the wind buffeting the helicopter made Paul's stomach turn.

Falmouth Harbour was very picturesque and a popular tourist attraction. The well-sheltered cove was crowded with fishing boats, advertisements for day-trip excursions and an abundance of fish and chip restaurants. But Anna drove straight through before heading onto narrow lanes towards a hotel built on a clifftop. The Trethanium was a very well-appointed establishment with a large roof-terrace restaurant. There were no spaces available in the front driveway so she had to use their overflow car park across the road.

She left the fleece jacket behind as it was just a short walk across the road to the hotel's rear entrance, where she found a row of Wellington boots left on shelves for the residents, along with umbrellas and plastic raincoats. She made her way through a corridor towards a small desk beside the entrance to the restaurant. The restaurant was empty so Anna then followed the signs for the bar. There were a few residents sitting on high stools around the small well-equipped bar, and a young girl in a white shirt and black skirt was serving. The room looked out on the spectacular sea views and opened, through two glass doors, onto a large restaurant terrace which was closed as it was out of season.

'I'm looking for Neil Baggerly,' Anna said to the barmaid, who checked her watch and suggested he might be in the dining room setting up for lunch.

'I've just come from there,' Anna told her. 'The tables are set but nobody is about. Is there anywhere else he might be?'

'Try the front of the hotel. We are expecting some guests to arrive.'

Anna went to go back the way she had entered when the barmaid told her that the main reception of the hotel was via another corridor. There were arrows pointing to reception, so Anna followed the signs down a staircase and out to the main reception area. This faced wide glass-fronted doors opening onto the narrow roadway. There was no one on the desk, but outside Anna could see a young dark-haired man carrying two suitcases from the open boot of a car. The glass doors opened electronically and he headed inside. The elderly couple on the pavement returned to their car to drive it around to the hotel parking lot where Anna had left her car.

'Excuse me, are you Neil Baggerly?'

He glanced at her as he leaned over the reception desk to remove a room key.

'You want to make a booking for lunch?'

'No, I would like to talk to you.'

He straightened, looking at her suspiciously. She came closer and showed her ID, saying, 'When you have a moment.'

Picking up the suitcases, he gave her a resigned glance and said over his shoulder that he'd be five minutes.

It was more like ten as Anna waited. He eventually returned and took the guestbook to jot down the time of the guests' arrival. She took the moment to have a really good look at him. He was not very tall, but was very striking in looks, with thick black hair combed back from his chiselled face. He closed the book and tucked the biro back into his top pocket.

'What do you want?'

'Is there somewhere we can talk?' Anna began.

'I'm on duty so whatever you want to ask me, do it here.'

'If you want me to air your dirty laundry in public I will.'

'Listen, I have been questioned over and over again. This is about Sammy Marsh again, isn't it?'

'Connected to him, yes.'

'Well, I've told a fat greasy guy everything, and then I've repeated it all to a tall, sandy-haired bloke. I haven't seen Sammy for over eight months. I knew him, yeah. I could get him the best table on the terrace in the summer, yeah, but I don't have anything more to do with him.'

'I really think you need to change your attitude . . .'

'I just *told* you. I'm on duty, we're short-staffed and I've got to man the desk and act as porter.'

Anna again showed her ID, facing him out.

'I'm not from here. I've come from London and this, Mr Baggerly, is a murder enquiry – so you *will* find somewhere for us to talk in private. And *now*, if you please.'

He sulkily picked up the phone and spoke to someone to say he would be in the other bar. He jerked his head for Anna to follow him.

The bar, which was close to the open terrace, was closed. Ungraciously, he pulled out two stools.

'Thank you.'

He shrugged as Anna placed her briefcase onto the bar and clicked it open, removing the photograph of Alan Rawlins.

'Do you know this man?'

Neil looked and nodded. 'Yeah, he used to have lunch here in the summer, but I've not seen him either for months, like Sammy.'

'Sammy Marsh? How well did you know him?'

'Not well, but like I said, I've been asked about him.'

'What about this man in the photograph?'

'Last summer, he'd come here for lunch and sometimes dinner.'

'What was his name?'

'Daniel Matthews.'

'Was he alone?'

'No, he was sometimes with Sammy and sometimes with another guy, or sometimes with four or five people.'

'How well did you know Daniel Matthews?'

Baggerly sighed and then looked her in the eye. 'I knew him. He was a heavy tipper so I always made a point of grabbing him as a customer.'

'You grab anything else?'

'What's that supposed to mean?'

'This man was homosexual.'

Neil looked away.

'Are you?' Anna enquired.

'That's my business.'

'It's also mine, Mr Baggerly. This man has disappeared, he has been missing for some considerable time and it's possible he has been murdered.'

Neil gave a soft laugh. 'Possible? Either he has or he hasn't.'

'You think it's funny? I need to talk to anyone who knew him. I need to find out who else knew him – and if you know *anything*, I suggest you straighten out and tell me what it is.'

'Straighten out?'

'Yes. We can either do it here and now, or I will have you taken into the police station for questioning. Now: just how well did you know this man?' She jabbed the photograph of Alan.

'Sammy introduced me to him a couple of summers ago. We had a few nights together, but he was an oddball and could get quite nasty and I'm not into that stuff. Also, he was with Sammy Marsh. Whether or not they were an item I couldn't tell you.'

'Did you score drugs from him?'

'Sammy?'

'Yes, Mr Baggerly.'

'Few lines of coke – that's my limit – but he could hoover it up, and didn't like to get down to it unless he was high.'

'You are referring to this man you know as Daniel Matthews?'

'Yeah.'

'You scored drugs from him?'

'I didn't score – he had them with him. I've never been with Sammy. He's not my type and besides, he's always got a bunch of guys fawning all over him. If I say Dan was a heavy tipper, Sammy used to be so stoned he would drop hundreds. Reason I was never too friendly towards him was because he was well known to throw his weight around. You never knew where you were with Sammy. One minute he was all smiles and the next he'd blank you.'

Neil Baggerly frowned. 'He never used to be like that – I'm talking about Sammy now. He was always Mr Sharp, but the last few times I saw him here he was well out of it. I kept my distance because the management here are very classy.'

'Was Daniel Matthews drugged up?'

'No, he would stick to soft drinks, but like I said, when he was alone with me he'd snort up a few lines.'

'When you were with him, did you go to his place?'

'No. I've got a room here. Apart from that, the summer is our busy time and I've not got a car. On my days off we'd go into Falmouth, but I never went over to Newquay, and he never seemed to want me to go there. In fact, I know he didn't like Sammy to know he was seeing me.'

'When was the last time you saw him?'

Neil closed his eyes and pinched the bridge of his nose. He recollected that it had to have been seven or eight months ago.

'He came in alone for some lunch and I told him that I wouldn't be off-duty for the afternoon and that I was also working that night. He said that he was not going to be around as he was heading back to London. Oh yeah ...' Neil clicked his fingers. 'Another thing, we always have all the newspapers, local as well as the London ones, and I gave him one to read because he was sitting by himself. It was the local one – about that girl they'd found dead, washed up on the beach. The coroner's report said that it was a heroin OD. Front page, it was.'

Anna waited as Neil licked his lips, frowning.

'I brought him some iced water and I said to him, joking, I said, nodding to the paper, that I hoped Sammy wasn't involved. At that he kind of freaked, rolling up the paper and slapping the table with it. He was really uptight, if you know what I mean.'

She nodded and waited, but Neil just shrugged.

'That was it. He got up and left without touching his food. When I went out to the back of the hotel to see if he'd really gone or whether he just wanted the lavatory, he was walking out. I asked him if there was something wrong.'

Neil described the odd look on Alan Rawlins's face, but he'd said nothing else and that was the last time he had seen him.

'What about Sammy Marsh?'

'Same day or night, Sammy was here asking if I'd seen Dan. I told him he'd been in for lunch, and Sammy never even waited for me to finish talking. He just pushed past me. Like I said, he was a weirdo.'

'Did you tell the Cornish police this?'

'Not about Daniel. They never asked me about him, just wanted to know the last time I'd seen Sammy.'

Anna held up the photograph of Alan Rawlins again.

'And you are sure that this man is Daniel Matthews?'

Neil laughed crudely. 'I'd know him anywhere – not that you can see it in this photograph. If you know what I mean.'

Unaware that Anna was driving to the Neve Hotel far beneath him, Paul was coming to the end of his tour of the beaches, as the pilot flew them over Polzeath and Padstow.

'We're turning back now,' Williams said.

Paul was grateful. His stomach felt as if it was lurching up into his mouth thanks to the helicopter constantly swooping low for him to get a good view of the beaches. The wind was picking up, and the single-bladed craft was bouncing as Williams pinpointed where one of the victims had been washed ashore; Constantine Bay, with its dangerous reefs.

'This beach is avoided by beginners. You get a tidal flow sweeping you onto the rocks and they can cut you to shreds, which is why our victim's body was so damaged.'

'How far to go?' Paul asked plaintively.

'About twenty minutes. We'll be coming over Newquay soon.'

Paul closed his eyes and whispered, 'Thank God.'

Williams smiled at the pilot, as they'd both noticed that Paul's face was ashen. 'There's a sick bag tucked into the back of the seat, should you require it.'

Anna almost had a head-on collision with a tractor as she drove slowly along very narrow lanes, with high hedgerows on either side. The sun had gone and the rain had started. It was light at first, but then it became a deluge and she half-wished that she had taken up Harry Took's offer to drive. She took the wrong turning over and over again, even though she was following the signs to the hotel. Twice she ended up in a field, through a cart track, and then turning back on herself she checked her map. The SatNav was useless. In fact, she had followed its instruction and that was the reason she had ended up in the fields. Covering her head with the borrowed fleece, she ran across to a farmworker and asked him the way. He laughed as he told her she was almost there and to continue on the narrow road for two miles and she would pass a small village and fishing cove. Three miles beyond that was the beach and cove and the Hotel Neve on the cliffs.

Soaked from just the few minutes of conversation, Anna set off and drove through a small village on a very narrow road with houses huddled on either side. It was impossible for two cars to pass each other and she constantly had to swerve into a tiny gap as a vehicle passed her. Eventually she managed to drive out of the village and she continued as instructed, next passing a cove with a small beach and sheltered by rocks. Hotel Neve was high up above it, with direct views of the cove and ocean.

The rain was still coming down thick and fast and she held the fleece over her head as she hurried from the car park to the hotel entrance, hoping it was not a wasted journey.

The hotel resembled a country house with antique furniture and Persian carpets in a panelled hallway. The reception desk was behind a windowed cubicle where a young girl was working at a computer. Anna waited a moment until the girl looked up.

'Could you tell me if Craig Sumpter still works here?'

'Yes, but he's not on duty right now. Lunch is over and dinner isn't served until seven.'

'Where could I find him?'

'He's probably in his room. The staff quarters are to the left of the reception as you enter. Do you want me to give him a ring and see if he's there?'

'Thank you.'

'Who shall I say is calling?'

'DCI Anna Travis.' She took out her ID and showed it to the girl, who glanced at it and then looked up.

'Police?' She rang an internal number, waiting a while before she replaced the phone. 'Not answering. He might be in the spa by the swimming pool. You want me to call there as well?'

'No. I tell you what – just point me in the right direction.'

'Turn right, go to the end of the corridor, then left and it's signposted.'

'Thank you.'

Anna moved along the thickly carpeted corridor lined with many sketches and paintings for sale, continuing along a second corridor down some stairs to the indoor pool. It was very warm and an elderly woman with a flowered bathing cap was doing breast-stroke in a very leisurely fashion. The spa and Jacuzzi area was through glass doors, and there was a beauty and hair salon which was closed. Racks of hotel towels were freely available. Pushing open the door to the spa, the smell of chlorine and bleach was overpowering. The Jacuzzi was empty and a slim young man was using a bucket and mop to clean it out.

'It's not working today,' he said pleasantly.

'Are you Craig Sumpter?'

He nodded. Anna moved closer and showed her ID. He tossed a wet sponge into the bucket.

'Is there somewhere we can talk?' she asked.

He hesitated and then gestured towards a sun-lounge with wicker beds, cushions and chairs.

'I'll be with you in a minute.'

The sun-lounge was cold. Anna watched as the rain lashed down on the large windows that overlooked the gardens and the cove, and sat staring out at the ocean until Craig came in, running his hand through his blonde hair. He was very slender with narrow shoulders, and he was wearing black trousers that looked as if they'd seen better days. His white shirt was clean and pressed, but it looked too large for him.

'Is this to do with Sammy Marsh?' he asked.

'In a way, yes it is. You knew him?' Anna asked.

'Everybody around here knows him, but this wasn't his type of place. He came here a few times, but not recently – maybe months ago. In fact, it was last summer – in June. He wasn't staying, just having tea out on the patio.'

Anna nodded.

'I've been asked about him a few times by the police, but that's basically all I could tell them.'

'Why do you think they questioned you about Sammy?'

'I'd been seen with him at the Smugglers café a few times. I worked the bar there when I first came to Cornwall and they said they were questioning everyone about him.'

'I'm going to show you a photograph of someone else. See if you recognise him.'

She noticed that Craig was nervous. He had an elastic

band that had been round his wrist which he was now threading through his fingers and twanging it. He was wearing rundown leather shoes and his foot twitched constantly.

'How old are you?'

'Twenty-one. I'm learning the ropes here as I want to get into hotel management.'

'This man?' She showed him Alan Rawlins's photograph. Craig looked at it and then back to Anna.

'What about him?'

'Do you know him?'

'Yes.'

'What's his name?'

'Dan Matthews.'

'When was the last time you saw him?'

'Why do you want to know?'

'Because he's missing and I am trying to trace him.'

'Has he done something wrong?'

'Just answer my question, Craig. When was the last time you saw him?'

'Over six months ago.'

'Did he come to see you here?'

'Yes.'

'Did you go to his flat in Newquay?'

'Sometimes.'

'Did you have a relationship with him?'

'Why do you want to know that?'

'Because we are very concerned for his safety.'

Craig leaned forwards. He had a pretty face with wide blue eyes and a small nose with plump girlish lips.

'I'm concerned too. He's not contacted me and . . .'

He blinked back tears, twanging the elastic band.

'Go on, Craig. It's very important.'

'He made me promises and I believed him, but he's not answered my calls and now he's not picking up his phone.'

'His London phone?'

'No, no, his mobile. I've sort of given up.'

'What promises?'

The tears were very close to the surface and he tossed his head back, sniffing.

'He said we'd move into a house he'd bought and he said that for my twenty-first he was going to give me a car.' He wiped his cheek with the flat of his hand. 'He said he was repairing a Mercedes, a 280SL. He said it would be my birthday present, but . . .'

'So you had a very strong relationship with him?'

'I thought so. I really believed him and I told everyone about the car.'

'When you last saw him, how did he seem to you?'

'Same as usual. We were going to look at his house, as he said it was almost finished. I'd helped choose some of the fabrics for his sun-lounge and . . . I can't believe that he was lying to me.'

'Did he say he was planning to move to Cornwall on a permanent basis?'

'Yes.'

'Did he ever tell you about his life back in London?'

'Not that much. He was always very cagey about it – I know why.'

'Why?'

'He was living with a woman. He said they were just platonic, but he never wanted to talk about her. He said it was awkward and that he didn't want to stay with her.'

'He never told you he was engaged to this woman?'

Craig looked shocked and then shook his head.

'Was he ever nasty to you?' Anna asked next.

'What do you mean?'

'Rough? Knock you around?'

'Dan?'

'Yes – did he beat you up at all?'

'No, never. He was really special. He was my first real relationship and he was always gentle and looked out for me.'

'Did you ever see him use drugs?'

'A couple of times he had some ecstasy tabs, but I wouldn't take them. He also smoked a few joints and I wouldn't even do that.'

'Why not?'

Craig turned away. His foot was still twitching and his hands couldn't stop twanging the elastic band.

'I've had a few problems with my kidneys. When I was a kid it was quite bad so I've been on medication. I'm scared to take anything that might make me ill again. I don't drink either.'

'You said you were working here to train in hotel management, but if you took up his offer to go and live with him, that would mean losing your job, wouldn't it?'

'No. He told me he was coming into some inheritance, a lot of money, and that we could look around to buy a small hotel. I couldn't believe it when he never wrote to me or texted or phoned. I've been in a right state because he promised me, he promised me.'

'Do you have any of his letters?'

'Yes.'

'Would you allow me to see them?'

'They're private.'

'Listen to me, Craig – you need to know that the man you knew as Daniel Matthews has been missing for some considerable time – and that is probably why you haven't heard from him. I'm sorry to say that we have grave concerns about his safety. In fact, we fear that he may have been murdered, so anything you can do to help me try to either trace him, or find out what has happened to him, would be greatly appreciated.'

'Murdered? Are you saying he's dead?'

'Possibly.'

The tears the young man had been trying to keep under control rolled down his cheeks.

'I loved him,' he sobbed.

'These letters, Craig – please may I see them?'

'They're in my room.'

'Will you take me there?' Anna tried to be gentle, to curb her impatience.

He drew a shuddering breath and then nodded.

Chapter Eighteen

Paul's legs felt like jelly as he got down from the helicopter. Williams found it amusing, saying that at least he hadn't thrown up. He put his arm around Paul's shoulders and guided him towards the waiting patrol car.

'Get a cup of our coffee down you and you'll feel better.'

'Promise?' Paul said with a weak smile.

When they arrived at the station Harry Took repeated to Williams that Anna had gone to talk to guys they had interviewed at the hotels. Williams didn't like it, saying sharply that he should have driven her as she was going to be hours, and with the weather getting even worse she would find driving hazardous.

They ordered sandwiches which were brought into the incident room on a trolley. Seeing them made Paul feel even worse. He also felt like a spare part. The trip in the helicopter had revealed nothing apart from the scale of Sammy Marsh's territory for drug-dealing. He sat at an empty desk as Williams asked his team if they had any new developments, listening to the latest reports: there had been no movement in any of Sammy's known bank accounts, no credit-card use, and the monies transferred to Alan Rawlins's account in the Cayman Islands were also untouched. Paul excused himself and went to the gents to put in a call to Anna, who answered abruptly, saying she couldn't talk, but that she would be heading back to the station shortly. She suggested he use the time to take a look over the Smugglers café, the known haunt of Sammy and Alan.

'It's closed,' Paul pointed out.

'Check it out anyway,' she said and cut off the call.

Paul next rang the incident room in London, only to discover that Brian Stanley was off sick and Helen was out of the station, on enquiries at Asda.

Paul was told that the manager had rung to say he had made a mistake and therefore the footage for the day Tina Brooks had purchased the bleach may not have been erased. Paul hung up, unconvinced that this would add anything as they already had the date and time on Tina's receipt and she was not denying the purchase of bleach and carpet cleaner from Asda.

He returned to the incident room as the team finished up their tea and sandwiches, and Williams gave him a side-long glance, knowing he would have been calling Anna.

'How's your lady boss?'

'Couldn't talk as she was busy, but do you think we could go and look over the Smugglers café?'

'It's closed. We've also checked it out and there's nothing there.'

'I know that, but just out of interest.'

'Sure – I'll arrange it.' Williams turned to Harry Took, who was still eating.

'Harry, wheel Paul here over to the Smugglers café. Call the guy that owns it and see if they can open it up.'

Paul caught the amused glances between Williams and Harry, feeling even more like a spare part as he delved into his pocket for some chewing gum, anything to take away the taste of bile still in his mouth.

The rain was still lashing down. Anna had to use the fleece to cover her head again as Craig led her out of the hotel via a back exit and around through the gardens to the staff quarters. He'd said he didn't want anyone from the management to see them go into his room as they didn't like their staff entertaining.

The staff accommodation was in a small single-storey building attached to the main hotel. Each unit had its own entrance door. Craig unlocked his, soaked from the rain, his blonde hair dripping.

It was just a single bedroom with a shower unit and a small kitchen annex, all very tidy. On the bedside table were three small framed photographs. Each one had Craig and Alan Rawlins together, sunbathing, dining out and walking close together on the beach.

'Who took these?'

'I did. My camera's got a timer on it. Dan bought it for me.'

Anna sat on the only comfortable chair as Craig opened a drawer in a small painted dresser. He took out a bundle of letters in their envelopes and then sat on the bed as he thumbed through them. A couple he placed to one side.

'They're from my mum,' he explained, looking up.

He then passed Anna four letters, all of which she noticed had peel and seal envelopes and therefore no chance of any DNA from Alan Rawlins's saliva.

'They're very personal,' he said quietly.

She opened the first. There was no date and no address, but she noticed a London postmark. The letter had been written over a year ago. The writing was neat in felt-tipped pen and it was rather touching, saying how much Alan had enjoyed meeting Craig and that he couldn't wait for when he would be able to see him again. It also mentioned he had enclosed some money for him to start saving for the surfboard he wanted. He had signed *Dan* and underlined it three times. The next two letters were similar in content, but more familiar, describing how much he had liked Craig's body and suggesting he start to work out in the hotel gym. Again he had enclosed money and again he'd signed his name as Dan.

Craig remained silent as Anna read through the letters. Nothing in them gave any indication of what Alan Rawlins's intentions were, although there was the promise of the Mercedes for Craig's birthday.

'How much money did he send you?'

'Two or three hundred. It's all in a savings account.'

There was something almost fatherly about the instructions to eat well and work out to build up his strength. There was a reference to when Alan would be next coming to see him and that he would be bringing some clothes for him and some new shoes.

'Did you reply to his letters?'

'No, as I never had his address. He said it wouldn't be a good idea, but whenever I asked why, he would change the subject. He told me he often stayed over at his parents' and I thought that maybe I could write to him there, but he said it wouldn't be convenient and that if I needed anything I could always contact him on his mobile.'

'Which you did?' She looked up from the letters.

'Yes, until about nine weeks ago.'

'Could you give me the number you called?'

He nodded and got up to write on a notepad as Anna

reread the letters. There was never a date or address. She concentrated on the contents of the last one as it looked different; the writing was hurried and slapdash, although it expressed as always how much he missed and loved Craig, but then came a passage about business problems and that he would not be coming to see him for a while. Anna looked at the date on the envelope: it was seven months ago. Underlined were instructions for Craig to stay well away from Sammy and to give him no indication that they were seeing each other. It was imperative they keep their relationship private; this was underlined twice. The next paragraph in the letter read:

> *I am having major problems and may have got in over my head. I have been foolish and I don't want you getting involved. If you don't hear from me for a while just know that you are the most important person in my life. I promise you the Mercedes is almost ready for me to drive it down for your birthday. I love you . . .*

Anna refolded the letter back along its creases and tucked it into the envelope.

'What do you think he meant by getting in over his head?'

'The costs of the house were mounting. He said he hadn't bargained for it in his budget and he needed a lot of money for the contractors. They were going to down tools if he didn't pay up.'

'When was this?'

'Oh, before that letter, but he was worried. He must have got himself out of trouble financially though, because he started making even more plans and ordered this expensive kitchen unit for the house.'

'Did you ask him about his problems?'

'Yes, he said they weren't to concern me, but he was a bit different.'

'How do you mean?'

'Very strung out and a bit tetchy with me, but I never asked too much as I didn't want him to get the feeling that I was in it with him for the money.'

Craig opened his wardrobe and began taking out various items: a fringed suede jacket, a suit and some shirts. All were new and bought for him by the man he called Dan.

'And shoes?' He bent down and brought out a box of suede loafers, before neatly replacing the items after he had shown them to Anna.

'He said he wanted me to smarten up. I don't earn much here, in fact I've never had much so I keep them for best – keep them for when I see him.'

He turned and the tears brimmed in his eyes again.

'You see, I really thought he cared for me, but to just cut me off like that . . . I don't understand it.'

He sat down hunched on his bed, and suddenly blurted out that it was his first time with a man, and that although he'd always known about his sexuality, he had never been with anyone until Dan.

'He told me how hard it had been for him, and that he had hated himself for years. That his parents didn't know – in fact, no one knew he was gay in London. He was tired of having to be so secretive.' Craig took out a handkerchief and blew his nose.

Anna stood up and passed the letters back to the young man.

'He's very secretive, Craig. In fact, his name isn't Daniel Matthews, it's Alan Rawlins.'

Craig looked up, shocked. 'Why would he lie about his name?'

'Because he was leading a double life here with you, but now what I am trying to uncover is who else knew.'

Anna quietly explained to Craig the discovery at Alan Rawlins's flat, the blood pooling, and how they had been unable to identify who it came from as there was no DNA to match.

'We don't know if it was Alan who died in his flat or whether he killed someone else. That could be the reason he has disappeared.'

Craig sat, dry-eyed now, listening. He seemed stunned and saddened, all at the same time.

'There was a Mercedes being reconditioned in the garage where he worked. He was telling you the truth about it, and I'm sure he did intend on driving it down here to give to you. He was waiting for the soft top to be delivered. But before he could do so, we believe something happened that resulted in either his committing a murder or him being murdered.'

Craig stood up and went into his small shower room. Anna thought that perhaps he had gone for some privacy, but he left the door ajar and then came out.

'He was very particular about his hair. He always brought his own shampoos and conditioner when he stayed here for the night. This is his hairbrush, razor and toothbrush.'

Anna could have kissed him! She opened her briefcase and took out a plastic evidence bag, slipping the items inside.

'Here's his mobile number you asked for. I've rung it loads of times but he never answers.' Craig began to cry again as Anna unfolded the note to look at the number.

She sensed something was not right. Taking her notebook from her bag she compared the number she had for Alan Rawlins's mobile recovered from his 280SL Mercedes. They were different.

'Are you sure this was the number?'

'Yes, positive. Why, what's wrong?'

'Sorry, my mistake. Nothing for you to worry about.'

Craig was very subdued as he walked out with her towards the car park. The rain was still heavy and he carried an umbrella to shield her.

'Thank you for your help, Craig. I really appreciate it,' she said as they reached the car.

'Do you think it has something to do with Sammy Marsh?'

She was halfway into her seat but now she stood up again. 'Why do you say that?'

Craig turned and pointed to the cove. 'A girl was washed up near to the rocks – teenager – they said she'd died of a heroin overdose. The last call I had with Dan, he spoke about it. He was very distressed, so much so I asked if he'd known her, but he just changed the subject and told me to never talk to anyone about him and Sammy.'

'So when you were questioned previously, you never mentioned this phone call?'

'No, but they never asked me anything about Dan.'

As she turned the car to head towards the cove and onto the road, she could see him in her driving mirror, the rain dripping off the big black umbrella. His sweet face and skinny frame shook as he gave a small wave of his hand.

Paul, accompanied by a very disgruntled Harry Took, plodded across the wet sands towards what looked like a rundown shack with a rickety veranda. The wooden steps were broken in places, and dangerous. They had had to wait for the owner to supply the keys, although they were hardly necessary as the door looked as if a hard push would have opened it, its hinges were so rusty.

Harry unlocked a large padlock that was looped through the door handle to a nail hammered into the wooden slatted frame. He eventually pushed open the creaking door and they went inside.

They could find no light switch so used a high-beamed torch, revealing a long bar rather like those in the saloons in cowboy films. Wooden chairs and tables were stacked against one wall, and empty bottles were visible behind the bar, along with old used candles stuck into their necks. There was a small raised stage where the bands would have performed, Harry told him, ladies and gents toilets, and behind the bar a door which led to a kitchen that was filthy, according to Harry.

'Hard to believe that come summer, this place is hopping. It's a big hang-out for the kids, especially the surfers,' he remarked.

Old surfboards were hammered into the wall alongside peeling posters of events and rock groups. Glasses and beer mugs were stacked on dirty dust-covered shelves, and a cutlery drawer was covered with spiderwebs.

'They make a fortune. Health and Safety have tried closing it, but the owner does a quick clean-up and re-opens. I wouldn't eat here, wouldn't touch a single one of their dodgy hamburgers, sausages and hot dogs . . . but it's the location, it's all about location and being right on the beach.'

Paul followed the beam of the torch as Harry flashed it around.

'What are you looking for?' the older man asked.

'Just getting a feel of the place,' Paul said.

'Oh right. Well, you seen enough now, have you?'

'Pass us the torch. You can wait outside, if you want.'

'Here.' Harry gave him the torch. 'Ugh, stinks of backed-up drains, if you ask me. Probably left the old used sani-bins in the ladies toilets.' Harry headed out to stand on the veranda and have a smoke. It was still pouring with rain and they had about a half-mile walk back to the car park, which he didn't relish.

Paul gave the main bar area a slow once-over and noticed that one table had been taken down from the stack and two chairs set beside it. It had candle drips and dirty glasses, and an empty bottle of vodka lay on its side. He went to look into the kitchen, which was, as Harry had described, filthy – plus sand had blown in through the cracks in the wooden slats.

Paul backed out, shone the torch over the bar area once more and then headed towards the toilets, the smell of drains growing more pungent the closer he got. He kicked open the door to the ladies, revealing a wash-basin and a single cracked toilet. The smell grew even worse. Paul was tempted not to bother looking into the gents, but thought better of it and tried to open the door with his foot. It was firmly stuck, but now the smell was overpowering. He gave one more shove and the door opened.

'Jesus Christ.' He could now see why it had been difficult to move – a pair of legs was pressed against it. Paul let out a yell for Harry to join him, as he tried to ease the door open further. Harry came back inside, shouting that it was too dark, he couldn't see. Paul aimed the torch towards him.

'You'd better get your people. There's a body rammed against the door. I think it's a bloke.'

Harry covered his nose and mouth, as the smell was sickening.

'You said this place had been checked out. By the stink in there, whoever it is has been here for quite a while,' Paul went on.

'Can you see his face?' Harry asked.

'No. His legs are blocking the door from opening.'

Harry backed away, saying they shouldn't move anything and he'd call the station. Paul, by now, had taken out a handkerchief to cover his face. He shone the torch on to the table.

'Looks like whoever it was sat over here. Maybe some drunk?'

Harry had gone back out to the veranda, swearing that his mobile was on the blink as Paul shone the torch back to the open lavatory. The light picked out a very expensive pair of crocodile boots. He inched closer and tried to gently ease the door wider to get a closer look at the body, but it was firmly wedged. He pressed himself against the wall to shine the torch round the narrow gap.

'They're on their way,' Harry shouted as he returned, banging into some chairs, which toppled over. He swore and rubbed his thigh.

In the beam of his torch Paul could see that the corpse was wearing a leather jacket; one arm was crooked over his face and the other was half-raised as if trying to shield himself. 'You want to have a look at him?'

'No, I fucking don't – and don't you touch anything, for God's sake.'

'He's wearing quality gear – leather jacket, croc cowboy boots.'

Harry edged his way closer to Paul, who handed him

the torch, then he peered around the door. The light wavered and went out.

'Shit.'

They were both now in total darkness, and the smell of the decomposing corpse was eye-watering. Harry gripped hold of Paul's arm.

'I'm gonna be sick.'

As Anna drove into the station, two patrol cars with lights blazing and sirens blasting almost ran into her. The rear car drew up and Williams looked out of the window, shouting something, but she couldn't hear what he said. Quickly she parked up and hurried into the virtually empty incident room where she was told by a DC that a body had been found in the Smugglers café.

'They got an ID on it?'

'Not yet – it was only just called in by Harry Took. He thinks it had been there for some time.'

'But wasn't the café searched?'

'Yes, weeks ago.'

Anna asked if anyone knew where Paul was, and then it dawned on her that she had asked him to check out the Smugglers café. She could hardly keep the smile off her face as she said it was a good thing her team were always so thorough. When she asked if someone could drive her over to the café, she was told that there wasn't a car available. She asked for directions and returned to her car to drive herself.

The beach car park was a hive of activity. Three patrol cars, an ambulance, and forensic and undertaker's vans were parked up. Although the Smugglers café was some distance away, it was easily picked out thanks to the arc

414

lamps lighting it up like a movie set. The rain had thankfully ceased, but it was bitterly cold and the wind was sharp; coming from the ocean it was freezing. Anna's fleece jacket was sodden and she was loath to get out of the car. To her relief she could see Paul heading up from the beach caught in her car's headlights, and so she opened her window and called out to him. He paused and looked around and then catching sight of her, hurried towards her car.

As he got into the passenger side his teeth were chattering, he was so cold. Anna kept the heater on full blast for him.

'I was feeling like a spare part and I was about to leave the café when I tried to open the door of the gents toilets,' he explained. 'Whoever it is, they've been dead a while, and there I was, trying to keep the scene from contamination when Williams and his heavies come charging in and took the door off its hinges. And boy, was he swearing. They'd apparently checked the place a few weeks ago.'

'Cut the chit-chat, Paul – anyone recognise the body?'

'We've not got a positive ID, obviously . . .'

'Was it Alan Rawlins?'

'Hell, no. Williams said straight off it was Sammy Marsh.'

Anna looked across at the beach. There were officers scurrying back and forth with torches.

'You think he'd been there a while?'

'By the stench, yes, and the way the body was lying it looked as if he'd been trying to protect himself with one arm across his face.'

Anna shivered and looked at her watch.

'We'll wait until they bring the body up then we'll head

back to the B and B. We're on the first flight out of here in the morning.'

Paul grinned. 'No train?'

'No way. And I'd say with them finding Sammy, their hands will be full here so I doubt they'll want us around.'

Paul asked if she had found anything for their case. She nodded and said it was not a lot, but enough for them finally to get some DNA to check with the blood found at Tina Brooks's flat. She also told Paul that Alan Rawlins had had *two* mobile phones – and she now had the number for the previously unknown one.

She stared from the window as a covered stretcher was brought along the beach with Williams following, talking into his mobile. She opened the driver's door but a blast of cold air made her shut it quickly.

Williams overtook the stretcher and waved towards Anna's car. She hunched her shoulders and got out, wrapping her thin jacket around her, and headed for the stretcher.

'Is it Sammy Marsh?' she demanded loudly.

Williams turned to ask the stretcher-bearers to stop.

'I'd say so. You want to take a look at him?'

Anna shuddered from the cold, but stood close to the stretcher as Williams unzipped the body bag.

'He's not a pretty sight. Don't know how he was killed, but he's going straight over to Pathology. Don't want to waste time examining here.'

Anna looked at the body; the long hair was matted and the face was ravaged, with his skin hanging loose and the open eyes sunken into their sockets.

'We'll check his fingerprints, obviously. There's no wallet or anything to ID him, but from the clothes I'm positive it's him.'

Anna shivered as Williams zipped up the body bag and gave instructions for the stretcher to be moved into the ambulance.

'That was lucky, wasn't it?'

Williams looked at her. 'What was?'

'That Paul wanted to look over the café. Apparently you'd already searched there, so it'll be interesting to find out how long he's been dead.'

Williams walked with her back to her car.

'You get anything?' he grunted.

'Not much, but at least I know it wasn't Sammy murdered in Rawlins's flat so I'll be returning to London first thing. If I could hang onto the car I'd be grateful and I really appreciate all of your assistance whilst we've been here.'

Williams knew she was being sarcastic but said he would have someone at the station come to collect the car in the morning from the station.

'No, not the station. We're getting the first flight to Gatwick. I'll leave the keys with the landlady and we'll order a taxi.'

Williams gave a curt nod, watching as she hurriedly got into the car and out of the cold. He knew he would be at the beach for some time as they checked out the interior of the café.

'Goodnight,' he said, watching as she began to back out, manoeuvring the car round all the accumulated vehicles. He was damned sure she must have gained some kind of a result, but as he had no direct connection to the case involving the disappearance of Alan Rawlins, he would have to wait to find out.

He blew into his freezing hands, turning to head back down the beach to the Smugglers café. Someone was going to get a severe bollocking if it was determined that Sammy had been murdered some considerable time ago and his body had been rotting in the gents toilet whilst they had run around like headless chickens, trying to trace him.

Chapter Nineteen

The first thing Anna did when they both arrived at the Hounslow police station shortly after eleven the next day, was to have the hairbrush, razor and toothbrush taken over to Forensics. She gave Brian the job of tracking down the phone company for Alan Rawlins's other mobile and didn't wait for him to explain why he'd not been around the previous day.

'I tell you who isn't alive any longer. They found the body of Sammy Marsh last night so you can write that up on the board with "deceased" underlined,' she announced.

She then went into her office as Paul related to everyone the trip to Cornwall, observing that whilst the Newquay police had been sitting on their butts, *he* had been the one to discover Sammy's body. Helen ignored him as she was viewing the hours of CCTV footage from the Asda store, beginning to think it was a waste of time, when she suddenly let out a yell.

'You are *not* going to believe this! Oh my God!'

Everyone looked over to her desk as she waved her hands.

'Let me replay it . . . yes, it's her! It's definitely her!'

Paul and Brian leaned on her chair as she rewound the clip and then replayed the sequence.

*

Anna was in her office on the phone to Langton, bringing him up to speed and loving it.

'Added to being able to hopefully get some DNA, we also know that the blood in Tina's flat was not Sammy Marsh's, as I insisted Paul search the Smugglers café where he found the body.'

Paul interrupted by knocking and walking straight in. 'Gov, you'd better come and look at the—'

'Do you mind?' she snapped, covering the phone.

'I don't think you'll want to wait – it's the CCTV footage from Asda and . . .'

She could tell from the look on his face that it was urgent so she stood up and told Langton that she would get straight back to him. She hurried into the incident room, where most of the team were gathered around Helen's monitor.

'What is it?' Anna asked as they parted for her to stand directly behind Helen.

'The store manager called in to say he'd made a mistake and that he still did have the interior store CCTV footage from the till that Tina Brooks was served at.'

'Yes, but she's not denying she bought the bleach, is she?'

'I know, and I found her on the CCTV at till ten buying the bleach and carpet cleaner just like she said, on the sixteenth of March, but the footage the manager gave us was for a two-week period, so I thought I would look beyond that day and—'

'Get to the point, Helen!'

'It's till number thirteen, the next day – the seventeenth. Let me just rewind it . . . no, sorry, too far. It's amazing, because each till has its own CCTV camera, as it's one of their biggest stores and . . . Okay, this is it.'

Anna watched intently as the footage played. Standing in line at till thirteen behind an elderly woman was Tina Brooks. She didn't have a basket or trolley, but carried her purchase in her right hand, placing it onto the counter as the cashier picked it up and ran it by the electronic bar-code reader. She then placed it into a carrier bag and passed it over to Tina.

Anna's mouth felt dry as she asked for the tape to be replayed. It was clear to every one of them that Tina Brooks was buying an axe, not an overly large one; but it was without doubt an axe.

'How long have you had this CCTV?'

Brian was red-faced as he confessed that he had been off sick when he'd been due to pick it up; Helen had thought he was checking it out with Asda, but due to the mix-up they had only got it the previous afternoon.

Helen explained that she had been wading through hours of CCTV footage as it covered days prior to and after Tina's purchase of the bleach.

Anna was shaking as she returned to her office to digest what she had seen. She had only just decided to re-arrest Tina when Paul returned, not even waiting to knock this time.

'There's more. We've fast-forwarded two days to see if there was anything and there is. It beggars belief. Come and have a look.'

The incident room was ominously quiet as Helen waited for Anna to rejoin them.

'This is two days after we now know she purchased the axe.'

Yet again, caught on the same CCTV camera, Tina Brooks was standing talking to the same cashier. She had the plastic bag in her hand and seemed to be angry. There was no sound, but the cashier was clearly pointing across to another area of the store somewhere off-camera.

'She might have been pointing to the returns desk. It's to the side of the row of cashier points,' Helen said.

'Do you think she's returning the bloody axe?' Paul asked in disbelief.

'Good work, Helen. Keep looking and see if you can find her at the returns desk,' Anna said. She looked at her watch and asked them to get a car ready to take her over to the store. Back in her office, she had to sit down to stop her legs shaking. It was hard to believe what she had just seen, even harder to get her head around the fact that Tina had not only bought something that could have been used to chop up the body, but might even have taken it back for a refund. She took a deep breath. It was a near-perfect way to get rid of evidence, but was it *too* perfect? Whatever she had thought of Tina Brooks before, she now had to reassess everything as she got ready to interrogate her as a cold and calculating killer.

The drive to the store was tense. Paul drove, with Anna beside him on the phone to Forensics, asking Liz Hawley to do her best to get a result from the items she had brought back from Cornwall.

'I need an answer on the DNA, Liz, as soon as possible. Do you think you'll be able to get it off the hairbrush?'

Liz never allowed herself to be pressurised, whether or not a result was urgent. She reported that they had two hairs, both with roots still attached, and she was confident they would be able to get the required DNA – but if not, she had the toothbrush and razor as back-up. She also asked if Anna wanted Toxicology to test the same hairs to see if they could determine what drugs might have been consumed.

'Concentrate on the DNA match with the blood pooling, Liz, then yes, go ahead and test for drugs. If there's no match, can you check it against the semen taken from the bedlinen?'

She rang off and said to Paul, 'They're confident we might get a DNA result. We just have to wait.'

Paul nodded as he drove into the supermarket car park. It would be a mind-blowing piece of luck if they were to also find that the axe purchased by Tina Brooks had been successfully returned and was still on sale.

Brian Stanley was making headway tracing the service provider from the mobile phone number given to Anna by Craig Sumpter. Although the number had not been in recent use, they would still be able to access the account and calls made from the mobile even without the phone itself. It was registered to Alan Rawlins, with an online billing account. Two and a half hours later, the waiting was over. Details began to come into the station listing numerous outgoing phone calls and texts. Brian's job was now to identify and cross-reference these with the numbers dialled from Alan Rawlins's other mobile. He divided up the lists with Helen to get the answers ready for Anna's return.

Anna and Paul were sitting in the manager's office. He was apologising profusely for the mix-up with the CCTV. They had already discussed the reason they were there, and the supermarket manager said it would not take long for him to confirm when the axe was purchased and returned as they had the dates and times from the CCTV footage. Anna and Paul watched as he used the barcode of an axe identical to the one purchased by Tina Brooks to check on the computer. After a few moments he turned to face them.

'We only had four on display between the dates you gave me. One was sold, but returned as not being suitable.'

'So you still have it?'

'Yes, we still have four on display. If there was no damage and it was never used, we would accept it on return. It was paid for with cash so we would have reimbursed the same amount. Because it was cash and not credit card, we do not have a record of the buyer.'

'Do you have a record of which axe was purchased?' Anna asked anxiously.

'Well, it has to be one of the four on display. Give me a moment and I'll double-check the barcode again, then get it brought up.' He turned back to his computer and tapped away for a moment before picking up the phone and asking for the floor manager in Home Improvements.

'Can you bring up to my office a fourteen-inch steel axe from the section with the electric equipment? It'll be with the screwdrivers and electric carpentry items. It's on shelf fourteen and the bar code is A4998652.' He laughed. 'No, I'm not unhappy with your work, it's a police matter.'

He replaced the phone and said to them: 'Worried I wanted to use it on him. Joke, just a joke.'

It was a long five minutes before the floor manager knocked and entered, during which time Anna was unable to chat; she was so eager to get her hands on the axe. The man carried the bubble-wrapped axe with a plastic cover over the sharp steel head.

'Was it returned in this condition?' Anna asked. 'By that, I mean with the bubble-wrap and plastic shield?'

'I believe so. It appeared to not have been used, which is why it was replaced onto the shelf.'

The floor manager hovered briefly before he was dismissed. Anna was eager to leave now, and after signing a document that released the axe to them as possible evidence, she and Paul were on their way once more.

Back in the car on the way to see Liz Hawley, Anna held the axe, now in an evidence bag, on her knee, not attempting to unwrap it or even look at it. She wanted it to go directly to Forensics for testing. She couldn't tell from the wrapping if it had been used. On first inspection it didn't look as if it had been, but part of the sellotape around the handle appeared to have been lifted open as some of the plastic bubbles were flattened.

In the forensic lab, Liz Hawley took the axe and weighed it in her hand.

'It's heavier than you'd think. I'll get onto this straight away.'

'Any news from the hair samples yet?'

'Not yet. We're working on it.'

'Soon as possible, Liz.'

'I know, I know . . . but you can't hurry the testing, you know that.'

'Yes. I'm really pressed though, Liz, so make it a real priority.'

Liz gave a rueful glance. 'One thing I can tell you straight off – the texture of the hairs you brought in from Cornwall don't match the single strand from the bed at Rawlins's flat. It's a different colour and it's longer.'

Anna thanked her and returned to Paul waiting outside in the patrol car.

'Brian's making headway with the mobile phone,' he reported. 'It was registered to Alan Rawlins and he's got a slew of dialled numbers to check out. It's a different make to the one we took out of his glove compartment.'

'Things are moving,' she said, slamming the car door.

'You going to make the arrest?'

'Not yet – just let me get my breath. Maybe it'll be third time lucky with Tina. She's walked out so far.'

'Yeah, but we didn't have her buying a fucking axe.'

'Question is, Paul, did she use it?'

The last person Anna wanted to see was Langton. He was in the incident room looking at the CCTV footage, and he turned smiling as Anna and Paul returned.

'This is what you would call a stroke of luck, to put it mildly.'

'Yes, we've just come from the store. The axe was returned and accepted, and Tina Brooks got a refund, believe it or not. It's with Forensics. You want to come into my office?'

Langton nodded and asked for coffee and his usual bacon toasted sandwich with no tomatoes to be brought in.

Anna took off her jacket and hung it on the back of her chair.

'I hate to say I told you so.' He grinned.

Anna really didn't want to get into an argument with him as she sat down. She realised her shirt was very creased and her hair hadn't had a comb through it since she'd left Cornwall.

'So, tell me – was it worth it?' he asked, tugging at an immaculate cuff of his pristine shirt.

'I believe so. As I said, we did instigate the discovery of

Sammy Marsh's body and so we can eliminate him as the victim of the murder in Alan's flat.'

'Fill me in on everything you gained from schlepping all the way there, staying two nights, and I hear you caught a flight back?'

Before Anna could make any reply, Helen brought in his coffee and sandwich. As he ate she opened her notebook and as briefly as possible gave him the details from the meetings with the two waiters, both of whom had been Alan's sexual partners. The last one, she added, had been more than that – a possibly permanent relationship.

Langton listened without interruption, making no notes, but after finishing his sandwich he irritatingly picked the odd crumb off his trousers.

'Thing is, Anna, you got entangled in this drug-dealer scenario when basically what you are looking at, and even more obviously now, is something close to home. Many cases have gone ahead without recovering a body, and although you are now aware that Alan Rawlins was friendly with Sammy Marsh and the other two gay guys, one his boyfriend, there's no evidence they were involved in the killing. Even if Alan Rawlins was getting into drug-dealing, it—'

'He was suddenly earning big money, paying out thousands for the house and then renting it out for three years,' Anna broke in. 'It is obvious to me that he was more than dabbling, and it could have proved to be a very strong motive ...'

Langton stood up, rubbing at his knee.

'If you prove that Tina Brooks killed Alan, for chrissakes the motive could be money! Could be that she found out he was a poofter and planning on ditching her for a twenty-one-year-old waiter. That could have created enough rage for her to be the one that smashed up the Mercedes and took an axe to his head.'

He winced as he sat back down again, still rubbing at his knee. 'Did I tell you I'm having a replacement?'

'What?'

'My knee. Apparently it's meant to be a virtually one hundred per cent improvement. It'll put me out of action for a while, but I'm on the waiting list.'

'Are you telling me this because the meeting is over?'

'Maybe. I just wanted to change the subject rather than repeat myself. Get her brought in and stop wasting bloody time running around the country looking for motives when you've had her in the frame since day one.'

'I'm waiting for the forensic.'

He leaned over her desk. 'Well, stop waiting and fucking get done with it. Now I am not going to get into a slanging match with you – that's an order, understand? I warned you that you're running out of time, Anna. I give you one more week. I don't want to bring in someone else to take over at this stage.'

He went to the door and yanked it open, turning back to look at her for a second before he walked out.

Just as the door closed, Anna's desk phone rang. Helen said that Liz Hawley was on the line and put her through.

'Anna?'

'Speaking. Have you got any results for me?'

'I have. The DNA profile from the hairs on the brush Mr Sumpter gave you is a positive match to the blood pooling. If, as it would appear, the hairs belonged to Alan Rawlins, then he is your victim. However, this still leaves us with no identification regarding the origin of the semen stain. We are obviously double-checking to make sure.'

'Anything on the axe?'

'Not as yet, but we are processing a minute speck of blood. We found it under the microscope, wedged between the axe head and shaft. To be honest I'm not certain it'll be enough to raise a DNA profile. It will take at least another twenty-four hours and it's possible that due to its size we may only get one shot at profiling it.'

'Liz, I don't have to tell you how important this is. If we can show that axe was used to assault or dismember Alan Rawlins, it'll crack open my case.'

'I hear you, and I can only do what I can do.'

'Thank you, Liz. I appreciate you working flat out on this. I owe you a drink.'

Liz laughed and said it would have to be a bottle of champagne.

Anna didn't feel elated, but the reverse. Her instinct was to wait for the results from the axe, and then if they failed she still had the confirmation that their victim was Alan Rawlins. Out of respect she put in a call to DCI Williams. She had to hang on for several minutes until he came onto the phone. He was cool, but polite, saying straight away that he presumed she wanted the update on the body in the Smugglers.

'Dead for about four weeks, maybe even longer. Fingerprints gave us a positive identification that it's Sammy Marsh.'

'How was he killed?'

'One gunshot wound to the back of the skull, second shot to just above his left ear. We recovered two bullets from his head and found cartridge cases at the scene. Looks like an execution, I'd say connected to his drug-dealing. The crime scene was pretty messed up. Christ knows how many people were tramping around the place, and the car park was awash due to the rain, but it looks as if whoever killed him first opened a bottle of vodka and had a few drinks with him, so we're testing for fingerprints and DNA on the glasses. They're not hopeful though, as they'd both been wiped, ditto the bottle.'

'Any witness?'

'Nope.'

'Well, we've had a few developments here. We now know the victim was Alan Rawlins. It's looking as if his girlfriend could be responsible. I'll keep you informed if there is anything that connects to your case, but I'd say it's doubtful.'

'Thanks for calling. Sorry you had a wasted trip and it was nice meeting you.'

He hung up before she could say anything more. Anna replaced the phone, reflecting that it had not been a wasted journey after all.

It was seven-thirty by the time Anna gave the briefing to the team. They began with a lengthy discussion of the phone calls made from Alan Rawlins's second mobile. There were numerous regular calls to Craig Sumpter, along with some to his parents. There were also frequent calls to Sammy Marsh, to the estate agents, and amongst those made shortly before he went missing was one to the spare-part company for the Mercedes soft top. It was clear from the dates of the calls that on the morning that Alan left the garage because of his migraine, he had made a surprising number of calls to Sammy.

Paul stood at the incident board by the lists of phone calls written down in the order they were made.

'So he gets off work because he says he's got a migraine. Tina collects him and leaves him in bed. But we can tell he had to have made all these calls on the same day. That would mean that Sammy Marsh was still alive, so we should pass that on to the Cornwall crowd.'

'Are there any numbers that you've not traced?' asked Anna.

Brian pointed to five long-distance calls which were underlined. They had been unable to get a trace on who they were to as they were all abroad, but they were still trying. Three were to Antigua, one to Los Angeles and one to Florida.

After the briefing Anna made the decision to rearrest Tina Brooks early the following morning. For now, she was tired out and couldn't wait to go home and get some sleep. Jonathan Hyde, Tina's brief, would be contacted as soon as they had her in custody at the station. If, as usual, he kept them waiting and then demanded a lengthy disclosure of their new evidence, Anna reckoned it would be around midday before questioning could begin.

Anna was prepared for a restless night, but she fell asleep as soon as her head hit the pillow. No sleeping tablets or even a few glasses of wine were involved. She was mentally and physically exhausted.

On the other side of London, Liz Hawley didn't often work half the night, but she and her team knew the urgency of the case. They had already double-checked their DNA match. They were now working on the microscopic speck of blood taken from the axe-handle shaft. Because it was so small she had instructed her team to attempt Low Copy Number on the sample and replicate the DNA cells over and over again so as to create a sufficient quantity for analysis. By morning she hoped they would have enough to test for a DNA match with Alan Rawlins's profile.

*

Anna was dressed and ready for action by seven. She drove to the station and already waiting for her were Paul and Brian. They used a patrol car to drive to Newton Court. Tina opened her door wearing a dressing-gown, her hair in large green rollers and a piece of toast in her hand. Without make-up she looked much older. She didn't put up any resistance, just asked if she could call her brief, but Anna said they would do that at the station. It took over half an hour for her to get herself ready. She had dressed in a demure, but tight-fitting dark maroon woollen dress with a white Peter Pan collar, her hair was gleaming and brushed up into a loose flattering coil and her make-up was thicker than she had worn before, with a dark red lip gloss.

During the ride to the station Tina sat in the back beside Brian Stanley, but as far away from him as possible, staring out of the window. Anna recognised her strong perfume, Shalimar, which permeated the patrol car. Paul took sly glances at her in the driving mirror. One time she caught him looking and outstared him. Her composure was unexpected; she didn't appear to be in the slightest concerned. The only things that seemed to be of interest to her were her manicured fingernails, which she constantly looked at and then patted the suede clutch bag she held on her knee.

Paul and Brian escorted her into the station and after she was booked in, a uniformed officer led her to a cell to await the arrival of her brief. In the incident room Helen asked if Tina had created a fuss when they arrested her and Brian shook his head.

'She's hardly said a word. Got all dressed up, stinks of some awful perfume that turned my stomach. She just sort of accepted it all, calm as a cucumber. Am I right, Paul?'

'Yeah. I've never arrested anyone who appeared to be getting ready for a cocktail party. She's freaky. The only time she got a bit rattled was when she wasn't allowed her handbag in the cell with her and we also took off her high heels. I reckon Travis was a bit side-tracked by her attitude. It took us all by surprise.'

'You think she knows it's curtains?' Helen asked.

Paul glanced at Brian and shrugged. 'You know the saying it's not over until—'

Brian was interrupted as Anna walked in to say that Jonathan Hyde was in reception and could one of them please bring him to her office.

Helen noticed that Anna was very tense.

'The guys say that Tina is very calm and didn't create when you arrested her,' Helen remarked.

'That's right. It wasn't as if she was expecting us – at least I don't think so – but she's certainly got her feelings under control.'

'Did she look scared?'

'No, Helen, she didn't.'

'She will be when she knows what we've got against her,' Paul predicted as he saw Brian bringing in Jonathan Hyde.

'Good morning, Mr Hyde – would you come into my office?' Anna said pleasantly and gestured for him to go ahead of her.

They all watched as Anna's office door closed behind them.

It was three-quarters of an hour later when Anna called through to Brian to bring Tina Brooks up from the cells and to put her into interview room one.

'With or without her shoes?'

'With, Brian, and she can have her handbag. It was checked, wasn't it?'

'Yes. It contained a compact, lipstick, credit cards and purse. That's it.'

'In five then.'

Paul straightened his tie. He was very nervous, knowing this was make or break, but at the same time couldn't think how Tina Brooks was going to be able to walk free again as she had done on two previous occasions.

Jonathan Hyde requested time to talk to his client and Anna agreed that he could be taken down to the interview room. Brian led him out and Anna emerged from her office. She looked at Paul.

'You ready for this?'

'Yes, ma'am.'

They spent some time arranging the files and photographs, and checking that there was a television set in the interview room so they could show the CCTV footage from the store. Another monitor screen would be up and rolling in the adjoining room to allow members of the team to watch the interview, which would also be audio- and video-recorded. It was later than Anna had calculated – now coming up to one o'clock – but she didn't feel like eating any lunch, nor did Paul. They sat ready and waiting for Hyde to finish conversing with his client.

At 1.45 p.m. a uniformed PC came into the incident room to say that Mr Hyde and his client were ready. Anna collected a heap of files, Paul carried the rest, and together they walked down the stone steps to the floor below and along to the interview rooms.

'Good luck.'

Anna turned to see Langton entering the corridor. She didn't need this and she stopped in her tracks.

'I'll be in the monitor room,' he said, almost cheerfully. She gave a brief nod and continued to the door of interview room one. She could see through the small window that Tina was sitting beside Hyde.

'Here we go,' she whispered to Paul.

They walked in and the door closed behind them. In the monitor room Langton sat on a chair and eased another closer to prop up his leg, before picking up the remote to turn on the monitor screen. Part of him would have liked to be in on the action, but instead he would watch it – watch it very closely as he was concerned that Anna had lost her ambition, lost what he had believed her capable of. He hoped she would prove him wrong. Her promotion had been very much down to him, but he was not a man to ever allow any personal feelings or previous relationships to interfere in his professional assessment. He could very easily make sure the next step of her career was to a desk job rather than heading up a murder enquiry.

Chapter Twenty

Anna cautioned Tina and informed her that they would be videoing and audio-taping the interview. Tina had remained impassive, staring at her folded hands resting on the table.

'We have acquired some new evidence that concerns you, but I would like to give you the opportunity of repeating exactly what occurred on the day of March the fifteenth. This would be when, as you have stated, you were phoned by Alan Rawlins, as he was suffering from a migraine and you drove him from his workplace to your flat.'

Tina sighed.

Anna had the statement from Tina in front of her. She continued.

'You have stated that you subsequently returned home at around six-thirty in the evening and discovered that Mr Rawlins was not, as you had expected, at home. Do you have anything you would like to add to this statement?'

'No.'

'You yourself did not report Alan missing, but stated that you felt he might have left you for another woman. We were subsequently approached by a Mr Edward Rawlins who was greatly concerned for his son's safety.

437

This was two weeks after the day Alan Rawlins had left work suffering from a migraine.'

Tina continued to look down, scraping at the cuticle of one of her manicured nails.

'Yes,' she agreed without looking up.

'Due to the fact there had been no movement from your joint bank account with Mr Rawlins, no credit-card transactions, and that by now it was almost eight weeks since he had last been seen, it was thought that something untoward might have happened to him. You allowed myself and Officer Paul Simms to search your premises and during this search we discovered that a section of carpet had been cut from under your living-room sofa. You stated that Alan had cut that section of the carpet as some wine had been spilled and he was concerned that the landlord would ask for damages to be paid.'

Paul passed over the photograph of the lounge showing the cut-out area. Tina glanced at it and then Paul took out the next photograph.

'During the search of your premises we subsequently discovered that a second area of carpet had been cut out. This was to the left side of the double bed in the main bedroom. That section would appear to have been replaced with the piece of carpet from under your sofa. Please look at the photograph, Tina.'

Tina stared at the photograph and pushed it back across the table.

'Forensics found no wine stain on the carpet removed from beneath the sofa or the underlay. However, when the inserted piece of carpet was lifted from beside the bed they discovered a bleach-washed bloodstain. The blood had in fact seeped through the underlay into and under the floor-boards. Due to the extent of the blood pooling it was doubtful that whoever had sustained an injury resulting in this amount of bloodloss would still be alive.'

Paul passed Tina the scene of crime photographs showing the bloodstained floorboards and the congealed blood underneath them. Again she stared at the photographs, but gave no reaction or reply.

Anna continued, her voice quiet and steady.

'Subsequently, to determine if there were other bloodstained areas that had been cleaned, the forensic team used a solution of Luminol which reacts to cleaned, or non-visible blood, by glowing in the dark.'

Paul showed one photograph after another of the Luminol reaction glowing in the hallway and on the bathroom tiles and floor. Tina didn't seem interested, but her brief scrutinised each photograph and then made notes.

'We now know through DNA testing that all the blood pooling, spattering and blood swipes recovered or revealed with the aid of Luminol belonged to Alan Rawlins.'

This was the first time Tina looked towards Anna. It was hard to detect what she was thinking or feeling as she quickly lowered her eyes.

'Do you have anything you want to say about this, Tina?'

'No.'

Anna nodded to Paul and he produced the receipt for four large containers of bleach purchased by Tina the day after Alan Rawlins had returned home with a migraine.

'It was determined that an extensive clean-up had been done in your flat. Bleach had been used to wipe around the walls and the bathroom. You have admitted purchasing containers of bleach and we have the receipt and CCTV footage dated the sixteenth of March confirming this. You have maintained that you bought it for use in your beauty salon, however we were unable to find three of the containers.'

Tina sighed, but still remained with her head down. 'I used them in the salon.'

'Did you also use this?'

Paul passed over a still from the CCTV. Tina frowned and picked up the photograph of her at the checkout till.

'You can obviously see what it is, Tina; it's you buying an axe.'

Paul passed across the second series of photographs – this time Tina at the returns desk with the axe.

'March the nineteenth, two days after purchasing the axe you are on camera returning it to the store to claim a refund.'

There was a pause. Tina crossed her legs and glanced at her brief, but remained silent.

'Would you please explain what this item was purchased for?'

'No comment.'

Anna leaned back in her chair.

'No comment? Then let me tell you what I think you used this axe for, Tina. To hack up Alan Rawlins. Having dragged his body into the bathroom you used this axe to slash him and dismember him to enable you to remove his body with ease.'

Hyde tapped the table with his pen.

'My client does not wish to answer this allegation, and without proof that indeed this axe was used in the manner you have suggested, she wishes to remain silent in the event she might implicate herself.'

'As your client has admitted that no one else was living at her flat on these dates, the implication is not just obvious, but shows she must have murdered Alan Rawlins,' Anna insisted.

'Then we reach an impasse because my client does not wish, as is her right, to answer questions relating to the purchase or return of the axe.'

'If there is an innocent reason then I'd like to hear it.'

'I have advised my client not to answer.'

'Why don't you advise your client to start telling me the truth? She has lied from day one. Alan Rawlins was murdered in the flat she shared with him.'

'If you have evidence to show that this axe was used to kill or dismember Alan Rawlins, then kindly present it, but it seems clear to me it was returned unused to the store and my client was given a refund. Is that correct?'

Anna leaned close to Paul and whispered. He opened another file and passed her the photographs and reports.

'I must inform you that we have identified and recovered the axe and it is presently with the Forensic Department who have discovered some blood on it. We are awaiting verification that it's Alan Rawlins's.'

Hyde reacted and gave a covert glance to Tina. She leaned close to him whispering, but he clearly didn't like it.

'The mattress removed from your bedroom, Tina, was bloodstained, and bleach had been used in an attempt to clean it off. Also discovered on the sheet on the bed when examined by Forensics was a semen stain and male head hair that does not match Alan Rawlins's DNA profile.'

The photographs of the bedsheet before removal were shown and Hyde replaced them in front of Paul.

'After you'd murdered him, Tina, who did you sleep with? Who was in the bed with you – lying on the mattress still stained with your boyfriend's blood? Did it make you feel sexy, knowing what you'd done? No one even knew he was missing, did they? Did you enjoy it? What kind of sick perverted woman are you?'

'My client has denied . . .' began Hyde.

'Your client is lying; you have the evidence in front of you. How can you explain this, Tina? What made you do it? Anger? Hatred? Did you find out that the man you intended to marry was a homosexual and was planning to leave you, not for another woman, but for a twenty-one-year-old guy? Was that what drove you to do this?'

There was a flicker of a reaction. Tina pursed her lips tightly and Anna stepped up the pressure. Paul passed her the photograph of the house in Cornwall.

'Look at the property he'd bought for his lover. He was intending to walk out on you and live with this boy. He was working on that snazzy little Mercedes as his birthday gift for that young guy's twenty-first. It must have made you feel old and worn and betrayed, considering all the money you'd managed to save was a paltry seventy thousand when Alan had thousands being hoarded in a bank in the Cayman Islands and had paid almost half a million for the lovely beachside house.'

At last Anna was getting through to Tina. She was wriggling in her seat, crossing and uncrossing her legs.

Anna kept up the pressure.

'Find it all out, did you? Find his mobile phone and start to put two and two together? It must have made the bile rise up, made you bitter and angry enough to want to kill him. You trusted him, you loved him and you'd driven him home because the poor lamb had a migraine.'

'I didn't know any of this until you fucking told me,' Tina snapped.

'You didn't know? You didn't have any idea that when he went to Cornwall for his supposed surfing holidays, he was screwing young pretty boys? He made sure you didn't know, didn't he? Used his former schoolfriends' names just in case the old bitch at home tried to catch him out.'

'I trusted him.' She was wringing her hands.

'You told me he never liked confrontation, never argued with you – but you found out about his other life, didn't you? You confronted him, you wanted to get to the truth and you wanted to know if he was about to leave you.'

'You couldn't have an argument with him – you don't understand. He would just walk away. He would not argue with me and you don't know what you are talking about.'

Langton leaned towards the monitor screen, muttering to himself.

'Do it, girl, push her – she's cracking.'

Anna did not feel as confident as Langton that Tina was opening up. She continued to goad the woman in an attempt to get her angry enough to either admit what she'd done or make a slip-up that showed her guilt; at the same time she was trying to fathom out what was constantly niggling at her. What was the missing jigsaw piece? She intuitively knew there was something else, but just couldn't place it. So she pressed on in the same manner, never taking her eyes from Tina's face.

'I know enough about Alan, Tina. He was never going to marry you, and when you found out just how much he had betrayed you, you were not going to let anyone else have him. He was weak, he was ill in bed, it was the ideal moment to kill him.'

Tina shook her head and laughed.

'You think you knew him? Well, let me tell you he was

never what you are trying to make out. Yes, he hated con-frontations, yes, he didn't like to argue – but you also never wanted to goad him into a face-off because ... because ...'

'Because what, Tina?'

She clicked her fingers.

'He could snap just like that. You never knew which way he would go, if he didn't like something. Everything had to be just perfect – and if it wasn't, he could get very nasty. And let me tell you, once was enough for me – just once – and I never ever got into an argument with him over anything again.'

'Was that when you killed him?'

'NO! You are not listening. I just said I did not argue with him. We did not argue because I knew it would be a waste of time.'

'Because he would leave you?'

'No, because he would win.'

'What about his friends? Did they also never argue with him?'

'What friends? I never met any of them bar a couple and they weren't my type. I was working hard to get my salon on its feet and by the time I got home I wasn't in the mood for entertaining anyone, never mind his friends.'

Langton swore. Anna was losing her pressure and Tina was now sitting up straight as if she was in control.

'Did you meet Sammy Marsh?' Anna asked, more than aware that she had let the interview go off-kilter, and she more or less threw the name in to give herself some time to try and get back on track. It was apparent she had taken Tina off-guard. Her reaction was interesting. She shook slightly and pressed back in her chair. Paul scrabbled through the file and passed over a mugshot taken of Sammy.

'Sammy Marsh, Tina – this man. Please look at the photograph.'

Tina swallowed, shaking her head.

'You have never met this man?'

'No. I don't know him.'

'You sure?'

Tina turned to Hyde and said she needed to use the toilet. Unable to prevent this, Paul informed the uniformed WPC waiting outside that she had to escort their suspect to the ladies.

Anna got up and followed. 'I want a female officer inside the ladies with her.'

Tina turned on her. 'For fuck sake, I need to have a wee! I've been here since early morning, all right?'

Anna ignored her as she hurried along the corridor.

'You need one as well, do you?' Tina shouted after her.

Langton walked out from the monitor room, catching Anna as she passed.

'You let her off the hook, Anna.' He was about to continue, but she ignored him, heading for the stairs to the incident room. A female officer passed her to do as requested and stay with Tina whilst she relieved herself. Anna told her over her shoulder to keep her eye on Tina Brooks. If necessary, ask for the lavatory door to be kept open.

Brian turned in surprise at seeing Anna.

'Get onto the station in Cornwall,' she rapped out. 'Ask them to get their lab to forward Sammy Marsh's DNA profile to Liz Hawley ASAP. I want it compared with the semen found at Tina Brooks's flat.'

'But he's dead!'

'He was alive until four weeks ago, so just get onto it. As soon as you get a result, interrupt the interview. Also, ask Liz if she has a result on the axe and get that to me as well.'

Anna turned on her heels and was hurrying down the stairs into the corridor when she caught the female officer returning.

'She all right?'

'Didn't like the door being kept open. She sort of looked like she was going to be sick, leaning over the basin, but then she straightened out. She's back in the interview room.'

'Thank you,' Anna said, hoping she didn't have to confront Langton. However, he was not in the monitor room but up in the canteen getting himself a coffee. By the time he took up his position Anna was already questioning Tina so he propped up his leg again. He had to take painkillers with his coffee as the trip to the canteen and back had made his knee throb.

Anna had jotted down notes to Paul, who glanced at them. She had underlined *Sammy Marsh*, asking if they had asked Tina about him in previous interviews. Paul began to thumb through his notebook.

'We have information that Alan Rawlins used recreational drugs. What can you tell me about that?'

'He never did that in front of me, and I've never done anything more than a spliff years ago. I don't do anything now, but I know he did sometimes.'

'What do you know he used?'

Jonathan Hyde was nonplussed at the new direction Anna was taking, but Tina's break had successfully calmed her down and she was more at ease answering the questions.

'What about heroin?'

'No, he'd never do that. Besides, I always knew when he'd done cocaine because it made him very hyper and he could get aggressive.'

'About what?'

'About me disapproving. Look, I'm gonna be honest with you. I know I have not been telling you some things, but it's only because it might have got me in trouble. I know I made Alan out to be the perfect guy, but he wasn't easy to live with.'

'So you argued?'

'No. I've told you he wouldn't – he'd always walk away and that used to drive me nuts.'

'Crazy enough to want to kill him?'

Tina raised her arms. 'I didn't, and you are trying to trip me up.'

'Trip you up? Tina, I am through with your lies. You have said that you, and you alone, were in the flat – so if *you* didn't kill Alan, someone else must have been there who did,' Anna persisted.

'I went out to work, you know. I was out of the flat every day when he was first missing; someone else might have come in.'

'Who?'

'I don't know.'

'There was no forced entry, so who else would have a key to your flat?'

'Well, you keep on telling me he had this boyfriend – maybe it was him.'

'And *you* keep on telling me that you were unaware of Alan having homosexual relationships, unaware that he was planning to leave you, and yet now you say that there could have been someone else who was able to enter your flat, kill Alan, dismember the body and clean up to the extent of changing the bedlinen ...'

'Yes.'

'Yes? So who was the other person who subsequently

447

had sex with you, or are you saying there were two other people in your flat?'

Tina became very agitated, slapping the table with the flat on her hand.

'I am telling you that when I came home, Alan was not there.'

'So why buy the bleach, the axe?'

'I've told you. I used the bleach to clean up my salon.'

'What about the axe?'

'I am not gonna talk about that.'

'Fine, then you will be held overnight in the cells until I have confirmation as to whether or not—'

'You can't do this.' Tina turned to Hyde. 'Tell me they can't do that to me. I've done nothing wrong.'

Anna started to pack up her files and suddenly Tina erupted, gripping the edge of the table and trying to over-turn it. The water bottles fell over and Hyde pushed his chair back to try and avoid the spillage as Paul grabbed the photographs.

'Sit down, Miss Brooks. SIT DOWN!' Anna shouted.

'It's Miss Brooks now, is it? I am telling you that what-ever fucking evidence you've got doesn't prove I killed Alan because I didn't. I DIDN'T!'

'Sit down. Mr Hyde, please control your client.'

Hyde went to grip Tina's arm but she shoved him away. He rocked backwards and then she was on her feet, running for the door. Paul was out of his seat, and as Tina grasped the door handle he prevented her from leaving. She turned and threw a punch at him. The door opened and the uniformed officer stationed outside the room stepped in as Tina struggled, frantically kicking and punching out. She was totally out of control, and as she was dragged back to the table, she tried to kick again.

Eventually, with Paul holding one arm and the officer holding the other, she caved in, her body sagging as she started sobbing.

'I think we should take a fifteen-minute break,' Hyde said, standing up.

As Tina slumped into her chair, weeping, Anna found some tissues to mop up the spilled water and threw the plastic bottles into the rubbish bin, then set her files back down again. But Tina got some kind of second wind as she reached over to grab the files, sending everything flying off the table again.

'Cuff her,' Anna said, and the uniformed officer drew one arm up behind her back until Tina was screaming. The policewoman pushed her face forwards onto the table. It was an ugly scene, and Tina was still fighting as her other arm was drawn back, but with Paul's help they cuffed her with her hands behind her back. Her eye make-up was running and her face was red and blotchy, but even cuffed she was kicking, swearing and trying to bite Paul.

'I want a break for my client,' Hyde repeated and Tina turned on him.

'Shut the fuck up. I done what you told me.'

'Miss Brooks, please calm down,' he said.

She snarled like an animal, her face twisting.

'Miss Brooks, MISS BROOKS, what the fuck do *you* know? I want to go home, I want to go home.'

'I'm afraid that won't be possible,' the lawyer told her.

She swivelled around and kicked out with her high heel, catching Hyde in the knee. He grimaced.

'Take her shoes off her, please,' Anna said.

'You're not taking my fucking shoes off me. Leave me alone.'

449

However, both her shoes were swiftly removed and she sat panting and gasping for breath.

'All right,' she growled.

Anna was still straightening out her files.

'I give up. I fucking give up.'

Anna stared as Tina closed her eyes, sighing but no longer fighting.

'If you're waiting for a result on the axe, it's a waste of time. They never used it, it wasn't sharp enough.' She looked up and glared at Anna.

'Do you wish to continue this interview?' Anna asked.

'Too bloody right I do. I've had enough.'

Hyde was rubbing at his knee, and shrugged as if to say to Anna it was not going to be a problem for him.

'I can't have the cuffs removed, Tina, but you can have them on in front of you so it's more comfortable. However, you have to behave.'

'Great.'

Paul removed the cuffs from behind her and she held out her hands so he could place them back onto her wrists. Anna signalled that the uniformed officer could leave the room, but to remain outside the door.

Tina asked if there was any more water left and Paul passed her one of the half-filled plastic bottles. She took two gulps and then held it out for him to take from her. She looked at her handcuffed wrists and gave a strange half-smile.

'Broken a couple of fingernails.' There was a pause as she remained silent, staring at her hands.

'If you are ready to proceed then, Tina?' Anna prompted.

'Yeah, yeah.'

'Previously you used the word "they" when referring to the axe?'

'Correct. He wanted it to split open the board.'

Tina glanced at Anna and then at Paul. She gave that strange smile again.

'You don't know what I'm talking about, do you? The surfboard – Alan's surfboard – that's how he was moving the drugs around, shipping them in and shipping them out.'

'Are you saying that Alan hid drugs in his surfboard?'

Tina gave a long resigned sigh. She then explained that along with Silas Douglas and Sammy Marsh, Alan had used the boards to hide drugs on trips back from Florida. Pure cocaine was made into a hard paste and then packed into the centre. They would then soak it, dry it out and mix it for distribution all over Cornwall.

'But then Silas met some heavy-duty drug dealers in Miami and the next shipment was heroin.'

'You are referring to *Silas Douglas* as being party to this?'

'Party to it? He was running the show. First along with Sammy, but then Alan got himself involved and started sharing the finances. He was making money hand over fist, but Sammy tried to screw Sal. He got his hands on one of the boards, took out the heroin and started dealing, but he didn't know what he was doing; the stuff was lethal. Alan got scared shitless. Kids had been overdosing on the stuff and so he wanted out. He was also scared of Sal, so he brought one of the boards back with him and hid it in our garage. He also had two hundred thousand in cash – Sammy's money. He said that he would pack up and leave England. He was certain that they'd never come after him because he'd always used other names.'

Anna held up her hand. 'Tina, I need to understand what exact part you played in this drug-dealing.'

Tina's voice was quiet and drained as she explained that

her relationship with Alan was, for the past year, more or less non-existent. She had found out about his homosexual partners and had first wanted to simply kick him out, but he had persuaded her that he would split his profits so that she would be financially secure. There was one condition, which was that she keep up the front of their so-called intended marriage. She knew about the property, she knew about his other bank balances, but because she also knew how he was making the money, she was certain that he couldn't back out because if he did, she would tip off the police.

'He got scared. He knew he didn't have all that much time, and he was planning to leave England and go into hiding. He'd got Sammy's cash and he'd also got a surf-board full of heroin.'

'Did he intend dealing it?'

'I dunno. He was so crazy around this time. To be honest I don't think he really knew what he was going to do with it – he just didn't want any more kids dying. He was snorting up coke so that made him even crazier.'

'Take me back to the morning of the phone call to you when he said he had a migraine,' Anna prompted.

'Well, he rings me up and says that Sammy had some-how got onto him, that he was gonna have to do a runner. He was shaking, and when we got home he said that he would pack up his stuff and be gone. I had to take the suit-case with the money to a locker at the salon and I left him at the flat and went to work in the salon.'

Tina continued to explain that she had put two fake clients into the appointment books. Often her clients would enter the salon via the car park and back door entrance, going up the rear stairs to where she did her treatments. The girls knew she worked up there and that her clients liked privacy so she was never disturbed. She was therefore able put the money into a locker and leave the salon without any of the girls seeing her. She subsequently returned to her flat around midday, not as she had previously admitted, at six-thirty.

Tina started to cry, pressing her hands to her eyes. She said that as soon as she had returned she knew something terrible had happened because Silas Douglas was there and so was Sammy.

'They grabbed hold of me, really terrified me, and they wanted to know where the board was and where the money was, but all I kept asking was where Alan was. I kept on saying that I didn't know what they were talking about and Sammy slapped me around. He really hurt me.'

Tina was shaking as she described them pushing her into the bathroom where Alan was in the bath, tied up, gagged and covered in blood with the bedsheet under him.

'Was he alive?'

'No, he was dead. He had this terrible gash over his face and head and they must have been beating him because there was blood everywhere.'

She went on to describe how she couldn't stop crying, repeating over and over that she didn't know what they were talking about, but did eventually tell them that the board was in the garage. They still didn't leave and instead they began to clean up the mess, making her help them wipe down the walls in the bedroom. Sammy had cut out a section of living-room carpet to cover the bloodstain in the bedroom.

'They said if I talked to anyone or told anyone, I would end up the same way as Alan. They got rid of the blood-stained sheet and pillowcases, and I made up the bed again so it looked as if nothing had happened. They were there all night, questioning me and mopping up, and the following morning they said I had to go and buy more bleach, which I did.'

'Where was the body?'

'I don't know. I never saw what they did with him.'

'Did you tell them about the money in the locker at your salon?'

'No. They said I had to go to work as normal, that they would finish cleaning the flat. They were still there cleaning up when I got home, and then they told me to go and buy an axe in the morning so they could split open the surfboard which was still in the garage. They were worried about anyone seeing them take it out, so wanted to wait until it was dark.'

'And they remained inside your flat all this time?' Anna asked, incredulous.

Tina nodded. 'I thought they were gonna kill me. I was terrified that someone would think I'd done it, so that was why I took the axe back.'

'And you just continued to go to work at the salon during all this?'

'Yes. It was unreal because the flat looked back to normal. It was all clean and neat, and it was as if it had never happened.'

She sniffed and Anna passed her a tissue.

'Oh God, then Sammy left and it all kicked off.'

'What happened?'

'Silas. I came home from work and Sammy wasn't there but Silas was still inside the flat and I thought he was going to kill me. He said the surfboard had been split open and it was empty.'

'So Sammy took the surfboard from your garage?'

'Yes, like I said. What I told this bastard Silas was that maybe Alan had picked up the wrong one. They were all decorated with customised stuff. Then he asked about the money again.'

She started to cry once more, sniffing and wiping her cheeks with the sodden tissue.

'He said that he would teach me a lesson and that if I was lying he would keep on coming back. He dragged me into the bedroom. I wouldn't even go in there because of what had happened and he raped me – the bastard raped me.'

'Did you tell him about the money?'

She gritted her teeth and shook her head.

Anna took a few moments to digest everything they had just been told, but Tina continued.

'Alan's father kept on calling and asking about him and where he was, and in the end I said to him that I didn't know and that I thought he'd left me. That's when he contacted Missing Persons and then you came round. That's the God's honest truth about what happened.'

'All right, Tina. You've really explained a lot, but one thing I can't quite understand is the fact that two men stayed in your flat and, as you said, removed a body and a surfboard from your garage, and yet nobody saw or heard anything.'

'You come in there at night and there's no one around. Most of the tenants go to bed at nine, they don't ever go out even. There's also a fire exit that leads into the back area and you could come and go that way. As I'm on the ground floor nobody would see you.'

'But they must have had vehicles to move the body and drove in and out with a surfboard.'

Tina shrugged and said that however they came and

went, she never saw what they drove or how they got the body out.

'Did they dismember Alan's body?'

'I don't know. I wasn't there.' Her voice was shrill.

'Have you taken the money out of this locker you say you used?'

'No, I just left it locked up at the salon. It's my money. Alan give it to me – it's mine.'

Anna decided that they would continue to question Tina the following morning and that she would remain in custody overnight in the holding cell.

'But I told you everything. I'VE TOLD YOU.'

'We need to check out your statement, Tina. Mr Hyde, do you have anything to say, as it's obvious your client has withheld vital evidence.'

'Because I was scared they'd kill me. I was raped, for God's sake! You can't keep me here.'

Hyde stood up and said quietly that it was within the law to hold her. Tina looked as if she was going to create havoc again, but instead she crumpled and sobbed, repeating over and over that it wasn't fair as she'd done nothing.

By the time Tina was taken back to the cell, Anna had already organised an arrest team for Silas Douglas. Langton had been waiting for her in her office.

'Owe you an apology?' he said quietly.

But she didn't feel elated, only exhausted from the lengthy interrogation.

'Maybe I owe *you* one. Bloody Silas Douglas was here and questioned at his car wash – he's got long red hair tied in a ponytail; we all screwed up. I didn't even notice what colour because he had this skull scarf around his head.

Now to make matters worse, I think we might have lost Mr Douglas.'

'What about Sammy Marsh?'

'I would say that Mr Douglas had a hand in his murder, but that will be over to DCI Williams. Let's just hope we can pick him up.' Anna sighed.

'Did you believe everything she said?'

'Funnily enough I do, but it's hard to conceive that they were able to murder and probably torture Alan Rawlins in her flat and no one heard or saw anything, let alone how the hell they got his body out without anyone seeing them do it. He was a big guy.'

'Stranger things have happened,' Langton pointed out.

'I guess they have, but if you don't mind I've got a lot of sorting out and double-checking to do before we have another interview with Tina Brooks tomorrow.'

He stood up and ruffled his hair, then lightly touched her cheek.

'Good work, Travis. Your instincts always were that this case was connected to drugs and you've proved me wrong.'

'Not altogether. You always maintained it was connected to Tina, but if I hadn't gone on the trail to Cornwall we wouldn't have been privy to so much information. I did make a big error with Silas Douglas.'

'You may be able to verify the rape if you pick him up.'

'If – and I would say he was also responsible for ripping the Mercedes apart, looking for the drugs.'

Langton looked puzzled.

'It was a car Alan Rawlins was working on for his boyfriend's twenty-first birthday,' Anna explained.

'Ah yeah.' He nodded.

She was eager for him to leave, but he still hovered with his hands shoved into his trouser pockets.

'Anything else?' she asked.

'Nope, but I'd throw the book at her and see if even more pressure gains further results. Right now she's saying she lied because she was frightened, but she's some bloody liar, and claiming that she had nothing to do with this drug-dealing doesn't quite ring true.'

'You suggesting we discuss this with the Drug Squad here?'

'I'm not suggesting anything, but I still think there's more to get out of Tina Brooks. She did a good job of lying to me about how she had always made a bad choice of previous boyfriends and was near to tears about Alan Rawlins disappearing.'

Langton paused before eventually walking out, leaving Anna to wonder if he was simply annoyed at being proven so wrong.

Silas Douglas's car wash was closed. They had a search warrant, but found nothing connected to their murder enquiry. His desk had been cleared of papers, and left charred inside an oil drum were fragments of magazines and what may have been receipts. They knew he owned the small block of flats adjacent to the building, one of which was his London base. They used the search warrant to force entry, but like his car wash the flat was devoid of anything of interest. It appeared to be very basic: a bedroom with en-suite bathroom, living room and kitchen-diner. They did, however, take numerous finger-prints, even though most of the flat had been very well cleaned.

Anna contacted DCI Williams to give him an update, at the same time asking if the Newquay police had anything further on the murder of Sammy Marsh. They had not, but Williams said they would put out a warrant in Cornwall for Silas Douglas, especially as Anna felt he would have been the prime suspect in Sammy's murder. They knew he had an apartment in Newquay, plus a workshop where he customised the surfboards, so both places would be searched for evidence. They also had the licence-plates of a motor bike owned by him and a Ford van, which he used to transport the surfboards. However, there had been no recent sighting of him.

Late that afternoon, Liz Hawley gave Anna the result from the axe-shaft. They were unable to get a DNA profile from the minute dot of blood. She said it might have occurred if someone with blood on their hands had held the axe, but no fingerprints were found on it, nor did it appear to have been used. She also by now had the DNA result from Sammy Marsh, and it did not match the semen sample they had from Tina Brooks's bedlinen.

If Tina was to be believed, she had been raped by Silas Douglas, and so Anna knew it would probably be his DNA. She felt very dissatisfied. Although they now had the jigsaw pieced together via Tina's statements, without Silas Douglas in custody it could not be 100 per cent verified. Nor did they have a corpse or any evidence of how the dead man's body had been removed from the flat or where it was dumped.

The key to the locker in Tina's salon had been taken from her and they found the suitcase containing the two hundred thousand pounds. The money was in used banknotes tied with elastic bands in bundles of tens and twenties and fifty-pound notes. So she had told the truth about that, and would be entitled to reclaim it unless they could prove it was the proceeds of drug transactions.

*

It had been a long day and Anna did not get back to her flat until after eleven that evening. Sleep was out of the question as she lay mulling over all that she had gained from Tina's interrogation. What she still could not come to terms with was the fact that Alan Rawlins had been so brutally murdered, his body removed and the flat cleaned up to disguise and hide what had occurred. Weaving through the mound of lies that Tina had told from day one meant a lot of sifting through notes and statements.

Tina Brooks had continued to live in the flat, knowing how Alan had died. She had gone about her daily business at the salon acting as if she was the estranged girlfriend and pretending that he had simply gone missing. She had denied having any knowledge of his sexual activities, instead weaving a picture of a gentle, quiet man who hated confrontations, who never argued and whom she planned to marry. She claimed to have seen Alan's bloody body in her bathroom, yet carried on going to work and even went shopping for the two purported killers who were still inside her flat. Could a woman be so traumatised and forced into doing terrible things, and then be raped and warned to keep silent or she would end up the same way as Alan Rawlins – yet never disclose the money she had hidden in her salon?

It was after two as Anna leaned back on her pillows, trying to ascertain if there was, as Langton had suggested, even more to get out of Tina. She had lied about ever knowing Sammy Marsh, lied about virtually everything – and even with her admission about what had happened inside her flat, she still claimed that she was not in any way responsible for the murder and had only acted out of fear.

Anna sighed, pushing away the mound of papers and notebooks she had littering her bed. But she still couldn't sleep, recalling how few personal effects were on display in Tina's flat when they searched it. The lone photographs, the ordering of the new carpet. She wondered, if Alan Rawlins's father had not contacted her via Langton, would Tina have simply moved on? That was another thing that Anna would have to face – informing Edward Rawlins of the outcome. This brought her back to wondering how his son's body had been removed from the flat. Did they wrap him in the sheet? The forensic team had found no bloodstains outside the flat or the surrounding area.

Tomorrow, she decided, she would take another look around Tina's flat and surrounds before picking up the interrogation . . .

When the alarm woke her, it felt as if she had only just fallen asleep. Disorientated, she threw the duvet aside, spilling all her notes and papers onto the floor. The first page of typed notes showed the lists of the phone numbers recovered from Alan Rawlins's mobile, with calls made to Florida, Antigua, Los Angeles – but they'd had no success in finding out the identity of the recipient. What's more, the calls had been made after 16 March – when Alan Rawlins was already dead.

Chapter Twenty-One

Jonas Jones was cleaning the glass panels in the reception doors of Tina's apartment block when Anna arrived, and she asked him to show her the fire exit and corridor to the rear of the building.

'Is it ever left open or used as a shortcut to the rear?' she asked.

'No, ma'am, it's a fire exit, but I've never seen anyone use it. It's near the basement entrance where all the central-heating and air-conditioning vents are. They were checked out by officers 'cos I had to unlock that door.'

Anna followed him, passing flats one and two as they went into a narrow corridor that ran the length of the building. At the end of the corridor was, as he had described, a small fire-exit door with a single bar across it. He pressed it open for her to pass through and step outside. Although the SOCO team had obviously checked out the area, this was the first time Anna had seen the rear of the building. The area was fenced in and covered in tarmac with an old rusted table and two chairs by the only tree.

'Do residents park back here?'

'Sometimes. They've got their own garages, but they're only for a single vehicle, so if they got people visiting they park here out of the way of the main exit.'

'You ever seen cars or vans out here?'

'Only when you people were around. They used this to park up and they sat at the table. It's for the tenants, but nobody uses it.'

'So you have never seen a motor bike parked here maybe?'

'Nope.'

'What about a Ford Transit van?'

He shook his head and repeated that he only ever came in for a few hours a week. Judging by the piles of dead leaves pushed up against the walls and around the fence, it didn't look as if he had swept up for some considerable time. Anna returned back through the small corridor, aware of how easy it would have been for a van to be parked up and a body carried out without anyone seeing it. Disappointed, she went back to her car not bothering to look over Tina's flat again.

By the time Anna arrived at the station, both Brian and Paul had been working on trying to get a trace on the three numbers. The Antigua and the Los Angeles ones they knew were to mobiles, but the Florida number was a landline.

'You got an address?'

'Yeah, it's a condo in Tampa and we're onto Interpol in the US to check out who owns or rents the place. We're waiting for them to get back to us.'

'Good. How about Cornwall? They had any result in tracking down Silas Douglas?'

'Nope. He's not been seen for weeks, but they got his Transit van hauled into Forensics; no motor bike though.'

'What about the Passport Office and Border Control?'

'They're checking, but as we don't have a date, he might have skipped the country.'

'Has to be after he came here, obviously. Keep up the pressure.'

Anna had only just sat down at her desk when DCI Williams called. So far, the Transit van owned by Douglas was as clean as a whistle, with no blood traces or finger-prints. 'The only thing we did pick up,' he said, 'was a few bits of chipped paint, plus some kind of mud grains which were caught in the rubber mats.'

'You found nothing at his place either?'

'Nope. He did a clean-out. Papers were burned and too charred to get anything from them, but Ballistics said that Sammy Marsh was probably shot with a 9mm Luger. The markings on the bullets and cartridge cases didn't match any previous shootings.'

'The time of death for Sammy was around four weeks ago, you believe?'

'Yes,' agreed Williams. 'Decomposition was pretty extensive so we'd thought longer, maybe due to the body being hemmed into the small space of the lavatory.'

'So if Silas Douglas killed him, he would have had to be in the country then, which will narrow dates down for us to try and get something out of an all-ports enquiry.'

'We're working on that, but my gut feeling is, because we've got no motor bike, he could have taken off and be hiding out in England, Ireland or even Europe by now.'

'Well, we'll both keep looking,' Anna said, with one eye on the clock. She could only hold Tina for thirty-six hours until formally charging her or getting a further extension at the magistrate's court. But she still wasn't ready to begin the exhausting process of going through the gruesome details of the murder or Tina's insistence that she had nothing to do with it.

Instead, she went into the incident room and told Brian that since Silas Douglas could have gone to Ireland or Europe with his motor bike by ferry, she wanted him to focus on the all-ports enquiry, circulate Silas's details and the number-plate of his motor bike. She turned as Langton made yet another unscheduled visit and once more she was forced to give him the latest details, which delayed her from beginning the interview.

From his attitude she felt as if he in some way disapproved of her continued search for Silas Douglas. She knew him of old; on such occasions he had a bad-tempered look and grunted, constantly gesturing for her to get to the point if indeed she had one.

'Of course I have one. We only have Tina's word for what happened in her flat: the rape, the body being removed and that everything she did was due to the fact she was terrified. She's still hiding something and I can't think what's niggling me.'

He nodded, rubbing his head, making his hair stand up on end. Then he clicked his fingers.

'I know! I know what it is!'

'Know what? What is it?'

He clicked his fingers again, grinning – and then pointed.

'You said they'd found some kind of mud particles in the footwell of Douglas's Transit, right? Yes – and when you did a search of her flat you listed thick bandages, tins of a substance she used for treatments at her salon for a seaweed wrap?'

'Yes, that's right.'

'The caretaker also told me that he saw the thick bandages tossed into the wheelie bin for her flat.'

'Yes.'

'It's a treatment she uses at her salon, Anna. It's a mud wrap. She plasters the mud over the body then wraps it with the bandages. Mud dries on the skin and the body loses water retention or something like that. You with me?'

Anna nodded, but she wasn't quite following.

'Now, you've got a bloody corpse leaking in a bathtub, but no blood apart from the bedside pooling, smears in the small hallway and some blood spray in the bathroom, correct?'

'Yes.'

'You could wrap a body in bloody sheets, but carrying that out has got to leave some clues. However, if she covered it in this mud stuff, then wrapped the body in bandages, it could have been inside the flat for days whilst they cleaned up. You said over and over that the cleaning of the flat had to have taken longer than just her going to work and returning.'

'But we are still going on her word that Alan Rawlins died on the day he left work, that both Sammy and Silas were there when she got home and that they had already killed him,' Anna said thoughtfully.

'You've seen how good a liar she is. At best, all you have her for is attempting to pervert the course of justice. I'm warning you though, she could get away with being seen as the innocent, terrified victim here. We know she's a bloody good actress. If defence put her in front of a jury, she turns on the tears, out will come the rape allegation – followed by a not-guilty verdict – and she calmly walks away from it all, passing Go and collecting two hundred thousand pounds. If you want her to go down for accessory to murder, you need to show she assisted or encouraged Sammy and Silas.'

467

Anna tried to take on board all Langton had said but knew that by now Tina's brief was waiting impatiently in the interview room.

'I'll do my best, but with only her word to go on it's not easy.'

Paul looked over to see if he was needed. They still had no result on the Tampa number and Brian was checking the possibility that Silas Douglas was in Ireland or Europe. Now Douglas was wanted for questioning about two murders, the hunt was hotting up.

'Okay, Paul, let's go for round two,' Anna said, heading for the stairs to the interview rooms. Langton watched her leave before he did another slow meander over to the incident board.

'Brian, what do we know about this guy Silas Douglas?'

'Not a lot, Gov. He's got family connections, well educated, trained as a carpenter and has a reputation for customising surfboards. He charges a few thousand as well, and he's been bringing them in from the USA for about three or four years. He runs this car-wash dump close to where he lives, full of Polish immigrants . . .'

'Any previous on him?'

'Nope. Travels from London to Cornwall for the summers and—'

'How did you get his name?'

'It was in Alan Rawlins's address book. Douglas gave up Sammy's name and showed us a photograph of Rawlins with pals. He admitted he knew Sammy Marsh again when we brought him in for questioning, and said Alan Rawlins had been in his surfing class.'

Langton sat down in a chair facing the accumulated evidence plastered across the incident board.

'Is he married?'

Brian dug around in his notebook, thumbing over pages.

'Yeah, divorced nine years ago, has one daughter.'

'Where do they live?'

Brian shrugged. 'I dunno but I can check.'

'Is he gay or straight?'

'Straight, but I dunno. He's got a ponytail like an old hippy with biker's leathers – huge guy.'

Langton ruffled at his hair again and then instructed Brian to dig up everything on Silas Douglas's background. He would be in the monitor room watching the interrogation.

Brian waited until Langton had left and then asked Helen to do it for him as he was still trying to work on what Anna had wanted.

'He's taking a big interest in this, isn't he?' Helen observed.

'He and Travis were an item a few years ago. To be honest, rumours were flying around that he'd pushed her promotion through. I think he's looking over her shoulder. This is the first Category A murder enquiry she's handled solo.'

'Well, the body count is mounting. It's gone from a missing person to a murder and then the guy in Cornwall, and . . .'

Brian was reading an email when he suddenly turned to Helen.

'Fuck, the condo in Tampa, Florida, is occupied by a Mrs Wanda Douglas. It's the suspect's wife, isn't it? Can you check with the General Registrar's Office for births and marriages?'

'I'm doing it, I'm doing it.'

*

Anna once again cautioned Tina and informed her that the interview would be recorded. Tina looked dishevelled and wore the same clothes as the previous day. Her eyes were red-rimmed as if she had been crying, her face devoid of make-up. Even her hair looked as if she hadn't bothered to comb it.

'You feeling all right, Tina?'

'Not really. I couldn't sleep. The place stinks and they gave me food that was disgusting.' She jerked her thumb towards Jonathan Hyde, saying, 'He got out of here so fast, he didn't make any arrangements for me to get a change of clothes. I've not got my make-up and ... so how do you think I feel?'

'Let's see then if we can get through this as quickly as possible. It will be entirely up to you, Tina.'

She shrugged and sat back in her chair. Paul, seated beside Anna, had all the files beside him in order and ready to take out for Anna when required. He was looking very smart and, unusual for him, was wearing a dark-grey suit with a white shirt and navy tie.

'Now this may sound repetitive, Tina, but I need for clarity's sake to know exactly the timeframe, going from the moment you received a call from Alan at his place of work which would have been the fifteenth of March of this year.'

'I was getting ready for work when he rang and said I had to collect him. He sounded in a right state. I asked if he was feeling okay and he said – well, he snapped at me – to get over to Metcalf Auto and pick him up, so I did.'

Anna nodded and Tina looked at her.

'You want me to go on? He was very anxious all the way home, said he would have to get out as some people were threatening him. He told me to take a suitcase and put it in a locker at the salon, that he couldn't stay at the flat and that he might go to his parents' and make arrangements from there.'

She rubbed her face tiredly.

'He was scared stiff, and I was worried about him, but he insisted I go to work. Anyway, I didn't get back home until, as I've told you before, around six-thirty or a bit later. I knew something bad had happened as soon as I walked in. The sofa was overturned, I remember that, and then this guy came at me from out of the bathroom. He grabbed me and pushed me back into the lounge. Next this other man, huge bloke with a ponytail, came out and he said the name Sammy and told him to leave me alone. He said that Alan had taken something that belonged to him and I thought he was talking about the money I'd put in the locker. I heard Sammy call the other man Silas and I realised from what Alan had told me who they both were. I got frightened and said I didn't understand what they were talking about. Sammy was screeching and swearing, and the big guy Silas had to hold him back. He kept asking me about a surfboard, where was Alan's surfboard. It was all so crazy and I said it was in the garage. Then Sammy left and Silas told me that if I wasn't telling the truth I'd get what Alan . . .'

She swallowed and down came the tears as she described being pushed towards the bathroom, how she had seen Alan in the bath with his head caved in and blood everywhere.

'I started screaming and he hit me across the face hard which knocked me over and he said to shut up so I went back into the lounge and just sat there.'

471

Tina continued to describe Sammy returning to say he wasn't going to carry the board in as he was worried about someone seeing him, so they said they'd wait until it was dark. They had asked her about money and she had pretended that she didn't know anything about it, and she'd remained sitting in the lounge. She saw them taking blood-soaked sheets out of the bedroom, rolling them up, and then they told her she had to help them.

'All the time I knew he was dead in the bathroom and I was terrified. They started cleaning the carpets, then they cut some out and they were in and out of the bed-room.'

'What time did they leave?'

'They didn't. They sat around until it was dark and then Sammy went and got the surfboard from the garage and brought it in. He started using a hammer, but it was just making dents and then they sent me out in the morning to get carpet cleaner and bleach for washing down the walls and the bathroom.'

'That was on March the sixteenth and you say you were kept in the flat that night as well?'

'Yes, they made themselves something to eat.'

'The body was still in the bathroom?'

'Yes, and then early next morning they wanted me to go and buy an axe. So they could cut open the surfboard. This time Sammy drove me to get it 'cos I was so scared they didn't think I'd come back. We went back into the flat but by this time Silas had used a hammer and screw-driver and he was in a terrible rage 'cos he said it was not the right board and again they came at me, but I swore I'd told them the truth and that I didn't understand what they were talking about.'

Tina sniffed and was passed a tissue. She blew her nose.

'They said I had to go to work and that if I told anyone about what had happened, I would be killed like Alan.'

'So it was now two days since you brought Alan back from his garage?'

'Yes. They made me help clean up with the carpet cleaner and bleach, scrub and turn the mattress, and change the bed and put a fresh set of bedlinen on it. They cut out the bloodstained bedroom carpet and put the other piece from the lounge over it. They moved the bed and I just had to do whatever they told me.'

Again the tears came down.

'I thought it was all over. I was just hoping and praying they would leave, and I was gonna go to the police, I was. Sammy went out and left me with Silas. He came onto me all nice and quiet and said I'd done very well, and then he dragged me into the bedroom and he raped me.'

Anna tapped her notebook. 'This was now the seventeenth, two days after you had returned with Alan?'

'Yes, but they had moved his body. It wasn't in the bathroom 'cos we'd been cleaning it with the bleach. I think they did it whilst I was at work.'

'Why didn't you call the police when you were at work?'

'I was too scared. They knew where I was and they said that if I didn't do what they told me to do they'd make sure I'd be implicated in the murder and that I'd be sorry.'

'What about the surfboard?'

Tina looked confused and then shrugged.

'I don't know. It wasn't left in the flat. When they took the body out they must have taken that as well. They did come in and out at night, but as I was at work in the day I didn't know what they got up to.'

Anna paid close attention to her notes. She turned one page forward and backward and then tapped the book with her pencil, repeating from her notes what Tina had said to her.

'"I couldn't have done anything about it. I was that scared. It was Alan's father who reported him missing and so I had to go along with it." You seem to have gone along with an awful lot of things, Tina.'

'I was raped. I saw the state of Alan, the blood in the bathroom. I knew what these two maniacs could do. I was terrified.'

'But you also had every opportunity to go to the police. You knew Alan had been murdered, you knew that drugs were involved.'

Tina made a gesture with her hands, touching her breasts as her voice quavered.

'I am just a woman and was so frightened. I honestly don't remember what I was even thinking.'

'But you hadn't been raped – that came later, on the seventeenth, didn't it? I just find it hard to believe that you could remain in that flat over two nights and then go to work as if nothing was happening when the man you have said you cared for and intended marrying was lying beaten to death in your bathtub. As I recall there's only one lavatory, so what did you do when you needed to use it?'

'I pissed when I got to work, Miss Clever Fucker. I never looked into the bathroom, bar that one time I told you about.'

Jonathan Hyde tapped her arm, saying quietly that she should watch her language. It looked as if she wanted to spit in his face, but then she gave a coy, whimpering smile.

'Sorry. I am so sorry. Please forgive me for swearing.'

'If you were so distraught, why take the axe back to the store?'

'I told you why – because it might have implicated me. I didn't want to be asked about it, it was never used.'

'So did Sammy or Silas accompany you that time?'

'No, they'd both gone by then.'

Anna looked up as there was a knock on the interview-room door. Brian Stanley was outside, indicating that he wished to speak to Anna. She got up, and for the record-ing announced that she was leaving the interview room and that it was five-fifteen in the afternoon.

Paul asked Tina if she would like more water, but she refused.

Jonathan Hyde sighed irritably, looking towards the door. Tina had been held in custody since the previous day. He knew they would soon have to either press charges or go before a magistrate to extend the custody time. He leaned closer to Tina, asking if she was in need of anything and she looked at him stonily.

'I need a bath and a massage – are you gonna give me one?' Hyde moved away from her fast.

Anna came back in, sat down and the interview con-tinued, with Paul stating for the tape the time that DCI Travis had returned.

'Tina, you have said that you had never met Sammy Marsh before, is that correct?' asked Anna.

'Yes,' she hissed.

'The other man was Silas Douglas – is that correct?'

'I didn't know his full name.'

'Really? Did he use another name when you knew him previously?'

Tina blinked rapidly and then swallowed.

'You did know him, didn't you?'

'No, I did not. I'd never met him before.'

'Do you know a Wanda Douglas, his wife?'

'No.'

'We have been able to talk to Mrs Douglas who is at present living in Florida, and she says that you did know her husband. In fact, you had a lengthy affair with him over nine years ago.'

Tina shrugged.

'So you see, I am doubtful about everything you have admitted as being the truth. You did know Mr Douglas . . .'

'He walked out on me. I never knew he was married. He lied to me.'

'Tina, you have also lied and I am now giving you one last opportunity to tell the truth,' Anna said.

'All right, I knew him from a long time ago, but I hadn't seen him for years, and when he turned up in my flat with that Sammy, I was shocked.'

Anna sighed and then it looked as if havoc was about to break out again. Tina began to push at the table, but this time Anna was faster. She stood up and warned the woman that she would be cuffed if she continued.

'I don't care what you do to me. I DON'T CARE.'

Thankfully she sat back in the chair and started to cry. 'Oh Christ, it's all such a mess. Everything is a mess.'

'Tina, if you start to tell the truth we can help you, but if we uncover lie after lie it only makes us even more suspicious. Continually lying makes it harder for us to believe that you were held against your will and that you never intended things to have happened in the way that they did. Unless we know the truth about what did happen, it's hard for us to understand your part in it all.'

Tina hung her head and then after a beat, continued, 'It was like it was happening to me all over again. It got that bad I didn't believe how I could be such a dumb bitch. One man after the other had taken money off me, made me promises, screwed me and dumped me, and with Alan I really believed it was different. It was different all right – he would go from me to his fucking little toy boys and pretend that it was my paranoia. If you knew how many times I tried to confront him, wanting to know why he wouldn't let me go with him to Cornwall, he'd just give me all this bullshit about needing space and needing time on his own, but he wasn't, he was screwing around and I was so determined to find out. I was living with him, for God's sake! He told me to go and get a wedding dress. He said to start arranging for a fucking wedding – and all the time he was planning on ditching me like all the rest of them.'

'How did you find out?'

'I knew that Sal was living down there or working the beaches with his boards so I called him up and asked him to check Alan out. I told him not to phone the flat but that I'd wait in a pub close to the salon for when he would call me, and I'd phone him from there. Those little cows at the salon are always poking their nose into my business. Anyway . . .'

She swallowed and then gave an open-handed gesture.

'He rang me back, said he had found out and that I'd probably not want to know, but I insisted. He told me that Alan wasn't even using his own name for one, but was a regular at all the gay clubs and was friendly with a real piece of work called Sammy who was running the drugs scene there. What I didn't know was that Sal too was in it up to his armpits with Sammy. He supplied the drugs, but I didn't know – I swear before God I didn't know.'

Tina paused for breath. 'At first I didn't tell Alan what I'd found out, but I had to get my own back.'

She pursed her lips, chewing the lower one until she calmed herself down.

'I wanted to put a knife through his heart. He lied. I could have got AIDS after he came back to me from fucking those waiters. He made me out to be a total idiot and then one night I couldn't stand it any longer and I confronted him. I told him what I knew about him and he wouldn't talk about it, he just ignored me until I started screaming at him, about how he'd wasted years of my life with his promises. I did fight with him, but he just gripped my wrists and told me to calm down and then afterwards he said he'd be moving out anyway. It was then he actually told me how long he'd been preparing to walk out on me, about the house he'd bought, the bank accounts – he told me all of it.'

'So did he also tell you that he was now involved with drug-dealing?'

'Yes. He said that was how he had made all this money, and then he said to me that he was doing some big deal and that he would give me a share of it. This time it was heroin: Sal was apparently bringing in a big shipment that would make everyone rich.'

The tears were gone. She sat almost composed as she said that she had found the suitcase with the money.

'I knew he was going to dump me and so I said I had to go and do something at the salon and I took the suitcase. I stored it in the locker in my treatment area upstairs. I knew it'd be safe as none of the girls are allowed up there. I felt really good – you know, that I was getting my own back on him – because no way was I going to let him just walk out on me. And then I phoned Sal and told him that Alan was planning on leaving, and that he'd even rented his house out in Cornwall. Sal was really uptight because he said Alan wasn't only walking out on me, but that Alan had got his hands on his last shipment so he was doing the dirty on him as well.'

Tina's part in the whole hideous scenario began to take shape as she continued to talk. It sickened Anna. Alan had rung her to collect him from work because he'd had a threatening call from Sammy and he was scared. What he didn't know was that Tina, through Silas, had been the one stirring it up. She knew they would both be there at the flat because she'd left the fire exit open and the front door on the latch for them to gain entry easily and unseen. Silas and Sammy wanted their drugs and the money; they didn't believe Alan when he said it had gone. Whilst Tina went to work at her salon, as she had admitted, and returned from there at the time she had always maintained, Alan was still alive, but he had been tied across the width of the bed, gagged and beaten. His head was over the edge of the bed and Sammy had put a pillow case over it to stop the blood splashing about when he hit him with the club hammer. Silas would then remove it to un-gag him and ask again and again where the drugs and money were and the blood from his head injuries flowed onto the carpet. Alan kept saying that he didn't know where the money was and he hadn't taken the drugs, so Sal would replace the gag and pillow case and Sammy then beat him again. Eventually Alan passed out and they left him there while they discussed what to do next. The pool of blood on the carpet got bigger and bigger.

'That crazy guy Sammy was using crack – he was totally out of it, irrational and gibbering – and Silas tried to calm him down. They had drunk the place dry – vodka, gin, anything they could find – then they'd taken it in turns to beat up Alan.'

She bent her head, and sniffed loudly. Anna passed her a tissue and she blew her nose.

'I didn't lie about the carpet, they did cut the piece out 'cos the carpet in the bedroom was so heavily blood-stained.'

'And you did absolutely nothing to help him?'

'How could I? Sammy forced me to watch Alan being beaten and said I would be next if I grassed on him or didn't do exactly what I was told.'

Tina continued, saying that she was genuinely scared. When she went to work the following day Alan was unconscious, and had still not told them where he had stashed the drugs. It was during the first night that Sammy went crazy and used the club hammer to beat Alan around the head.

'Sal knew that Sammy was too drugged-up to know what he was doing and he insisted he leave, saying he would do the clearing-up. That's when I went out to get the bleach because there was so much blood that needed to be cleaned up.'

Tina described how between them she and Sal had carried Alan's body into the bathroom using the duvet cover, and hoisted him into the bath whilst they cleaned up the bedroom. Tina had taken off the bloodstained sheet and winter fleece undercover which, she said, had prevented most of the blood soaking through to the mattress and in her haste had not seen the specs left on the edge. The duvet had been on the floor at the end of the bed and was not bloodstained so she removed the cover to use it to drag Alan to the bathroom. Tina had then placed all the bedlinen into a black plastic bag, which Sal later disposed of, and she then remade the bed with a fresh sheet and duvet cover. Sal had turned the taps on to wash away some of the blood from Alan's head. Sal had been driving his pickup truck, but had left it parked a few streets away. The main problem was how to get Alan's body out to his truck without being seen . . .

And then the most shocking part of her statement came when Tina realised that for all the punishment he'd taken, even with his immense loss of blood, Alan was still alive.

'He was lying in the bath and suddenly came round and started thrashing about like mad. The water must have revived him because Sal thought he was dead. The blood was going everywhere, up the walls and on the floor. Sal put his hands round Alan's neck and started to strangle him but he didn't have it in him to finish him off. He was unconscious again but there was a faint rasping of air from his mouth so Sal suggested using the axe to finish him off and then chop him up, but when I said go on then he bottled it again.'

It was so incongruous; Tina gave a strange laugh, which made her telling of the murder even more repellent.

'I gave him a mud wrap – well, it's called seaweed wrap but it's a mix I prepare. He was always so prissy about his legs and his bit of extra weight and I kept jars of it as he would do it on his own thighs.'

It was hard not to show disgust as Tina giggled when she described how she and Sal had covered the dying man with the thick solution and then wrapped the big wide bandages all over him. Even his head and face were tightly wrapped.

'He was finally dead so it meant Sal could carry him out into the truck and leave no tracks, 'cos Alan wasn't bleeding like a stuck pig any more! Bandaged up there was nothing. Then when it was done we had another clean-up. When the mixture had dried out, Sal carried the body out. He's as strong as an ox – carried Alan all by himself, 'cos I was still cleaning.'

She had a strange almost euphoric look on her face as she went on.

'I didn't lie about the rape. After all we'd just done together, he suddenly turned on me and threatened to kill me if I ever told anyone. He said he would take care of Sammy, but he would also take care of me if I double-crossed him. He then dragged me into the bedroom and he raped me. I swear to God that I am telling you the truth. I was raped.'

No one spoke. There had been far too many hideous details to take on board. But the silence was broken when Tina suddenly gave a soft laugh.

'You want to know how dumb I am? For a while I sort of wondered if me and Sal could get back together. I asked him about his wife and he said he never saw her – that he was divorced from Wanda. He even lied to me again about that. I am such a fucking idiot.'

Anna felt that she was anything but, and her cold-hearted revenge on Alan Rawlins beggared belief. However, Anna was now convinced that Tina had told them the truth at last.

Returning to her office, Anna slumped into her desk chair. Tina Brooks was to be held in the station cells and taken before the magistrates the following morning, when she would be charged with the murder of Alan Rawlins.

Silas Douglas was arrested at Dublin airport about to board a plane to Florida. DCI Williams said he would come to London and interview Silas after Anna had finished interviewing him about Alan Rawlins's murder.

Silas was represented by a very high-profile solicitor, and refused to answer any questions, responding to everything with 'No Comment.' But thanks to Tina's statement and the forensic evidence, Silas Douglas was charged with the murder of Alan Rawlins. When DCI Williams, who'd come up to London as soon as Anna had finished her interrogation, interviewed him, he again refused to answer anything, and with no substantive evidence against him, he was not charged with the murder of Sammy Marsh.

As with most cases, the winding-down always felt tiresome, a form of drudgery that had to be got through. The adrenalin of the hunt and enquiry were gone and the team were left with the wretched conclusion of a sickening murder. The two surfboards in Alan's room at Edward Rawlins's house had been removed and sent to the forensic lab for examination. As expected a large quantity of raw heroin was found concealed within the boards and its street value, when mixed with cutting agents, was estimated at nearly two million pounds. Tina was not granted bail by the court and was sent to Holloway Women's Prison to await trial. Silas was also denied bail and sent to Wandsworth Prison. Although Tina had never admitted to any part in the murder of Alan Rawlins, she was without doubt accessory to it. The CPS had decided to accept her plea of guilty to involuntary manslaughter and then they could use her statement as evidence against Silas at his trial for Alan's murder. She would get a more lenient sentence for turning Queen's evidence, but her appearance in the witness box would help prevent Silas putting all the blame on the late, unlamented Sammy.

Alan Rawlins's body was never recovered, and the sad task of giving his father the details of his demise was left to Anna. Mrs Rawlins was by now installed in a home and Alan's father was preparing to sell the family house. He listened as Anna told him without going into too much explanation about the death of his son.

'It's odd, isn't it? You know, if I hadn't loved him enough to worry and want to find him, but had just accepted that he had gone off somewhere, none of this would have had to be uncovered.'

His small chiselled face looked worn and tired as he gave her a sad, watery smile.

'To be honest, I think it would have been better. I am sorry that I ever contacted you, but I did, and I found out layers of lies. I found out that the son I thought I was blessed with was perverted and not even my own blood – bad blood – but at least it's over.'

Anna received no thanks for the hours of diligent police work. Instead, as she drove home she kept on thinking about what Mr Rawlins had said. It was perhaps over for him, but not for her. In a few months she would have the lengthy trial and be on trial herself as she would be questioned by the defence team about her actions and decisions throughout the investigation. It was depressing, and she had never felt this way about any other case she had worked on.

*

When she let herself into her flat, the depression persisted. She threw her briefcase and car keys down onto the sofa as she picked up a half-filled bottle of wine, poured herself a glass and sipped it as she walked into her untidy bedroom where she kicked off her shoes and sat on the bed.

The telephone rang and made her physically jump. She leaned over to the bedside table and answered.

'It's me,' Langton said.

'Hi. I've just got home.'

'You sound depressed.'

'Funnily enough, you just hit the nail on the head.'

'I know how it is. It often happens, even more so on a seedy case like this one, but you never gave up, Anna.'

'Thank you.'

'You want a bite to eat?'

'No, to be honest I don't.'

'Okay. I'll be there in half an hour. Get your glad rags on and we'll go somewhere special.'

She laughed.

'That's better. You'll get your second wind, Anna, believe me, and you impressed me. My little protégée is proving to be everything I thought she would be.'

'So I'm your protégée, am I?'

'Just joking. Get in the shower, get dressed and be ready in half an hour.'

She let the phone drop back into place, already feeling better.

She had just managed to shower and put on one of her best and most flattering dresses before the doorbell rang.

'I'll be right down,' she said into the intercom.

She didn't use the lift, but ran down the stairs, and there he was, waiting for her. He gave her a good look up and down, smiling his approval, and then hooked one arm around her shoulders.

'You hungry now?'

She nodded.

'Then let's go eat, DCI Travis.'